Colbert Kearney teaches English at University College Cork.
This is his first novel.

The Consequence

The Consequence

COLBERT KEARNEY

THE
BLACKSTAFF
PRESS

BELFAST

● A BLACKSTAFF PAPERBACK ORIGINAL ●

Blackstaff Paperback Originals present new writing, previously unpublished in Britain and Ireland, at an affordable price.

First published in 1993 by
The Blackstaff Press Limited
3 Galway Park, Dundonald, Belfast BT16 0AN, Northern Ireland
with the assistance of
The Arts Council of Northern Ireland

© Colbert Kearney, 1993
Typeset by Paragon Typesetters, Queensferry, Clwyd

Printed in England by
The Cromwell Press Limited

A catalogue record for this book
is available from the British Library

ISBN 0-85640-506-X

CONTENTS

BEGINNING

SUNDAY AFTERNOON: 24 AUGUST 1986

This is not exactly the letter I promised you as the airport bus
began to pull away. When I said I would write in a week or
two I had in mind something more straightforward than this
and very much shorter; but things have taken several turns
since then.

At the moment I am living alone in a friend's house near
Clifden, in Connemara – I don't think you were ever in these
parts – on the extreme west coast of Ireland. (Get a map, find
Dublin and then move in a straight line to the west coast and
fidget around till you find it.) From where I sit I can look
down at a lake and beyond it at the Twelve Pins, the
mountains of Connemara. There is almost total silence: sometimes I hear the wind in the trees, very occasionally the dulled
noise of a car passing on the road some fifty metres from the
house. There is a stereo here with an interesting selection of
tapes and records but I have forbidden myself the consoling

distraction of music. (The television comes under the same ban.) I quite like this world as it is, the orchestra of my breath surrounding the solo of a scraping ballpoint.

But what, you are asking, am I doing here?

I could say that I am on holiday or that I am working, that I am taking a break, getting away from it all, relaxing or whatever. I myself don't know exactly why I am here but I do know that it is, as I always tick on the questionnaires, *none of the above*. I am here because Kate suggested it and made all the arrangements. I am here because on Friday 8 August, in Stockholm, a thousand and more miles away, you took me on the ferry to the museum on the island in the harbour. I am here because of a million things, one of them the promise I made to you as the bus driver closed the doors and turned out into the traffic.

I was exhausted when I got back to Cork that night but that was only to be expected. A week later I was still exhausted, still incapable of doing any work, still unable to get back to normal life again. (As usual, I use the term loosely.) Ten times every morning, ten times every afternoon, I sat down to write to you but I couldn't even manage a thank-you note. Kate is a stickler for such courtesies – even in the case of 'an old girlfriend' – and asked me several times if I had written to you. One afternoon she reminded me that I had been home a fortnight and still hadn't written. Suddenly, it seems, I became very rude. I certainly didn't intend to be – at the time I didn't even think I was; I thought she was overreacting – but she was very upset and I saw the children look at me the way children on American TV programmes look at stepfathers, and though I wanted to explain to her and the girls that I was sorry, that I hadn't meant to upset Mummy, that I wasn't feeling very well, all I could do was plod up the stairs, slam the door of my study, bite the inside of my cheek and hope that the tears would not begin to flow.

After an hour or so Kate came in and we sat in the armchair hugging each other, each of us trying to take all the blame for what had happened. Eventually the children were summoned to join the general hugging and I gave them some money to get ice-cream down at the Cross. When Kate brought up the subject of the book I could not deny that it was partly the reason for me being out of sorts. Inevitably, she suggested what she had always suggested: that I should go away by myself for a few days, a week, and decide, once and for all, without any interruptions or interference, what I was going to do about it. In the past I had always resisted this idea but this time I could only agree that it would be worth a try, that I could always come back after a couple of days if it wasn't working. Typically, Kate had understood me and the situation much better than I had and she had already been on the phone to a friend of ours – a cultured solicitor, if you could imagine such a creature – who has chosen a leisurely life in an architect-designed house in Connemara in preference to whatever professional gents do in cities and towns. He is, of course, a bachelor and thus a great attender of cultural jamborees and, by a coincidence not lost on Kate, this was the season for cultural jamborees. The Yeats School was just drawing to a close and the summer scholars were girding their loins for the Merriman. In fact, Kate had the previous day – last Thursday – failed to reach Bernard at his home but got him in Sligo, had established that he was going on to Merriman and that his house would be vacant, offered him my services as a house-sitter for the week and told him I would arrive on Sunday.

And here I am, having arrived a couple of hours ago to find the key where it was supposed to be and the house filled with vases of fresh flowers and socially acceptable weeds. A note on the table welcomed me and informed me that in the fridge there was a bottle of reasonable champagne with which to toast my safe arrival. I checked the bottle – much better than reasonable – and decided that I would use it to toast the end of my stay here – if I felt I had achieved anything worth toasting.

And so you will gather that I am here in some comfort. The house is at the end of a twisting lane, about three kilometres from the local town. It is appointed to the requirements of a bachelor hedonist with ample means and an interest in

literature: there are books everywhere and there is a very
pleasant little room on the ground floor which I will use as
my study. One wall, that facing the lake, consists of a large
window and a door; behind my head there is a slit of window
to catch the evening sun, on my right-hand side another slit to
make sure no light is lost on this little cell. To give you an
indication of the creature comforts here: there is a sauna, a rare
luxury in Ireland and one I hope to be able to resist. I cannot
explain this suspicion of pleasure except as part of my
preparation for a week of industry and assiduity. (Strange phrase
that: my final report from school commended me to the world
at large as possessing among other virtues those of industry and
assiduity!) Fortunately for me, despite all these amenities there
is a strong sense of being alone, of being in a hermitage: as I
look out across the lake and towards the hills there are only the
telegraph wires to remind me of social relations and the
external system that provides lighting and hot water. People do
not occur except as indistinguishable figures moving like flies
around the cottages on the top of the ridge on the left-hand
side of the lake, or as blurred shapes in stationary boats at the
far end of the lake.

Have you figured out by now the connection between my
stay here in Connemara and our visit to the Museum of
Modern Art?

As I came up the steps of the underground station and
checked to see how many entrances there were, I was
reckoning that I hadn't seen you for fifteen years and
wondering if it were possible that neither of us would
recognise the other. It was a very busy part of the city and the
more I watched the endless traffic, human and mechanical, the
more anxious I became. Yet I recognised you when you were
at least a hundred metres away: no problem. I could hardly see
your face at all as it was crisscrossed by hundreds of others, but
there was no mistaking the walk. The bouncing hair, the tilt of
your face, the thoughtfully determined way you cut through
the throng, your hands in your pockets, the sun glinting on
your glasses: it never occurred to me that I could possibly be

mistaken. You were not nearly as sure when I called your name and you turned to see me at less than ten metres: foreign accent, short hair and what else?

What I wouldn't give to have a videotape of those first few minutes. All I remember is the look of confusion in your face as I shook hands with you. (I suppose it was quite a normal thing to do but it felt so strange to me that I almost clicked my heels and bowed abruptly.) What did we say during the first few awkward minutes? (While examining each other as discreetly as possible.) On the way to the apartment block and up the stairs? (It must have occurred to you that my accent had changed a good deal?) And then, at last, finding ourselves across the table from each other – fixed in space, a defined distance apart – looking at each other (mostly when the other was looking the other way) and asking questions that began to bridge the gorge of fifteen years, fifteen years of me, fifteen years of you. And time and time again returning to the relative safety of what we felt relatively sure of, relatively less uneasy with: the one world we shared for a short while fifteen years before.

How's Hamlet today?

I had totally forgotten the phrase: my words of welcome as I opened the door of my rooms. (Even, as you reminded me sternly, when I knew you had finished your chapter on the tragic fate of that Scandinavian prince.) A huge wave or surge of something – call it memory or nostalgia or what you will: they are all wide of the mark – flooded my veins as you spoke the words. How could I have forgotten something that was such an intimate part of those days in Peas Hill.

Peas Hill!

How could you? Yes, the name of the hostel. Your turn to light up at the rediscovery of a lost name, a lost tang, a forgotten sense of one's own body, Bruch's Violin Concerto. Under the archway between the old dons fondling second-hand books on David's stalls and the students worshipping the latest stereos in University Audio. The waterfall of returning images: the bicycle rack; Dolly's morning cackle as – having disregarded the *please do not disturb* – she assaulted the living room with her carpet-sweeper; sitting by the gas fire at night waiting to see if somebody else would answer the phone downstairs; those blasted bells on Sunday morning.

Not only had our perception of our attitude – our understanding of our understanding of the past – changed; we had even retained a different selection of past experiences in our memories. Maybe we should never speak of memory, but always of memories.

Let's go to the museum.

Travelling across on the ferry I took a few photographs but without much enthusiasm. All I needed, I joked to you, was proof that I had been here. But even as I joked, even as I smiled...

The exhibition I enjoyed enormously. I was in the mood for sculpture, for solid objects in three dimensions before our eyes. Remember the group of six wooden figures, minimally humanised by a process of broad planing and, as if to correct this residual sentimentality, each figure left short at least half a limb? But the piece that really seized hold of me was the enormous contraption which loomed like a giant spider over a grand piano. I forget the title – if I ever knew it – but I am not likely to forget the thing itself. It took up an entire room of the gallery, extending up through the ceiling line into the raised skylights. It was the quintessential nineteenth-century factory machine – one of those enormous pieces of apparatus that fed thick fibres onto a loom, or one of those black hoists – I can't think of the correct name for them – that bring men and minerals up from the mines beneath. It was a wilderness of black cogs and wheels that moved black beams that pulled ropes through creaking pulleys in order to transfer the effort along another beam, through another joint, another rope. I can't remember the source of the energy – was there an engine? I can't recall hearing the sound of an engine – but wherever it came from, that simple energy was conducted through a crazy labyrinth of mechanics until, having filled the room with its elaborate travail, it returned to move a single small lever along a plane, say a couple of metres in length and one metre above ground level. The movement was sporadic – the arbitrary product of apparently random kinetic sums – and was twofold in nature: the lever moved a certain distance along the plane, stopped, changed its angle so that the back rose and the front fell, resumed its angle and its variant stations along the plane, pausing again to allow the lever to tip over and then resuming its progression. The tip of the lever was covered with a piece of white cloth – simply tied on with twine – and as it fell it struck the keyboard of a perfectly average grand piano which stood there to the right of the contraption as we looked at them. The cloth was the glove of this mad mechanical pianist, whose grand gestures reached through the roof, whose creative groans could be heard on the tensed ropes and anguished pulleys, whose virtuoso performance consisted of hitting one – if he was lucky, only one – key every ten seconds or so. *Bing:* the finger withdraws, the body straightens out, moves – with a gargantuan series of grunts and toiling efforts – to another part of the keyboard and drops: *bung.*

I laughed aloud, thought it the wittiest thing in years. All that laborious industry to produce so little. And behind it the strange imagination making music not by conventional means or skills or inspirations but by a process we think of as being the very opposite of artistic creation so-called. But, think about it: this music, this piano-playing, arose from a strongly individual imagination and was generated by a conventional process. The imagination of a contemporary sculptor; the process of an ancient phase of creation, nineteenth-century industrial production. The machine was mining music, not from the depths of the earth but from the kinetics of industrialisation: it was playing the music that lurks beneath the whirling of a spinning jenny, behind the slamming of looms. Perhaps what was sounded on the piano was the music coal-miners heard as they paused from hacking and hauling to wipe their foreheads, lick their lips, and listened to their thoughts in the tunnel. .

When we had seen most or all of the exhibits it was time

for lunch. We bought coffee, bread and cheese and tarts to eat in the courtyard. It began to rain almost immediately but rather than go indoors we moved to a canopied table and continued with our discussion – whatever it was. Maybe I forget what we were talking about because I was distracted to notice a woman pointing a telephoto lens at me, or at least in my direction. I tried to forget about her but each time I looked up, there she was, in the cloisters at the far corner of the quadrangular courtyard, still training her camera on me and, presumably, still taking photographs. I pointed her out to you and joked that she must be a CIA agent and that the only way to get rid of her was to point a camera back at her. I took out my camera, put in a 135mm instead of the 50mm I normally use, and aimed it at her. Instantly she moved behind an ornamental shrub and almost immediately afterwards she packed her camera away and left. You must admit that even you were amazed.

Just then we were joined at the table by three people, a nurse in charge of a mentally handicapped couple – a man and a woman, probably about the same age as ourselves. The nurse – a woman – was chain-smoking and looked utterly drained. You and I tried not to look away, even when the couple gurgled and gestured strangely, slopping their coffee and crumbling their cakes as they tried to conduct them from the table to their mouths. We wanted to hide, not to show them how unsettled and disgusted we were. I remember finding it quite difficult to hold on to what I was saying. I remember you asking me not to speak so quickly and I remember the thought lodging in my mind that you knew no English, or didn't know enough to follow what I was saying, and there was something I wanted to say to you, only I couldn't think of how to begin it. And no matter how hard I tried I kept forgetting words and clicking my fingers in annoyance and then slipping back into English and apologising for doing so. You told me to speak English if I wanted to, asked me if I was feeling all right and I said I was fine: there was something I wanted to tell you, something I found very difficult to talk about, something which would be difficult for you to understand, not because you didn't know enough English – you are, after all, as academically qualified as I am – but because what had happened was hard to understand.

That's it as I remember it. You know the rest. The relief of being able to talk about it, the release that came once I managed to begin. I was suddenly happy – no, it's not too strong a word – to be talking to you, to be looking for and always finding the movements of understanding in your eyes. There had once been a time when we had shared a good deal of our thoughts and somehow I knew I could count on reaching some trace of that; at the same time, we had been many years and hundreds of miles apart and it was something of an extraordinary chance that we were sitting there, about as far from the orbit of our normal lives as possible, almost out of the world but not quite.

Know something? I can see it all now much more clearly than I could then. In the process of writing it down it all fell into place – well, more or less. Most people, I imagine, looking at the music machine – you must write and tell me the correct title – would identify with the sculptor – the creator, the human being whose mind designs the labyrinth and gives the starting push; but I immediately saw myself in terms of the machine and specifically the tip, invisible within the white rag, which was directed up and down the keyboard by the Machine. I wasn't the player: I was being played by some Thing, by a Machine which I could not stop or understand or even see. All I knew was a series of notes which made clear sense to me but which, I was absolutely convinced, made fuck-all sense to anybody else.

You saw the woman with the camera. You must have; you said you did. We joked about her. She was there, half hidden by shrubbery but half revealed as well. She did have a camera, one with a long lens that you saw her point at me, at us, in our direction. (I checked behind us: there was nobody else, nothing else she could have wanted to photograph: the people lining up in the self-service restaurant could not be seen, not even with the best lens in the world, because they were

distorted behind the glass, down which the heavy rain was
falling.) Why did I suggest that she was CIA? I was joking: I
mean I didn't ever really, fully, believe that she was an agent of
the CIA or of any other such group – although I presume there
is a thriving espionage community over there – but, then again,
the thought not only crossed my mind once, it has stayed there
ever since, however strangely angled, and here I am writing
about it two weeks later in Connemara.

And here in Connemara I think I can rediscover the path of
my thoughts in the museum. The museum of featureless faces.
The hooded agent of the music machine. The woman pointing
a camera from behind the shrubs. The nurse exhausted from
supervising the couple. The pattern as clear to me as a simple
sentence in a foreign language: *On prétend qu'ils ne sont pas
intelligents.* The elements would not have made the same simple
sense to anybody else, I know, but it was as if somebody had
made a public announcement in Irish and I was the only one
there who knew Irish. The series of images joined together like
a string of words in a syntactically correct sentence: *Tá an bád
ar an tír.* Rather like the notes struck on the piano. Notes that
were simply incoherent to the average ear with the normal
notions of what constitutes a musical phrase. Notes that would
have been fascinating for a mind interested in statistics or
random numbers or whatever.

I began by trying to tell you how surprisingly relaxed it felt
to be with you. I had been anxious before meeting you,
fearing some kind of rejection or deflection, afraid that we
would be formally polite and no more. I don't know whether
I had decided not to say anything about the book or whether I
just let the whole business get overlooked in the welter of the
first few hours' conversation. The first evening, alone for the
first time, sitting and smoking on the balcony as you got
dressed to go out, it struck me that my position was rather like
that of a man who has just escaped from a repressive regime
and been granted political asylum in a sympathetic state. Eating
our lunch in the museum, the image returned to me and I
began to tell you about it; it was then I had that difficulty in

speaking clearly. It was as if the words crashed in my mind before I could utter them. Of course I had not found political asylum; I had found... My thoughts skidded to avoid the phrase that loomed up in front of them. Even now I have to force myself to confront it on paper: mental asylum. Don't be upset if I try to explain the process as it works in English: you will of course understand it but perhaps not as feelingly as I, because of where and when I grew up, understand it. From the beginning asylum meant the medical prison in which lunatics were confined; when later on one heard of dissidents seeking political asylum one understood what was involved but one never managed to unremember the first frightening flavour of the word which suggested a granite-walled bedlam beneath a brimmingly full moon.

The same old terror rose up in my throat as I sat on the balcony and I had to come in and busy myself changing my shoes. It throttled me again in the museum and I thought for a while I would vomit. The other version of the facts, the awful possibility, seemed confirmed everywhere. I was not the controlling machine, mine was not the composing perception. I was the hooded tip of a small lever at the end of an elaborately long process, the beginnings of which were unknowable to me. The notes I struck were not really struck by me: I was merely the agency through which something else operated. And so it was more likely than not that the woman with the camera was an agent of the state I had escaped from, that there was no complete escape, not even here. I had been so innocent to fall for talk of political asylum: because of who and what I was, I had made my own way to the madhouse, offering them my wrists. And I was there already. Jesus! were you my nurse, my supervisor? Did I only imagine that you were, that you looked like... how could I know what you would look like now, after fifteen years? I mean, more or less anybody could... How could I know anything?

Look at the far end of the table I am eating at: there was nothing remarkable about them being here in this quadrangle – a quadrangle in a museum! – they were there just as I was

there, thinking like me their thoughts of cause and effect and
understanding it all, understanding it all except the incoherence
of the nurse who could understand so little, who was always
too tired to understand, who did nothing but yawn and smoke
and look at her watch.

I suppose I controlled myself fairly well – I had been in
similar situations before – but I was almost epileptic with the
realisation that I was about to tell you the whole story and,
even when I managed to strike something like a conversational
rhythm, the mad thought prowled the edge of my mind: that
you were not you at all, not the body or the mind I had once
known, that you were a nurse, playing along with my fantasies,
happy to answer to any name, to recall any memory, as long as
it kept me quiet and relatively happy.

It must have been a strain for you but you too managed
well. (Don't I recall something about you working as a nurse
during a college vacation?) Remember? You said of course you
wanted to hear about it, the whole story, sounded interesting,
not at all crazy, but I needed to relax in order to remember all
the details and you needed to sit down comfortably somewhere
in order to pay proper attention. Well done: you got me out
of the museum, back into town and, after a longish walk, back
to the apartment. We had talked of eating in the university
quarter that evening but you suggested we postpone that:
instead, I would get some wine while you cooked a vegetarian
meal.

And thus, before, during and after that immortal dinner –
we acknowledged the memory of our old friend B.R. Haydon
(1786–1846) – you heard the whole story of *Gone The Time*.

Postprandial, drinking Mouton Cadet, I related how I had
tried several times to extricate myself from the fiction that I
had accepted publicly, told you that I had made several efforts
to give my side of the story, that I had a few hundred pages of
typescript but no idea what to do with them. Not only did I
not know what to do with them – whether to continue with
them, to show them to somebody, or what? – I didn't know
what they were, what they were intended to prove or show or

establish. I hadn't even looked at them for ages yet I had guarded them as if they were my most treasured possession. At one stage – you were running water into the sink – you said that you would love to read them.

Well, here they are on the table in front of me now, almost radioactive with reflected emotions. Even now I am free to choose. To parcel up the five folders and post them to you. Or not. To burn them. Or not. But am I free? It was painful for me to build up the typescript in the first place and it is not easy for me even to think of reading through it again. But I know that I cannot simply walk away from it. Because I know – and by that I mean something more fundamental than 'I think I know' – that I must go through it again at least once. Because I know that this is a last chance, for good or ill, for better or worse, till death us do part. If I leave it go now, as I have before, I will leave it go for ever, leaving a sore tooth at the back of the mouth, gradually getting used to the pain, knowing that by the time the tooth has died I will have forgotten that it ever even bore a nerve. My only chance is while the pain lasts.

My instinct is to avoid all emendation and revision. Remember when we used to develop and print our own photographs in black and white? Remember watching the image form in the developing fluid, waiting for the right moment before arresting the process by immersing the paper in what we called the 'fixer'? I would like to fix – for once and for all and, as I have already admitted, for better or worse – my image of the events in question.

There is something I keep trying to remember: were you ever in Connemara? I know you were in Dublin and Cork the summer Kate and I were in California – you sent me some photographs afterwards – but I cannot recall any mention or image of Connemara.

When you were in Ireland you must have come across postcards of Connemara or calendars or even boxes of biscuits with images of Connemara, because the landscape has always been a favourite with painters. Several of the better known

Irish painters spent entire lives painting it and so sometimes it is hard to appreciate the excitement of the actual geographical formation because one's senses have been drugged by conventional reproductions. Today – for the first time, I suspect – I have taken pleasure in the landscape. The scene I look out on is fairly typical of this part of Connemara: a ridge on the left, trees (not that common) on the right border; descending foreground of garden grass falling away to rough vegetation and brown bog, middleground a lake, background of hills rising to mountains and a vast sky above. What no verbal sketch could communicate – and this is why the painters moved in – is the range of constantly shifting light. Not only is the weather inclined to change rapidly from dull cloud to rain to rinsed sunshine but all of these changes are often to be seen in a single perspective. Just now it is generally cloudy and so the line of light changes from bright green grass to darker green grass to blue water to grey water to white water to very dark green bushes to grey-blue hills to pale blue mountains to white sky to blue sky to grey sky. Shortly there will be a shower, the sun will break through and re-create the entire scene. I was never one to linger on scenery for longer than it took to take a photo, but I have been spending hours watching the weather re-dress the landscape, waiting especially for the lake and the hills to change from dull two-dimensional forms to massive volumes of glistening life.

I had better stop this twaddle and get on with the job. But first some tea.

Decision: the various sections stay as they are. I may add the odd explanatory note but no major changes or rewrites. The only kind of coherence I can hope for lies in the incoherence of the typescript: I could give it a new coherence by rewriting it from here and now but that would not be something slightly different, it would be something else altogether. You might as well record the notes played by the contraption in the museum, speed them up and add a backing: you could if you tried get something that sounded more conventional but what would be the point? I might as well set myself up with easel, brushes and watercolours – the owner dabbles, of course – and try to paint what I see before me.

The folder which contains the first section of the typescript has BEGINNING written on the cover in thick black felt-tip. As far as I remember it was written during the Easter vacation, not all that long after the events it sets out to describe. It is self-explanatory and needs no introductory comment.

I do not know what has possessed me to begin this: the very last thing I ever wanted to do was write about myself and the only reason I type these words is because I feel I owe them to others, living and dead. My own preference would have been for silence but we all live in one world or another and ultimately it is dangerous to resist that proposition. As I begin I find some little comfort in my suspicion that having written twenty or thirty pages or so I will stop, read back over what I have written, throw it aside for a couple of days and then read it again, feel a little silly, find some reason to postpone continuing for another while and then find some excuse for abandoning the idea altogether. It was ever thus.

But, of course, dear reader, you know now that my suspicions were groundless. Dear reader: who and where and when and how are you?

All I know now is now your past: the times and places in which the page you finger was conceived and developed.

All I know now is the fear that my desire to go forward will be forever frustrated by a current of eternal retreat, that in order to be as fair as possible to the identity of one particular moment I will backpaddle myself – and everybody else – into the whirlpool of explanation.

In Ring Street, Inchicore, Dublin, around the corner from the three-roomed redbrick house in O'Donoghue Street where we lived till I was six, there was a series of shops. Outside one of these shops – I presume it was a greengrocer's but I am not absolutely sure and the name escapes me for the moment – there was always an open sack. I can't remember what it contained – flour or oatmeal or salt? Assume it was oatmeal –

but I can never forget that printed in colour on the front of the sack there was an image of a man – sturdy, bearded, booted, dressed in a loose-fitting suit of rough material, sitting cross-legged, smoking a pipe, an idealised farmer, suggestive of fresh strength and natural virtue. And what burned this swain into my mind was the fact that as he sat cross-legged – on a stool? – he had a patting hand of approval on a sack of oatmeal and on this sack there was printed the image of a man who was sturdy et cetera, who was in fact the image of the man on the sack outside the door. And of course this man in turn had his hand on a sack and so on and on and on, deeper and deeper and smaller and smaller until... But until what? There was no until about it. It was always happening: even though the sack sat there slumped against the wall, it was alive with little farmers with their hands on even smaller sacks of whatever it was and even as you thought about it there were more of them being made and no matter how fast you tried to think about them you could never catch up with them because they had been at it even before you saw the sack, even before you came around from O'Donoghue Street, even, maybe, before you were born. I used to stand for ages at the far side of the street, almost afraid to go any closer, paralysed by the sight of this sack as it shimmered in the sunshine. When I worked up the courage I walked over and approached it carefully, got down on my knees to see how many men I could see. I could see only a few and soon the man was no longer the rich detailed figure of the sack outside the shop but tiny smudges on the tiny hairs that made up the twines that made up the sack. But just because you couldn't see them, that didn't mean that they weren't there. Or did it? Didn't it have to stop somewhere? But where? When the eye of the man who painted the sack could no longer see what he was doing? And another thing: the sack was outside the shop in Ring Street but where was the cross-legged man with the pipe and the beard? He didn't look like anybody I had ever seen in Inchicore. He was a bit like the man on the packets of Player's cigarettes, the sailor who lived in a house in the woods called Nottingham Castle in England. Maybe the man on the sack was sitting down and smoking his pipe in England. It was all right to think about where he was but when you realised that the sack was alive and changing all the time you felt dizzy and you even felt afraid of something. It was like when Mrs McDonald said that God had no beginning. She said it was a mystery and you couldn't understand it no matter how hard you racked your brains.

What must – or may – seem odd is the claim that I have never wanted to write this, a claim mocked by the very words with which I record it. I am not sure that I am capable of explaining the thought behind that claim but I accept that some form of explanation is called for.

I have in my time written some prose fiction and some verse. (My time = some time ago.) In fact, from about the age of fourteen my ambition was to be a writer. I suppose there were times when like my contemporaries I wanted to be a Hollywood star, a Presley or a Lennon, an Elliott or a Puskas – how many other masks are piled up in the basement of recall? – but, if asked, I would have settled for James Joyce or, during some short periods, for John Keats. When I first read the *Portrait* – going home one night on the Finglas bus during the Easter vacation of 1960 – I was overwhelmed by the power of Joyce. In the days afterwards I was haunted by his writing. I suppose I still am – in different ways and for different reasons and by different parts.

Keats has always been my favourite lyric poet, has always spoken clearly to me.

At secondary school I wrote some verse and some articles for the school annual. None of the verse – published or otherwise – was any good although it occasioned a predictable amount of happiness and excitement. The essays were not much better, competent bright-boy stuff, and recently I was half amused and half embarrassed to find one of these innocent essays listed in what purported to be a scholarly bibliography. I am not sure if this is the place to go into the details; perhaps at a later stage it will seem opportune to recall some of that excitement. And excitement is a very weak term for the psychic and nervous eruptions associated with those early effusions. I never saw myself as in any way bohemian then. There were others who affected pocket hankies, shrieky manners and sought to be excused from playing field games. I was never part of that. I was an industrious student and knew that, for all the talk of intellectual nourishment, my first task was to win scholarships at examinations. And I was addicted to sports of all kinds – especially rugby (scrum-half), tennis and athletics (sprinting and what is now called the triple jump). I was associated, I suppose, with literary interests but only because I was known to derive pleasure from the prescribed texts and to admire writers – Joyce again – who were more generally regarded with suspicion.

As a student at UCD I published a few short stories – in English – which were generally praised. A reviewer in the *Irish Times* made some knowing noises about the inevitable influence of O'Connor, which was a reasonable guess but wrong because – amazingly, as it seems to me now – I hadn't read O'Connor. (I read a good deal, I suppose, but was less than voracious when it came to the Irish short story.) One of my stories – not the O'Connoresque one – I can still read with a kind of pleasure and recently it has acquired an added significance for me. (I'll come back to this in time.) It tells of a student visiting his pregnant girlfriend in her basement flat. These fictional events had absolutely no analogy in my circumstances: the only sexual relations I had at the time were with myself. While writing the story I gave the student a name which is very common in Ireland but when it came to the final draft I decided to change the name because it was the name of a close friend of mine. Shortly after the publication of the story, this friend took me for a walk and told me that his girlfriend was pregnant. I remember at the time wondering if he blamed me in any way but I reminded myself that he could not have known that the character in the first drafts had borne his name. (Actually he blamed the Holy Spirit, being – at least consciously – innocent of the spirit of primary ejaculation.) There are creaky lines here and there but it's not a bad story.

I had not intended making any further comment on this story for the moment but I might as well get it out of the way now: I have always felt since writing that story that the strongest proof of its value as literature was this uncanny relationship with the facts of life.

Though it sometimes seems otherwise – especially to those who teach English – the fact is that very few people are willing to admit publicly that they try to write fiction or verse and those few who do – however marginally – soon acquire the reputation of being literary. In that sense, I was perceived as literary while at UCD. I didn't write very much there – less than half a dozen stories, a few pieces of sentimental sexuality in sonnet form, a translation of the choral odes of *Oedipus The King*, one rather long and reasonably competent poem entitled 'The Will and Testament of Larry Lynch' – but nevertheless it was not unusual for friends to make jocular remarks of my yet-to-be-written and bound-to-be-acclaimed novel in which they would all appear in naughty disguises. It may be that I even began such a novel. I can recall two consignments of prose fiction but cannot be sure if they were one and the same project. There was at least one chapter based on my experiences as a diet waiter in Butlin's Holiday Camp in Bognor Regis. There was also a typescript version of the adventures of a student living in digs on the North Circular Road – location details from the house of a friend – and enjoying at UCD the kind of existence which Mr Donleavy had recently made fashionable. Nothing came of all this. I was diverted by lust or learning or conviviality or something yet to be named. I seem to have lost the typescripts, I who tend to hoard the most patently worthless rubbish.

Verse had become my favoured medium towards the end of my time at UCD – probably because of romantic complications but possibly because of a refined form of laziness. I cannot recall writing any fiction at Cambridge – apart, that is, from a doctoral thesis that identified the anonymous and pseudonymous writings of the painter B.R. Haydon – but there was a fair amount of verse. Again the Muse was *Libido Tortuosa*, but now there were allusions to Palestrina.

But this is all too much and too little. Let's not dwell on my desertion of the Muse; the facts are simple enough and easily checked. As my academic life became more organised I gave less and less of my time to fiction or verse. During my ten years as a lecturer in English in Cork I did almost no so-called creative writing – a few stabs at verse, the odd beginning at a novel, one go at a play. (I have, of course, published a slim sheaf of critical stuff.) The other fact – which is not so easily checked and for which there is only my word – is that throughout all this literary inactivity I have consistently experienced a sense of obligation to write and a sense of guilt at my failure to fulfil that obligation. Although, by most counts, my life and my academic career have been quite full and successful, I have always felt that there was something more important that I was avoiding and that that something was writing. As I have already suggested, no year has passed without some stillborn fragment; no year has begun without resolutions of increased efforts. I have tried to shift the blame, find an explanation, understand it all: academic work kills the creative impulse (oh, dear!) or, try again, happily married life does not allow the carelessness which is a necessary condition of good writing (pull the other one, do, please!). There may be something in one or both of these but the sum total is something short of a scapegoat. A last fact: to this day, despite my best efforts, I can find no sufficient explanation either for my continuous failure to do something I believe I want to do or for my guilt, which has lost none of its bite over twenty years.

There is every chance that this is connected with friends who are now dead, especially with one man who more than any other sponsored my intellectual life. Mind you: he never urged me to write or castigated me for not writing – simply showed the most extraordinarily generous interest in the merest thing that came from my hand.

I realise that I have not made myself very clear but I also realise that it would be impossible to do so without greater length and greater detail. Yet, these few details will serve as a context for what follows. To the implied psychiatrist I would like to make it clear that I have considered the consultation room but – wisely or not – I have preferred to put my tattered faith in this more primitive process.

One final point. I am setting out to give an account of recent experiences and to relate them to parts of my past life. I do not want to write a fiction. Devotees of contemporary literary theory need not get excited. I want to write what earlier writers would have termed *a true account, the true history*. I intend to do my best to describe what happened as fully and as honestly as possible – that is to say, not fully and not honestly but not in an intentionally or misleadingly partial way and not consciously dishonestly. For example, I will report conversations verbatim as if I had a tape, although I assume that the reader will know that I am remembering and reconstructing within the conventions of fiction. Yet my objective is not fiction – I cannot stress that sufficiently – and anybody interested will often be able to check this by reference to public documents and, should they wish to take things further, to living people.

And so here goes.

On the morning of Monday 11 February 1985 I arose at seven thirty and washed and dressed before coming down to breakfast with my wife, Kate, and my three daughters – Sally, ten, Cliona, seven, and Maeve, five. I had my usual breakfast – a soup-mug of home-mixed muesli, a slice of toast, two mugs of coffee – while listening to the news on the radio. I cannot recall any particular items of conversation or of news.

I probably consulted my Collins Academic Year Diary and read there that my first lecture was at ten o'clock – on *Hamlet*, one of the two prescribed texts for a second year course on Shakespearean tragedy – but I had made a more or less firm arrangement to meet a colleague at half past nine to discuss some departmental business. (It had to do with a complaint from a graduate student that she had been sexually harassed by a member of the department.) The three girls left the house at about half past eight and, as they normally did unless the weather was too bad, walked along Wellington Road to their school on St Patrick's Hill. Kate worked mornings as PRO for the Cork Theatre Company; I normally dropped her outside the theatre at about twenty-five past nine and then continued on up to college.

It was quite sunny in a frosty February way as I pulled the kitchen door behind me. The garage is at the back of the house and so usually, by the time I have taken the car out, closed the garage doors and driven around to the front of the house, Kate is waiting at the front gate. This morning she was not there and so I sounded the horn. She appeared at the front door, signalling that there was somebody on the phone for me. I do not consider myself a rude person normally but neither do I consider it rude to refuse to come to the telephone when I have already started my journey to work and especially when I am in a hurry to keep an appointment. I sat in the car until Kate came running down the steps and I understood from her that the phone line was still open and that it was for some reason necessary for me to take the call. Making little effort to hide my annoyance I switched off the engine, walked slowly up the path and into the hall, picked up the phone and said hello. I did not recognise the voice at the far end.

– Fintan. Glad to have caught you. Kate has just told me you are in a hell of a rush and so I won't keep you a second more than is absolutely necessary. How are you this morning?

It was that of a man aged about forty, English accent, somewhere around London, public schoolish, professional manner.

– Good morning.

– I just wanted to say that everything is moving according to plan and we are just tying up a few loose ends, making sure that everything is in place for the launch in Grogan's on Friday the twenty-second between five and seven. Have the books arrived yet? What day is it today?

Monday. Yes, you should have them by now. They were sent, a dozen –

– Who is this?

– Hello. Is that Fintan Kearney?

– Who is that?

– Is that, let me see, is that Cork 351740?

– Why?

– I wish to speak to Mr Fintan Kearney, please.

– This is 351740 and this is Fintan Kearney; now who the fuck are you?

He broke off for a moment and I guessed that he was muffling the phone while speaking to somebody in the room with him. He came back.

– Fintan, the line must be bad at your end. This is Peter, Peter Oldham at Hollinsfords. Can you hear me?

– Yes.

– I'm calling about the launch.

– So you like playing with boats. Congratulations.

– Yes, and we shall have some fun launching your boat in Grogan's.

– My boat?

– Yes, we shall crack a bottle over *Gone The Time* and ask God to bless all who sail in her. Are you looking forward to it?

– Look, I'd like to have the time to chat to you about life on the ocean wave but I'm afraid I am one of those unfortunates who have to work for a living and I am pushed for time at the moment. So I'm going to hang up now. All right? *Au revoir, matelot.*

– Are you sure you're Fintan?

– That is perhaps the only thing I am sure of; of that and the fact that I did not, do not and will not own a boat.

– Fintan, can you hear me properly? I want to talk to you about the book. I can hear you perfectly. Is Kate still there?

– You can hear me perfectly?

– Yes.

– Well, hear this perfectly. This is Fintan Kearney, about to be late for an appointment because I am talking into my home phone which bears the number 351740. I am about to hang up and go to work but, on the off chance that you are the victim rather than the perpetrator of a joke, I will go beyond the requirements of the Geneva Convention and give you the following information: I have not the slightest idea who you are, what you are talking about or why you are talking to me. Over and out.

I slammed the phone down, pulled the hall door behind me and ran down to the car. As I started the engine and shot off Kate put her hand on my elbow.

– I gave you that telephone message, didn't I?

– No.

– I was sure I saw you put it in your top pocket.

– No.

– Let me see. Yes, I did. Here it is. You'll remember to call him this morning?

– Who?

– Your friend in RTE.

– Who? What are you talking about?

– I told you this morning in the bathroom.

– What? Told me what?

– This friend of yours called last night when you were out.

– Called to the house?

– No. The phone.

– Hm?

– You'll never guess. Dan Henegan. Remember him?

– Uh-huh. RTE.

– That's what I said. He says he taught you how to play rugby.

– Latin. What did he want?

– He wants you to take part in a programme he is producing, he called it something Arts. I told him that the launch would be on Friday the twenty-second – Peter Oldham rang for you as well last night to confirm the date and when I told him you weren't in he said he would ring this morning before we went out. Anyway, your friend said he would try to come along but wasn't sure he could make it. He wants you to give him a call this morning to see if you can find a suitable time to record the interview. I told him that you would probably want to do it the afternoon of the twenty-first or the morning of the twenty-second. Was that all right? I mean, there's no sense in going up twice in one week or so, is there?

– No.

Rather strangely – or so it seems now – this conversation was interrupted and was never really resumed that morning. As we were in the middle lane in Brian Boru Street Kate remembered that she had letters which needed to be posted urgently. First of all I had to beg and bully my way to the right-hand lane and then further endear myself to the mass of traffic by parking illegally outside the post office – thereby jamming an entire lane – for as long as it took Kate to jump out and stuff the letters in the box. When eventually we got back into the correct lane Kate was talking about Dan Henegan's career after Garbally and we were still on this when we made our second illegal and (for others, especially a red Volvo) infuriating stop outside the theatre. As she turned and stepped out of the car:

– Don't forget to ring him as soon as you can: he said he would be there from about nine thirty. Will you be able to collect me at one? I'll wait outside for you, OK? Unless it's raining. If it's raining, give me a blast on the horn: I'll be waiting inside the door. There was something else I meant to say to you. Oh, yes: you better make arrangements to cancel your lectures on the Thursday and Friday. We can go up on Thursday morning. The girls will be staying with the Montforts on Wednesday night so we could go up on Wednesday evening if we wanted to. Think about it. I suppose it will depend to some extent on your friend in RTE. Anyway, must go: give me a call if you get the chance.

As I nodded my head and looked at my watch, Kate sat back in, leaned across and kissed me:

– I am really looking forward to this, know that? I am going to enjoy myself.

– OK. Out you get. Time to go.

Standing outside the car, waving and laughing as she shouts through the weaving pedestrians:

– It's gone the time already!

How did I manage to drive from the Grand Parade to the English department of University College Cork without mishap? I parked the car at the back of the English department and walked down to the shop on the corner of Gaol Walk. I had not smoked for two years and it was only about half nine in the morning but what I wanted was a cigar.

Down at the corner shop I tried to buy a single cigar but had to buy a packet of five. On my way up the stairs to my office I knocked on Jim Roche's door.

– Morning all!

As I reached my door I heard him open his and shout up.

– Ready for coffee?

– Sure. Just give me five minutes to straighten some things here and then I'll be down.

– Fine. I'll wash a couple of mugs and get some milk.

– Five minutes.

Behind my desk I lit a cigar. The first drag almost choked me but I had the faith of an old addict: I knew it would help me gather myself together. There were telephone calls I did not understand, one of them from a person I did not know. But Kate seemed to know all about it and to take it all in her stride. She seemed to know that I had written a book called *Gone The Time* which was about to be published by Hollinsford of London and launched in Dublin on Friday 22 February 1985.

The only problem was I had not written any such book.

Reviewing what I have written so far, I must confess to a feeling of disappointment, even of frustration. Although I have described the principal events of the early morning, so much seems to be missing – especially the feeling within my limbs, within my head, a feeling of the absolutely ordinary beginning to disintegrate like a sand castle in the wind. (There: I try to forbid myself such similes but they intrude.)

Why I didn't confide in somebody? I honestly don't know. I mean: confide in whom? Kate? She was at work and I would see her at lunch time. My colleague? Absolutely dependable, so why not? Because I think – I know – I believed that there was an easy solution to whatever was happening, that somebody would laugh and then we could all laugh together, that somebody would pull a string and the knot would disappear. If I had my time over again I would have consulted a lawyer. My instincts are to avoid officers of the law and legal practitioners at all costs – or even, unlikely though it would be, at no cost – but experience has made me lament the lack of an official document, not open to any doubt, dated 11/2/85 and containing, properly witnessed and in the acceptable jargon, my account of the morning's events. A lawyer could have rung Hollinsfords and made enquiries concerning their forthcoming publications. Why didn't I contact a psychiatrist? Two reasons. Firstly, I do not believe in them; I would as soon have gone to a priest in confession. Secondly, though my head knows better, there is some backward part of me which persists in associating psychiatry with what used to be known as lunacy. And I did really think that, despite the fact that I could see no strings or shoes beneath the curtains, this was some kind of practical joke that we would all laugh at before the day was done. Touchingly optimistic? Consider the alternatives. Selective amnesia? Paranoia? Schizophrenia? Insanity? I hadn't changed – no matter what else had. I was the same body, same clothes, same mind, same office, same job, same colleague downstairs. Better than most people, I could remember almost everything of my shared experience with the human race. Apart from one detail: the writing of a book. And so there had to be an explanation and that explanation would have to have something to do with a hoax or a practical joke. How had they come up with the title? It was a matter of staying calm and waiting for the others to give themselves away.

Another explanation for my failure to confide: I would have to admit to a certain congenital distrust of the total and spontaneous honesty which so many of our elders and betters propose as *summum bonum*.

Am I unusual in that I have had moments of giddiness when I distinctly heard the voice inside explain how everything would be much the better for a brief spasm of chaos? I doubt it: I imagine most people can recall similar temptations. Though I have had such moments I have never really felt myself in danger of actually falling into the whirlpool. In fact, if the truth were known, I tend to be slightly proud of the fact that I am not weak under pressure, that a youthful immersion in Manichean cosmology and scholarship examinations has given me a kind of strength under fire.

I conducted myself quite normally and in character when I joined Jim for coffee and confabulation. I had asked him to consider the case of the graduate student who had come to me with her complaint. I believed every word she said but was inclined to advise her to forget about it: she had reacted to my apparent nonchalance by collapsing into sobs and giving details of her humiliation that she had previously withheld. There was, as far as we could see, nothing that we or she could do about it. There were no witnesses, no marks; the charge would be denied. Jim wondered what we should say to her.

– Tell her to make sure it doesn't happen again. Anyway: I'd better be going.

– You have the second years at ten, don't you? Before you go, cast your expert eye over the opening par of this.

It was an undergraduate essay. I glanced through the first page, concentrating on syntax and punctuation. Then I checked back on the name of the student. The syntax gave the game away.

– A palpable plagiarist.

– Yes, but cunning or accidental?

– I'd have to read it all.

– I'll leave it in your tray.

– Fine.

And then it was time for me to head up to room G19 and *Hamlet*.

By what some people might take as a strange coincidence – I wish I could ditch the mystical terminology but that's what it was, a coincidence – I can actually reproduce part of the lecture I gave that morning because I used the typescript of an address I gave a few years ago at a conference of English teachers. It was not my custom to use a prose text for lectures; I preferred brief jottings to remind me of the main points and of the texts I wanted to refer to. This use of a written-out text was an experiment that was abandoned immediately afterwards.

In my previous lecture I had argued that the opening scene of the play was designed to make it impossible for the audience to reach a confident conclusion as to the nature of the Ghost. The Ghost was a mystery, as instantly acceptable, as utterly satisfactory and as far beyond our rational comprehension as, say, the Fairy Godmother in *Cinderella*. In the opening scene the characters 'analyse' the appearance of the Ghost, several 'interpretations' are offered but no 'right answer' is given – certainly not in the earliest parts of the play and it is there that our expectations are formed.

That is a general paraphrase of brief notes; what follows is a careful transcription of material I used for my lecture and that I still possess in my file, marked 'Shak Trag 2PH 3/12' (Shakespearean tragedy lectures for second year students, pass and honours, third lecture of twelve-lecture course). I began with a summary of the previous lecture, continued with a close reading of two passages – Hamlet on 'seems' and Horatio's account of the Ghost – and then used the following section of the typescript.

> Hamlet's encounter with the Ghost confirmed his own intuitions, his 'prophetic soul', that the Danish court is in fact a sham, a rotten core covered by a skin of legal dignity. An uncanny encounter at midnight enabled him to see through the disguise and now he realises that he must look at life again and disabuse himself of the common sense and the common sensations he has always taken for granted at face value:
>
> > Yea, from the table of my memory
> > I'll wipe away all trivial fond records,
> > All saws of books, all forms, all pressures past
> > That youth and observation copied there . . .
>
> He will begin again with a proposition which is apparently simple but one which undermines the human ability to share a sense of actuality. Nobody, nothing is to be trusted: just now when he needs all the support he can find, Hamlet discovers that he must operate in the dark.
>
> Although the audience sees a world of which Hamlet is only a part, its perception of that world is strongly influenced by Hamlet's description of it. Hamlet's own world is curiously bifocal: he moves in the environment he had known since childhood but is convinced that all he sees may be a visual illusion. He is rather like a man walking through a suspected minefield, seeing only the surface but obsessed with the invisible threat beneath. Hamlet tries to make sense of his world – to relate the surface appearance to the inner truth – but again and again he fails. The best analogy for his situation is that of the dreamer in a nightmare and this analogy throws considerable light on the dramatic technique of *Hamlet*.
>
> The essence of the nightmare is freedom from the laws which govern – or at least seem to account for – waking phenomena. The laws of gravity are suspended, clocks and calendars no longer apply and fantastic changes of shape, colour and behaviour are the norm. Very often the subject is convinced of the existence of a barrier between himself and the other characters in the nightmare. It may

seem that he is strangely powerless against them, that they enjoy abilities denied him, that they conspire against him for no apparent reason, but there is nearly always a feeling on the part of the dreamer that he is somehow normal in an abnormal world.

It was at this stage that I detected a certain unease in the class. I went back over the points I had been trying to make, restating them as simply as I could, but many in the class seemed lost. I asked for questions. As usual there was a long pause but after a while I noticed two girls pushing each other light-heartedly and I guessed that each was prompting the other to ask the question. Eventually I elicited the question: was I saying that Hamlet dreamt the whole thing? Some of the class laughed at this but I made my disapproval clear. It was a very interesting question and showed that somebody was awake. No, I was not saying that Hamlet was asleep but I was working up to the point that the dramatic style of the play owes much to or is analogous to the common human experience of nightmare. Again I tried to interest the class in this idea but again I felt that I was losing them. Any questions? At all?

After what felt like hours, I was rescued by one of the brighter students who asked me to explain what I had meant when I said that the Elizabethan audience would, certainly by the end of Act One, have known what kind of play *Hamlet* was and what to expect of the central character. I accepted the question as my release from typescripts and nightmares. It was a topic I could lecture on in my sleep and so, having written REVENGE PLAY and MALCONTENT on the blackboard, I slumbered through the remainder of the lecture.

I decided against reading the newspapers in the common room and made my way back to the English department.

Transcribing that portion of the lecture, I could not avoid noticing the relationship between it and my own circumstances. I would wish to make two points which are easily verified. A: The topic of the lecture for that day had been decided by me and advertised in a handout given to the students the previous week. B: The typescript was about four years old, had been heard by some hundred delegates at a conference and had been read and commented on by two colleagues.

It may be that whatever text I was using would have acquired a personal resonance on that day. Perhaps. 'La Belle Dame sans Merci'?

I have an image of myself crossing the bridge on Gaol Walk and making my way quietly towards the buildings which housed the English department. I am fascinated by my apparent calm: I experience a kind of alienation, a feeling of being more than usually alone. It is in some ways like a hangover, a dull wasteland of discomfort in which every now and then a bubble of residual alcohol bursts, two clumps of dazed neurones collide and then, ugh, back in glorious cheek-warming techni-colour and nerve-grating hi-fi comes a digitally transcribed replay of the awful moment of the previous night – the unbelievably gauche remark, the oh so uncharacteristic revelation of one's casual lust, the wine stain spreading through the carpet. Similarly, into the routine of my Monday morning come regular summonses back to the world of the phone call and the conversation with Kate. Must be some kind of a dream. A nothing. Nothing more than imagination, a fiction of some kind.

Fiction. A book floated into my mind when I was seated back in my office. *I'm Not Stiller*, written in German by a Swiss writer, Max Frisch. (I am not sure about these details; my copy of the book is in Dublin.) I bought the Penguin trans way back: I remember reading it on a train, presumably the train to or from school, probably not long after I bought . the Penguin *Portrait*. It is a Kafkaesque story of mistaken identity and I found it pleasantly tedious during my first and only reading: it bored me at a time when I believed that boring German novels, especially those sanctioned by Penguin, should be part of the diet of any serious student of literature. (I must read it again; perhaps I am being unfair to it.) I remember almost nothing of it except the thickness of the style – perhaps the translator's contribution – and the fact that it told of a man who was arrested as the eponymous Stiller. Surely this novel can hardly have touched me as did, say, *Ulysses, Emma, A Handful of Dust*?

But what was I doing? What was all this about? Jesus, I had to cop on. All this stuff about Max Frisch was fishing in the whirlpool. I had to wake up. I was in the back room on the top floor of number 8 Bloomfield Terrace. Not in a fucking Penguin book.

A braver person, a more honest person, would not have behaved as I did. The courageous course was obvious: call Kate and arrange to meet her in a café without delay. I should have checked my filing cabinet for typescripts (second drawer from bottom) or for evidence of publication (contracts and agreements). Instead, I lit yet another cigar and felt suddenly in danger of being sick. I had to get out in the air. To the Lee Fields. Take the car and be there in two or three minutes.

This I did.

Off Grafton Street in Dublin there is a pub called McDaid's. It consists – or did the last time I put foot inside it – of a compact high-ceilinged room with barely enough space for the bar, the gangway and the seats affixed to the wall. It stands – like a true corner boy – where Harry Street meets Chatham Lane and has been quite famous for some time now, having been haunted by several celebrities-to-be in the fifties and written about by friends-of-the-famous-dead in the seventies: at one point in the late sixties the place was seldom free of some form of recording equipment. The late sixties were my years there. When I came back to Dublin in the early seventies I headed straight for McDaid's but – like all pubs – it had changed almost as much as I had in the meantime. Staff and regulars looked increasingly uneasy as the bohemian boozers and oddballs of other days were pushed around by toughs in black leather who kept their business and themselves very much to themselves. But then a most remarkable thing happened: though the name and the building – and, I imagine, the latest wave of clients – remained where they were on the corner of Harry Street, the essence of the pub transferred to a different street where it lurks beneath a different name. For the essence is a man of Chaucerian warmth, a truly great barman, a genius of sociability: Paddy O'Brien. Paddy worked in Harry Street for many years and was so much the heart and soul of the place that when he moved to Grogan's of South William Street some two hundred yards away, the odd assortment of artists, artisans, able-bodied seamen and unsteady academics, painters and punters, actors and ex-actors, took up their drinks, as it were, and traipsed across the rubble after him and continued their conversations in the new place.

This decline and fall and resurrection, this modern metamorphosis, was all in the future when I, a student at UCD, became an habitué of McDaid's of Harry Street.

The heart glowed and the bosom expanded. In entering McDaid's I was following a short but substantial family tradition: my father was not unknown there; Uncle and several relations were very well known there. I was delighted to be recognised in such a place, to be so-and-so's son, nephew or cousin or whatever. I was just out of a secondary boarding school in the country and for me this was it: McDaid's, bohemia, Grafton Street, downtown, life. I was now a student in the only sense in which that word could then be used on its own, meaning a university student. I had longed for this state of grace: lectures, zipped briefcase, duffel coat, sitting beside girls, discussing Joyce over pints in smoky pubs. Nor was I, for the most part, disappointed. I had a duffel coat and a new zipped briefcase and during my first year I attended almost all my scheduled lectures. And in time it became a daily routine to drink coffee with girls in the pubs near college – Kirwan's and Hartigan's of Lower Leeson Street – and I even remember once talking about Joyce at the back of Kirwan's. That kind of thing was fine, especially if the girls were there, but if analysis of the deep structures of life was what you were after, McDaid's was the place.

Fortunately, McDaid's was not to the taste of the average student and this suited the three or four of us who liked to leave the groves of Leeson Street and tarry awhile with the apostles of the counterculture. All kinds of images come flooding back. Passionate dialogues on the nature and function of the metaphor conducted with Platonic assiduity while sharing the corner behind the telephone with big red-faced street-traders. The way the telephone would ring for ages before anybody picked it up. The inscription above the phone: $e = mc^3$. Plans for a life of bohemian pleasure hatched on bar stools and continued – with a truly peripatetic grace – in the downstairs toilet, a dark subterranean stall to which one descended by means of an almost vertical stairs – presumably a relic of former times, for only a black joker could have designed such an obstacle for a pub – and in which the radiance of the plans became tainted with the reek of urine, tobacco and beer-laden breath. Several rainy days and nights when Paddy, noticing that I was at the end of my funds, put up free drink with a gruff generosity.

And a cast of thousands. Solicitors and junior doctors slipping in for a quick gin and tonic. Gamblers leaning on the bar, sipping slow pints and reading newspapers between regular sorties to the bookies. Literary cells – poets of all ages, attendant women of uncertain age – sprawled around a table, talking loudly about horse-racing and Auden and the likes. Telephone engineers – ill-kempt beards and donkey jackets – applying Marxist theory to drink and sex and Sean O'Casey. And the academics: one of them crouched over the bar stuck in a book on theoretical mathematics, looking up to survey the crowd as he sips his pint and then returning with audible relief to his book; the other, tall and thin and unsteady as he sets his watch by the clock above the bar and marches across the traffic to Earlsfort Terrace, ten minutes less late than he thinks. There were some more irregular regulars. Even in those optimistic times before the North blew up, McDaid's had its share of men known for their politicial convictions. There were others – quiet, carefully dressed men who never shouted or laughed aloud – whose activities were well known to the police. And the endless stream of eccentrics, most of them alcoholic, passing through from one strange place to another. And moving around among them all was Paddy, peppering the place with jokes and jibes and greetings. He had assistance – Jim with his serious face and occasional smiles, John the elderly potboy always trying to crack jokes – but Paddy was the sunny centre of things.

I loved the summer evenings, say around seven, when the door was still open and the place fairly quiet. One in particular has remained in the memory. Four of us there, drinking slowly, talking quietly, taking our time. The summer of 1967, the summer after graduation, Barry Mullins, Donncha Kinsella, Caroline O'Neill and I, yawning on the fatness of the summer evening air. A good year. I felt on top of the world, a graduate student at UCD but earning some money as a tutor in the English department, spared the indigence of student life but still innocent of the responsibilities of real employment. Barry was in Foreign Affairs and, we all felt, destined to travel to foreign countries, to become *au fait* with the wines and women of distant cities. Donncha and Caroline were engaged, the first of our friends to make that ritual contact with the outer world. I am not sure that we understood what was involved in their plans any more than I understood what a mortgage was: marriage was something we all expected to experience some time or other in the middle to long term.

At about nine o'clock the place began to fill up and the four of us decided to have a meal in a nearby Chinese restaurant, the Kum Tong at the top of Grafton Street. We waved farewell to Paddy and said that we might drop in later just for one on the way home. Walking across Grafton Street, it struck me that we had all set ourselves on roads that would take us away from Ireland for at least three years. Nobody knew when but it was certain that Barry would be posted abroad. I intended to sit for a travelling studentship, the only virtue of which was that it enabled successful candidates to spend three years working for a doctorate in the foreign university of their choice.

What did we talk about when we were seated at our usual table in the back corner of the Kum Tong? No idea. Certainly not politics: we were genuinely apathetic, regarding politics as an optional interest and one that was dominated by clowns with simple minds and concentrated energies. Barry and I spent a good deal of our time together talking about literature but we would have skirted the subject in the company of Caroline and Donncha. (Barry and I spent a good deal of our time together talking about sex but, again, not in company.) What did we talk about? The weather? Music – classical or pop? No, not really. I imagine we talked about people, new people – strangers to the others – whom we had encountered at work. And we would have laughed at them, at their stuffy ways and ridiculous routines. Because we were still between two worlds, still able to take adolescent pleasure in the adult world.

We lingered over the meal for so long that we decided it was too late to do anything except slip back into McDaid's. We were lucky: the place had filled up but just as we came in the door Paddy called us over to the table at the far end of the bar which was just then being vacated. Everything seemed to be arranged for our pleasure: the anecdotes and the quiet laughter came as regularly as the drinks and the cigarettes. And I felt a kind of bursting sensation, a high contentment, realising that it would never be quite the same again, not for us, not in this particular way, never again; things might be better but never like this. And such stirrings of pre-emptive nostalgia contrived in the commotion of last orders to evoke a family favourite:

> Farewell companions, my knights of red ochre,
> Bravely you've bent to the rule of the poker,
> Blazing a trail for the baker and broker,
> Far from the village we tarried so long!

I must have lost myself in my own thoughts for suddenly into remembered silence comes the clamour of Paddy banging the empty glasses on the counter and shouting that it was gone the time, come on now ladies and gentlemen, well gone the time.

Watching the others finish their drinks and gather their things, I knew that if ever I wrote a novel based on my experiences as a student in

Dublin I would call it *Gone The Time*. I can still feel the *frisson* of conception, still see the scene before me as if it were a painting. People looking in the back door to see if drink was still being served. A man on the telephone, with his back to us, trying to call a taxi. At the far end of the bar – by the seat, our customary seat, inside the front window – a red-haired medical student was stuffing a half-bottle of gin into his pocket and listening to Paddy. Donncha was putting on his mac and straightening the collar with his right hand while helping Caroline put on her coat with his left hand. And I thought that the difficulty of such a book would not be the recovery of incidents – far from it – but the task of editing and shaping the *copia* into a copy that had the same clarity as the scene in the bar had for me there and then. The epigraph stared me in the face: $e = mc^3$. And if possible the final lines would describe Paddy shouting that it was gone the time, ladies and gents have yis no homes to go to, well gone the time.

No copy came from my vision of McDaid's. Not that I had any ideas about charging home, pulling out the typewriter and working through the night. I assumed that I would wait a few months or years or whatever until I was ready or the time was right. Or whatever. But two years later I was somewhere else, drinking a different beer in a different pub with different friends. I was delighted to have escaped from Dublin and had no desire to spend my time re-creating a life which had come to seem dull and repressed. I preferred new beginnings to old memories.

But something too much of this. Time to return. Where was I?

Walking along by the Lee. I have always liked walking along rivers; I suppose everybody does. Why? Does the moving water promise to clean and forgive? Does it offer us the simplest and clearest image of the transience of all things, even those things we think of as fixed? For some reason I had come here and somehow the terror began to eddy. My mind sported and played, careless for minutes on end of the frightening possibilities which lurked 'neath each green leafy shade but always returning with a gradual qualm to the reason for my presence by the river. And then another effort to push the trip switch of the brain. Way, way back, perhaps as far back as I go, as a child in bed, huddled up beneath three or four blankets and a huge black belted overcoat, the cogs and pulleys of the brain groping for something on which to engage.

Thinking. I am thinking. I am thinking about thinking now. Or am I simply thinking?

Thinking about what?

It.

What is *it*?

Thinking about thinking about thinking and so on.

I see.

And is it possible to get off this roundabout of thinking about thinking about thinking? Thinking about *it*? Is it?

Yes. Experience teaches us that it is merely an occasional occurrence, that the bulk of your past life has not been spent thinking about *it* but about many other things.

Fine, but how can I stop thinking about *it* now?

I don't know just now. Can you imagine yourself stopping?

Not just now. But I agree with you: I am bound to stop soon. The brain will blink and –

And next thing you know you'll be thinking about something else.

Like what?

Like somebody you met today, a conversation you had, thoughts. Like that image you have of people coming back to Cork from a successful Munster Final in Thurles: the back of a pub packed with caps and blue striped suits and huge tobacco-stained fingers and shrieks of victory and then the sudden reverential silence as a thin man with watery eyes, purple veins on his upper cheeks, a bony triangular nose, begins to sing 'The Banks': Ah, how often my thoughts in their fancy take flight...

By the way?

Hmmn?

You've done it.

Done what?

You are no longer thinking about *it*.

Jesus!

It did happen. Right under your nose. As I told you. As you knew well it had to. As it always has and always will.

Do you know something?

What?

I was stopped but now you've started me again: I'm thinking about *it* again.

Not quite.

Explain please.

Escape led to a consciousness of the escape and that brought you back not to thinking about thinking but to remembering about remembering.

Same thing.

Don't be ridiculous. You might as well say red is the same as yellow just because they are both colours. Remembering about remembering is a totally different *it*.

Even now, walking along the Lee on this fatal day, although there is a tightening sensation inside and outside the skull and fear crackles in the disturbed branches of the trees, I know that I can absorb the thought that the escapes will for ever be merely brief interludes between returns to lengthy terms in the prison of thinking about thinking about thinking. Frightening though it is now, it is nothing compared to the boiling silence of childhood: in the boxroom bed there was an overwhelming fear that the brain was going to break up and crumble because of the constant circling. Like a motorcyclist on the wall of death who discovers that the throttle is jammed and he has no way of slowing down, no way of getting off except by jumping. Of course it's different now. I know so much more than I did when I cowered between the hairy blankets and waited for time to skip ahead towards morning and the world of other people. I can exercise a good deal of control over my thinking. I think I know most of the escape procedures.

It was time to start walking back to the car. The thing to do, now as ever, was to bear up and act as if everything was under control. Which it was. Apart from some little short circuit somewhere along the line. I looked across the river and up at that line of splendid grey buildings on the crest of the ridge. Time to go.

When I got to the theatre a few minutes after one, Kate was waiting outside, looking all excitement.

– Field Day are coming.

– Great.

– There are still one or two things to be worked out – accommodation and dates – but that's no problem. Must get working on the advance publicity immediately. Do you know anything about this play *Double Cross*?

– Not a lot.

– Do you have any lectures this afternoon?

– No, I've kept it free so that I can try and finish this essay on Joyce.

– Will you be able to give me a hand?

– Hah?

– I don't want you to write it for me, just look over it.

– Look over what?

– The advance publicity. I want to get something into the *Examiner* and onto local radio as soon as possible: just a general piece about Field Day coming to Cork with their latest play et cetera.

– OK. We can look at it tonight.

Back home I was making coffee when the phone rang.

– Hello.

– Fintan? Howya? Tom Dolan here.

Tom was a former student of mine who was now working for the *Examiner*. I never knew him particularly well but he had been very good to Kate when she looked for newspaper coverage.

– Tom. What can I do for you?

– The *Examiner* want me to do a piece on you and so I was wondering how and when and where would suit you.

– What did you have in mind?

– About an hour. In your house, if that suits you. It's only down the road from me. Or anywhere else. I don't mind so long as it's not in some crowded smoky pub.

All I could do was make a mumbling noise.

– Your house would probably be best. I was thinking of a photograph of you with Kate and the kids. If that's OK with you. Huh? Are you there?

– Sure. I'm listening.

– I thought you had been cut off. Anyway: maybe you want to think about what arrangements will suit you.

– OK.

– Somebody else is doing the review. What I will be doing is a feature, more of a general interview, personal rather than literary, if you know what I mean, but basically about the book of course.

– How do you mean?

– It's really up to you. Whatever you want to talk about. Well, I've heard that the plot resembles your own life somewhat.

I was suddenly at a loss, about to panic, when Kate came into the kitchen and silently asked who was on the phone. When I told her it was Tom Dolan she signalled that she wanted to talk to him afterwards. I am not exactly sure what ridiculous excuse I gave him – I think it was something about not being permitted to give interviews until after the launch – but it enabled me to hand him over to Kate and while they were discussing the Field Day visit I decided to skip lunch and head for Mayfield pool.

– Bye, Tom, talk to you soon and thanks again. Will I put you back on to Fintan? OK then. Bye for now. What did Tom want you for?

– An interview.

– What did you say? I hope you were friendly.

– Of course I was. I know he is a very good contact for you and, anyway, I like Tom. I said I was tied up at the moment but I would get back to him next week. He seemed happy enough.

– But you will do the interview?

– Next week.

What had happened to me on the phone with Tom Dolan? Why had I lied about a publisher's ban on interviews? (Had I lied?) That was simple: I lied in order to avoid giving an interview or at least to postpone it for a week or so. So what? Was I worried about telling a lie? No, not really, perhaps not at all. So why was I interrogating myself like this? Not because I had told a fairly trivial lie to Tom Dolan. Because I had told the other lie: for the first time I had underwritten the fiction that I was the author of a book called *Gone The Time* which was about to be published. I hadn't said anything to Kate or to anybody in college that could be construed as an explicit acceptance of the allegation. I had watched my words carefully all morning, even in the bosom of my own family, and then blown it all during a telephone call. It was frightening to think how easily one could slip into somebody else's thinking, some-body else's world. It wasn't that I believed it – it wasn't even that I could imagine myself believing it – but I had behaved as if I believed it, and not only that: I had as good as gone public on it by speaking to a journalist. Why?

I had made a mistake, a tactical mistake, a fairly natural mistake in the circumstances. Circumstances? I had been surprised, ambushed by the telephone. I could have told the truth, so to speak: I could have laughed at Tom and told him that it was all a joke. A joke? A laughing matter? With Kate and Cliona and Maeve listening to me. Whatever it was, it wasn't a joke – not within the normal meaning of the act. A hoax? Perhaps. If not a hoax? A mistake? Whose mistake? Whose hoax? Kate's? No, I was convinced that Kate was as much a victim as I was. There was a book. I knew nothing of its gestation but Kate accepted it as if she had known about it for some time. The guy from London knew about it; it was taken for granted in the English department and the *Cork Examiner*.

Driving up to the pool, the thought occurred: it made no sense to try to make sense out of it. It was a mistake to look for the mistake somewhere. Everything would become clear. All would be explained. And all manner of things would be well.

Under the water the words boomed: *I've heard that the plot resembles your own life somewhat.* Did he tell me that or was he asking me a question? What did that sentence mean? The more I repeated it to myself, the more opaque, the more meaningless it became, especially the enigmatic – inane? – 'somewhat' barely hanging on at the end. But then again it didn't matter a shit what the sentence meant: the important thing was what Tom Dolan meant and that much was fairly clear. Bubbles. *I've heard that the plot resembles your own life somewhat.* Mustn't tire myself out too quickly or I won't be able to complete my twenty lengths. *I've heard that the plot resembles your own life, so what?* To hell with this. I tried to drive past the voice but there was no mistaking the bubbles. *Absurd that the plot resembles the only life you've got.* Faster and faster. I knew that if I went hard enough I would be too tired to think, that the sounds of my breathing would fill my head, that my trunk would bump with the pounding of my heart and my arms and legs would cry out for rest. Come on! One more length. And just one more: the very last one!

Back home Kate was busy with paperwork and didn't want a cup of coffee. I put my towel and togs to the wash and retired to my study where I opened my Joyce folder and tried to find some point of entry. I had been working on an essay for some time – what I had before me was the second typed draft – but not only could I not become interested in it, I could hardly understand it. Paragraphs that I remembered forming and re-forming in order to be as elegantly precise as possible now

made no sense at all. The punctuation throughout seemed intrusively
bizarre. I was beginning to realise that the more I forced myself to read
the essay the more incomprehensible it was becoming. Footsteps on the
stairs. Kate at the door.

    – Like some salmon later on?

    – That would be nice.

    – Do you have a drop of wine to go with it?

    – Indeed I do; and some to go before and after it as well.

    – I'll feed the girls and get them up early. Eat about half eight or so?

    – Perfect. I'll look after the wine and then work up here for a while.

At last I had something to do, some action in which I could lose
myself. I got two bottles of white (just in case) from the pantry and stood
them out in the back yard to chill. I cleaned and polished two cut glasses,
asked if I could be of any use in the kitchen and then returned to my
study. I was lost in the essay when the girls came in to kiss me good night
and tell me that they were going to bed a little early because Mummy
and I were having a special dinner.

As I walked down the stairs I knew that the time for confrontation
had come.

I am obliged to preface my account of what happened that night with
two brief notes on the wine.

1: I have often drawn Kate's attention to the wicked intelligence
which ordained that the common bottle of wine should contain 75 cl.
(approx.). So great is the force of this convention that when bigger bottles appeared in supermarkets they did not, as one might have expected,
contain one or even two litres; they contained 1.5 litres, double the
normal contents. Why has the litre bottle not yet prevailed? No doubt
the wine companies would come up with all sorts of reasons – most of
them to do with the welfare of the customer – but I prefer my own
explanation. Which is: that the average person who likes to have some
wine with their food would like to have half a litre and that, consequently, a couple would prefer to consume one litre. But given the
inviolability of the standard measure, what happens? The couple must
either limit themselves to 0.375 litres each and retire unsatisfied or they
can open a second bottle and face a further choice: whether to consume
the half-litre each and cork the remainder for some other time or to

finish off the second bottle, thus drinking more than they originally desired, getting more intoxicated than they would have chosen but – and this is the logic that clinches the issue halfway through the second bottle – not wasting half a bottle of expensive wine by recorking it and throwing it there *sine die*.

2: The bottles I had chosen were a Pouilly Fuissé and a Muscadet. Lest this give the impression that we drink beyond our means, I must explain that our apparent extravagance was due to the happy carelessness of an employee in Dunnes Stores in Ballyvolane. Among the bottles on the shelf were two which, to eyes unexcited by wine, looked very similar: a Muscadet and a Pouilly Fuissé, the former priced at £2.99, the latter at £11.99. However, an employee whose task it was to stick the price-stamps on the bottles had failed to distinguish between the two and that is why, one afternoon as Kate did the real shopping and I browsed among the wines, I found before me a dozen bottles of Pouilly Fuissé clearly priced at £2.99, a dozen bottles that shortly afterwards made the short drive to our house.

My reservations about the accuracy of the following sequence are basically due to the fact that between us Kate and I finished both bottles of wine. It's not that I felt particularly drunk at any stage but of course I wouldn't have felt particularly drunk if I had been a teeny bit jarred. And, looking at the situation in reasonably dispassionate retrospect, even though I think I remember everything that happened in the manner in which it happened, I must presume that the consumption of the equivalence of at least one bottle of wine did alter my normal perception of events.

During the meal, while savouring the food and chatting with Kate, I tried to plan my opening statement as carefully as any chess challenger, mentally testing one after another, anticipating Kate's response to each and then trying to figure out my reaction to her response. As things turned out, this was a waste of time. When we had come down to the cheese, I took the used plates and cutlery out to the kitchen, came back and sat down.

– There's something I want to talk about, well, something that I find it very difficult to talk about.

Kate was cutting herself a piece of cheese and spoke without looking up.

   - I know what it is. It's the book, isn't it?

   - How did you know?

   - What else could it be?

   - I don't know.

   - No, it could only be the book. Will we move over to the fire?

   - No. Let's stay here. Why could it only be the book?

Did I have any idea what it had been like living with me for the past year? If I had, I would have no doubt that no matter what was on my mind it had to have something to do with the book. It must have been the nearest thing to a male pregnancy: about the only thing I didn't do was crave lumps of coal or bars of soap – presuming, of course, that I hadn't done so in private.

   - Come on.

It was very easy for me to say 'come on'; I hadn't had to put up with me for the first few months. I knew what was going on; Kate hadn't a clue. Except that she knew something was going on: it was obvious that I was up to something – running in from college and rushing up to the study for hours, having to be called several times for meals instead of constantly asking when meals would be ready, going silent all of a sudden in the middle of a meal, sometimes for minutes on end, the rest of them looking at me and trying not to burst out laughing. Not that it mattered to me whether they did or not. Would I like some more cheese; the Brie was beautiful. No, on second thoughts, it wasn't so much as if I was pregnant, more like as if I was having an affair.

   - I never realised you had this talent for comedy. You should never drink anything but Polly Fussy.

Did I ever wonder what it was like for her, not knowing what I was up to? What was she supposed to think when I seemed to lose interest in almost everything except disappearing up to my study or suddenly driving off to Mayfield or going for long walks God knew where? She was telling me that it did actually cross her mind that I was meeting somebody.

   - This is very good.

It was very easy to joke about it now but those first few months were no joke. Just as she was about to go lampy from living with a mute I began to talk and once that happened she thought I would never stop.

Then everybody else had to shut up and listen to my stories, breakfast dinner and tea. Not so much telling stories as trying to remember things that happened when I was a child, the names of the guys I was at school with, the things some of the neighbours used to say, the songs my parents' friends used to sing – everything you could imagine, Jesus, from old programmes on the radio to she didn't know what. She would have another glass of that excellent wine and might God bless the girl in Dunnes.

– Her very good health and yours. You must have known what was happening?

Well yes, she had always guessed that I was writing something, but what kind of a something? She had thought it was a book about Eugene.

– I was writing about Eugene: there was the essay in Irish on his English poetry and the essay in –

But that was different. They were just articles, the kind of things I was always doing, something to get interested in but not the sort of thing to blow my mind altogether. No, what I was up to was different. I was digging up long-forgotten stories about Eugene in the classroom, seeing how many of the boys' names I could remember, trying to relive the Finglas of my childhood. And I seemed to be understanding things for the first time, things I had more or less taken for granted. One night I had come down late and described what it must have been like for Eugene to live out the country, miles from a sleepy little village, and then to see the peaceful fields ravaged by bulldozers, dumpers and the men who built row after row after row of almost identical houses into which were poured the hordes of runny-nosed gurriers in short corduroy pants who squashed into the little village school and sat before him, the mystified in front of the amazed. Kate was dying to read it, to meet the other woman, so to speak.

– Why didn't you ask me?

I must be joking. She knew me well enough to wait: no way she wanted the snot cut off her and so she waited. Once or twice she dropped hints about not having anything decent to read but I made it clear that whatever I was writing was not ready yet. Not ready yet! And this after months of activity upstairs. Of course by then she realised that there was more to the book than Finglas and Eugene, that I was also doing something about Garbally and UCD, that she would have to wait. And by the way her glass was empty again. I was too kind. And then ... She would never forget the way I walked out of the front room, saying that I had something to show her, and I went upstairs and came down with the typescript, hundreds of pages high. Did I remember? And she remembered being staggered at the size of the thing: in three parts, each jammed into an envelope file, each one bigger than the average thesis. Did I remember what I said when I gave it to her?

– What?

– 'It's not as good as I hoped it would be but it's more or less the best that I can do. I'd like to know what you think of it.'

What a memory!

She remembered everything about that night: sitting in the front room, listening to the tape I had made for the Joyce course, I knew the one, with 'Marble Halls' and 'In Happy Moments', and then suddenly there I was with the typescript. Did I remember which day of the week it was?

– Let me see ...

Sunday night. The Easter vacation. Very late, in fact it was almost certainly Monday morning when I placed the typescript in her hands.

– The typescript?

I was to shut up and pass the cheese. She had thought that life would return to normal now that the thing was written but no such luck: it was bad enough waiting for a reply from the publisher but it was worse when it was accepted. And so ...

– And so what?

– And so, when you told me tonight that there was something you wanted to talk about, I knew it had to be the book.

– You are, as usual in matters of faith and morals, absolutely right.

– Well, it's not as if it wasn't clear to a blind man that something was bugging you for the past few days and especially yesterday and today. I mean, even Sally wanted to know what was wrong with you: she asked me why you weren't happy now that the book was about to be published. She said you were going round like a zombie and she was right.

– Yeah: I did feel a bit off, I suppose. I had a lot on my mind. It's hard to put it into words.

– May I try a guess?

– Be my guest.

– Haw-haw. Anyway. I have always felt – and I know you will say I am being silly – I have always felt that you were half hoping that it would be turned down.

– What makes you say that?

– I don't know. I've always felt that. I think your whole attitude changed when the book was accepted for publication. Am I right?

– I don't know.

– Oh, come on. First of all you said that no Irish publisher would touch it and you sent it to London; as soon as Hollinsfords accepted it you changed your tune and said you were sorry you hadn't sent it to Wolfhound or some Irish publisher. I mean, at one stage you wanted to withdraw it and send it to that Irish film company, what do you call them?

– Strongbow?

– Yes. And then the closer you come to publication the more faults you find with the book.

– Isn't that only natural?

– I don't know. Why should it be? I think it's great. The publishers think it's great. Why can't you think it's great. Or why can't you at least be happy about it? Is it because of what you have written about somebody like Eugene?

– What do you mean? Why Eugene? Why pick on Eugene?

– There you go again. I didn't say Eugene, I said somebody like Eugene. Eugene or Brendan or anybody else for that matter? You did say at some stage that it was a mistake to call the Eugene character George Rivers. I can't see anything wrong with it; seems fine to me.

– I wish to Christ I had never heard of the same fucking book.

– How can you say something like that? You spend ages working on it and there you are, lucky enough to have it snapped up immediately by a famous publisher. Most people would give their right arm to be in your position and all you can do is complain. It's a mystery to me.

– You haven't written the fucking thing. Here let's finish this bottle.

– I'm fine for the moment; help yourself. Look. If it wasn't good, you wouldn't have sent it to anybody; if it wasn't good, nobody would have accepted it for publication.

– They'd print shit if they thought it would sell.

– Maybe it proves nothing, but I think it's very good and I think people will enjoy it. Why not you? Why not sit back and enjoy the experience. It's not every day you have a novel published. And if it means so little to you, think of us. Think how much it will mean to me and the girls and your mother and father and lots of other people. Imagine what it will be like for Sally and Cliona and Maeve to see their Daddy's book in Easons and the Mercier. You will have to excuse me for a moment. I must go to the toilet. Have you any idea how thrilled the girls will be? Think about it.

I am. I have been thinking about it for the past hour at least. I have imagined myself playing the part, accepting the evidence, speaking my lines into a hundred recording devices, laying false claim to a book somebody else had written. And that was an undeniable fact: somebody else had written the book which bore my name, somebody else had chosen and set a selection of characters and incidents from my life. I had planned to sit here and explain all to Kate, but what had happened? I had grabbed at every crumb of information concerning the book, trying to surmise something of its form and contents. I was annoyed with myself for not speaking out quickly and clearly but what annoyed me even more was knowing that, initially at any rate, I enjoyed the effort of reading the book through the medium of Kate's comments. Part of me was waiting for her to come down from the toilet and scatter another series of clues; the other part was preparing to make a clean breast of the whole business here and now. No great problem making a clean breast of anything in the decent obscurity of a confessional; quite another thing to sit with Kate, pass the cheese and explain that I have absolutely no notion of what she is talking about, that I have what I take to be an adequate sense of the past year with one slight exception: my memory does not include such minor phenomena as the drafting, writing and re-writing of a book, the exchange of many letters with the firm of Hollinsfords, the checking and correction of proofs, the signing of contracts and, finally, the destruction – by burning or shredding or dumping in the bin – of notes, drafts, *disjecta membra*. Try telling that to Kate. Try explaining to the girls that Daddy didn't really write the book with his name on it in Easons' window. Kate closing the door and sitting down at the table, looking quizzical:

– I suppose it would be making pigs of ourselves to open another bottle.

– Indubitably.

– We'd be bound to regret it.

– Absolutely.

– There is a bottle outside. Not quite up to what we have been drinking but...

– Yes please.

I managed to get the other bottle, uncork it and bring it into the dining room – all without serious mishap. Kate had moved over to her armchair by the fire.

– This is the Muscadet which the little recording angel in Dunnes thought was the same as the Pouilly Fuissé. It would be nice to think that we could make the same mistake. Try it.

– Thank you. It looks nice anyway. I've been thinking.

– Was that wise? Did you bring over the cheese?

– Beside you. As I say, I've been thinking. I used to think, in fact I still think, that what's wrong with you and this book thing is that you are afraid. I still think you are afraid, although now I am convinced that you are afraid not of the thing I thought you were afraid of but of something else. Jesus: I'm getting myself into knots. Can you follow me?

– I'm there before you.

– Where was I?

– What used you think I was afraid of?

– Oh yes. Now I know. I used to think that you were afraid that people would dislike what you had written about them or about places like Garbally or UCD, but I don't think that bothers you a lot. You never know, but I don't think so. Maybe you had, still have, second thoughts about what you wrote about people like Brendan and Eugene, maybe even about your own family and so on.

– So what is it that bothers me?

– You. Casement Kelly.

Jesus!

– Explain.

Casement fucking Kelly!

– Right. But don't stop me. I know it's a novel and all that sort of thing. I know you have taken me through all this before. I know that there are major changes here and there, that there is no mention of certain things that you consider very important in your life – ninety per cent of everything you've ever thought, eaten, drunk, heard, seen, ninety-nine per cent of your bowel movements and all that. We've been through all that before. And I know that your name is not Casement Kelly. I know all that and I have no answer for it but the fact is that Casement Kelly is you to a *t*. When I read about him I see you, I hear you, I know you. And the same will happen with anybody who knows you and who reads the book. You know that Jim Roche will recognise you. You know that. And what's more: you know that you recognise yourself in Casement Kelly – which is hardly surprising seeing as that's why you made him the way he is. But this is what worries you now. It's the kind of thing that has always turned you off.

– What kind of thing?

– Standing up in public and being what you would call 'serious and sincere'. There's even something in the book about it – I forget where – but you know the bit when somebody wants him to address that meeting in UCD?

– The Literary and Historical?

– Yeah. The same thing exactly.

Casement Kelly. Roger Casement? But I am far from charmed. And Kelly the boy from God-knows-where.

– Say what you like. Say that you know more about the theory of it than I do – I don't care – he is exactly as I would have imagined you. I couldn't be so sure about the other characters. This is not nearly as nice as the other stuff; what is it?

– I told you. Muscadet. The stuff that your woman mixed up with the Pouilly Fuissé.

– Oh, yes.

– This is the stuff that is meant to be sold at £2.99. You need to take one decent mouthful to get yourselves properly introduced; it's not really meant to be sipped.

The phone barged in. As Kate rushed to put down her glass and pick up the receiver I whispered to myself the name of Casement Kelly, convinced that it would start a landslide in my brain. Casement Kelly. Nothing.

It was Kate's mother on the phone. She wanted to confirm that she would be able to babysit the girls while we were in Dublin for the launch. Putting the phone down, Kate went over the arrangements again. I refilled the glasses and tried to seem pleased. But it was futile: I gulped what was left in the glass, reached for the bottle and muttered something to the effect that I was not looking forward to the business in Dublin.

– Oh come on. No more of that kind of talk. We're going to enjoy ourselves. I can tell you one thing, I'm going to enjoy myself and fuck the begrudgers.

– Who will probably be there in some strength.

– Well, I can assure you that they will want to look out for themselves because I intend to have a ball. Is there anything on the box?

– I think there's snooker on 3.

– No thanks. I'm off to bed. I'm bushed.

– I think I'll watch the snooker for a few minutes.

– Hurry on up. I'll be perished.

– I won't be long. Few minutes.

With a crackling of static the grey screen cleared to a pattern of coloured balls on green. *Gaza per undas*: the world made flat. Formed and fixed. His opponent having become the horrified victim of a kick, Steve Davis moved in and began to clear the table with what he made seem a boringly facile inevitability. The spectrum of victory and defeat. The yellow, the green, the brown, the blue, the pink, the black. Into my life had come a book, written by me, an autobiographical novel, based on episodes from my own past, characters based on people I had known, one of them based on what seemed to some people myself.

Steve Davis was cruising. I knocked off the television.

I had not done it. That much I must hold on to. No matter how difficult it was to square it with the remainder of my universe, it was ultimately as simple as that. I had not done it.

I had not done it. It was not I. And even if it was I it was not me. Time for bed.

Within the rules and regulations laid down by the only court which ever commanded my belief – that of the one, holy, Catholic and apostolic – I was innocent. Well, at least, not guilty. I had no clear knowledge, no full consent, absolutely no intention, in fact no cognisance at all other than a highly dubious retrospective induction.

– You awake?

Garbally, Dor 8, *prima luce*, frost on the window, echoes of a remembered bell. A yawning brain revolving back into the whorl of night: nocturnal emission or masturbation? Theologically speaking, did you know what you were doing? Theologically speaking, no. I knew what was happening but I did not know what I was doing. Because I was not doing anything: it was doing me down there. Of course, it must have been triggered by thoughts up here. Yes, but clearly I was sleeping innocently through the thoughts; it was the result down there which woke me up up here. Yes, indeed: it was one up for me and a total defeat for cultural evolution. I had squared the circle in my sleep.

Sweet sinless sleep. The bright day to come.

– Night.

I would live to laugh at this, just as I lived to laugh at my little morning agonies in the dormitory, realising that it was all a question of sweet sinless sleep . . .

Light frost on the window. Kate telling me to get up quickly. Nearly half eight. Going to get the girls up. Never set the clock alarm. My throat. My head. Half past eight. Jesus. Tuesday. First years at eleven. Last night. Wine. Shit! Still there. Up.

After almost half an hour of shouting, pushing, bickering and arguing, of gobbling cereals and trying to agree on what Sally and Cliona would buy themselves in the shop in lieu of lunch, of insisting that in future the rules of the house were going to be strictly enforced et cetera, after all the commotion and turmoil that always happens when the electric lark fails to sing, I dropped the girls within fifty yards of the school and then came back and picked Kate up and dropped her and the core of her breakfast apple outside the theatre and then came home again to have my own breakfast and try to prepare myself for a major statement on dramatic irony to the first years.

I was walking down the front path at about twenty to eleven when a registered parcel arrived by post.

– Mr Kearney.

– Morning.

– Sign this for me, please? Not a bad morning. Thank you.

Kate does some occasional work for a market research company and so we are used to having registered parcels arrive and I have come to be on small-talk terms with the delivery man. I signed where he indicated, mumbled some reaction to his remark about the morning and then took the parcel back into the house. I was about to leave it on the coffer in the hall when I noticed the English stamps. It was not for Kate. It was addressed to me. It came from London, from Hollinsfords, and the customs declaration identified the contents as books.

Although I was already in danger of being late for my lecture and despite my unwillingness to believe in the actuality of the parcel, I began to rip it open with barbaric zeal, ravaging the outer box, tearing the inner brown paper wrapping, discovering within, half a dozen copies of a book, the pristine white of the pages, the blue of the jacket. I picked one up. On a background of sky blue, a border of blue, black, yellow and green, the colours of the UCD arts undergraduate scarf. Across the top: a photographic image of the stump of Nelson's Pillar and the GPO. Centre: a profusion of neo-Celtic ornamentation: pseudo-Celtic monkish figures which turned out to be students – duffel coats, surplices and soutanes (Jesus!), football gear, bent over books, between pints of Guinness and clouds of cigarette smoke, leering at pre-Celtic maidens as tumultuously-titted and as boulder-buttocked as anything *après At Swim-Two-Birds*. Supporting all this activity the title: *Gone The Time*. Across the bottom border, in clean white capitals, my name. I went to open it but something froze my fingers, a fear of what I would see, and to this day I have never been able to let my eyes rest on a single word of the text.

I remember very little of the lecture except that there was a fair amount of laughter and good humour. Normally I tend to go one or two minutes over the allotted time and normally, when teaching the vast hordes of first year in one of the library theatres, I hang about to allow those in a hurry to get out. On this occasion I surprised them, finished at six minutes to, and was halfway down the aisle before anybody realised I had finished. I made straight for the security booth and rang Kate at the theatre. I wanted to see her immediately. No: there hadn't been an accident, nobody was hurt or sick or even dead; there was something I wanted to talk to her about immediately. Anywhere we won't be interrupted. Take a coffee break. The Imperial. Fine. Ten minutes.

Kate was in the Imperial when I arrived. She looked very anxious.

I explained.

– Look, don't worry. Everybody's fine.

– So what's wrong?

– I'll explain. Have you ordered coffee? Thanks. Now the reason I wanted to meet you like this is because I have something important to say to you and I thought it would be easier if we were by ourselves rather than at home with the girls and so on. No, don't raise your voice. Just listen for a while.

– It's to do with the book, isn't it?

– Just listen and don't say anything for a while. Remember last night when I told you I had something to tell you? Well, I never got round to telling you the most important thing. Even now, I don't know how to begin.

The coffee arrived and while Kate settled for it I tried to find some reasonable beginning. In vain.

– This book. I didn't write it.

– What do you mean?

– I didn't write it, I didn't . . . write it. I know nothing about it, nothing about the book. The first I knew of it was yesterday.

– This is *Gone The Time*?

– I didn't write it.

– What do you mean?

– I can't say it more clearly. I didn't put paper in my typewriter and type out the words which are in the book called *Gone The Time*.

– You did. I know you did.

– I know I didn't. If I had done it, I would know.

– Do you mean that somebody else wrote it?

– I don't know. All I know is that I didn't.

– Then who did?

– Don't ask me. I don't know. I suppose somebody wrote it but I didn't.

– Somebody? Who?

– Not me.

– Who sent it to the publishers?

– Not me.

– You're not joking, are you?

– No, I am most definitely not. I wish to Jesus I was. I wanted to tell you this last night but I never got round to it.

– But why didn't you tell me before this?

– The first I heard about this book was yesterday.

– I don't know what to say.

– Nor do I. I know how strange this must sound to you. I thought it was all some kind of joke or some kind of I don't know what but . . .

– What if I told you that I know you wrote it?

– It would change nothing.

– That I saw you writing it? That you asked me to post the typescript for you? Remember when you were going to send it by college post and I said that I wouldn't take any chances, I would send it by registered post?

– I don't know what I would say. I know that you have read the book, even though the copies only arrived this morning.

– Who else could have written it? It's all about you.

– I know that. I gathered that much from you last night. I just don't know.

– I can show you contracts that you have signed. I have them at home. We can go and look at them now. Will that convince you?

– No.

– You can see your own signature!

– That will only convince me that I am legally responsible; it will change nothing else.

Kate was shaken but practical. Clearly she believed this was merely a temporary fit of nerves, that it would be wrong to berate me, to make a fuss, to treat me like somebody with a problem.

– Let's go home and talk about it over lunch.

– What about the theatre?

– That's OK. I told them I mightn't be back. Where's the car?

– Across the road.

On the way home Kate asked me to give a full account of everything I knew or thought about the book, from the beginning, whenever that was. Back home, she went upstairs and brought down a number of documents relating to the book: there were contracts that I had signed and there were two or three letters relating to the publication of the book and bearing my signature. Very calmly she assembled the irresistible argument: there were these documents, there were other documents, there was her own witness, there was the awareness of others. Did she want me to go up to my study or into my room in college and find other correspondence and notes and drafts for the book?

– No.

Kate was taking cold meat from the fridge when, without turning, she asked in a very casual tone.

– When did you first realise?

– Realise what?

– That something was wrong.

They were her words. I remember the precise tone. I remember the qualm that spread out from my spine as the words hit my ears and assembled the idea in my mind: there was something wrong with me. Angels and Ministers of Social Welfare! Buzz-buzz.

– Maybe you've overdone it, spending all summer on the book and then going straight into teaching.

I knew what was coming.

– Why don't you nip up to Joe and have a general checkup? Can't do you any harm, can it?

– I don't need any pills.

– You may be physically fit and able to play squash but –

– But that doesn't mean that there's nothing wrong with me mentally? Is that what you mean?

– Now that only shows how jumpy you are. You're emotionally knackered.

– Tired and emotional.

Kate looked helplessly and came over and hugged me.

– Don't be like that. I'm serious. You had no real summer holiday and you've been working hard since October. Even at Christmas you were reading stuff to do with college. I've told you to take things easier but when you feel tired you play squash and then when you feel exhausted you go for a swim and a sauna. You need a rest...

A cottage by the sea where there was no dramatic irony, no subversive puns. Fresh salty air and Monteverdi.

– They say it's like having a baby and I suppose there's something in it. I mean, you carry the thing inside you for months, feeling it getting bigger and feeling that it is becoming more and more a part of you and you have to sit and stand and walk and everything in a certain way because of it. You know? And instead of this thing that you came to live with, there's a baby and you love it but in the beginning it's very strange and I suppose that's because it's out there; it's no longer inside you.

– What I have is a touch of postnatal depression.

– Don't be so quick to make a joke about everything. What's your schedule like? Can you take a few days off and . . .

– And what?

– And just do nothing. Mess about in the garden. Listen to the stereo. Have a liquid lunch in Henchy's and that'll put you to sleep for the afternoon. Fester in front of the telly for the night. Or go to the pictures. What?

– I don't know. I suppose I could try. But I don't really see the point.

– Just to get away from things for a while. I'm going down to collect Maeve. There's some nice cooked ham there; make yourself a sandwich.

Just to get away for a while. And in a little while all will be well. Maybe I am depressed, simply depressed, in need of a rest. Maybe it's a form of hangover, like the hangover after alcohol when the conditions are ideal for the demons of guilt and despair and self-disgust; life seems bleak for a while but then something – the chemistry, I suppose – changes and after twenty-four hours you notice that the sun shines, that it is reasonable to make new plans, that the plans you made when still hungover are no longer suitable. Maybe we see only what we digest. Maybe I would feel better in a day or two; maybe I would see better in a day or two and I would recollect all this as mere moodiness. What did I have to eat on Sunday? Chicken.

Cooked ham. Make myself a sandwich. Have it in my study.

I was still staring at the typewriter when I heard Kate and Mary Montfort push in the front door and urge the children to wipe their feet. I need to prove to myself that I could still move and so I went down to say hello.

– How's Mary?

– Look who it is: the famous writer.

Mary had a copy of the book on her lap. Kate picked it up and waved it at me:

– Well?

– Well what?

– What do you think of it?

I sidestepped to the cooker to check if there was any tea in the pot.

– Jesus, you were right, Kate. He's more interested in his tea. I thought he'd be over the moon.

This became my preferred tactic, my favourite pose – debonair, nonchalant, insouciant, dismissing the book as just another of those things – but though it worked well enough with friends like Mary Montfort, it was not a role I could play with my own family. Shortly after Sally came in from school, I heard her running up the stairs to my study, bubbling with excitement, and I knew she would have the book in her hand. For a few minutes she was almost incapable of speech: all she could do was hug me and emit a high-pitched moan of pleasure. She couldn't wait to bring the book into school and show it to the girls in her class: oh, please, please, please, Daddy, I beg you, please let me bring it into class tomorrow and I swear I'll keep it perfectly clean, honestly, I won't let anybody else touch it but me.

– You better check with your mother.

– She said it depended on you. Oh please!

– OK.

– Thanks! Oh, I can't wait.

She clattered down the stairs, crashing into Mary Montfort who was preparing to leave. Five minutes later Sally was hurtling up the stairs again: this time she paused outside the door, knocked and opened it slowly and assumed her thoughtful, intellectual frown.

– Daddy, would this book be suitable for me?

– To read?

– Yes. I would love to read it. Mummy said that the story is like you growing up with Con and Nana and going to school and all that. I'd love to read it. But only if you think it would be suitable.

– What did Mummy say? Does she think it would be suitable?

– She said that she would leave it up to you.

– And what do you think she thinks?

– Well, I think she thinks it would be fine for me to read it.

– And how old are you now?

– Almost eleven.

– Well, I suppose that having lived with Mummy for almost eleven years you should have a fair idea of what's on her mind.

– What do you mean?

– I mean that if you think Mummy thinks it's suitable, I think you're right to think that Mummy thinks it's all right and if Mummy thinks it's all right it must be suitable for you.

– So I can read it?

– Nobody knows if you can read it. What I am saying is that you have my permission to try.

– *May* I read it?

– You may. On one condition: that you do not ask me to discuss it with you. If you have any difficulties with it, ask Mummy. OK?

– Yippee! Thank you, thank you, Daddy! Don't worry. I'll keep it perfectly clean. Bye.

– Sal.

– Yes, Daddy?

– Remember one thing. It's only a book, a story. You might think at times that it's me or Con or Nana or somebody else, but it's not: it's only a story.

– But it's a true story, isn't it?

– That's hard to say. Only the really good stories are true stories.

– But this is a good story, isn't it?

– I can't say whether it is or not. Only the people who read it can say that. Maybe you'll know when you finish it. If you really enjoy it, if it's as good as Roald Dahl, then you can be fairly sure it's a true story. I know this is difficult to understand. All I want to say is that you should read it just as if it was written by Roald Dahl –

Her happy, intelligently tolerant face before me.

– Go 'way and read it and maybe we'll talk about it when you've finished it.

As she kissed me and left the room I felt a tightening of the rope.

And that is where and how the first section of the typescript ends. I will resist the temptation to offer a detailed analysis of my present perception of this account of my former thoughts and actions – no point in that – but I would like to add a little something by way of explanation.

You must have asked yourself at some stage why I allowed the situation to develop at all: why did I not simply put my foot down and make my position unequivocally clear? After all, am I not a mature, educated and reasonably responsible person? Not normally thought of as lacking in confidence? Used to dealing with people, singly and in small and large groups? Used to stating and defending my point of view? Well? Yes, yes, yes. Then why?

Well, partly for the reason already given in the typescript: had I taken a stand and held out against all the evidence, it would have had very unpleasant consequences not only for me but for Kate and the girls as well. And then again, I think it's fair to say that the typescript underplays the effort I made to convince Kate of my position. I really did make an enormous effort; it's just that it seemed so ineffective. I wanted to hold to the truth. When I made that first substantial compromise, I walked away convinced that I had condemned myself to a life of lonely guilt, that I had traded my centrally heated world for some *film noir* alley in which I would creep from lie to lie, living on my tensed nerves, concealing my terror with an unblushing smile and a throwaway line. But it wasn't like that and this is something else which the typescript fails to describe adequately: it was very easy, hardly any problem at all. I am not saying that I was always idyllically happy with what was happening but I cannot remember any desperately anxious moments or periods of unbearable suspense. I was apprehensive as I drove into college after my talk with Kate but not for long. I soon learned that it was infinitely easier to behave as other people expected me to behave than it was to agonise over my own individual sense of everything. It's not that everybody I met alluded to the book – almost nobody did directly – but everything they said and did assumed that I was happy or anxious or proud or embarrassed or busy or absent-minded or whatever because I was the author of a book which, even though it had not yet been published, had begun to be spoken about by those in the book business and by those who knew me.

It was even easier on the phone. Calls began to come in from well-wishers and from friends of mine to whom Kate had sent complimentary copies. I was quite anxious when Kate announced that Donncha and Caroline wanted to talk to me but – yet again – no problem: they had no objection to the selves they recognised in the book – in fact, if anything, they seemed pleased – and they thrilled with expressions of admiration for the book – a little sharp at times but then what did you expect? – and with hopes of getting together after the launch. Tim Plummer rang the same night – also from Dublin – and said that he had enjoyed the book enormously, even the bits where he thought he recognised himself, and that he would be at the launch – if the Garbally past pupils did not have a picket on it. And of course my father rang to say that he had read the book the previous night and enjoyed every bit of it, unable to put it down till he finished it at three in the morning. A few days later Barry Mullins rang from London: he wasn't able to give it his full attention yet – Anne was devouring it at the moment – but he had dipped into it here and there and had found it intriguing. My sister Maura called from Montreal and said she and her husband Michael were 'bucking' that they would not be able to make it over for the launch. There were other phone calls during the days that followed – even one, on the night before we went to Dublin, from Alec Maturin in Australia. We hadn't seen Alec – a close friend from Garbally days – for about ten years. He began by laughing incredulously at the discovery that I had not lost my sarcastic tendencies and by considering himself lucky to have escaped so lightly. No, but seriously, he was only joking: the book was a very interesting study of growing up in Ireland in those days and he had derived immense pleasure from reading it – even the section on Garbally.

After a week of this, having encountered colleagues and neighbours and old friends, the pretence no longer cost me a second thought. Except with Kate and the girls. With Kate I spoke of the matter as little as possible: I asked her to make whatever arrangements were necessary for Dublin and I always allowed her to answer the phone just in case the call had something to do with the book. She obviously knew that I had mixed feelings about the business but, just as obviously, she believed that they were a kind of first night nerves which would vanish as soon as the curtain went up on the launch in Dublin. The girls were another matter altogether. Sally was old enough to take a quiet pride in events, old enough to be interested in the practical side of literature – royalties, the arrangements with libraries et cetera. Cliona was giddy at the prospect of her daddy being famous, being interviewed on radio and television, having his picture in the papers, and she wanted to know if she could have a copy of the book for the parents of her best friend. Maeve was delighted to join in the general excitement. I changed the subject as quickly as I could.

And that is essentially how I bridged the interval between the events covered in the opening section of the typescript and those described in the second part, entitled LAUNCH, which deals with the publication party in Dublin and the events which immediately followed it.

LAUNCH

Kate and I drove to Dublin for the launch in Grogan's on the morning of Friday 22 February 1985. Kate was in a holiday mood and, though I say so myself, I managed to conceal my thoughts – even when we met the publisher's representatives, Peter Oldham and his assistant, Heather Hiley, for lunch in the Shelbourne.

I don't know what Peter had made of my behaviour on the phone the previous Monday week. Since then I had left most of the arrangements to Kate and had not spoken to Peter until we greeted each other in the foyer and went straight in to our table. He was disconcertingly professional, always behaving like somebody who had done a crash course on how to be the life and soul of any party but always seeing the world in terms of publicity. Even while he was giving you a pain in the arse you had to admire his thoroughness. Faced with the task of generating some interest in a rather pedestrian book by an unknown author, he had read it carefully and found his opening in the person of Brendan Behan. He studied Rae Jeffs's book on Behan and learned something of Behan's genius for publicity. Peter decided on a launch in a

Dublin pub at which he would assemble as many relations as possible –
preferably relations who had connections with Behan and/or the IRA –
then add alcoholic beverages in large quantities and await developments.

– I gather from my Dublin spies that we shall have some colourful
characters at the launch this afternoon?

Although this was clearly a question, I chose to take it as a statement.
Anyway, what did he want me to say? In the embarrassing interval I
pretended to see an acquaintance heading into the bar and, *mea culpa*,
left Kate to deal with Pete and Heather and timetables and various lists
of people. Sitting at the bar with an inferior pint and a half-corona, I
felt confused, grumpy and guilty. The grumpiness was due to the
confusion, the guilt to fact that the half-corona was in clear breach of
Cliona's injunction on smoking. Looking at the reflection of my face in
the mirror, I realised that this was the last chance to come clean, to be
honest with other people. It would be natural for me to make some kind
of a speech and there, in front of the scribes and the cameras, I could
simply say that I had not written this book at all. Thank you very much.
That will be all. No further questions, please. No more. Sorry. Now
why don't you all drink up and fuck off.

But no. No, I didn't want another pint. No, I didn't want to finish
the cigar. No, it wouldn't work, not as I would wish. Still inspecting
the reflection of my little known face in the mirror, I realised that at this
stage the best way of preserving as much of my privacy as could be
preserved would be by going through the motions of the launch, playing
the relatively easy part of author, and letting the comedy run its course,
from the crisp copies picked up freely at the launch to the faded copies
picked up for rapidly decreasing amounts in second-hand bookshops.
Having come this far, I might as well go the few hundred yards, the few
hours, the few gestures, between lunch time in the Shelbourne and
wherever we would have dinner after Grogan's. Easier said than done.

At about two thirty Peter and Heather took a taxi to Grogan's. Kate
and I waited in the Shelbourne until my mother and father arrived and
then the four of us rambled over at our ease. I was only mildly mollified
to think that in their very different ways my parents would enjoy the
little sideshow, that they would both take pleasure and pride in what
they saw as a great occasion for me. If only they knew.

As we reached Grogan's the women were palpably more enthusiastic than the men. My father and I are known to be slow starters in such matters. Unlike my mother and Kate. And unlike the owner of the voice which was rending the air of the lounge as we walked in.

– And all I'm telling you is that you are more than welcome to a glass of beer. Personally I am not in the least interested in what you are drinking. Nothing personal: it's just that I couldn't give a shite. For the moment I am only interested in little me and what I want is a Jameson, a large Jameson and red, and I also want a pint of stout and yis can chalk it up to whoever is running this effort.

Poor Peter: he was learning the hard way that even the ghost of Brendan Behan is not raised without a certain rattling of the crockery. Poor Pete, his diplomatic demeanour was wilting under the Gatling gusto. I almost felt sorry for him. Almost. As the other three looked on in some discomfort I shouted across the room.

– Make it three more pints and a vodka and white while you're buying, will you, Pearse.

Pearse had turned away from Peter to look behind the bar when he heard my voice.

– Will you look who's here. Come in, come in, come in. I thought I was going to be stuck with this creeping Jesus here. Howya, Maisie. And Kate girl, come here and give me a kiss. Fresh and well you're looking. And how's the quare fella? Have you got the children with you?

– You must be joking. I try to keep this kind of thing a secret from them. Did you call for those drinks yet?

– O'Brien, will you for the love of somebody come up here and serve drink. Me brother's here, and me favourite nephew.

Paddy arrived, ruddy and warm like the sun itself, beaming at the company.

– Oh thanks be to God, there's respectable people here. Bejaysus, Con, I thought I was going to be stuck with this crabby huer. He thinks he can come in here and drink all before him for nothing. The nice gentleman over there asked him if he would like a glass of beer and bejaysus you'd think he was after asking him for the lend of a pound. He ups and ates the arse off him.

– Fintan, will you for the love of Jaysus, Con or Kate or anybody, get me a drink before I tell the true story, the story that wasn't told in that effin' book, no, nor in any other shaggin' book.

Peter stood back, perplexed, unable to interpret the apparent discrepancy between the language and the open happiness that animated our faces. Pearse and I hugged each other and exchanged our passwords.

– Fuck the begrudgers.

– And their friends in America.

People were beginning to arrive and there was the usual amount of saying hello and shaking hands and introducing. As Paddy brought the pints over and I was informing some old UCD friends that Pearse was the rightful lord mayor of Dublin and future high king of Ireland, Peter was attempting to retrieve the situation. He called Kate over, had a quick pow-wow with her and then presented himself before Pearse with humorous humility, shaking his hand and showing no sign of ever letting it go again.

– Dear me, yes, indeed. My humblest apologies. Indeed, if I had known that you were Pearse, the famous Uncle Pearse who rewarded rhetoric with shining shillings, well then it would have been my pleasure to get you a drink, any drink you wished. You should have introduced yourself. I thought you were just somebody who stumbled in not knowing what was happening.

Peter had made several, well it would be severe to call them mistakes but it would be inaccurate to call them anything else.

– Is it trying to cod me you are? Who the fuck do you think you're talking to? Somebody who stumbled in not knowing where he was? Listen here, fellow me lad, we were here before you were pupped, do you follow me? We were here before yis came over and, mark my words, we'll be here when yis have all gone back. Shining shillings how are ye. Are you in the right shop yourself or what? Are *you* the full shilling? Holy Jesus tonight!

At this stage the thought struck me – coinciding with a nudge from my father – that Peter had suffered enough and that it was time to mollify Pearse. But it would have been like trying to hold back the tide: Pearse was already in song, his face contracted in the pure love of tribal play, his fist pumping the air as he sang with pride and malice:

No longer hands are willing
To take his dirty shilling

And Ireland's boys have told him what to do.
He has lost his occupation,
Let us sing with jubilation
For Sergeant William Bailey tooraloo.

I had intended – as my father had intended me – to shut Pearse up
but blood is thicker than water and tradition stronger than all but the
very odd individual talent: here was a family song that we had sung
together on so many sacred occasions in the past that it bonded us like
psychic superglue. It was time to choose between Britannia and the Boys
of Barr-na-Sráide. No contest: fuck the begrudgers and lurry him up
he's no relation. Hardly a beat was lost before there were three of us:

[Pearse] Tooraloo! [Us] Tooraloo!
[Pearse] Tooraloo! [Us] Tooraloo!
[All] He has lost his occupation,
Let us sing with jubilation
For Sergeant William Bailey tooraloo.

And so things were flying and, to the innocent eye, all in the best of
good order. Peter, knowing on which side his bread was buttered,
grinned and applauded, not yet ready to risk another verbal. Uncle
Jimmy had appeared at the door while the chorus was in spate and he
contributed a glistening smile and a gentle hurrah. He was the harbinger
of a host of others who would have come at decent intervals but who
rushed together to hear the singing. Before long there was fair crowd
present – friends, relations, colleagues, journalists. My sisters Eileen and
Eva came in together and made straight for Kate, signalling that they
would leave me to Pearse for the moment. Seamus Routledge was there,
a friend since the Finglas days with Eugene. I was sorry not to see more
from the Garbally days but such is the usual diaspora that the only close
friend was Tim Plummer who, with his customary social efficiency,
managed to bring along two others whom I had not seen for years. I was
glad, as always, when Donncha came in, kissed Kate, shook my hand,
wished the book every success and pulled me up to the bar, saying that
Caroline would be along later when she had arranged with the solicitor
how much she would be suing for. (Donncha had been talking on the
phone to Barry Mullins who had tried in vain to get back from London
for the launch and who wanted to have another more select launch in

a couple of weeks' time.) Just then a platoon of academics arrived and were profusely and esoterically benign in their comments about the book, their leader, Henry Keating, brandishing a review copy that contained a quiver of page-markers. The last thing I wanted was a discussion of the book with people who had actually read it carefully and so I decided that what these intellectuals needed was a lesson in Hiberno-English dialect as a moulder of the Irish national character. I introduced them to Pearse, suggesting that they decide among themselves which of them was deserving of the title as the wisest person in Ireland; Henry was learning his first lesson in the discourse of confrontation as I escaped back to my pint beside Donncha at the bar to have a welcome sip, bum a cigar from Tim and see arriving a few of the usual huers who are so confident of themselves that they assume a welcome where there is none.

Meanwhile, Peter was delighted with himself, the centre of his own show, surrounded by people making enquiries about the book, its price in Irish pounds, whether there was VAT on books in Britain, how many copies they hoped to sell here, there and anywhere else, where he was from himself and how often he had been to Ireland and so on. Peter saw overwhelming interest but he was unaware that it was overwhelmingly self-interest: few of the enquirers went back to their drinking without a display copy of the book and Auntie Maureen won the award for the most artistic stroke by asking Peter to autograph the book.

Suddenly Peter was excusing himself, politely but urgently, and I wondered what he was up to. Had he lost control of his bladder? No: he was insinuating himself through the crowd and towards the front door. To what? To whom? Well, well, well, what have we here? Malachi Murphy, *enfant terrible* of Irish journalism, had arrived and was surveying the scene with his customary combination of contempt and discomfort, knowing that he was more capable than any of the other journalists present but knowing equally well that it would be many years before they treated him as anything other than an overread intellectual wise-arse. Peter Oldham descended on him as on the long-awaited VIP, shook his hand, guided him to food and drink and then steered him into the quietest corner. In no time at all Malachi was smiling and not long afterwards it was Malachi who was doing most of the talking and Peter who was nodding like an old hen in absolute concurrence, absolutely unable to agree more. At the time I was at a total loss as to what was happening; looking back, I would guess that Peter Oldham simply flattered Murphy who, being human, was happy to hear that word of his important achievements in Irish journalism had reached London. Eventually Peter saw me staring and invited me to come over but I pretended not to understand him and went over to see how my beloved uncle was faring among the academics.

By now he was enthroned on a bar stool attracting a growing percentage of the attendance. My heart surged as I saw him assume what I always called his 'crabby' face – a look of sincere sympathy with the sorrows of this fleeting life mixed with a hint of imminent vengeance on those responsible, some of whom, to judge from glances that shot out of Pearse's eyes, were not a million miles away and who might do worse than get out now while the going was good and they still had the use of both legs. This aspect, reinforced by assorted mutterings and tuttings, generated a certain amount of trepidation – not to say fear – among those present who did not know Pearse and who were anxious lest they might find themselves involved with the unattractive side of a hooley, namely the shuffle of bodies in conflict and the screams that accompany breaking glass.

– Dearest Uncle, I have to warn you that if you persevere with this show of Christian charity I will find it difficult to keep a straight face.

He leaned back against the bar and moved his head up and down.

– Oh, is that so? Is that a fact? Listen to him now. Now that he's written a fucking book, we'll all have to listen to him. Next thing he'll be teaching his granny how to suck eggs. Are yis writing this down for the papers?

Pearse had scored: he didn't know it, but I was just becoming aware of the fact that there were professional reporters nigh. I had no objection to oral reports but some vestige of something led me to consider it improper to be the subject of written columns in the press. It was time to distract Pearse before he gave the journalists the inside story of a lifetime. Looking at Pearse with as much mock-taunt as I could manage, I intoned maestoso:

> Sad is the theme of my muse and my story,
> Gone are the days of the snug and its glory;
> Dark are the clouds that are hovering o'er me . . .

Pearse jumped down from his seat of judgement, gripped one of my hands in his right hand, punched the air defiantly with his left fist and hit the final line with gusto, belligerence and the smiling contentment that comes with memory of past sins and past victories:

> DOWN in the village we tarried so long!

And then, with a little vocal shuffle, the run-in to the chorus:

> Heigh-ho! *slán* to the revelry,
> Shouting and drinking and singing so merrily,
> Red nights we never again shall see,
> Down in the village we tarried so long . . .

By now Pearse had pulled my father in and we were a trio for the finale:

> Farewell companions, my knights of red ochre,
> Bravely you've bent to the rule of the poker,
> Blazing a trail for the baker and broker,
> Far from the village we tarried so long!

As I considered how often I had sung or heard sung the final verse without ever really understanding any of it, there were various shouts of wellbeing, a variety of appreciations from those who had been listening, including a request for more, but I suggested to my father and Pearse that it was time for a quiet pint and while my father requested the kind offices of Mr O'Brien, Pearse put it to the company that if they wished to hear more songs they should sing them themselves. And the devil thump and thank the begrudgers. And their fucking friends in America.

And so, seated on a stool, I repeated the oft-told tale of that sunny morning on the Claddagh, when my father and I had heard Pearse's voice drift in song across the depressed docklands, singing of summer. That same bright morning when Paddy Melvin, having fallen off for the third time, dropkicked the bike against a warehouse wall and proceeded on foot. The same that oftimes hath . . .

– Answer me this.

It was my father speaking quietly, making sure we were not overheard.

– Why did you change that in the book?

I felt my face go red and tried to cover it by taking a long slug from my pint.

– How do you mean?

There were some details – only a participant would have noted them – in which the account in the book differed from the story I had just retold. I could say nothing. All I could do was shrug and smile and hope that my father would not insist on some answer. Pearse saved me: turning around on his stool and surveying the scene, assuming his most oriental aspect, grinning from ear to sardonic ear, his chin thrust forward, his eyes like jewels of eternal life encased in a face of hard lines.

– I love this. I fucking love it. The whole lot of them, look at them, mooching here and mooching there and wondering who's looking at them, who's listening to them, like, bejaysus, I don't know what, like a lot of hens seeing what they can pick up be way of something for nothing or a line in the paper or maybe even they might get their face on the paper. Ah, will you look who's here.

Niall Murtagh had arrived. Although Niall and I were at UCD at the same time, we didn't really get to know each other until three or four years later when Niall was beginning to make a name for himself in politics. I never thought I would like somebody with Niall's political views but in fact I found him personally irresistible – generous, humorous and almost totally free from arrogance. Malachi Murphy, to judge from his blank stare, would find my compromise morally and intellectually reprehensible. Niall, I knew, would find Murphy's earnestness unacceptably tedious in somebody over the age of twenty-five. (Niall's voice pained: As soon as somebody identified the little shit for me, I understood why his style was so acned.) Malachi Murphy would recognise in Niall's public and private life the contradictions and evasions that were the inevitable consequences of a reading of history which was blind to the firm ideological assumptions of its claimed immunity to ideological bias, a reading based on premises which had been exposed and discredited in many parts of the world. (My imitation fails to suggest the attractively truculent shape and rhythm that his zeal normally imparts to his material.)

Niall burst upon the scene with the vigour of a public man, checking and computing all, dispensing a rich repertoire of recognition and greeting – facial, manual and verbal. He walked over to Kate, kissed her, shook hands with my father and mother, pretended to punch my Uncle Pearse, signalled that he would be back to him in a minute, then turned to me and congratulated me.

– Thanks for coming. I gather you are involved with the mighty today.

– Thanks for remembering to aşk me. I am honoured to be here with yourself and Kate and this élite gathering of the Kearneys and their allies. I am glad to see them all looking so well and almost equally glad to see that several gentlemen of the press are looking so wretched. Little do they know why I smile at them.

– What will you have?

– Prudence instructs me to order nothing. I had an extremely demanding night last night and this morning with some members of the Bundestag who are supposed to be studying our little democracy. A likely story if ever there was but one has to pretend to believe them until they get jarred and, say what you like about them, they all have at least one hollow leg.

– You better have something to keep one of your hands occupied.

– Would you mind if I asked for a Perrier?

– Not at all but you can ask Mr O'Brien for it yourself.

– That is not a pleasant prospect. But I daren't start drinking again for another few hours at least. Turn then, most gracious advocate, thine eyes of mercy towards us. Paddy!

– Yessir?

– Would you have such a thing as a bottle of Perrier water?

– I would, and more than one.

– Could I ask you to pour one of them into a glass and add some ice and lemon.

– Ice and lemon. Like in gin and tonic?

– Exactly. As in gin and tonic.

Paddy knew that he had Niall over a barrel and played with him for a while, much to the amusement of all, especially Pearse, who declared to God that he was no longer puzzled about the state of the country now that he knew what our leaders were on. Niall entered into the spirit of the occasion while he was there but after about ten minutes he pulled me aside and whispered that he simply had to get back to the office but that we would shortly make amends with a little snack and some wine in his place. Little did he know as he danced and gesticulated his way out that he had left on the gathering a character or spiritual mark that would last, if not for ever, then for as long as anybody was interested in the fate of *Gone The Time*.

Pearse and my father were in the process of forgiving Niall his political sins when a tall stooping dark figure filled the doorway and inspected the crowd with an obvious lack of enthusiasm.

– McCann! Frank McCann! Come over here and talk to us. Don't mind that shower over there.

– Agh, Pearse, how nice to see you and in such friendly form too. How's Con? Fintan? Thank you very much for the invitation. And thank you very much for the book. Most enjoyable.

– Don't mind the fucking book. That'll be there tomorrow. Get a drink into you while it's going free. And relax.

– Pearse, you're incorrigible.

– Am I? Is that what I am? Well, you learn something every day. And me thinking I was an ordinary working man.

– Pearse, not even you ever thought you were ordinary but before we get involved in matters of controversy I insist on congratulating Fintan here on his book. Which I found very interesting. Even if a trifle exaggerated here and there. Ha-ha. Excellent on Brendan and excellent on your good self, Pearse. Less excellent, if I may say so, on yours truly but that's a small point. Good Lord, Con, did you ever see me throw a tantrum or pull my hair – even when I had enough hair to pull. But of course I am being facetious: lovely book, lovely read. I am reviewing it for the *Times Literary Supplement*, you know.

For the first time of the afternoon I wanted to ask somebody a question – I wanted to know why Frank McCann had not included Eugene in his remarks – but with characteristic tact Peter Oldham pulled me aside to discuss the formalities. He would initiate proceedings and make sure that everybody present knew the names of the book, the publisher and the author. Then he would introduce me and I would make my speech. He didn't want to seem to be telling me what to say but if he might make so bold he would suggest that I begin by thanking anybody

I wished to thank, family, friends et cetera, then perhaps a mention of the publisher, making sure to get the name across clearly, and then after that whatever I wished, a story perhaps, or even a song, and something which in his opinion was always a winner and which I should be well used to, being a university lecturer, an invitation to those present to ask questions about or make comments on the book. Still trying to hear what was passing between Frank McCann, my father and Pearse, I told Peter Oldham that it would be better if he did what he considered necessary, that I would make a speech which might contain a story but certainly not a song and which would be unlikely to last more than a minute and that would be the end of things as far as I was concerned: there would be no questions, no discussion of the book one way or the other. He gave me the look he had been giving me all day with a decreasing effort to disguise it: he was doing all this for me, so why, if I wouldn't do something for me, could I not help him help me?

– Fine. Well it's not really fine but if you won't do it there's very little I can do other than remind you that all this is designed to get people to read the book and they won't read the book if they don't hear about it.

Nothing from me.

– Right. Well. That will be it then. I shall come back and simply say that there is a limited number of copies for sale and that Heather will be in charge of that and that you will be happy to autograph them and so on.

– I'm not signing anything, certainly not copies of the book.

– Oh, come on, Fintan.

– Look, Peter. Don't worry. Most of the people here don't buy novels anyway and so they won't be pushed about autographs.

– But why are you doing this? You seem to be setting out to exocet the launch. Why? Just tell me why?

– It doesn't matter, Peter. Really, it doesn't matter here. The people who matter here won't miss it.

– Look, I don't want to pull rank or anything like that but I know this business. I know what I'm doing. Believe me. Trust me.

– Peter, I know you know your business. And I do trust your judgement. Do whatever you think is best. Just don't expect me to do anything other than what I have said I will do.

– But I feel responsible for what happens here today.

Nothing from me.

– And believe me things are going well. I just don't want things to fade out now. Do you know how I feel about this?

– Peter, I do. As I have said, I know you know your business: I have admired your skill. In fact, I will exonerate you completely in my speech.

I thought for a moment that Frank McCann was about to go.

– Peter, excuse me, but there really is nothing left to say. I am not being an artistic prima donna – the type gives me a pain in the arse – it's just that I am allergic to this kind of speech. (No, he wasn't going: just nodding politely at Gus Martin.) I could lecture to millions for hours and it wouldn't bother me one little bit. But. Different strokes and so on. Don't worry about it. I have to see this gentleman here. He's reviewing it for the TLS, you know.

Peter was not exactly revived by my claim to be about to nobble a director of the Abbey Theatre. Maybe he knew I was lying; maybe he knew that when it came to fiction a glowing review in the TLS could make a difference in terms of copies sold that staggered into double figures. Not that I cared one way or the other; I wanted to have a quick word with Frank McCann about what he had said about the book.

He was back with my father and Pearse and they were talking about Eugene and more especially about his funeral in Ballinasloe. I listened in and while waiting for my moment I pondered what Frank McCann had said when he had come in. Here was a man who, from a helpful distance, had known the story of Eugene and most of the characters and relationships involved. Although, in my opinion, he was too much a man of the theatre (too much an expressionist) and too successful a public figure ever to reach the precise frequency at which Eugene existed, his was a perspective worth noting. It was obvious to me that he was less than satisfied with the portrayal of Eugene in the book and I wanted to know why.

Between the arrival of the complimentary copies and the launch I had been frequently tempted to read the book. I handled copies on several occasions, always surprised when I did not experience some kind of electric shock. Once, alone in the house, it occurred to me to open it and read the first complete paragraph on the right-hand page. The object of these *sortes Vergilianae* was not to discover what lay ahead of me but rather what lay behind me. Surely, I reasoned with myself, surely one glance at the actual writing – not the story or content but the syntax, punctuation and so on – would tell me with absolute certainty whether I had arranged these words as they sat on the page. And myself replied with absolute certainty that indeed they would. And that very moment I was seized by an absolute fear and never since then have I been tempted to open the book. Subsequently I have read – and heard – quotations from the book but as I made my way across Grogan's lounge after Frank McCann I had not seen or read or heard one line.

What did I know about it? That most if not all of the events depicted were – as far as I could judge – clearly based on incidents in my own experience. That there was a strong satirical element in the book, the tone being characterised by a kind of sarcasm or sharp wit. That Kate thought well of the book, that she had read it carefully – probably in search of the me who lived before we met – and she had never indicated that she found the characters in the book portrayed as significantly different from the same characters as I spoke to her of them. Similarly my parents, both of whom claimed to have read and enjoyed the book: they expressed no great surprise or dissatisfaction. (My father had suggested that I had confused one or two details but he was content to believe that I had done this intentionally.) Uncle Jimmy had said it was a lovely book. Tim Plummer had ho-hoed about the part that dealt with Garbally and had said that I would be *persona non grata* there but I gathered that he had not felt it was inaccurate in any serious way and after all he came to the launch and was as gregarious as ever. Donncha and Caroline accepted that they had appeared in thin disguise in the book and Donncha, while joking about the reactions of various other participants, had said that it was a bloody great read and congratulated me in his usual warm way. By the day of the launch I had accepted that – by some mysterious process – the book reflected my mind even if it did not issue from my labour. Hence my unease at Frank McCann's remarks.

In order to get a few minutes with him I told my father and Pearse that I wanted to introduce Frank McCann to Jim Roche. It was a reasonable ruse: my father knew that Jim was a writer of plays. I asked Frank what he was drinking and took him to the bar.

– One thing I'd like to ask you. You weren't happy with the stuff on Eugene in the book, were you?

– Ah no, Fintan, I wouldn't say that I wasn't happy. Not at all. It was fascinating.

– But?

– No 'but' at all. I read it through and found it fascinating. You seem to have taken me up wrong.

– But you've already as much as said that the treatment of Eugene was less satisfactory than, for example, the stuff about Brendan Behan.

– Did I say that? I don't remember saying that.

– You implied as much. In what way was it less satisfactory?

– Oh, it would take a long time to explain.

– But just give me some kind of a rough idea.

– Let me see. How shall I put it. Yes. Well, I always considered Eoghan – you call him Eugene but I always think of him as Eoghan – I considered Eoghan a remarkable man.

– So did I.

– Yes and I know you acknowledge your indebtedness to him. You certainly did that.

– But?

– Oh, I should never have let you get me into this corner. You're an awful man, you're worse than your father, you're even worse than Pearse. We'll talk about it some other time. Enjoy your moment of triumph here.

– Look. Between the two of us. I'm not interested in praise or criticism, when I ask you this. I don't want to be flattered nor am I inviting you to point out my mistakes. I am interested in what you said for reasons outside aesthetics. Now, you knew Eugene well and you feel that I ... that the book makes him out to be less than ... that it does not do him justice.

– Oh, it certainly does him justice as a teacher.

– He was my friend.

– He was my friend, faithful and just to me.

– So here you are to speak what you do know. Did the book make him out to be less than he was?

– Oh no, not at all. Please don't believe I could think that.

I had to try something.

– Embittered?

– Eoghan could be very bitter. At times, only at times. I don't think you exaggerated his bitterness; I think you explained that you eventually came to see that he was only human like the rest of us and not the great genius whom you idolised at school. It must have been very difficult for you to ... how shall I put it?

He had tried his best, I thought, and I couldn't keep at him like this. It was time to lay off.

– Look, I'm sorry to be keeping at you like this. It's just that ...

He smiled conclusively and his face jerked up.

– Look, your friend over there is signalling to you. I think he wants to start the speeches. You'd better go over and do your stuff. Your audience awaits you.

Peter was indeed about to formalise the event and wanted me by his side as exhibit B. Exhibit A had never been out of his hand – right way up and front cover out – since the first punter had come through the door. I stood beside him and he coughed and smiled and sent out concentric circles of attention waves. His patter was no empirical improvisation; he knew exactly what he was doing – establishing his name and that of the publisher as the first order of business, smiling in order to make it clear that we were here to have fun and not just to talk about the book business, flattering the press but not obviously. Held up the book and said that the cover made quite a nice photograph, brilliant designer of whom we will hear a lot in the future, mentioned the name of the book and the name of the publisher, massaged the guests in such a way as convinced most of them that they were honoured to be among those everybody wanted to meet and lucky to be having such a good time as they were obviously having, mentioned how often he mispronounced my name as Key-arney, silly English never get it right in Ireland, always thought it was Brendan Be-han until that morning when he learned that the *h* was silent, about the only silent thing about the bold Brendan, ha-ha, had never actually encountered him in the flesh but judging from what he had heard and read and especially from his reading of the character of Decco Deane in *Gone The Time*, oops! had he let a cat out of the bag? He did hope Fintan would not be annoyed with him: obviously time for him to shut up before he dropped any more clangers and incurred the wrath of the Kearneys and their allies which he could imagine being a wrath to be reckoned with indeed. And so, thanking everybody for everything and hoping that if anybody, anybody at all, wanted any further information or details about *Gone The Time* published by Hollinsford at ten pounds, sterling he feared, they would approach him or his assistant, Heather, take a bow Heather and let them see you, but not just yet, not before they listened to the man of the hour, and it was with great pleasure and even greater confidence that he called on Fintan Kearney, now that was better wasn't it, the author of *Gone The Time* and, he was sure, many other works in the future.

– Fintan Kearney!

I am a professional lecturer. Sometimes I face three different roomfuls of people one after the other and I am never in the slightest way nervous or anything like that. However, this situation called not for a lecture but for what is known as 'a few words'. Pitched halfway between an address and conversation, it is a form of speech I have never been comfortable with – despite much practice introducing guest lecturers and so on – and the circumstances in Grogan's that afternoon made me as ill at ease as I had ever been since... I don't know, certainly since my student days. I was on the verge of panic when my attention settled on Pearse up at the bar. There was something in his ironic grin which made me feel that maybe I could get through the next few minutes.

I had already decided that the best way of dealing with the question of autographs was to make it clear that I was not signing any and to wrap this announcement up in some kind of joke or anecdote. That was no problem: I knew I could always come up with something in that line. No, my problem had to do with precision of language. I would say that it had to do with telling the truth except that such a term has moral connotations and what was driving me was not moral. I was not philo-sophically or ideologically or even theologically committed to telling the truth. If I had been I could hardly have gone through the business of the launch – accepting the congratulations of friends like Seamus Routledge, Donncha Kinsella and Tim Plummer – without standing in the middle of the floor, screaming for attention and announcing that I was not the one who had written this bloody book.

Nor was I about to make such an announcement now – I had been through that before. And yet – and this is where the suspicion of superstition comes in – even though I was not going to make any explicit disavowal of the book, what was uppermost in my mind as I cleared my throat was the firm resolve not to make any explicit verbal admission of authorship. I was going to equivocate. I was going to tell a moral lie but my words would be innocent. This idea had been with me for some time beforehand but Frank McCann's remarks on the portrayal of Eugene left me no room for doubt. Irrespective of moral or legal or economic factors, I could not give my word or my name to a book that was in danger of being conceived as unfair to the memory of a man who had been an important part of my life and who would be for ever part of whatever it was that is me.

And so, concealing all this as best I could, I coughed, and began, and it was as if I was in a dream, alienated from the words which came from my mouth.

– I suppose the first thing for me to do is to welcome you here and thank you for coming and hope that you enjoy the nearest mere mortals can get to a free lunch. I see so many good friends in front of me that it would obviously be impossible for me to go through a long list of individuals and, equally so, it would be tedious for you to have to hang around and listen to it. There have to be exceptions. I have to thank mine host, Paddy, for existing. I must also thank my Uncle Pearse for many things and not least for introducing me to Mr O'Brien. And I must also thank my parents for introducing me to Pearse. And I should, by the same token, thank whoever introduced my parents to each other but, as the man said, about that of which we cannot speak we should remain silent.

It was working. I was getting away with it. I could feel my face returning the smiles of those in front of me.

– And so to work. As a member of a union of professional talkers, I am unhappily aware of the fact that I am not being paid for this speech and so I promise to keep it to a minimum. I had better say something about this book, although to tell the truth I have no desire to talk about it and I see no good reason why I should be expected to do so. Peter suggested that one of the characters in it bore a striking resemblance to a certain Dublin writer not unknown to several people here. The exact relationship between that character and the other fellow is tricky and is, or was recently, a fashionable topic for discussion in universities and so we can leave it to the academics. At the risk of undoing the good work of the alcohol, I want to call as my witness a gentleman of the French nation, late of this life, Monsieur Barthes. He had a certain talent for selling books – his own books – by the use of slogans, and one of his better slogans was that as far as the reader is concerned – especially perhaps those readers in the French income tax service – the author of a book is dead. Most people who have ever spoken to an author about his or her book will know what Monsieur Barthes was on about: the author seldom has a good grasp of what the book means to the readers and there is no basis for thinking that he more than anybody else knows what the hell happens when the book is being read. The author may remember what cigarettes he or she smoked or what music they listened to while writing the book but that's another matter altogether; he or she knows nothing special about what happens afterwards, when the book has been published and placed in the hand of a reader. And that's my roundabout and smart-arsed way of saying that I haven't the inclination nor the intention nor, as I see it, the right to talk about the book which is the occasion of this free drink. Another and not unrelated point. Don't worry: three or four minutes at the most. And by the way, I don't expect anybody to listen to any of this: if you prefer, get up to the bar and get stuck in there or, indeed, if you want to withdraw from this talk and close your eyes and contemplate the hollowness of all things human, well – off you go. The final point. Some of you have asked me to autograph copies of the book and I have put you off, saying that I would explain later. Well this is later and here is me explaining. My unwillingness to scribble my signature on copies of the book is not entirely due to my admiration for and belief in the formulations of Monsieur Barthes. No. A little anecdote will have to serve as my excuse. One night I attended a poetry reading in Cork. There is no need for me to name the poet: his remarks in this anecdote will identify him as surely as if I mentioned the volume of his poetry which I carried in my pocket. After the reading, back in the house of a common friend, I sidled up to the poet and asked him to sign the volume for my wife Kate, who could not attend the reading because she was about to give birth. I was a little embarrassed to ask anybody to autograph a book and very embarrassed to do so with such an unlikely sounding story. Would you mind signing this for my wife, please. He was happy to do so and when I suggested

that he must have a pain in his arse from signing books, he laughed –
there, I told you I would identify him – and told me that he was so well
used to it he just took it for granted. We got talking about wives and
he pointed out that his wife maintained that in the unlikely event of his
books ever becoming valuable – now I've given the game away completely – in the unlikely event of any of his books ever becoming
valuable the most valuable would be those tiny few which were not
autographed. And that, citizens, is the case for the defence. Again,
thanks to you all for whatever it is that is happening and my advice is
to get to the jar while the going is good. Thank you.

Several people came up and congratulated me but I don't know who
they were or what they said. I only remember my hands shaking as I lit
a cigar and inhaled deeply. That was something I would not like to
repeat; but Jesus! the worst was over and I could lose myself among old
friends.

The press corps saw that the pleasant part of the function had come
to an end and so most of them whipped out notebooks and began to
ask questions of me, my family or anybody who had ever known us in
our actual lives. Photographers kept pulling me into various groupings
and then badgering me for the correct names, left to right, and the relationships. Perhaps the most common question was whether Brendan
Behan was an uncle on my mother's or my father's side. A few wanted
to know how this guy Eoghan Ó Tuairisc – how did he spell it? – was
related to me. I was not asked if Ciarán Fitzgerald was a relation, merely
if he and I had played rugby together. An *Irish Times* man – a social
diarist rather than a books-pager – asked if I was going to be the heart
of the rowl and provide them with the *clef* that the book was a *roman à*.

There arose in the room that tone – suddenly louder but less in-
tegrated and obviously the work of raucous individuals – which is always
the prelude to dissolution. As the last late questions were being asked
and one more photograph taken with Pearse, I had to find out what the
arrangements were. Kate and I agreed that we needed a substantial meal.
Neither my parents nor Pearse wanted to hear about food: they decided
to head off together and leave Kate and me to our own devices. While
I was talking to my father, Kate was trying to organise something later
with Tim and Donncha and Seamus Routledge. Simultaneously we
were both of us saying goodbye and thanks and shaking hands all over

the place. At one stage Kate asked me if we should invite Peter and Heather somewhere; I said that for my part I would rather not spend any more time with them. Then Kate got on the phone and the rest of the evening was laid out. Tim had to go home for a while but was on for a few jars later: he would be alone because Fay had to stay at home with the children. Seamus was also going home but would also be on for a few jars later; he too would be alone because Fran was tied up in some way or other. Caroline had to go home because she had promised to feed Niamh Minogue, who was on a working visit to Dublin. (Niamh had been invited to the launch but couldn't make it.) Eventually Donncha solved the situation. I would go home and have dinner with them. Kate would go home with Tim and have dinner with the Plummers. Seamus would go home and have dinner in his own house. Then we would all meet in Donncha's house at about half nine and from there we would head for a pub in Leeson Street. Agreed.

And so it worked out. More or less. Almost.

The main topic of conversation on the drive out to Merrion was San Francisco, whither Donncha was bound on business a couple of months later. I was relieved to get away from the book and launched into a commercial for San Francisco and environs, its cultural and meteorological climates, its food and wines, especially the Chardonnays of the Napa Valley. Donncha, politeness itself, asked if I had made any arrangements for the publication and distribution of the book in the US; not at all comforted by the fact that I was telling the truth, I said I knew absolutely nothing about such arrangements and then redirected the conversation back to the University of California and how Berkeley got its name.

Back at the house, Caroline released the babysitter and busied herself in the kitchen while Donncha and I organised the children and the drink. I became really conscious of something that I had known for several weeks: that people who had known me anyway well at UCD immediately recognised Donncha and Caroline as the originals of two characters in the book. As far as I could make out – from earlier phone calls and from snatches of conversation in Grogan's – neither Donncha nor Caroline were angry or offended: if anything at all, Donncha seemed pleased but it was characteristic of him to be pleased rather than displeased and he would have been happy to contribute in any way to what he saw as my success. (At some later stage Donncha conceded that the only cavil they had was with the names I had given them: he thought Diarmuid Kennedy sounded like a Kerry footballer, while Caroline, admitting a soft spot for the name Louise, made it quite clear that Mulrooney was not a surname she would have chosen herself.) Judging from the sparkle in his eyes as he plonked himself down in the armchair opposite me, Donncha did not expect the remainder of our common acquaintance to be similarly satisfied with their fictional reflections. He raised his lager:

– Have you had any complaints yet?

– Who'd complain?

– Who indeed? And if they did, who'd mind them? Look, here's to *Gone The Time* and I only hope that everybody likes it as much as I did and what's more, I hope people buy their own copies, not like me, thanks very much by the way for sending us a copy. I don't pretend to know what art is but I thought it was a bloody good read and I hope you make a fortune out of it. Good luck!

– Your imminent beatification!

– Fuck the begrudgers!

– Your eventual canonisation!

– I always knew you had it in you.

– O ye of great faith!

We drank our imported lager. I began to unwrap a half-corona but Donncha would not hear of me smoking such common crap on this of all days. He had, for entertainment purposes, a special box he would like me to sample. Which I did with pleasure.

– What has the general reaction been like?

– To tell you the truth, I don't know. So few people have read it.

– But what were they saying today?

– You wouldn't pay any attention to what is said at a launch. It's like an official communiqué – only there is less substance beneath the verbal glazing. How do you think people will react?

– You mean the people who are in the book?

– Uh-huh.

He started to laugh and then hummed and hawed for a considerable time.

– I don't know. In different ways.

– What about Niamh, for example?

– She's read it. Did Caroline not tell you? You know she stayed here last night? She's up in town on business. She read right through the book in bed. Niamh's quite happy with it; in fact, I'd go so far as to say she likes it. Maybe not every little detail but, well, you know . . . She seemed relieved.

– Relieved? Doesn't sound as if she enjoyed it.

– Oh she did, she enjoyed it right enough. I heard her say it herself. At breakfast this morning. How's the cigar?

– Fine. So why the relief?

– Why do you think?

– You tell me.

– Well, if you heard that Niamh had written a novel based on her experiences at UCD, what would you feel like?

Good question. I would be terrified.

– I would rather that she didn't do anything like that. I think she should stick to whatever it is she is doing so brilliantly at the moment.

Donncha smiling broadly, breaking into a laugh.

– What would you be afraid of?

– Afraid of? *Moi*? Publish and be damned, I say.

– Talk about hypocrisy! Let us say that in her situation you would be a little anxious.

Indeed. The thought shot across my mind that, though my feelings for her were uniformly affectionate, Niamh was perhaps the last one of my acquaintances whose public account – however oblique, stylised and transposed – of our time at UCD I would welcome, or of anything else if it came to that. Why? The awkward age? Probably.

– Conceded.

– Well, when she got to the end of the novel she was relieved because, I suppose, like the rest of us, she recognised most of the people in the novel – especially in the final section – and she knew other people would recognise her. I mean, we were bound to be worried. I was worried. And I wasn't your girlfriend.

– A technical term from a more innocent age.

– It doesn't take a lot of imagination to guess that, well, you could have embarrassed her if you had wanted to, or if you hadn't cared. Come on: you know what I'm talking about. You knew how people would react. You knew who would be happy and, you huer, you knew who would be anything but. Here, let me put another bottle into that.

– It tastes so good I can't refuse.

– Agh no, joking apart, Niamh was quite happy about the way you dealt with the relationship between Casement and Orla. In fact, Caroline thinks the best part of the book is when they meet at the beginning of second year, remember, when he's coming up from the Annexe and she's going down. I heard herself and Niamh talking about it last night and again this morning: they say that it caught the atmosphere of the Terrace to a *t*. And I agree with them. It made me feel eighteen just to read it.

– I was ever the romantic sop.

– You were in my bollox.

– I protest!

My objection was overruled by the voice of Caroline coming up the corridor from the kitchen and seeking assistance. I offered my services but Donncha told me to shut up and mind my own business. I boasted of my kitchen skills but was pooh-poohed and told to get myself a drink, to relax. Caroline was adamant and pointed to the shelves.

– Why don't you get yourself a decent book? Niamh should be here any minute now.

I pulled on my cigar and tried to take stock.

The Annexe. Queues. Crowds. Conversation. Coffee. Condensation. Perspiration.

In my time University College Dublin was housed in a building on Earlsfort Terrace which had been designed for one of those Great Exhibitions at the beginning of this century. The only part of the original design that proved really suitable was the Great Hall, which was used for examinations and graduation ceremonies, the core of the academic system. (The hall has since become the National Concert Hall, a change that lends an archaeological interest to this memoir.) Behind the building were Iveagh Gardens which, given the prevailing climate, were only used for pleasure during the summer months; otherwise they were merely paths one took through dripping grass and trees and past heaps of mouldering neoclassical statuary on monastic walks or on the way over to the restaurant or the society rooms in Newman House on Stephen's Green. There were only two places for the students to congregate: the foyer, where seats were few, and the Annexe, a

subterranean café where one could smoke and talk for ages over a cup
of dreary coffee – that is, if all the tables were not already taken by others
who were smoking and talking for ages over a single dreary cup of
coffee. Later on, in second year and third year, our particular group
graduated to spending hours over coffee – or, occasionally, over
alcoholic beverage – in Kirwan's, around the corner in nearby Leeson
Street; but that was later. I came back in some triumph for the beginning
of second year: I had got a first-class honours and a scholarship in the
first arts exams and, equally prestigious, I had had an adventurous summer, working on a building site near London and then spending several
weeks in Hamburg at the invitation of a pen friend. So there I was with
a scholarship and a fund of stories of the pubs and clubs and characters
of London and Hamburg, Soho and St Pauli, a whole new vocabulary
of jackhammering and subbing – not to mention bilingual jokes – there
I was with all my riches and nobody to share them with. I sat on our
habitual seat in the foyer – under the English Lit notice board outside
the council room – and waited for some friend to come on the scene.
Now that I think about it, I couldn't have known all that many people
very well; even so, those I knew were all somewhere else. I decided to
finish my cigarette and head down to the Annexe.

At the time I didn't much like going alone into places like that – pubs,
cafés and the like – because I didn't like the prospect of being seen looking around the crowd and recognising nobody. The alternative – to join
the queue and hope to see somebody on the way to the cash register
– was fine until you found yourself standing there, cup of coffee in hand,
briefcase under oxter, trying to put the change back into your pocket
and all the time sweating away in a damp duffel coat. And, worst for me,
looking out through misted glasses, afraid to miss an acquaintance, more
afraid to stare at a stranger. But I pushed myself into gear, stepped on
the remnants of the cigarette and headed through the press, past the
entrance to the library, past the L and H notice board, past the entrance
to the toilets and down the crowded steps to the Annexe. Almost all the
faces around me were familiar, some of them nodded greetings, some
smiled, but there was nobody whom I felt I could stop and talk to about
the summer or even about the examinations and what subjects we were
taking for the BA. There were people I knew slightly from last year's
lectures. There were some I knew less well from societies such as the

English Lit or the Cumann Liteartha. Down at the first turn of the steps I could see the girl with the extraordinarily beautiful red hair, what was her name? can't remember it just now, there was always a sudden rush of whispers when she came into the physics theatre for English lectures, and who was that she was talking to? Yes it is, isn't it? Yes, Niamh.

She was Ismene or Antigone and I spent a lot of time with her when we took the play to Galway. I'll say hello to her. Just casually as I go past. Yes, of course, her name is Niamh. It doesn't matter about the other one: you can just nod at her, she won't know your name either. Yes, she will: of course she'll recognise you. Jesus, imagine if you look over at her as you go past and you say Hi Niamh and she just looks over at you and looks through you as if she had never seen you before in her life and, Jesus, knowing you, you'll blush and sweat and feel awful for an hour afterwards. No thank you very fucking much. Just keep going down, pretend not to see her but keep your eye open just in case she goes to say anything, so that you can stop and act surprised and try to work out if she just wants to smile or wants to say hello and leave it at that or if she wants to talk. Maybe she will want to talk; she was really nice during the play. Even though she was obviously a girl who could take her pick, you know, all that talk about tennis clubs and dates and dress dances and that kind of thing, she'd always be a member of whatever it was; she wouldn't be short of guys after her, that much was clear, she knew guys doing law and engineering and that sort of stuff. Just walk by and if she says hello then fine and if not, just keep going. Just keep going: you can always meet her later in the year, see her hanging about when it's less crowded and there's less risk of getting confused. Just keep going; maybe one of the guys is down in the Annexe.

– Fin!

Yes.

– Hi, Niamh. Welcome back.

Of all the fucking stupid things to say! Cop yourself on and move in to the wall or you'll block everybody's way. The other wall! How can you talk to her through a stream of bodies! Jesus!

– You too. And congrats on the exam.

Will I ask her how she did? Will I? What if...

– Do you know Gráinne? You two know each other, don't you?

No. Well yes. Just to see at lectures, the English lectures.

– Hello.

– Hi.

Fuck: what to do? Better not give the impression you're hanging on, that of all the thousands of people around you, you don't know one well enough to go off with and talk to about the summer and things. After a pause she speaks.

– Did you go away for the summer?

– Yeah. I worked in England for a while.

– What at? Canning peas somewhere, I suppose?

– No. Building site. London Airport.

– You're joking!

What did she mean? That I didn't look strong enough for work on a building site? That guys who do Greek and wear glasses don't work on building sites? The girl with the red hair spoke.

– Niamh, look, I'll leave you with Fin and see you at French at three. I promised Anthea I'd see her in the ladies' room five minutes ago. She'll kill me.

That's my cue: time for me to go. Before she says sorry. I'll say something about seeing her later on in the week.

– Are you going down?

Casually. Matter of fact. Don't fidget, leave your fucking glasses alone.

– Yeah, I was thinking about it. Just to grab a cup of coffee and see who's back.

– It's bedlam down there. Gráinne and I tried it for a while but we got fed up standing there being pushed around.

– Look, Niamh, I'll see you later. Bye for now. Bye, Fin.

– Bye, Gráinne. See you later.

– See you.

Gráinne fought her way up the stairs. A crowd was coming down like a flood. Niamh was crushed up against the wall. She elbowed whoever it was and then looked across at me.

– Let's get out of here for a start. Isn't it ridiculous that you can't sit down somewhere quiet with a cup of coffee?

Say something. Do something. Now's your chance.

– They serve coffee over in Kirwan's. But maybe that's crowded too.

Oh, come on. Talk about subtlety. Take it easy for godsake.

– Kirwan's sounds great. Couldn't be as bad as down there. Will we go over to Kirwan's?

Will we? Will we?? Will we??? Yes. We will. Yes.

– Why not?

– Let's go. And you can tell me about your summer. I'm dying to hear about it. Come on.

An omniscient narrator – some tall clerical student of philosophy who stood in front of the Pax Romana notice board – would perhaps have noticed my awkward movements as I bumped through the mill, ushering the sandy-haired girl towards the door; poised there in his sable suit of celibacy, he could hardly have resisted the temptation to laugh at the phenomenon of his fellow man in heat. Surely, losing sight of us as we went beyond the corner of the main office, he would have felt vindicated in his sense of sexual lust as the most demeaning of the natural addictions and the one that testified most incontrovertibly to the enigmatic nature of an omniscient God.

There were, as I recall, two moments in my early life when the actuality took on the quality I later came to associate with Bo Widerberg's film *Elvira Madigan* – sunshine, harvest colours, soft focus, slo-mo and a Mozart andante. One was during my first year at secondary school, coming back from confession on the second day of the retreat, having made a good confession for the first time in four or five years. It was lunch time: I should have left the queue and been in the ref in time for grace but I had waited for the retreat priest, willing to disregard mere college rules in order to reach out for that divine light that I had been deprived of for years, to shake myself free from the webs of lies and deceits that had almost become part of me. All it needed was one brief act of honesty such as the retreat priest had described with overwhelming passion; all I had to do was kneel in front of the screen and tell this almost total stranger the truth. I remember hearing the words come from my mouth. I remember the gradual realisation that there would be no explosion. I remember sensing the entire atmosphere change, as if a sun-shower had come and undone the pressure behind the thunder. I remember making my way back, past the forbidden aura of the sacristy and the red carpet of the priests' staircase, past the reek of the kitchens, past the weeping walls carelessly decked with assorted coats and jackets, down the corridor towards the screech and clatter of the junior ref, across to the table in the far corner, to sit beside a stuck-up student who wasn't interested in games or anything, to be confronted by a soggy white mousse of overcooked cabbage and know that I could not answer those who asked me why I was late. And it was as if I wasn't walking but moving through the atmosphere, sensuously sensible to each individual molecule and the waves in which they made the air in my face, loving how the saddle-shaped erosion on the limestone steps told the stories of generations of unpolished shoes, wanting to kiss the over-varnished doors on the press outside the main ref, wanting to feel even the unloved towels, separated socks and limp underpants that were thrown on the window beside the press as items of misdelivered laundry, feeling my feet hover on the wooden boards of the corridor, hearing the voices in the junior ref as a symphonic climax in which massed choirs were reinforced by triumphant brass, delighted to sit down and eat among my fellow students, my fellow human beings, feeling for the first time that my neighbour too, a proper little consequence, had a life and a past and a family and emotions just as much as me, as much as anybody else, and maybe he was trying to help, really trying to help when he told me and the others the correct way to lay out cutlery and explained that a person didn't *drink* soup, and I smiled at everybody who looked up at me and I knew that nothing could spoil the warm glow of the moment, nothing, not even the soggy white cabbage that I forked into my mouth and, thanks to the grace I had received as a gift with absolution, I overcame the temptation to gulp it whole and, while still smiling, I chewed it to the last stringy sinew before allowing it to slide slowly down. A new life began among faces and trees and buildings that exuded their own glow as these things normally do only through the lens of a great lighting cameraman.

And another and at least equally tremulous life began, a *vita nuova*, as in slow motion, soft focus and to a musical accompaniment of which the andante of Mozart K.467 was but an imperfect transcription, as I followed Niamh out the front door, into the deliciously cool October sunshine, past the cherry blossoms now all déshabillé, through the black gates and...

– Can you get that please, Fintan. It's only Niamh.

Caroline's voice. The doorbell.

– I'll get it.

And then Donncha's voice coming up from the kitchen.

– Get her a drink and tell her to make herself comfortable; I'll be up in a second. Tell her that there's a bottle of Black Bush in the cabinet. And grub will be up in twenty minutes.

It was Niamh all right; I recognised her head movements through the glass of the front door.

– Hiya, Niamh. Long time no see. You're looking well.

– Thank you. I feel lousy, absolutely exhausted. Where did you come from? I thought you would be signing copies somewhere.

– No. Not quite. Come on in here. Caroline and Donncha are in the kitchen and have ordered me to order you to relax in here with a bottle of Black Bush.

– That's very nice of them. Caroline! I'm back. Anything I can do for you?

– No! Tell Fintan to get you a drink and we'll be up in a couple of minutes!

– Say when, Niamh.

– That's plenty, thanks. No, just by itself. Where were you sitting? Jesus! I needed that more than I would like to admit. You're not looking too bad yourself. Cork must be agreeing with you. You still have all your hair: you must be the only person of our age who is not going bald.

– We go grey, not bald.

– I thought you would be singing 'McAlpine's Fusiliers' by now.

Our student days had coincided with the ballad boom and we had spent many early morning hours sitting around in bare flats, sucking bottles of beer and singing of the oppression of the irrepressible working class.

– I doubt if I remember the words but I remember enough of the monotonous tune not to want to sing it ever again. I doubt very much if I have sung it since I was in UCD.

– Well, here's to your book and I hope you sell the film rights for a least a million dollars. Well, tell me all about the launch. How did it go? Hey, by the way, where are Kate and the kids?

– It's complicated for the moment. The kids are in Cork and Kate is about a mile from here eating with some friends of ours. The idea is that we will meet Kate and a few others later on for a quiet jar.

– Were your mother and father there? I hate to think how long it is since I've seen them.

– Oh they were. And Pearse. Remember Pearse?

– Pearse? That's your father's brother, right? He used to be in Peter's Pub with the Behans? I thought I recognised him in the book.

– Right. Well, he was in good form and sang several songs and offered a commentary on much of what went on. I confess that there was one point when I joined him in song but that was only because I was sober.

– Well, you still haven't told me: how did it go?

– I would imagine it was a relative success: the people from Hollinsfords seemed to think it was wonderful – whatever they mean by that. There was free jar: normally people think that's wonderful. Hold on till I dispose of this wonderful cigar.

– Have you taken to smoking cigars? Or is this merely for the occasion?

– Only for the occasion, I hope; I was, to the extent that it is possible, a reformed addict. One day at a time, sweet Jesus.

– You used to smoke at college, didn't you?

– You must be joking. Smoke? Like a bloody chimney, non-stop when I had the money.

– I don't ever remember you as a heavy smoker. Were you really? Well, anyway, what did they think of the book?

– Who?

– Anybody? The people at the launch?

– Very few of them seemed to have read the book. The journalists just look through the publicity, the stuff the publisher gives them.

– Somebody must have read it and talked to you about it?

– Oh, yes. My mother and father think it's great because my name is on the cover and because they like to recognise people and events in the book. Like most people, I suppose. Pearse claims that he read every word of it and enjoyed every word of it but, to his eternal credit, he's lying: he probably glanced through it and decided that it was just another book in which characters he knew appeared in some form or another. And anyway, he has an instinctual sense of the status of little novels in the great scheme of things. I mean, you don't expect people to come up to you and tell you that they thought your book was a load of shit; I'm sure there are lots of people who will think that, but they will only say it in private and in the safety of a review.

– Donncha and Caroline liked it. I liked it.

– Great.

– Is that all you have to say?

– What else is there to say?

– Are you really as cool and conceited as that? Does it not mean anything to you?

– What?

– That people have enjoyed the book?

– Yeah, it does, I suppose. I mean, I don't feel whatever you said I was: conceited and cool and so on. I am curious about the book. I like to know how it strikes certain people or at least how certain parts strike certain people. For example, I suppose about twenty people came up to me this afternoon and praised it but as far as I was concerned I couldn't care less, honestly. I couldn't give a shit what they thought about it or what they said about it. But then this guy came in, a friend of my father's and somebody who worked with Eugene, and something he said, I'm not exactly sure what it was – something about the book being excellent in all sorts of ways or whatever – I don't know exactly how he put it – but he seemed to suggest that the portrait of Eugene Watters was somehow unfair or false or whatever.

– In what way?

– I don't really know. I tried to get him aside for a chat but you know how it is at these freebies.

– This is the George Rivers character? I didn't really know Eugene Watters – only met him once or twice with you – but I could see immediately that the George Rivers character was based on him.

Smiling at me, adults remembering childish things:

– You were crazy about him, you were, thought he was the last word. I couldn't understand what you saw in his writings but, mind you, I read very little of his stuff, just a few poems that were difficult and a novel about Wolfe Tone, was it?

– No. About the French landing at Killala.

– Oh yes. Wasn't it called *L'Attaque*? Yes, that was quite good as far as I remember. He was . . . unusual. And was he very conscious of his protruding eyes?

– It never occurred to me that he was, but then all sorts of things about Eugene never occurred to me. For me he was, literally, a superman: it never occurred to me till much later, till I was working in Cork, it never occurred to me that he was subject to such emotions as fear, loneliness, doubt, loss or that he gave a fish's tit about what anybody thought of him.

– But you brought that out in the book, I think: you know the part where he is thinking about how the professors in the colleges were unable or unwilling to face up to his work but that maybe the students would be less blinkered and that some of these students would go on to be professors and journalists and broadcasters and the like.

– But would you say that the George Rivers character was –

There were sounds in the kitchen, footsteps in the corridor and I couldn't formulate the question before Caroline came in, smiling ironically:

– No need to ask what you two are talking about. Well, Niamh, have you listed his mistakes?

– No, she hasn't. Come on, Niamh. This sounds interesting.

– Now, Caroline, don't misquote me: I never said anything about mistakes. I never used the word.

Donncha's voice preceded him into the room:

– I beg your pardon, Niamh Minogue. Did you or did you not say, last night, in my presence, in this very room, that, never, never, never, did you ever, to your certain knowledge, wear your hair in a ponytail?

– I did, and I say it here and now for all to hear: I never wore my hair in a ponytail when I was in college. Can you imagine me at a lecture in a ponytail?

Niamh was looking over at me as if she were inviting me to confess that the author of the book was in error. I tried to produce what novelists describe as a 'disarming smile'.

– Never?

– I did when I was at school, at secondary school, I mean, but never at – oh come on, Fin, can you really imagine me in a ponytail?

Could I? I could; but was I remembering a past actuality or simply imagining what had never existed in actuality? Strange how few photographs of those days. Compared to now, compared to the time immediately after UCD. Was it money? Did we not have cameras? Or were we in transition between despised Box Brownies and unaffordable SLRs? What photographs did I have of Niamh? Did I have any? I don't think so. Did I have any photographs of UCD? Aren't there photographs of graduation? Of Eugene, yes. And of me: tight, short hair, tight suit, thin tie, cigarette in hand. And isn't there somewhere a photograph of Niamh's mother? Or do I just remember her being there when photographs were taken?

Frustrated, Niamh turned to Caroline.

– Caroline, back me up. Am I right or wrong?

– I don't know, Niamh. Like I told you last night, I'm not too sure about it. Honestly.

Donncha was laughing loudly.

– Very well then. Case dismissed for lack of evidence. Come on, Niamh, your next accusation?

– I made no accusations. You'll give him the wrong impression. I liked the book, liked it a lot: first book in years I've read through.

Suddenly Niamh studied the pattern in the carpet. Caroline flashed an impassive stare at Donncha who immediately stood up and rubbed his hands together.

– With all due respect to this bloody book, there is a more important matter to be looked after. I refer to alcoholic refreshment. Let me refresh your glasses before we go inside to eat. Do you want to finish that first, Niamh?

– I'm fine as I am, Donncha.

– 'Deed and you are not. Here, give me your glass a minute.

– I'm fine, fine for the moment.

– Fintan will have another bottle, love. Won't you, Fin?

– No better man.

– Yourself, Caroline?

– I think I'll follow Niamh's example and hold off and have some wine with the dinner. Dinner will be ready in about ten minutes at the outside. Fin, Niamh and I were just saying – when was it, last night or this morning? – anyway, we were just saying how incredible it was that you were able to make the Terrace come alive again. How did you do it? I mean, you must have an amazing memory. I remember hardly anything at all.

– I remember even less. Here: you can pour this yourself. Just because you write a fucking book doesn't mean that I'm going to pour your beer for you.

– I was saying to Niamh this morning that I doubt if I had thought of the Annexe for what – at least fifteen years? Donncha was away when I read the bit about you and Niamh on the stairs down to the Annexe and I kept wanting to phone him up or phone Anne or somebody just to say yes, that's right, that's what it was like, that's just what it was like. I think you got the atmosphere right, too. You're shaking your head, Niamh, but I thought you agreed with me.

Niamh continued to shake her head and smile.

– I agree with you about the atmosphere of Earlsfort Terrace but, as I've already told you, I think it is silly to say 'the bit about you and Fin on the stairs' or whatever.

Donncha emboldened:

– But the characters are based on you and Fin.

Caroline in support, convivially:

– No matter what you say, Niamh, they are. It's obvious to everybody else. I know that they are characters in a book and that they have different names and so on, but the fact remains –

Niamh, blushing a little and smiling that old smile:

– The fact remains that the book is a fine piece of writing, as far as we can judge. And as far as we can judge, the last section is an accurate picture of life in UCD in our time – the way we spoke, the things we did, the societies, Kirwan's and the flats and so on and so on.

– I don't really see what you are getting at, what sort of distinction you are making. I know that Diarmuid and Louise are not really Donncha and me but in a sense they are: I recognise them as being based on us and so do most other people, including you.

Niamh – as in a hundred mental photographs – blinking and raising her eyebrows, licking her upper lip and moving her head from side to side:

– Of course you recognise a certain similarity but there are thousands of things that you and Donncha did and said and thought, by yourselves and together, things that are not mentioned in the book.

Donncha, smiling across at me and then returning his gaze to Niamh, studiously:

– Of course, but we recognise what is there.

– But what if there were things there that you did not recognise, maybe because you did not remember them, maybe because they never happened to you?

Donncha, slowly, cautiously, but eventually with a show of non-chalance:

– Then I wouldn't recognise them.

– Or you wouldn't recognise the character as yourself?

– I wouldn't recognise the character as myself. Just as I don't recognise Casement Kelly or Orla Dineen as myself because I recognise them as based on you and Fin here.

Caroline, standing up:

– Oh, Donncha, you're just looking for an argument. Come on, folks, dinner time. And notice how quiet Fin is over there: uncharacteristically quiet. But maybe he's right. Let's change the subject to Northern Ireland or something uncontentious, please.

Niamh, draining her glass and standing up:

– Fine, I agree: but just let me finish the point I was trying to make, and Fin, please back me up on this.

– One last point. Last points, please!

– I can see that there is a general, a vague similarity between the Orla character and me but –

– Oh come on, Niamh, there's more to it than a vague similarity. Several other people I've spoken to see more than a vague similarity.

– Probably because they see that Casement Kelly is based on Fin and they know that we went out together for a while in second year.

– There's more than that involved. Do you mean to say that you do not see yourself and Fin and Gráinne in the bit about the Annexe?

– OK. Perfect. Take that example. You recognise Orla as based on me?

– Of course.

– Everybody does. Everybody I've spoken to.

– But it's fiction, that's all. It never actually happened. Fin made it up. I am the first to admit that it gives a very good impression of what life was like in Earlsfort Terrace in those days but . . . it never happened. Simple as that. Tell them, Fin: tell them it never happened, you just made it up.

Three faces directed at me: Caroline enquiring, Niamh incredulous, Donncha grinning.

– It's fiction.

Caroline incredulous, Donncha still grinning, Niamh unsatisfied:

– Come on: that's not enough. Donncha and Caroline believe that something very similar to what happens in the book actually happened to you and me and Gráinne. But then, they also believe that Orla is an accurate picture of me; so I suppose they'll believe what they want to believe. Come on, please, just once: tell them you make it all up or that at least you change your memories to suit yourself or the story or whatever.

– What do you think?

– That you're mainly interested in telling a story that will interest the reader who has never heard of any of us. That you base the story on your own experience but that you change things and shift things around and add things and subtract things – whatever you think the story needs. Take the part about going to Galway. Now we know, the four of us here know, that there was the incident with the cow outside Kinnegad – I know because I was in the bloody car with you and Barry and Anne and I had the glass in my face to prove it. OK: that happened and the main details are given in the book but – and this is the important part as far as I am concerned – the book goes on to include a lot of things that probably make it a better story – in fact I would say that they definitely make it a better story – the book goes on to include a lot of things that never happened. I mean, all that drama on the seafront at Salthill and all the excitement in the hotel. To say nothing of all the talk about *The Táin* and whatnot. Now, I'm not saying that this didn't all go on in your mind, and I'm not saying that it isn't all great fun; what I am saying is most of it never actually happened outside your mind. All we did when we got to Galway was get drunk and go asleep.

– Not a bad idea at all. I'm afraid I can't comment on the Galway episode because neither Caroline nor I went that year.

– I think Donncha had his fill the previous year.

– Jesus, I'll never forget that fucking play we did, never. Come on, let's eat and drink and forget about plays in Irish. Bring your mug, Fin, if you want to stick with lager. We can continue our literary criticism inside.

An opening, a palpable opening.

– Oh, no. Let's give the book a rest for a while, at least while we are eating. I get enough lit crit shit at my work. For me it is not an aid to digestion: in fact, it tends to give me heartburn in the high hole of my arse. And so, good friends, sweet friends, I pray you all: no more about the fucking book tonight.

And it seemed then as if it might work: the others all agreed that they were more interested in eating. I was following Niamh and Caroline out to the dining room when Donncha called me back.

– Here, take a couple of these cigars with you for later on.

– No, honestly, thanks: I've got some in my coat pocket.

– For the love of James Joyce, take the fucking things. If you're really going to be a famous writer the least you can do is accept a good cigar when it's offered.

– K.M.R.I.A.

– *Gesundheit!*

– I suppose it is a consideration these days; still it's never nice to be refused.

– What are you on about?

– I'm going to nip upstairs for a sec. You go on in.

– You know where it is?

– I do indeed. But tell me this: where's the toilet?

– Just...

– OK. Only testing.

In the toilet I spoke to my reflection in the mirror, one of the few indisputably accurate early warning signs of approaching inebriation. I was less than civil in my remarks: ominous. Watch yourself. Going down the stairs, that is. You've had a fair amount today; started early. Behave yourself.

– This potato soup is simply delicious.

– It's a cinch to make.

– Cinch for you.

– No, honestly: you can take down the recipe before you leave. Absolutely straightforward.

– How did you get on today?

– Fine, I suppose. They all seemed content.

Niamh was in Dublin for a week, instructing trade union officials in the mysteries of advanced personnel management. Sounds interesting.

– It is, I suppose. Most of the time. But absolutely exhausting.

That tone of voice, that manner, that minimal glance, that total lack of doubt. Left you in no doubt: she was good at whatever personnel managers taught. Listen. Change the relationship. See it his way. The way people see each other and themselves.

– But how?

Examples from elsewhere. Talk them round. Images of themselves. Other cultures. Provided it has a strong economic basis. Talk, talk, talk: talk most people into anything if you keep at them long enough. Basic interrogation techniques: series of individual encounters followed by a group discussion.

– That, of course, is a good day. There are times you might as well be talking to a fucking brick wall – if you'll pardon my French. Here, Caroline: let me give you a hand with these.

– Not at all, Niamh. Stay where you are. I can manage – or at least the dishwasher can. Donncha, some more drinks?

– I do humbly beg youser pardons; more booze.

– Come on, Caroline. I insist. I'll take this lot out.

Does the voice change more imperceptibly than anything else? Voiceprints. I would still recognise that voice instantly. Twenty years since we were in college. Wouldn't it be marvellous to see me as she sees me? Maybe not so marvellous. Happenings I can only guess at. Seems thinner to me now; that means that she is probably much thinner. Or does it? Personnel management. Discussing self-images and relationships. Changing people in order to make more concrete blocks per diem, more blocks of cheese, more blocks of tinned meat. So what do I do, I suppose, except the same thing: change people's image of themselves, of the world, so that they turn out a better product in the schools? A more enlightened population? A population less likely to allow themselves to be turned into blocks? Lovely thought. Symbiosis. Still together after all these years.

– Now everybody help themselves while things are still hot. It's not great but it will have to do.

– Looks great to me.

– Me too.

Still crazy after all these years. No, not really; although something always there, erupting now and then when triggered, like a hiccup. Emotion recollected in embarrassment. Innocence recollected in disbelief. I like the brandy 'cos it makes me randy but (crescendo) give me the vino.

- Wine, Fin?

- No thanks, I'll stick with the lager.

- As odd as ever.

Still. After all these years. Niamh's cross look.

- Writing this book seems to have affected you.

Smile at her.

- If I am affected by anything it is more likely to be alcohol.

- I don't know, really, but I would guess that you are no longer able to distinguish between what actually happened and what didn't happen but might have crossed your mind as being useful for the book. That's not very clear, is it?

- Can you say it again?

- I thought there was to be no more talk of this masterpiece for the moment.

- Hear, hear.

- Fine by me.

- I'm afraid there is no dessert but there's fruit and plenty of cheese. And coffee for everybody?

- A drop of cognac, anybody?

Oh no. Not for me. Strong black coffee.

Niamh adamant, a sprout couchant upon a fork rampant, but the mercy of God is revealed through the telephone. Caroline took it. Kate, just checking to see that all was well. Well actually she had a suggestion. She had just been on the phone to Seamus, making final arrangements to meet in Leeson Street, when Seamus had pointed out that we were all at the moment, though in three different houses, miles closer to each other than we were to Leeson Street. Why didn't we all come over to his place? Kate said she would consult the others and get back to him. Tim agreed that Leeson Street made no sense and suggested that we all meet in his house. And this is what Kate wanted to fix up: was that all right with us? Caroline looked at Donncha, whose face lit up with sudden relief. Could he speak with Kate for a minute? Not at all: he was delighted that nobody was in favour of Leeson Street. He had always had reservations about that and had only gone along with it because of the book and the special occasion and so on. Now, he had a suggestion: why didn't we all come over here? Plenty of room if anybody wanted to stay and no end of drink that we were all more than welcome to. Kate would have to put it to the others and get back.

And the upshot was that Kate rang back shortly afterwards to say that herself and Tim and Seamus would arrive in about an hour.

In that case, cognac for all, coming up. In that case neither Donncha nor I wanted dessert or coffee. When it was suggested that the men withdraw into the front room and allow Caroline and Niamh to do an initial clear-up, I was unwilling to protest. I wanted to get away from the table for a while and I wanted, if possible, a quiet smoke. The initial transition to cognac achieved, I more or less agreed that Kate and I would stay the night: the brazen fumes dissipated most of the defensive tension of the day and a quick refill marked a sudden sense of wellbeing that could have been mistaken for that state normally designated by the term 'merry'. There was another pool of brandy for me when the ladies returned from their toils; Donncha decided to pass for this one and Niamh and Caroline agreed that wine would be wiser for the moment. It was generally conceded that Hanrahan was correct in remarking that we would all be pissed before the night was out, an allusive proposition to which my later reflection in the bathroom mirror would nod agreement. The bell ringing; shuffling in the hall; faces coming around the door.

– Look at them, they're pissed.

– Langers.

– Absolutely scuttered.

Tim was a stranger to all except Kate and me but his social talents meant that his arrival quickened rather than interrupted the flow of hilarity, allegation and riposte. Despite various edicts and proscriptions, with the late arrivals came a resumption of talk about the day, the launch and the book itself. Seamus and Tim referred to themselves by their fictional names and rounded on me ironically for the cruel sentences I had passed on the realities they had shared with me. Seamus had a few yarns about schooldays in Finglas and recounted events and remarks that I had inexplicably failed to exploit; Tim pretended – I still presume he was pretending – that he had met one of the priests from Garbally who had expressed amazement that such a nice boy could have developed into such a shit as to write such lies. Kate was allowed to pass judgement on all matters of dispute while all right of reply was denied me. Donncha consoled me with more cognac and another of his knock-me-down cigars; for as long as there was laughter I would laugh. Kate commented on how much or how little I had changed from the times of the various narratives and she urged Donncha and Caroline and Niamh to come up with memoirs of those innocent Arcadian days which seemed hardly credible now. Is it possible that we were ever that innocent? In action if not in idea? Wave after wave of laughter came with ever more rollicking crests. Niamh was telling the story of our production of *Oedipus* when Tim –

– Excuse me, Niamh, for interrupting, but it's only just struck me. You're Orla!

Even Tim was taken by the reaction. Donncha and Caroline howled with laughter. I closed my eyes and wished to Jesus that I could close my ears. Kate and Seamus knew enough to catch a hint of embarrassed dissent. Tim's puzzled eyes panned the room. Niamh blushed, paused, blushed some more.

– No I fucking am not!

Somehow the situation was saved, and more or less all manner of thing was more or less well, probably because everybody, including Niamh – and even including myself most of the time if the truth were told – was having too good a time and the millilitres of alcohol were not going to be pushed about by a few blushes. And I suspect that everybody thought they knew the score – the whole business of the girlfriend and all that. I don't know how it was all smoothed over but Tim was quite brilliant, I thought, the way he had Niamh smiling in next to no time at all. Before you could say when! Caroline and Niamh were telling girly-tales from the days at UCD, mostly to the effect that anything more unlike themselves than this Orla character would be hard to imagine. Not that she wasn't perfect for the book, if we knew what they meant; just that she wasn't particularly like any of our group.

It was, by general acclamation, a great night and time to go. Despite the urgent whispers of Caroline, Tim and Seamus launched themselves into the early morning air with rebel songs and slogans. Caroline took Kate upstairs to show her where we were sleeping. Niamh padded out into the kitchen in bare feet and announced that she was going to wash up. Donncha and I raised our voices to tell her that we would if we could but we were not able. Donncha asseverated that we would have one for the stairs, would we not? We would: it was all we were fit for.

What did he do then but put on a record – the old DGG box of Beethoven 8 and 9 that I had given him as a wedding present – but for whatever reason I kept thinking of the Pastoral and that got me thinking of Eugene and though it hurt me to do it, I had to ask Donncha to turn the sound down or take it off altogether.

Now, I am convinced that I know what happened after that but not quite so confident as to how it happened as it happened. It seems at least probable that Kate and Caroline came down and failed to dissuade Niamh from bustling about in the kitchen. There was a division of labour among the women: Caroline tidied up in the dining room and in the drawing room and took things to the kitchen, where Niamh and Kate were doing Trojan work on assorted ware, including, and perhaps especially, two glasses which they were scouring with whiskey and gin respectively. Donncha and I could not fail to notice that whatever was happening in the kitchen was punctuated with gasps and screeches of hilarity that were becoming more and more frequent, more and more altitudinous, more and more stomach-tribulating, more and more sinus-stuffing, more and more and more suffused with tears. The extra-human sounds pertained less to domestic science than to the contact of glassware.

There was no evidence to suggest that they were going to come back in and share their merriment with us.

– What, in the name of Jaysus, are they finding so funny at this time of night or morning? Will you answer me that?

I would and I could and I did.

– Not difficult to say: us.

– The thought had crossed my mind.

– Could you make it?

– I'm not sure.

– Are you willing to try?

– I am, if you are.

– Come on, so.

And without causing any permanent damage we made it out to the kitchen where we saw our wives and Niamh with tears of laughter running down their cheeks and when they saw us loom before them in the doorway they did even laugh the more, banging their glasses on the table, closing their eyes, slapping their thighs and suchlike. Nor were we left to linger in ignorance long as to the source of their merriment. Kate had, casually, *en passant* and with no expectation of more than a sentence or two by way of rejoinder, mentioned to Niamh that, though she did love me dearly now, it had often occurred to her that had she encountered me at school or at UCD she would probably have thought me an awful shit: if she had been Orla and had been confronted by such a moody bastard she would have told him precisely what to do with himself.

– Gratuitous instruction indeed. I think I will subject myself to one last cigar.

– Here, have one of these.

– Too strong. One of my stoggies will serve.

I busied myself with searching for and peeling and lighting a cigar, hoping that the Lord or his nominee would steer me through these troubled waters. And things did indeed fare better than a convicted sinner had any right to expect. Niamh simply agreed with Kate and expressed the difference between the me she had known at the time and the character she had read about in the book in such a colourful way as to endear her to Kate instantly and for life. Niamh's contention was that that section of the book was an accurate representation of the general atmosphere of UCD and, filling her glass and inviting Kate to do likewise, as one woman of the world to another, she illustrated her thesis by relating several anecdotes concerning the sexual mores of the little boys at UCD in the sixties. Caroline came in to remonstrate but stayed to corroborate Niamh's thesis with a further selection of incidents from the same time, all of them supporting the same less than adulatory presentation of the student body, male and female, but, inevitably, mainly male. Just as Donncha and I descended onto our chairs, Caroline precipitated the spilling of a bottle of tonic water by mimicking Donncha's first formal declaration of his desire to go steady with her. It was too late for me to retreat: Kate had seen to her great glee that Niamh and Caroline had me in their sights.

– Niamh and Caroline agree with you about UCD: that it really was as innocent as you made out.

– I refuse to comment on the grounds that anything I say may tend to cause me to have my head eaten off.

– Aaw, he's afraid to say anything.

– Well, you have to remember how shy he is.

– Would you say shy? Or sensitive?

– Both: shy and sensitive.

– I know he is shy and sensitive now but was he always like that?

– But of course.

– And I thought it was my influence.

– 'Fraid not, Kate: he was famous for his quiet and shy sensitivity. Whenever you mentioned his name to anybody they always said: You mean the shy guy in English?

Despite the volleys of laughter that marked the passing of each comment, Donncha was almost asleep; the only thing between him and unconsciousness was the pain of trying to stretch out on a kitchen chair and the firm resolve of his spouse that he was not to get away so lightly.

– Donncha dear, wake up. Kate doesn't believe us that Fin was famous for his shyness and his sensitivity when he was at UCD. You tell her.

– You lot are only taking the piss but I think it's true. The reason he wasn't famous is that we were all shy in those days, at least most of the people I knew. I was anyway, and I would go so far as to say that Fin was too. And so were you in your own way. There were those who were obviously shy and uncertain of themselves and there were those who managed to hide the fact that they were shy and uncertain.

It occurred to me that I should agree with a good deal of what Donncha had said and offer some qualifications of my own but the Three Graces – or Fates, perhaps – were in no mood for such twaddle: they simply exploded in derisive laughter at Donncha's observations and prescribed another drink.

– Come on, Caroline, you knew him as well as anybody else: what was he like, really?

We were in the badlands now, the territory of the drunken truth-tellers. How drunk were we?

– I wasn't gone on him in the beginning but you have to remember that I had a very sheltered upbringing. I was very prim and proper. I thought people only used bad language when they were fighting on the street.

And there I was, the Finglas Kid, pissing on the pillars of respectability, watching them wince as I told them to fuck off, very rude, very crude. And didn't anybody tell me to cease such obscenities, to shut up? Of course. And? And I urged them to ask my arse.

– But he didn't give a shit about the lectures or the lecturers. He found the whole middle class thing very funny. I know I am making it sound more political and radical than it ever was. I don't know. He just made it clear that he didn't give a shit about things that I had been brought up to believe were important. I mean, I had never used the word shit in my life.

Saint Fintan the Foul, virgin and nihilist, preaching to the middle classes.

– But, Niamh, what in the name of God made you go out with him?

– Look who's talking: you married him.

– Oh, yes, but he's such a sweet person now, not like the prick you two remember – if you'll excuse the expression.

Was this really happening? I wanted to go to bed.

– Is this really happening? I want to go to bed.

– Sit down and keep quiet. Or better still: have another drink. Ladies, may I?

– What a good idea.

– Well, just one last teeny one for me.

I really should go to bed.

– Let's see can I answer the question: why did I go out with him?

I want to fast forward. Anywhere: just out of here.

– It was a long time ago: seems like another lifetime. I mean, I remember going home for Christmas in second year, when I had been going out with Fin, and I remember sitting on the bed and talking to Marion – Marion's my younger sister – and I remember her getting progressively more horrified as I told her about this Dublin gurrier who used bad language and didn't go to mass and didn't believe in anything at all except maybe literature and drinking and singing ballads. Poor Marion: she thought I was on the top of the slippery slope. Little did she know. Little did any of us know. I mean, I was thrilled to bits to think that anybody thought I was in danger of –

There was a crash but strange to relate it was not the announcement of some apocalypse, merely Donncha falling to the floor.

– Time for bed, Donncha dear.

Caroline was waking Donncha. Niamh and Kate were cleaning up, washing the glasses and putting them away. They were still talking and laughing as I made my way up the stairs. Even if I had wanted to hear more I couldn't have stayed: my eyelids were like lead and the tree outside my window was bending and bending and my story was ending and ending and ending...

But it was not: Kate was shaking me, telling me to wake up and get a move on, that the others were all up, that I had to get out to RTE to be interviewed. With the swishing of curtains came the painful suspicion that all Kate said was true.

As I watched my hand trying to lift the mug of coffee and steer it towards my mouth I decided it would be prudent to ring RTE and check on the arrangements. And as well that I did: there were problems. Needless to say, they were not on my side – I was merely possessed by a horde of demons – but Dan Henegan claimed to be in trouble, in some doubt as to when and even whether he would have studio time that afternoon or evening. I seized the opportunity to imply some mild annoyance and postpone the interview *sine die*. I'd had enough. I wanted to get back to my own world – my own bed, my own coffee, my own music and, most of all, the girls. And so after expressions of mutual gratitude and solemn promises to meet again, Kate and I bade farewell to Donncha and Caroline and Niamh and headed for the warm south, full of the true, the blushful Hippocrene.

During the fortnight after Grogan's there was hardly a day which did not bring some news of the book in some form or other. So much so that I came to take it all for granted – like the rain. I avoided people as best I could. I spent as little time as possible in college, arriving in time for my classes and leaving immediately afterwards without checking my room or my pigeonhole for correspondence. I tried to keep myself as busy as possible with college work, correcting essays and preparing lectures. I completed a draft of the essay on Joyce and immediately began a revision even though the term was due to end in a couple of weeks.

I could not resist reading the reviews.

With one notable exception they were the usual congeries of predictable opinion and bland inanity. I found them very disappointing, not because they failed to praise or fault the book but because they told me so little about it. But Kate cut them all out and I confess I did pore over them, examining the sparse quotations with minute fascination. None of them managed to avoid using one of the following terms in a prominent position: 'sharp' (the favourite by far), 'unsentimental', 'ironic', 'cynical'. Almost all the reviewers alluded to the thinly disguised presence of Brendan Behan and commented that this was an interesting addition to the existing portraits. Three reviewers referred to Eugene Watters by name. Another wrote that 'the character of George Rivers must surely have been based on an actual teacher who exercised a powerful and not unmixed influence on the author's development'. One wrote that the book was at least as interesting for the insights it offered into the Irish educational system of a generation ago as it was for its manipulation of plot and character. Whatever that meant, if anything. There were many phrases which I doubted meant anything at all but no more than usually crop up in Sunday reviews. Several – only one of them a professional writer of fiction – used the term 'academic', each intending – as far as I could discern – a different meaning: if there was any common factor in these usages it was the suggestion of excessive self-awareness. Only one critic – a total stranger to me – was wholeheartedly hostile. The piece, gleefully entitled 'The Cobbler's Last', was short and savage and dismissed the material as uninteresting, the style as pretentious, and the author as fortunate to have a permanent and pensionable post to fall back on.

But I was probably the only person disappointed by the reviews. Anybody interested in the fate of *Gone The Time* – and probably a great many more who are not – will know that the launch of the book was a great commercial success, bringing the product and its producers to the attention of an unusually large section of the market. The amount of coverage – all the national newspapers, daily and Sunday, everything from *Image* to *Hot Press*, all the important radio and television magazine programmes – was several times what the most optimistic of the Hollinsford people could have expected. Some would argue – with justification – that a good deal of this was down to a fluke, but that would be unfair to those who organised the launch.

Take the bulk of the press coverage. I had reason to study this carefully and what I found most interesting about the reports was their consistent failure to describe what had happened in Grogan's that evening. I do not mean to suggest that the journalists were wilfully false or that their virginal copy was perverted by malignant editors. Nor would I attribute their inaccuracy to the amount of drink that the journalists and some of their more colourful informants consumed. All journalists have to satisfy the requirements of their own style – whether it be a particular linguistic barbarism, a recognised formula or a strictly enforced number of words – and though such pressures could be easily noted, they were not nearly as obvious as the strange pressure which made almost all the reporters file an almost identical copy. True, they all witnessed the same event but that does not explain their agreement among themselves, for the event they witnessed was very different from what took place. To see this as a fluke would be to miss the point.

Which is that a professional publicity team decided that their assault on the Irish media – European and Asiatic papers please copy – would be three-pronged.

Gone The Time was presented to the public not as the first novel of an unknown lecturer in a provincial university but as another product of that genetic complex – the Kearney/Behan/Bourke – which had for generations been providing the people of Ireland with entertainments ranging from the national anthem to the Four Provinces Ballroom. I was identified in a series of alliterative oppositions too tedious to recount in full. I was the one, it was implied, who had gone to boarding school rather than borstal, who had preferred the Athenian to the Abbey stage. Mine was the cold eye of the Kearneys, the implied comparison being with the less critical perceptions of the Behans and the Bourkes. (My mother's people got short shrift for no other reason than that they were neither famous nor notorious.) This, of course, was madness but there was method in it. Somebody had done his or her homework and realised that with Irish people generally and with Dubliners in particular the dominant emotion is a deeply sentimental tribal nostalgia. Just think of the true love that emerges after a gallon of Guinness, that slobbering pas- sion for the green green grass of home, for that gang that sang heart of my heart, alive alive-oho. Think how those bleuried eyes wander into astral strabismus as the pulp behind them is pricked by the memory of a damp valley, a grey river, a straggle of hovels. And, most ludicrous of all, think of those true-blue Dubs – some of them with connections in the city stretching back over more than one generation – who sway with nostalgia as they sing of Anna Livia Plurabelle. The Hollinsford people drifted the old blue fly down by the Liffeyside and in next to no time the punters were happily munching it, triple-hook, line and sinker. Some of the resultant headlines were hilarious and even I was amused to learn that I was supposed to have written 'a detailed reconstruction of an earlier and happier Dublin' or 'a fascinating history of several of the city's most colourful septs'. Septs!

But the most typical headline was something like 'Cousin of Behan Writes of Rare Oul' Times' and the second prong in the attack was none other than the archetypal Dubliner himself, the late Brendan Behan. Hats off to whoever decided to make BB patron saint for the day. Despite the fact that the launch took place twenty years after the death of the boul' Bren' and that none of those present had ever been at one of his famous press occasions, a casual reader would have been forgiven for assuming that Behan had actually been there in all his earthly amplitude. Any report which did not work a reference to BB into the headline had one in the first few lines. The spirits of Dicey Riley and Dunlavin, of Granny Grunt and assorted quare fellows and hostages, captains, kings and people of no standing all jostled and jingle-jangled from here to the greater Crumlin-in-the-Sky. There were rather arcane versions of it – 'Jackeen ag Caoineadh an Bhaile' – and several variations on the theme of 'Belfield Boy', a rhetorical victory over the fact that the UCD of the book was located in Earlsfort Terrace and not on its present site at Belfield. There were genealogical errors – with and without photographs – and it was interesting to consider the moral permutations suggested by these errors. There were all kinds of other errors but who cared? Before long all notices but one had become secondary.

The ultimate proof of the skilful professionalism of the Hollinsford people – and the third prong of their attack – was their selection of Malachi Murphy as a primary target. Remember that Malachi Murphy was – even more than now – the maverick of Irish journalism, disliked and envied in equal parts by almost all of his professional colleagues. They had not forgotten how he had made his triumphal entrance into Irish journalism with a series of articles on the principal faults of Irish journalists – they had once again chosen to imitate the British rather than continental models et cetera, now stuck with a journalism aspiring to nothing higher than bum'n'tit politics, nothing more permanent than last night's dress dances et cetera, unless editors show the courage et cetera the press will attract neither writers nor readers from the new highly educated generation. And so it came to pass: Jesus Christ his own precursor. Nobody could be seen to reject Murphy – lest they be accused of stifling criticism of themselves – and so all doors flew open. Suddenly Murphy was everywhere – radio, television, dailies, Sundays, magazines – laying down the new gluten-free wisdom on everything from AIDS to Wittgenstein. And he was good copy because he had the true talent of the journalist – an instant and apparently informed opinion on every topic. Three years' sociology at the University of East Anglia had given him the Key to Knowledge and a loathing of authority. He had a brain – that much was not in doubt – and he used it to process all material through the filters of à la mode sociology in order to produce findings that were always radical and fresh and modishly abrasive. He could take a topic that had been worked to death by other journalists and, reinterpreting it in the light of Marxism and/or feminism and/or poststructuralism, make it as good as new. Drama, fiction or verse, ancient or modern, male or female, there was nothing on which he could not promulgate an instant, incisive and interesting verdict. All you need is context: the best angle is your own angle.

But though undeniably the brightest, probably the best, journalist in Ireland, Murphy was not personally popular – either with his colleagues who resented his facility or with the politicians who couldn't quite cope with his absolute contempt. Who or what prompted the Hollinsford people to get to him? Who marked their card? Who tipped this outsider?

Even I noticed that there was something afoot in Grogan's but could make nothing of it: it seemed strange, miscalculated, maybe even self-destructive, but time has proved that it was an inspired move. In the following Sunday's *Independent*, Malachi Murphy's column – 'The Sunday Supplement' – was entitled 'The Perrier Generation' and took as its text *Gone The Time*.

It was a remarkable piece of writing – no matter what way you look at it: it is probably fair to say that it turned the publication of a fairly pedestrian novel into an event of cultural impact. Nobody else in Ireland could have done it. (Again I ask: who pointed Pete?) The other journalists did their predictable thing: a photograph, a social headline and

two or three paragraphs of chat. The reviewers, some liked this, some
that, others that and this and so forth: most of them had something to
say about the actual persons and events they detected behind the
characters and action. And had it not been for Malachi that would have
been it: the social occasion of the launch quickly forgotten and the book
dismissed to the decent obscurity of the magazine section. But Malachi
Murphy, the master of significant contexts, transformed the book from
a novel to a text and transferred it from new fiction to news and current
affairs. As a result of this metamorphosis the book was discussed on such
popular radio magazine programmes as *Morning Ireland, Day By Day,
Women Today,* the *Gay Byrne Hour* and, the publicist's dream come true,
on *the* television programme, the *Late Late Show.* Inevitably, the book
became a best seller in Ireland.

My own particular misgivings did not prevent me from admiring
Murphy's dexterity: in one article, produced within a week, he pleased
himself by attacking – without mentioning his name – Niall Murtagh
and by denigrating – without, of course, seeming to do so – the author
of *Gone The Time*, and he also laid up credit with Hollinsfords by giving
the book a push such as they could never have imagined. In the process
he emerged as an author of at least equal importance as the author of
the original book.

Murphy used his customary opening move: though the author
thought he was writing a nostalgic narrative of the subjective past, what
he had produced was a scathing indictment of the political present. The
central character was not so much a portrait of the artist as a young man
as the genealogy of a generation, the generation that is assuming political
power in Ireland today. As a novel in the traditional sense *Gone The
Time* was as interesting and accomplished as most of the other thousands
of narratives that were bought or rented and then consumed carelessly
in libraries, cinemas and sitting rooms all over the country every day and
night – no more or less; but as a pathology of the current ailments of
the Irish body politic, an account of the origins and developments of
those ideological formations which the narrative tries to conceal and
suppress, it was the most interesting text of its kind to appear in Ireland
for a generation.

The key term was 'generation'. The Free State had been achieved by
the revolutionary generation, hard men, brave and sometimes brutal but

nevertheless honest men who were genuinely gripped by the ideals of freedom preached by Pearse and others: the hearts of this generation of men – and women – were eventually broken by the civil war or the sterile political structures it produced. Power passed to the next generation, the post-revolutionary generation, mostly the sons of the revolutionaries, most of them born in the twenties, and it was this generation who, despite their utter failure to effect worthwhile change, were still clinging to power: pathetic, in their defence it could be said that they had preserved some shadow, however grotesquely misunderstood, of the ideals they had inherited. But the post-revolutionary generation was finished; no longer able to convince themselves or the people, they stood by the window, glass in hand, perplexed by history. The eighties saw the arrival of the third generation, those who are beginning to replace the old guard. According to Malachi Murphy, these are the scrapings of the bucket, the verrucas on the snow-white feet of Cathleen the daughter of Houlihan. They grew up in relative luxury, comfort, went to university and, crucial to Malachi's analysis, were the first generation to enjoy cheap air travel in the sixties. They had all the advantages of education, travel, communication; they were the ones ideally placed to realise the social and political ideals which had begotten the Free State; they were in a position, no longer blindfolded by traditional notions of language, nationality or religion, to reform the state along enlightened lines. But the signs were that, far from improving things, this shower were leading the march into a black hole of intellectual, spiritual, political and financial bankruptcy. This was the Perrier generation, producing endless bubbles of gas that vanished when they made contact with actuality, utterly lacking in any national spirit, failing to tap the natural resources of our own country and preferring to buy whatever Europe advocated, the ultimate morons of consumerism. Trapped by their own inanities between a dead past and an unimagined future, between the hangover of tradition and a gutless, witless fear of action, they stumbled from crisis to crisis, from mortgage to mortgage, from fetish to fetish, from the heroic fantasies of whiskey to the repentant belch of Perrier water.

Or words to that effect.

Within a week the phrase 'the Perrier generation' was everywhere in the media, within a month it was as embedded in the language of Irish political commentary as 'champagne socialist'. I am not sure of the order in which things happened but two or three days after the review a government spokesman who was being grilled on *Today Tonight* tried to deflect the interviewer by reaching for his glass and saying, 'I hope this isn't Perrier water.' He succeeded: the camera went in on the glass and the interviewer felt obliged at the end of the interview to explain the reference as best he could and this, of course, involved mentioning the book and the author. Shortly afterwards John Bowman, interviewing an elderly and particularly primitive junior minister, asked him if he was a member of the Perrier generation. And then an opposition spokesman insisted that there were no Perrier people in his party: he and his party supported the Buy Irish campaign and would always drink Irish spring water in preference to any imported product. It was only a matter of time before the phrase was given official recognition and used by Gay Byrne both on his radio programme and on the *Late Late Show*. It was beyond a sales manager's wildest dreams. Money could not have bought such publicity.

Everybody was happy: Hollinsfords had a best seller, Malachi Murphy's guru status was raised several notches, the bottlers of spring water – foreign and domestic – tried merrily to cope with the increase in sales, Kate was proud and the children thrilled, friends and relations rang to congratulate, media people clogged the phone.

Everybody was happy except me. I had hoped that, after the little ripples of publication and review, the book would sink peacefully in a trough of uninterest, but I had reckoned without the power of the press.

I didn't actually hear the stuff on the radio about spring water and the post-revolutionary generation – not because I avoided it, but simply because it was unexpected. I was asked to appear on the television *Late Late Show* but declined, saying that I had no opinions on the matter one way or the other. The representative of the programme was initially surprised and eventually surly: if that was the way I felt, that was my own lookout. Kate's reaction was not entirely dissimilar and she thought it best that word of my refusal be kept from the children. Kate and I watched the show and saw Malachi Murphy go through his paces, smiling contemptuously at a brace of politicians who insisted on revealing the high regard in which they held themselves, each other and the Irish people. But it was soon obvious that the audience was not interested.

The host tried to enliven the occasion by inviting questions but this didn't work out either. From the floor two would-be politicians tried to demonstrate their intelligence and humour; the other guest on the panel – the author of a new book on the death of Marilyn Monroe – did not feel it would be proper for her to comment on matters relating to Irish politics.

Kate was amazed at my casual acceptance of the reviews – good, bad or otherwise. I too was amazed, not that I felt either pride or resentment, but that I was beginning to accept the public relationship of myself and the book as an accomplished fact. When Dan Henegan rang again and suggested another date for the interview, I accepted that too.

I could have done it from the Cork studio but I decided to use the interview as an excuse to have a quiet evening with my father and mother. I went up by train on the afternoon of Thursday 7 March. My father met me at the station, we had a quick pint in Ryan's of Parkgate Street and then back to the house for dinner. They were eager for news of the book; I kept asking about various friends and relations. Pearse wasn't well.

Mammy came round to the pub with us after dinner and insisted on buying her round: brandies to toast the book. We remembered every little detail of the launch in Grogan's and agreed that we hadn't seen Pearse in such good form for ages. Daddy told us how he had met Mattie O'Neill who had told him that Pearse wasn't well and had had the doctor to the house. To ward off evil spirits I called for a last round of brandies.

When my father knocked at the door next morning I woke up tired and hungover and wishing that I had never agreed to the interview. I didn't feel up to a bus journey and so I accepted his offer of a lift into town. This meant that I didn't really have enough time to wash and shave properly: I was able to supplement my breakfast in Bewley's of George's Street but for the remainder of the day I felt internally and externally scruffy, especially when I arrived at RTE.

Dan Henegan came out to reception – how was everybody in Cork's own town? – and brought me to the studio. After the usual introductions it was down to voice levels, suggested lines of interview, countdown and red light. There was a brief introduction in which the interviewer referred to the Perrier generation phenomenon, related it to the book, gave two or three brief quotes from reviews, and then sum-marised my life and times in one long epileptic sentence. And then a gasped breath arrested in the form of a semi-colon. I was, he half asked, half accused me, looking at the notes on his clipboard as if he thought they might have changed in the five seconds since he had last glanced over them, was I not, forty years of age: did I not think it, aagh, 'premature' to publish at such an early age what was, he was willing to grant, an autobiographical novel with the emphasis on novel, but what was also undeniably, and here he tended to agree with almost everybody who had reacted to the book in public, an essay in autobiography with the emphasis on autobiography?

I didn't think my response was in any way 'snotty' or 'facetious' or 'unhelpful'. I remember feeling that two could play this game.

– Do you mean as a general principle?

Smart-arse was not amused. He waved play-on but I just continued to look at him. Eventually he growled intellectually.

– Yes. First of all. As a general principle. Let us deal with the general principle first.

– When you use the term 'premature' in conjunction with a specific numeral, are you primarily concerned with the literary quality of the book or with the moral fate of the author?

And that was the end of the first take. The interviewer waved his hands terminally and then stormed out of sight until he appeared behind the glass panel. After a while Dan came out and put his arms around me and said that there was no problem, a matter of clearing the air, taking five and beginning again. Everything he did or said implied that the interviewer was a bit off form and that we all had to make allowances et cetera.

Take two. They ran the tape of the intro and then began recording again. This time things seemed easier, more relaxed.

Towards the middle of the novel there was a section in which the central character discovers the work of Joyce: was Joyce a major in-fluence on me? Plain sailing: I launched into a long press release on the likely relationship between Joyce and the average Irish adolescent male with a taste for literature, keeping to the high seas of generalised com-ment for as long as I was allowed. Had it been for me as it had been for the central character in the book? Again, no problem. I responded as if he had asked me in what order and at what age I had first read Joyce's works. No personal details other than age, educational establishment and the fact that I had grown up in Dublin, travelling hundreds of times on the Finglas bus under Butt Bridge, up Gardiner Street, along Dorset Street, looking back over my shoulder towards Eccles Street, turning left into Whitworth Road et cetera. I was about to meet the funeral party from *Ulysses* at Prospect Road when again he interrupted me.

– Do you see any similarities between your work and that of Joyce?

– None.

– I am thinking particularly about the manner in which you, rather in the manner of Joyce, have obviously exploited family and friends and relations and that sort of thing.

It was downhill from there on. I tried to divert him but he kept at me about this. He came out with a series of identical questions about family and friends and relations recognising themselves and others in the novel; my replies seldom went beyond three syllables. No. Never. Not at all.

– Surely you're not going to sit there and maintain that while you were writing this book you never realised that you were basing your plot on your own experience, your locations on places where you yourself are known to have lived and studied, your characters on relations, friends, acquaintances?

– Yes.

– You must be playing with words. Is 'realise' not the right word? Something like that?

– Yes.

– What word then?

– You talk about me writing this book called *Gone The Time*. I didn't write it.

And that was more or less the end of the interview. He asked me if I was being obsessively precise, if I was insisting on some term other than writing, if I would prefer 'composing' or 'creating' or 'dictating' or 'publishing' or whatever. I replied that I was splitting no such hairs, that I simply wanted to say that I had not written the book. Of course he asked another string of questions about who wrote it and how come my name was on it and so on; I just repeated the fact that I had not written the book and was not, therefore, the person to whom these questions should be addressed.

There was a peculiar hum in the air as he rounded off the interview and got the signal that we were no longer being recorded. For my part, I got out as quickly as possible and nobody, not even Dan, objected to this.

And a few hours later there I was looking out the window of the Cork train and thinking: hey, you've done it. I felt a huge relief, kept taking long deep breaths.

By the time Kate and I were having our after-dinner coffee I had recounted the affair in RTE and it had become a joke. I was only joking.

As I had to explain to the reporter from the *Examiner* when he rang the morning after the interview was broadcast. Just a prank. Well, it wasn't easy to explain it in a few words. OK: there was the idea that language existed before you and me and that it was by means of language that we experienced the world and had whatever ideas we had and so you could say that the so-called author didn't write the book but that language was writing the book or indeed that the book was writing him or her. An academic joke. Well, no: I didn't suppose that it was the kind of joke that would appeal to everybody. Well, yes: I had already admitted that it wasn't a side-splitter, it wasn't funny-ha-ha. Oh, come on: how could anybody be guilty of irresponsibility on a radio arts programme? Bad manners perhaps or poor judgement but not irresponsibility. For fucksake. No, I couldn't say how I would behave if I was to do the interview all over again: it just seemed like a good idea at the time. What would I say to the charge that I was simply looking for attention for the book? I would deny it. OK. Anytime.

I had hardly put down the phone when it rang again: a friend's voice smiling, to say how much he had enjoyed my Derridean pose, my postmodernist performance, the eighties equivalent of being drunk on television in the fifties, that Brendan Behan would have been proud of me, that it should sell a few copies anyway.

Term ended that Friday and I was certainly ready for the break. I planned to fill in the few weeks by immersing myself in domestic maintenance by day and slumping in front of the television by night but things didn't quite work out like that. By the following Friday lunch time not only was all the maintenance done but the back garden had also been dug, weeded and raked. There was nothing left for me to do but give my study a general tidy-up. By the time I plonked myself down in front of the television that night my study resembled a scene in a Sunday supplement. Saturday morning found me sitting at my typewriter, wondering what the hell I was doing there. I had decided to eschew any academic work during the vacation but it was as if I could no longer control myself. I took out the draft lecture on Joyce which had been giving me trouble and suddenly there was no problem at all: I could now see what the central point of the argument was and out it came fluent and pleasingly pitched for oral delivery and, later on, publication in a journal.

And so there I was on Monday morning – 25 March 1985 – with a clean desk in a tidy study and an overwhelming feeling that I owed somebody or other a letter. I just sat there, staring out the window and trying to think, only moving to change a cassette. At some stage I began to tidy the books I had been using for quotations and references in the Joyce lecture, moving them from the desk to the shelves behind me. My attention fell on the Penguin Modern Classics edition of *Ulysses* with Lawrence Mynott's portrait of Joyce on the cover: dicky bow, hat at a jaunty angle, cigarette in tanned fingers . . . And it struck me, not for the first time, that portraits of the older Joyce – the Parisian author-of-*Ulysses* Joyce – always reminded me of Pearse. What was it? Certainly not the dicky bow nor the hat nor the little rounded glasses – none of which Pearse ever wore. The cigarette in the stained fingers was familiar but hardly enough to set up a similarity. Was it the thin moustache – what we used to call Pearse's ronnie? (When was Ronald Coleman on the go?) And of course the hair, the greying hair pushed straight back off the furrowed forehead. And those rough brown furrows in which I used to move my soft white fingers were, like Joyce's, the marks of an attitude of sardonic sentimentality, a wild careless wilfulness and, most of all, a pervasive generosity. An extravagant, licentious disposition. I was about sixteen when I was surprised by the collection of photographs in Ellmann's book: not only did the physical similarity to Pearse make my skin tingle but it even crossed my mind that the body they buried in the snow in Zurich in 1941 wasn't that of Joyce at all, that after *Finnegans Wake* Joyce had decided to get away from it all and return to Ireland and that he had settled down in Raheny with his

Galway wife and his children, pretending to be a house painter. (*The Dalkey Archive* had not been published at that stage.) Joyce as Pearse; Pearse as Joyce. It was an idea worthy of Joyce, one that would have tickled Pearse. Had I ever mentioned it to him? Maybe I'd mention it to him the next time.

And then I began to write. I put a sheet into the typewriter and the words hopped up before me: I do not know what has possessed me . . .

And that, as I've said, is how it all started on Monday 25 March 1985. I was convinced that *it* would also be finished on 25 March 1985, presuming that *it* would consist of about twenty pages of typed A4, but *it* was full of surprises. After three or four sessions at the typewriter I knew that *it* would involve much more than I had imagined. I wasn't in any sense writing to Pearse and I don't think I was ever writing for Pearse; it's just that I was conscious of his presence in the scheme of things whatever it was.

Whatever it is.

The first burst of energy produced almost all of what you have just been reading. In June we travelled to the US where I taught two courses – partly to finance the family holiday, partly to keep myself busy. I brought the typescript with me but hardly looked at it before we returned in September. The break had not whetted my appetite for what I was now beginning to think of as a task. I tried and failed to write a link between the two parts of the typescript. I wanted to continue the second part but could find no way forward. I often thought of giving up but never managed to resign myself to the decision. When I tried to force myself to confront the typewriter I ended up yawning and walking away; when I chose to forget about it, sit down and read a book, I always found myself heading upstairs with an idea for the typescript. All these ideas failed, were crushed up and thrown in the basket. Then one morning – it would have been in late

November or early December – my father was on the phone and he mentioned in passing that Pearse wasn't well. I realised that time was running out, not only for Pearse but for all of us. I also realised that I wanted to write down an account of Pearse to which I could put my name, an account which I could confidently place in his own hand.

By Christmas I had a draft of the Pearse narrative and looked forward to hearing his reaction to it. When I saw him in hospital I realised that we would never discuss it – or anything else. Pearse's funeral made me want to get back to the typewriter, to express my feelings in a way that would be out of place at a funeral – or at least at one of our funerals. By the time I had finished writing farewell to Pearse I had already conceived the sections on Eugene Watters and Brendan Behan and by the end of second term I had completed them. What is now the final section was drafted during the Easter break.

By then I had been involved with the thing for a year but the longer I spent with it the less I understood it. Did I have preliminary sketches or final drafts? Was I going to link and/or interweave the sections into a traditional synchronic narrative or was I going to leave them as they were? If and when the thing was finished, what was I going to do with it?

I was really perplexed by the time I met you after the conference, even more so when I got home. Which is, of course, why I am here in Connemara.

I need to walk into Clifden and get a blast of fresh air and prove to myself that people who know nothing of any of this still manage to lead reasonably contented lives. And if I am to do any or all of these things I had better get going because I think there's a drop of rain on the way.

PEARSE

A drop of rain? Would you believe a hurricane? Yes, a hurricane in Connemara. I don't know if it got as far as you: did you feel or hear of Hurricane Charlie? The tough guys in the meteorological office have pointed out that what we got here last night was merely the tail of the hurricane but it was still enough to stir the heart and ruffle the landscape. Even now, ten o'clock the morning after, the clouds are scurrying across the sky as if they were trying to get out of the way of something and I would suspect that a fair amount of damage has been done. The house and I seem to have escaped.

It built up so gradually yesterday that I hardly noticed anything unusual till I heard doors slamming and windows creaking on their latches. I like to keep the door of my scriptorium ajar but it kept banging shut and I got fed up opening it again. I wasn't feeling the best but I put it down to the typescript and the sense of being confined, but dogs bark before earthquakes and – who knows? – maybe I sniffed the

storm. When I had finished my stint on the typescript I
mooched around for a while and then, inexplicably, turned on
the radio. It didn't work. I then broke one of my resolutions
and switched on the television. Sure enough the six o'clock
news had pictures of waves crashing over seaside walls, boats
being buffeted up against each other, rivers bursting their banks
and, inevitably, well-fed farmers prophesying doom. I decided
to light a fire.

My first real taste of the wind was when I went outside to
gather kindling. Most of it had just been ripped from the trees
but I found enough dry stuff to get me going. There is a deep
atavistic pleasure in sitting inside by the fire and listening to the
storm outside: it must be one of the basic human delights, so
rooted in our pre-history that no amount of central heating and
double-glazing can eradicate it. With a great feeling of
primitive man – and the help of a microwave oven – I cooked
my meat and two veg and ate them by the fire, listening to the
squalls building up into howling gales as the rain crashed against
the windows. And then suddenly – all my actions seemed
sudden and apparently senseless – I knew that nothing would
do me but to don boots and raincoat and head out into the
storm.

And out I went. I had no idea where I was headed and
cared less. I felt a rush of elation as I reeled before the wind
for the first time and tasted the first drop of rain to roll down
the side of my nose and into my mouth. I was on the road
into town and just kept going until I heard traditional music
coming from a pub. I paused a while before deciding to make
temporary contact with this abstruse form of human society for
as long as it would take me to drink a couple of pints.

The bar – neo-plastical, stuffy, sweaty and noisy – was filled
with tourists and the music was aimed at them but I overcame
my instinctual snobbery in the matter of pubs and called a
drink. Maybe I was still high on the primitive sense of revelry
in the hovel: I kept thinking of *King Lear* every time the door
opened and oilskinned figures came dripping in. I stuck it for
about an hour and then left. The music was poor – songs and

tunes learned from recordings – and the tourists only exaggerated the artificiality. I preferred the wind and the rain and fought my way back to the house and to bed.

This morning it was as if the storm had been all a dream. No damage to be seen from my scriptorium. Just a sheaf of typescript marked PEARSE. The first part of it was written before I went to see Pearse in Jervis Street hospital, the second shortly after his funeral.

Number 25 O'Donoghue Street, Inchicore, Dublin. The weatherboard slithers across the step as he pushes the heavy hall door in, humming as he hangs his coat behind the door, coming in a shadow over by the window, rubbing his hands and singing, talking to me, stories heavy on his breath sweet and dancing in his moist eyes friendly, hugging me into his stubbled cheek, into the rough green material and shining buttons of his jacket. Uncle. Just Uncle, never Uncle Pearse till years later and then – but that was years away when I was big too.

I don't know where he comes from. Daddy and Uncle are Nana's boys. Everybody calls Daddy Con. My name is Fintan. Daddy calls me son. Everybody smiles when they talk about Uncle. He is a character. Uncle has a special way of looking at you. He thinks I know why he is smiling and he winks at me. But I don't really know. I suppose I'll know later on when I'm big. Mammy and Daddy know where Uncle is when he isn't with us. When he comes it's always a surprise. Mammy says look who's back on the land of the living. And then Nana shakes her head from side to side and Mammy goes out to the gas stove to make a tea. Mammy and Nana try to give out to Uncle but nobody can do that to Uncle. They say you couldn't be up to him. And Mammy says the style of that and Johnny idle. Mammy says things like that: sometimes you have to know what she means before you can understand her.

Uncle is big but he can be great gas. Uncle is not like anybody else. When somebody gives out to him he jeers them and makes faces at them and sings and does his little dance. He moves his fists in and out. He has golden buttons on his jacket and he gives me a sixpence when he has been away. He opens the heavy hall door for me so that I can go down to Monsie Ward to buy dates and the *Herald*. The dates are for me and Mammy, the paper for Daddy when he gets home.

Daddy comes home every night. He sleeps with Mammy in the big bed at the far end of the bedroom. He calls Mammy Mary when they are by themselves. Everybody else calls her Maisie. I only call her Mammy. I sleep in a little bed down by the fireplace. Sometimes I hear Mammy and Daddy talking in bed. They whisper so as not to wake me or the baby. Maura the baby is in the cot over by the window. She is as good as gold. I can look across at the window and even when it's the middle of the night I can see the apple tree in the back garden and then the back wall and then the trees in the grounds where the big children all walk in the possession and they sing 'Flowers of the Rarest' and Mammy and Daddy stand on chairs among the gooseberries at the back wall so that they can see the people singing to Mary – Mary the mother of Jesus – and Daddy lifted me and there were hundreds and hundreds of people and I scraped my arm on the top of the wall. Daddy can sing 'Flowers of the Rarest'. Pearse sings 'Have you heard of Mickey Hickey and the Harp and Shamrock Band'. When he says mother of Jesus it's not a prayer; Daddy says mother of James's Street.

Sometimes when I am in bed I fall off the windowsill very slowly through the soft air and down onto the black tar on the roof of the kitchenette. But I know when I land on the soft tar that I am still in bed.

Uncle is big but sometimes he is bold and gets into trouble. When Mammy and Daddy went around to confession Uncle was sitting on the sofa. Mammy said Uncle would mind me but he fell asleep and I had to shake him to stop him snoring and talking to himself and to get him to mind me. He said I could mind myself. I said I couldn't because I was only a baby. And he fell asleep again and I told him I would tell Mammy and Daddy. His eyes were all watery and tired but after a while he started to smile at me and pulled me over and gave me a hug. And then he took a heap of money out of his pocket and he told me if I said fuck he'd give me a shilling, a big shilling with the silver bull on it. And I said fuck and he gave me a shilling. And then he said say it again and I said fuck and he gave me another shilling and he was laughing and I looked out the window to see if Ward's would still be open but it was dark and Uncle said say it again and he laughed and rooted in his pocket for more shillings and he said he would be fucking broke with me but he was laughing to himself all the time and saying that I was a great little fellow all the same. Mammy and Daddy came back from confession and I told them that I could say fuck. And they looked at Pearse and they looked at each other and I could see that Daddy was very annoyed but he put his finger on his lips and shook his head at Mammy. Auntie Annie and Katty Barnes came to see us and they brought sweets for Mammy and Daddy. They said it was very late for me to be still up and Mammy said she was just getting me ready for bed. I had to go to bed when Annie and Katty Barnes came to the house. I could always hear them laughing, especially Daddy, when I was in bed. And now Mammy told me to say night-night and had I a kiss for Annie and Katty. I didn't want to kiss them because they were lipsticky and there was an awful smell on their necks and in their hair and I said night-night and they said that I was a good little boy and maybe there was a sweet for me if I gave them a kiss, a kiss for a sweet, and I put my hand out and I said fuck. Annie nearly choked on her cigarette and they looked at Mammy and Daddy and I said fuck again but they gave me nothing and I began to cry and Daddy said it was time for bed and they all said good night and waved when Daddy carried me around the corner of the stairs and up to our bedroom. Daddy and I had our snuggle, the special snuggle we always have when I am crying, and Daddy said we would say our prayers and we'd be all right. And we had to whisper them so as not to wake the baby.

God bless Daddy. God bless Mammy. God bless baby Maura. God bless Nana. God bless Uncle.

When Uncle was working in England Mammy sent him hundreds of cigarettes folded up in the *Irish Press*.

When Uncle is here Mammy is always joking him about Galway. There is a photograph of Uncle and other people on horses but they are not dressed like the cowboys.

And when Mammy saw the photograph she said oh look at would-be-if-he-could-be and everybody laughed. Uncle and Auntie Bridie are going to live in town in North Frederick Street, across the road from Walton's. Their house is a basement. A basement has white walls and a window high on the wall where you can see the feet of the people walking along the street. It's dark. Auntie Bridie is strange, she has big eyes and long hair like a girl, and she talks funny: that's because she comes from Galway. People were all dressed up drinking bottles of stout and singing and Uncle had to sing 'Galway Bay', the *old* 'Galway Bay', because everybody shouted for it and when he was singing it the men were trying to put him off and the women were shaking their heads and smiling.

Mammy said you'd miss Pearse, and Daddy and Nana said you would and then they looked at me and asked me did I miss Uncle and they knew I did.

Uncle always put on his soldier face and stuck out his chest when he asked you anything about Irish. Daddy and Uncle liked Irish because their daddy fought for Ireland and Nana got guns past the Black and Tans in her shopping bag. That's why they were always asking me to say the poem whenever anybody came to the house.

> Sínte ar thaobh an tsléibhe
> do chonaic mé croppaí bocht
> Bhí an drúcht go trom ar a éadan
> agus piléar trína ucht.

Daddy and Uncle were always talking and singing about the men who died for Ireland. When they were little boys their daddy was taken away by British soldiers and before he was taken away he came into their room and said a prayer with them and at the end of the prayer they said God bless Patrick Pearse and all the men who died for Ireland. Daddy and Uncle always called him my father. They never said Daddy. Maybe that was because he was dead. He died before I was born but sometimes I can see him sitting in the armchair beside the fire listening to the radio and looking very cross. He talks to me when we're alone in the room but he doesn't say much to me and I'm afraid to talk to him and ask him what it was like when he was fighting for Ireland. He is very famous because he was in 1916 and he wrote the songs that the Irish soldiers used to sing when they were fighting for Ireland. Peadar and Nana were very poor. We didn't know how lucky we were.

Uncle's new house in Raheny was great. There were woods behind it where you could play and climb trees. There is a photograph of Nana and me in the woods. Uncle is in it too and Mammy and Daddy. Nana and Daddy and Uncle all sit there in the grass with their heads back, looking away to the side. Maybe they were looking at the mansion that had been burned down by the men fighting for Ireland. It was Peadar Kearney who told them how to keep their backs straight and how to look as if they were cross. Mammy and I are looking at the camera. When Mammy saw the photograph she said: that's nice oh look at full front. I asked her who was that and she said she didn't mean anybody but I knew she meant the way Pearse looked for the photograph and maybe the way Nana and Daddy looked as well. Somebody told me to straighten up but the sun was in my eyes and the grass was itching behind my knees and I was thinking that once upon a time the mansion had beautiful curtains and carpets and shiny wooden floors and now there was only sooty stone and the smell of dogs on the clay in the cold dark corners. It was a pity to see the lovely house like this but it was their own fault. The Irish had suffered even more. I loved Uncle when he sang.

> Now how often we've been flattened out
> Our history books can show
> And Mother England battened on
> Our misery and woe
> She slaked us and she baked us
> Till the snivellers cried Amen
> But the world knows that Ireland rose
> From out the dust again.

And whenever Uncle sang that song Daddy would join in the chorus and afterwards they always told the story. It happened before I was born but I knew everything about it. When Daddy was only Con, when he was just getting big enough to go into pubs by himself. He was two years younger than Uncle. That was hard to understand because Daddy always talked now as if he was bigger. Daddy heard there was a great singsong in the Black Lion. The Black Lion was the pub down beside Lavin's where Mammy bought the colander. There was a shiny black cat over the front door with white eyes and bright red lips. So down Daddy went to see for himself. (Will I ever forget this!) And Daddy saw that there were scarlet women singing in the Black Lion but he was careful to stand at the far side of the bar. (Jesus, Mary and Holy Saint Joseph, can you imagine your man here?) Daddy was delighted when Uncle came in because he didn't want to be standing there by himself.

   – I didn't know that it was this sort of a place?

   – What sort of a place?

   – You know. Your women over there. Are they regulars here?

   – I've no idea.

   – Have you seen them here before?

   – Me? Sure I never come in here.

Never in his life, says he to me and then what happens but one of the quare ones and I can still see her face made up to kill, thick with make-up she was, white with powder, and she brings the house down with some song that was all the rage – I forget what it was – and next thing she puts down her glass and licks her lips and I thought for a moment but I knew I had to be wrong that she was looking over at me and I'm sure I blushed (Agh Jesus, me little brother was blushing) and I turned away to say something to Pearse here and next thing I hear your woman calling for the best of order please and it's her noble call and it gives her great pleasure to call on a great favourite with one and all, none other than the one and only, let's give him a big clap, Mister Pearse Kearney, come on now Pearse. I nearly dropped. I nearly died and your man here beside me as cool as you like. And eejit here believing him that he'd never seen them before. And there's everybody in the bar clapping and calling on Pearse and especially me bould Rory O'Moore. The best of order please for Mister Kearney. Come on now Pearse. Give us tower and steeple. And out steps your man there and no more bother to him.

     Oh you've heard of revolutions
     And you've read of bloody wars
     And you've seen our land disfigured
     By the cruel Saxon scars
     You've seen our best go sailing
     In the ships from vale and hill
     But there's hearts and hands in Ireland boys
     To fight for freedom still –
     For it's a grand ould country every time
     With its trees and rivers, rocks and soil and clime –
     We're God's own people
     And we shout from tower and steeple
     It's a grand ould country every time . . .

I couldn't understand why the scarlet woman would want a song about the Irish fighting against the English, why she'd shout across a crowded smoky bar and make Daddy turn red with embarrassment. And the way Daddy looked, even after all the years, you could see that he was embarrassed that Pearse should know those scarlet women, even if it was only the way people know each other at a singsong. But anybody who had heard Uncle singing that song would want to hear it again. Even ourselves, didn't we always ask him to sing it when there was a singsong? The way he crouched down and shot his eyes all over the place and worked his fists in time with the music, the way he hammered out the chorus and – most of all – the way he went down on his knees and pretended to cry like a baby drying the tears from his eyes.

> We'll spend our time in praying
> While we're waiting for the day
> And we'll pray for Mother England
> Till we're bald and blind and grey...

And then he would get up slowly, squint his eyes and grin:

> And we'll pray that dying she may die
> And drowning she may drown
> And if ever she chances to raise her head –

And here he'd stamp his foot on the ground and even kick a table or chair if there was one handy –

> We'll pray to push her down!

And he'd wave his free arm round and round to make everybody join in and shout out the lines together.

> For it's a grand ould country every time!

Every time.

I used to love going over to Uncle's house in Raheny and always I hoped there would be a singsong when the men came back from the Manhattan. There was always a singsong when there were other visitors, from Galway maybe, or one of the Behans from England. While the men went down to the Manhattan the women stayed chatting in the living room and the children played, either on the green in front of the house or in the woods behind. There was nobody for me to play with – Pearse's children were too young to play real football – and so I used to read the paper or a book or walk in the woods or listen to the women talking until the men came back from the pub, carrying bottles of Guinness in stiff brown paper bags. I remember one Sunday in the summer when Mammy kept asking me why I didn't get out in the air and not be hanging around the house on such a lovely day. She knew I was listening to herself and Auntie Bridie. I told her I had nothing to do and nowhere to go and she gave me the money to go to the pictures. I saw *The King and I* at the Fairview and I thought it was all right but the best thing about it was that it passed the time while the men were in the Manhattan. I hurried home to be there when the men got back to the house, laughing and talking out loud and making a racket when they knocked at the door. I loved to see them come in. Uncle would be a little jarred and would make no bones about it. Mammy would say oh look at Diamond-Eyes and Daddy would say that they had only had four pints and Mammy would laugh. Pearse would sit in an armchair, smiling away and allowing the younger children to clamber all over him, burning themselves on his cigarette, scattering ash everywhere.

– Bride, what about something to eat?

Bridie and Mammy would tell him to look after himself or say that the meat was all gone but Uncle knew that they were only joking. Bridie would get up and go out into the kitchen and Uncle would see to it that the children would get glasses and a corkscrew. It was a madhouse with the children running around and screaming and laughing and crying. Bridie would ask the children to leave their daddy alone but Uncle would sit forward and look surprised.

– Leave me alone? Not at all. Don't mind them. Come on me little darlings and give your daddy a kiss, a huge big kiss and a love.

Bridie spoke in her soft Galway way and unless you knew her you'd think there was going to be a row.

– And what about me, Pearse?

– And now then Bride, there's no need for you to ask me that. My own Bride, my own Galway girl.

– I'm far from Galway now, Pearse.

And that was signal enough for Pearse to tell Bridie to never mind the plates or whatever, to give him her hand and he would look up at her with his glistening eyes, glance around the room and then he'd begin, almost speaking the lines as if no music could explain how he felt about Bridie and himself and how they met in Galway. And of course it was always 'Galway Bay', not the song that Uncle said was rubbish, but the *real* 'Galway Bay'.

   – Give us the *ould* 'Galway Bay', brother.

> It's far away I am today from the fields I roamed a boy
> And long ago the hour I know I first saw Illinois
> But time nor tide nor waters wide could wean my heart away
> Forever true it turns to you my own dear Galway Bay.

   – Me life on ye, Pearse!
   – Rise it, Pearse.
And Bridie would pretend that she didn't like the song.
   – Oh, Pearse, if you're going to sing, sing something happy.

But Bridie was happy that her Pearse was singing about Galway. No matter what any of them said, they all loved the songs that made you want to cry. They'd all smile their sad smiles and nod their heads as if they knew the story of the man who wrote the song. I had to keep my eyes on the floor when Daddy sang 'My Mary of the Curling Hair'. Mammy used to keep everybody waiting when she was asked to give them 'Teddy O'Neill'. She used to frown and look up at the ceiling when she was singing. Uncle would look straight into your eyes, especially when he knew you were biting the inside of your cheek to keep the tears in.

> The blessings of a poor old man be with you night and day
> The blessings of a lonely man whose heart will soon be clay
> It's all of heaven I'll ask of God upon my dying day –
> My soul to soar for evermore above you, Galway Bay.

Sometimes when he was singing about God or heaven Uncle would look up at the ceiling like a saint in a stained-glass window and sometimes he would even bless himself. Auntie Bridie would tell him to stop because she didn't like any joking about religion. That was because she was from Galway and down the country all the people were holy. Mammy and Daddy were very strict about going to mass and confession and so on but they weren't holy, not like Auntie Bridie. Neither was Uncle and when he got warmed up or when he had a few jars he'd take the holy name in vain – and he'd say Jaysus which made it a bigger sin – and sometimes under his breath he'd say worse things. Once, I heard him talking to a neighbour in Raheny, telling him a story about meeting somebody and the neighbour laughed when Uncle said: I told him to go and ask me arse. You'd have to laugh at Uncle when he was giving out about somebody. No matter how bad his language was. It sounded so funny. Daddy always said jacksie. That sounded funny too.

Sometimes in summertime we walked from Finglas to Raheny, Maura and me walking beside Daddy, Mammy pushing Eva and Eileen in the big pram, taking the back road and sauntering on for mile after mile past farms and cottages, past the airport and on till we hit the Manhattan road and we knew we were almost there. One day Maura said she was too tired and she wanted to get a bus.

– There's no buses out here, Maur.

– We could get a bus into town and then another one out to Uncle's.

– But that would take us all day and we'd miss the lovely walk.

– It's not a lovely walk. I'm tired. I hate walking.

It was nice walking out the country in the summertime but Maura was just looking for trouble.

– I hate going to Uncle's. I don't want to go any more. I want to stay at home and play.

That wasn't a nice thing to say about Uncle. Just because she was a girl, she was allowed to say what she liked. It would serve her right if somebody told Pearse what she said but Daddy would never do a thing like that. Even now he was putting his arm around her and trying to keep her happy, walking ahead by themselves. After a while Maura looked up at Daddy and I knew she was going to say something stupid.

– Daddy, why do we walk to Uncle's? Is it because we haven't the money to get the bus? Is that why we don't get the bus? Daddy?

Gawney! Wouldn't you think that one would get sense. Imagine saying a thing like that to poor Daddy.

– But, Maura, it's nice walking like this and we'll get the bus home.

– But, Daddy, we'd have to get the bus home anyway. It'll be pitch dark when you and Uncle come back from the Manhattan.

Janey Mack! she really is thick. Can she not see that Daddy is going red and smiling in that sad way? It's awful when people say things out like that. I had to start telling Mammy about school so that we wouldn't hear the other two talking.

One afternoon in Raheny Dominic and Josephine were over from London and Josephine sang 'My Ain Folk' because she was from Scotland. She didn't want to sing but Mammy and Bridie kept at her. You had to do that with visitors. Josephine wanted to talk about politics with the men but when they came back from the Manhattan the men wanted to sing. (Josephine got up to go to the pub with the men and Mammy and Bridie began to laugh. Of course Josephine stayed with the women but all the same I think she was serious about wanting to go.) That night Dominic sang 'The Zoological Gardens' and I thought it was great. When we were going home on the bus I was sitting with Daddy and I told him that the song about the zoo was great and I said it was his father's best song and when he told me that it wasn't one of his father's songs I felt awful. As if I had let the Kearneys down or something. And I tried to think of something to say to him to make up for it but I could think of nothing and all the time I was looking out the windows of the bus at the people waiting for the late-night buses, the words and the swings of the song were going round in my head.

> Thunder and lightning, it's no lark
> When Dublin city is in the dark
> And if you've any money get up to the Park
> And view the Zoological Gardens.

It was nice to listen to the radio and imagine what Mockingbird Hill looked like but in a way it was even better to have songs about the places you knew yourself. Every Saturday morning the team used to go to play matches in the Fifteen Acres in the Phoenix Park and sometimes on the way home we used to walk around by the zoo and look in through the railings and wish we had the money to go in.

> I brought me mot up to the zoo
> For to show her the lions and the kangaroo;
> There were hemales and shemales of each shape and hue
> Up in the Zoological Gardens.

Most of all I loved it when the songs were sung in a Dublin accent because then you knew it would be real and funny and not sad like in the olden days. Josephine had shouted out thunderin' Jaysus instead of thunder and lightning when they all sang the first verse again at the end. Mammy had laughed with the others but you could see that Daddy thought it was wrong to use language like that in front of the children. Although there was only the grown-ups and me. The others were upstairs, asleep or playing. And if you thought about it, he was right: it was taking the holy name in vain. And Daddy always said that his father was no prude – far from it – but he always insisted that language like that was the sign of a limited vocabulary. And he was right there too, if you thought about it. Maybe the others didn't think about it, maybe that was it. But still, you really had to laugh it was so, well, funny.

– What are you laughing at, son?

We were standing on Eden Quay waiting for the 40 bus.

– Huh?

– You were laughing away to yourself. What were you laughing at?

– I don't know, Daddy. I was half asleep.

And it made me feel sad to tell Daddy a lie but what could I say? I could easily have told the truth but that would have made him sad. And I would rather tell a lie – a teeny little lie – than hurt Daddy. I put my arms around him and he put his big warm hand on my cheek and pulled me into his hip.

Uncle nearly made you cry when he sang 'Slán Libh' or 'Galway Bay' but it wouldn't be long before he'd have you laughing again when he would say terrible things about some of our relations and he would scrunch up his face and curse them bejaysus so help me Christ for a bunch of bloody johnnycomelatelys. And if somebody said that he was getting very crabby he'd agree.

– I am. You know that? I'm very crabby and will I tell you why? I'm crabby when I think of certain people, no names no pack drill, certain people who are where they are for one reason and one reason only and that is – are you listening to me? – and that is because they lied, lifted and looted from others. Now I'll say no more but you know who I mean. Bejaysus, when I see them there in their power and their glory, looking bejaysus as if they owned the place, but one of these fine days by Jesus I'll let them know that if they don't know where they came from there's people that do, people who remember them when they didn't have two makes to rub together, when they didn't have an arse in their trousers, are you codding me or something, will you go 'way outa that. Not an arse in their trousers.

And sometimes Mammy and Daddy would talk about Pearse. Daddy would say:

– Isn't he a gas man, me same brother?

And Mammy would nod her head and smile and say:

– Agh sure he's as good as gold in his own way.

– A gas ticket.

That would be on the journey home, one bus into town and then another bus out to Finglas and sometimes we would have to let a bus go without us because there was a pram on it already and Eileen and Eva would be asleep before we got home. Maura would often get crabby and say that she didn't want to go to Uncle's again. Daddy would look at me and say that she was very tired and not to mind her, it was time for her bed but it wasn't only that and he knew it. Girls wouldn't like Uncle as much as boys and Maura never sang 'Deep in Canadian Woods' or learned 'Sínte ar Thaobh an tSléibhe'. When we were going home Uncle always gave me more than he gave Maura but I suppose that was because I was the oldest. He'd give me something for myself and then he'd give me something else and tell me to divide that among the others. He was very generous. Mammy said that he was always good-natured.

It was ironic, I suppose, me going to school in Galway of all places. Because Galway was part of Uncle's world. He knew all about Galway because of Auntie Bridie. Before I went to Spiddal to learn Irish I only knew about Galway from watching the Galwegians who came up for the matches at Croke Park: real culchies with their red faces and yellow boots, just like the men from Kerry, and screeching and whooping like Indians when they got a score. Chrisht. When Ireland lay broken and bleedin' she called for the men of the wesht. Uncle used to tell us to stop if we called the country team culchies. We said we didn't mind being called jackeens but Uncle said that was different. He was treated like a prince when he went down to Galway.

– Your da tells me you're going to school in Ballinasloe, huh?

Uncle put on his serious face whenever he talked about school. He didn't care much about school himself – that was because they were poor when he and Daddy were boys, I suppose, and had to go to work when they were fourteen, but you couldn't imagine Uncle studying every night for a scholarship. It was like Irish: Daddy and Uncle were always going on about Irish and how it was no burden to carry and things like that that sounded as if they had heard their father saying them when they were small, but why didn't they learn Irish now when they had the chance? Daddy would have loved to stay on. You could imagine Daddy studying, writing out his lovely clear figures and letters, always checking his sums, never taking them down wrong from the board. And he was a dinger when it came to mental arithmetic, so cool and quick you couldn't believe it the way he always saw the short cut. Daddy had a lot of Irish – he wrote a whole letter in Irish to me when I was in Spiddal – but Uncle only knew things like *dia 's muire dhuit* and *slán leat* and *sláinte*. And, of course, *éist do bhéal* if you said something he didn't like. *Éist do bhéal agus bí i do thost agus ná bí ag caint mar sin*. And the way he snapped at you, you knew that he had learned that from his father.

– Remember who you are and where you come from. You're a Kearney, remember that. No matter what happens, you're a Kearney. Don't let your father down; Con and your mother have put a lot into this school business. Don't let any of us down. You're getting the sort of chance that none of us ever got. Remember that. Work hard now, won't you?

– 'Course I will.

He roughed my hair with one hand while he put the other into his pocket.

– Here, take this. Will you take it and stop annoying me. Take it for luck. *Slán leat*.

And then when I was a good bit off, he'd shout out so that people would hear him and I'd be embarrassed.

– And come here. Watch yourself down there in the bogs of Galway. Watch yourself bejesus that some of them wild fellas don't ate you for their dinner, do you hear me? Bejesus, Greek and Latin how are ye, boy; get yourself into a mill with somebody from Castlegar and see where your Greek and Latin'll get you.

And yet if Galway was part of Uncle Pearse's world, boarding school was something we could never really share together; going to Garbally was going away from Uncle Pearse – and from a good deal else besides. It would have been perfect if he – and the others – could have got excited about Greek and rugby and athletics but he didn't. Maybe he couldn't; maybe I didn't try very hard. Exams and scholarships were mentioned and that was it. But I had no complaints. As the scholarship boy, the boarding school boy, the first of his family ever to et cetera, I was given the treatment. And because I was still sufficiently ordinary – faithful to Irish, to Dublin, to Croke Park, to Uncle – I was very special indeed. It's not that I tried to please anybody other than myself. I was enjoying all the new things that I was discovering at school but I was still fiercely attached to family, football team and Uncle.

Looking back, there is always the temptation to think that we understand what actually happened but all we can do, short of writing a book, is tick the boxes of convention. I could say that I moved from a working-class world to a middle-class world, from an urban environment to a rural environment, from a culture that was predominantly oral into a world dominated by reading and writing, a world of copybooks and textbooks and notebooks – but what would be the point? I might as well say that I went from Leinster to Connacht. Or – and this is perhaps the least ludicrous description – that I went from short trousers to longers.

Presumably, a year or two on, we had defined our roles: inevitably, I became more the secondary school boy, he more the happy-go-lucky uncle. Presumably we became objects of amazement to each other. Presumably – this the most embarrassing hypothesis – there were times when I tried to score against him with learned allusions to the literature of Greece or some such branch of the arcane. But he always had something that no teacher had. He was real in some special way. You knew he had been where life was lived wildly and carelessly. And he had a way of doing things that was all his own.

Like the time he took me to have lunch in a restaurant in Galway. One summer when I was staying in Spiddal I heard a heavy motorbike bumping and growling its way up the boreen and wondered at such an intrusion into the Gaelic calm of Connemara. It was Pearse. He was down for a few days in Galway, had borrowed a motorbike and a leather jacket and had come out to bring me back into Galway for the day. Could I, would I come? Try and stop me. And we tore along the ten miles to town.

I was nervous about going into the restaurant. I would have preferred to go to a pub with Pearse but he said that I had to have something to eat. Although I wouldn't have admitted it out loud to anybody – not even if they tortured me – I was afraid that Pearse would make a show of himself, that he would not use the right knives and forks and so on. And then, when I picked up the menu, I turned red as a beetroot and wished I had never heard that motorbike. Pearse took the menu from me.

– Don't waste your time with that. Sure that could mean anything or nothing. What we need is the latest information. Daughter! Will you come over here a minute and look after this poor unfortunate *garsún* from Dublin.

He had gone too far. This was too much: I was fifteen or sixteen at the time. I was sure the waitress would look through us. She stopped and turned. Not a bad-looking bird.

– When you get a minute, girl. No hurry. Take your time. We can wait.

She was standing beside us, beaming at Pearse and talking to him as if she'd known him for years.

– What can I get ye, lads? By the way, the sole is off and the lamb is off.

– I told him not to bother with the menu. Come here, darling, and listen to me. What we want is a good feed and, you know what, we'll leave it up to you. Whatever you think.

It's not that she never looked at me – she did, as if I was a child – but she stood there beside Pearse, as if he was her long lost father, as if, instead of being embarrassed, she was only delighted to be helping him rather than serving the other customers. And the food came and it was lovely and it was everything we liked and lots of it. Every time she came with more food she had another chat with us, about being from Dublin and what did we think of Galway and how she was in Dublin for a while with her sister who was a nurse but she couldn't stick it and back she came. When she brought the pot of tea for Pearse – I had coffee – he wanted her to sit down for a chat but she had to say that she was awful sorry but she couldn't, much as she'd love to. We were sorry to have to let her go and serve other tables but we were glad that we had met her because she had certainly looked after us. Pearse sat back and lit a cigarette.

– Like princes.

– Can I have one of them?

– So you've started?

– Not really. I started but I gave them up. I only have the odd one on special occasions.

– Oh, I see. I understand.

After our dinner we rambled round Galway for a bit. It was a beautiful sunny day and Pearse pointed out various places that had stories attached to them. Then we went back to the bike and roared out to Oranmore where he had a few pints in MacDonagh's and I had as much Cola and Tayto crisps as I could manage. Was it that there was always a singsong in MacDonagh's? Or only when Pearse was there? We weren't long in before a strange man entered and blessed all there and asked if anybody would treat him to a glass of porter or would they prefer he went further on. His speech was so strangely clear and polite that about six of the locals signalled to the bar that they would pay for the drink for the travelling man. We all looked at him as he waited for his porter to settle and then drank it.

– I'm much obliged to ye all, gentlemen, for your kindness and gracious hospitality to a man of the roads on this hot day. I've come from Gort today but sure what does it matter where I've come from or where I'm going to? I've been on the roads for fifteen years now and it's on the roads I'll die, with the help of God. And so, gentlemen, to thank you all for your kind hospitality, I would like to sing a little song, if that's all right with the man behind the bar.

> At Boolavogue as the sun was setting
> On the bright May meadows of Shelmalier,
> A rebel hand kept the heather blazing
> And brought the neighbours from far and near.

The travelling man sang with a direct style and a strong voice that rang through the silent bar like a bell. He just stood there in the middle of the floor, his eyes shut tight and his hands held out like a priest at mass, his voice falling and his passion rising as the English got the upper hand at Vinegar Hill and time began to run out for Father Murphy and the Irish. It was a song we knew well from singing it at home or at Croke Park when Wexford were playing. It was a song that always made you shiver at the end.

Gradually I noticed that the locals were raising their eyes from the floor and glancing at each other in an uncomfortable way. The signals led you to look over to the door. There, looking increasingly embarrassed by the behaviour of his fellow countrymen in 1798, was an Englishman. He couldn't have been there very long either or we would have noticed him. You knew he was an Englishman because he couldn't have been anything else. He was dressed from top to toe in tweeds and was holding in his left hand a fully assembled three-piece fly rod and in his right hand a glass of Guinness. His tweed hat was decorated with flies. He didn't know where to look as the travelling man collapsed onto his knees to mark the death of the rebel priest.

> The Yeos of Tullow took Father Murphy
> And burned his body upon the rack.

Here he wrung his hands in grief and then spat violently on the floor in front of himself.

– The bastards. The dirty English bastards.

But he was soon up again to finish the song and look forward to the time when the Boys of Wexford would be back again in another fight for freedom. There was a burst of applause for the song but you knew that there were people who were a bit uneasy about the English fisherman who was, after all, doing no harm. He might look a bit stupid to us but sure we all have our own little ways and surely the man was entitled to drop in for a jar – if that's what he felt like – and to drink it without having the national skeleton rattled into his face.

– Here you are. Get that into you.

Pearse had got the singer a glass of Guinness. At first I thought he had got him two glasses, but no; one glass he gives to the singer, the other he carries over to the Englishman by the door. He takes his empty glass from him and gives him the full one.

– There you are. Sure a bird never flew on one wing.

The Englishman was flabbergasted.

– That's extremely kind of you but, really, thank you, I couldn't possibly...

– Don't mind that kind of talk. Just drink it up.

– Well, if you insist. It's extremely kind...

– You're more than welcome.

– Your health!

– And the same to you.

– And may we all be as happy this time next year.

– With the help of God and the aid of a few policemen. And having an even better time than we are now – if that's possible.

And there was a general murmur of approval and agreement from the bar, followed by the odd hoot of happiness, as we watched the travelling man drain his glass, refuse another drink, bless us all and take to the road.

– What about a song from yourself, Pearse?

– Will you go 'way outa that and let me have me pint in peace.

But of course there was no way they would let him off. The singing had started and they had heard Pearse before.

– Give us a Dublin one, Pearse.

– Leave him sing what he wants.

So he sang 'Galway Bay', not the curse-of-God rubbish that Bing Crosby was moaning and groaning about, but the *real* 'Galway Bay', the *ould* 'Galway Bay'. And there on the edge of Galway Bay he let rip.

> Had I youth's blood and hopeful mood and a heart of fire once
> more
> For all the gold the world might hold I'd never leave your shore,
> I'd be content with whatever God sent, with neighbours old
> and grey,
> And I'd lay me bones 'neath churchyard stones beside you,
> Galway Bay.

The place erupted when he finished. Men came over to shake his hand and ask him what he was having, to bless him for singing that song again, to assure him that he never lost it, to pray that he would never lose it.

Neither of us was able to finish all the drinks that were bought for us on the strength of Pearse's performance. Pearse had to mind himself for driving the motorbike – not that that was any great problem because it was only a stone's throw from MacDonagh's to the Melvin house where he was staying with Bridie's mother and brother. So we had several for the road, said goodbye to all – we had both shaken hands with the Englishman before he left a couple of hours earlier – and stepped up from the pub into the blinding sunshine.

– Did you enjoy yourself?

– Oh, I did, Uncle. It was great.

– Sure, they're God's own people. Come on till we see if Granny Melvin has kept a bit of tea for us.

There must have been times when he looked at me and thought that I had all the makings of proper little bollix; I can't remember suspecting that, presumably because, having all the makings of a proper little bollix, I misinterpreted his glance as one of simple bewilderment. And conscience is not so kind as to permit me to believe that there was never a time when I thought him – in spite of all – a little tedious, limited. Although memory is kind enough to spare me the details.

But still and all I can say this much: I always knew he had a generous heart and I always loved him. Always. Against the odds, against what I took to be my wishes. To my own confusion and maybe even that of others. Even – especially? – when he had failed utterly to defend whatever position he was trying to maintain in the face of reason and logic. Even when he snarled or seemed to have given in to envy or self-pity. But even his faults were part of his generosity. You knew he could never maintain the serious face, the embittered tone, that he would always put on his other face, his funny sneer, as if to stick his tongue out at whatever universal law or god had just slapped him in the face.

There he is: that's me Uncle. The black sheep. And here am I embarrassing him and me, talking to him like this, writing the kind of thing that we would never talk about. There was never any of that in our family. Not that I ever heard of, anyway. If you should ever read this, Uncle, you don't have to say anything: next time you see me, call for a couple of pints, put on your crabby face and talk about some subject of common interest which you wouldn't mind being overheard in Grogan's.

May we never forget the happy days with the bucks of Oranmore, nor the feeling of stepping down into the cool shade of MacDonagh's on a bright summer's day, nor the pure freedom of a sunny Sunday morning walking down the Claddagh, drinking illegally and swapping songs with the locals, coming outside once in a while to look at the gleaming warehouses, the blue ocean-water, the wide sky and you wouldn't call the queen your aunt.

And God be with the days in McDaid's, our undergraduate days – if you'll pardon the expression. Down in the village we tarried too long. And, I suppose, on somebody else's time. I should have been up in the library at UCD; where you should have been only some unfortunate contractor knew. And who knows now? And who cares? We thought we were doing wrong but that was only because our understanding was limited at the time. Now, older, uglier and wiser, we know we were right.

And what about the Manhattan? The evenings there after the matches in Croke Park? Where, in your presence, as was only right and proper, I took my first drink in front of Daddy. (Drinking pints! I ask your holy pardon this blessed night!) Where, again with a certain element of congruity, the first allusion was made to my adult status. (Heard your father caught you with your trousers down.) Where Mr Maguire directed his grim northern sneer at anybody who spoke during the Angelus. Who'd believe that now? We have heard the chimes at six. And the various owners who came and went after him and your various relations with them.

What about the new barman who asked you to use the ashtray and not be spilling ash on the floor? Remember that? They had just done the place up. I don't know why I'm asking you if you remember; I wasn't even there at the time. The first I heard of it was one night Daddy and I met you over in Raheny and we were looking for parking near the Manhattan when you said that we'd go to some other place. Why? Because the Manhattan was gone to the dogs altogether, an awful kip. Come on: why not the Manhattan? And, of course, you were barred. Not for the first time. Nor the last. And then we heard the story of the ashtray. There you were minding your own business as usual, dropping in for a pint on your way home from work, as you were entitled to do. And you heard this voice – hey, watch the carpet, will you – but you assumed it was meant for somebody else and you went on minding your own business, reading the paper and sipping your pint. Hey, watch the carpet, will you, and use the ashtray. You looked up and he was talking to you. The cheeky, pimply-faced jumped-up potboy, two steps from the bog and here he was going on about the carpet. A right cnat, the ringer for his oul' fellow, a barman in the Dragon, a miserable oul' moan from the County Kildare that was forever boring the arses off half the bar with his funny stories.

– Are you by any chance talking to me?

– You're dropping ash on the carpet.

– I most certainly am not.

– I saw you dropping ash on the carpet.

– You did no such thing.

– I'll show it to you if you like.

– You'll do no such thing, you impudent little pup. You'll show a little more respect for your customers and less for your bloody carpet. I'll thank you not to talk to me in that tone of voice. You can save that for when you get home. In the name of Jayses, who do you think you are? Standing behind the bar there like a mule looking over a half-door. Waltzing in here and talking like that to people who have been coming here for years, people who sat here when there was nothing but tables and chairs and a flag floor. Carpets, be Jayses, and what would you know about them, except maybe if one of them jumped up and bit you? It's far from carpets you were reared; you were lucky if you had lino and thankful to God that you had it. Keep your ash off the carpet. You can keep that oul' guff for your oul' fellow at home. Coming up here, be Jayses, and acting as if you owned the place. Do you want to walk all over us while you're at it? Ride roughshod over us all? Do you think you're back in the County Kildare now or what? Back on the farm with your ass and cart, your yella boots and your Curragh cap. Be sure you have it on the Kildare side, do you hear me now? And if you know what side your bread is buttered on you'll learn to pull a proper pint and look after them who pay your wages and not make a fucking idiot out of yourself by talking about things you know nothing about. And you can tell whoever is in charge of this glorified kip now, that I am taking my custom somewhere where I know I can sit down and drink me pint in peace without being bothered and insulted by ignorant gobshites from the County Kildare or anywhere else.

– And off you went?

– Off I went and across the road.

– With never another word?

– Well, I wouldn't say that. The pup behind the bar went mad altogether and told me to consider meself barred. I told him that I would consider meself well rid of gobshites like him and out I went.

– Just like that?

– More or less. Ah, sweet Jesus, I enjoyed it. It did me heart good to see the look on that young bowsie's face.

And so if you were barred – and you were – you got your money's worth and anyway you can't get rid of a bad thing and before long you were back in the Manhattan as if nothing much – well nothing extraordinary – had happened. Of course what was par for the course in the Manhattan would have raised eyebrows in other establishments.

> And in Kilkenny it is reported
> On marble stones there as black as ink,
> With gold and jewels I would support her
> But I'll say no more till I get a drink.

Will you ever forget the night of 'Carrickfergus' and the new barman? That was as mad as I ever remember the place, and I mean mad, not just funny. I really thought the barman was going to do for somebody that night and my only fear was that it might be me or Daddy. Anything you got you would have had coming to you. You kept starting 'Carrickfergus' and the barman kept warning you to stop. The regulars were falling around the place but the barman was coming to the end of his tether.

– Pearse. Final warning. Next time you're barred and I don't care who's with you.

You were on for anything that night and off you went again:

> I wish I wa-as ...

The barman wiped his hands, threw the towel on the ground and came out from behind the bar. He was in a lighting temper and I thought for a moment that he was going to grab poor Jimmy, who was the nearest to hand and who was incapable of any rapid physical action. But no bejaysus he just pushed past him and started down in our direction – we were sitting down where the toilet door was in the old arrangement, I don't suppose it's there any more – and Daddy muttered something about go easy and I said nothing because I knew it was too late, but of course nothing would do you but to go on –

> ... in Carrickfe-ergus –

and just as the barman was passing, didn't the door open and who stood there but Mr Goggins, arriving in for his nightly glass of stout half an hour before closing time, on the dot; the old gentleman had been doing it for years before the place had become a bedlam and was too well-bred to risk causing anybody the slightest offence by taking his nightly glass anywhere else. A quiet old man who retired from an office in Gilbeys to dedicate himself to caring for his invalid wife and growing roses in the back garden, maybe he thought that every pub had degenerated to the same extent as a natural consequence of independence or the emergency or the plan for economic expansion or something; anyway, pleasant as ever, he didn't like to give any sign of what he must have thought of the hippos with whom he took his nightcap in what was by any standards an alcoholic zoo. Despite the fact that he lived in a different world for twenty-three and a half hours of every day, he did his gentle best to be one of the boys. And that was why, having heard from outside the sounds of singing and laughter, he threw open the door of the Manhattan, confronted the suddenly silent clientele and warbled in his puny little voice:

I dreamt that I dwelt in marble halls...

It was as far as the poor man got before the barman pounced.
   – I'll give you marble fucking halls!
   And then grabbing the old gent by the collar of his jacket and the arse of his pants, he pushed him out the door.
   – You're barred, d'ye hear me, you're barred. Now home with ye to your bed before I call the guards.
   What happened in the end? I can't recall. I know that poor ould Goggins was not let in that night, that he made a timid appearance the following morning to ask what had he done wrong, that when he was let back in he was happy as Larry to tell the story of how he was barred for singing. And then a couple of years later we were talking about the same night and I asked if there was any word of old Mr Goggins and I heard how he had died, how nobody in the Manhattan even knew about it, how several regulars had wondered aloud if old Mr Goggins was sick or something, if anybody knew which house he lived in, but nobody got round to doing anything until it was too late and somebody was reading the paper and came across the notice of Henry Goggins of Rose Cottage, Raheny, whose funeral to Kilbarrack

cemetery would take place . . .

But what happened that night I can't recall. Maybe I am inventing an ending but is it the case that our friend the barman decided that he would serve everybody one last drink and that was it, no singing, no messing, no nothing? And that he looked as if he meant it?

You can tell me your version of it when we meet.

January 1986.

As I knelt in the church in Raheny, less than a hundred yards from the Manhattan, my greatest regret was that I would never have a chance to show him the typescript. I could have sent up a draft – and I intended to as soon as . . .

As soon as what? What were you waiting for? An order of the court?

I don't know: I think I wanted to finish it, to make it better. Maybe I wanted to see how the whole thing would turn out. And I was in no hurry: I thought I had all the time I needed, another summer at least.

I had my suspicions when Daddy rang and told me you were in Jervis Street and that I should think about coming up. I brought your section of the typescript with me on the train but I couldn't bring myself to look at it. When I saw you asleep in the hospital bed I knew that time had tricked me, that you and I would never speak again, that the imagined night in the Manhattan would never take place, that we would never piece together the story of Mr Goggins – if that was his name.

All we had was a cold day in January when I followed your coffin into the same Kilbarrack cemetery. I don't remember very much about the burial. As I got out of my father's car I saw Paddy O'Brien walking by himself and looking a bit lost and so I went in with him. My mind was on the white horses of the sea as the priest went through the words and the water and the decade of the rosary. We were all about to move away when Rory began to sing:

> Sisters and brothers, comrades all,
> Who trod the olden road with me,
> Who answering a nation's call
> Dear Mother Ireland swore to free.
> To you who carry on the fight
> My share of deathless hope I give
> Before I pass into the night – *Slán libh*.

At first I was embarrassed – I thought it was a poor choice of song, about as congruous as the decade of the rosary – but after all, I reminded myself, it was one of your father's songs, one of the songs you sang yourself, a song that most of the people present would consider a good choice for a funeral or the end of a party – in your case the same thing. And certainly the sound of Rory's voice being blown around the graveyard caused us all to think of the reality that had been obscured by the mummery of the religious ritual. Your singing days were done. Never again would you rise from your chair and take the floor for the second verse. Never again would you mark the simple rhythms with outstretched hands. Never again, between the lines, would you mutter about your poor father and the hopes he once had, wonder what he would make of the world in which his song was being sung.

> Your work allows no time for rest,
> Your longest life's the merest span:
> Your cause, the bravest, noblest, best,
> That e'er inspired the heart of man.
> Fight on! Fear not, for God is just;
> The tyrant, too, shall cease to live;
> And pray for him whose bones are dust – *Slán libh*.

As a youngster you had seen the Dawn of Freedom, the Triumph of Justice after Centuries of Oppression, and you had known that your own father had played his part. But shortly afterwards you had seen him stare with disbelief at the stories of the civil war. When did it strike you that this is it, that Easter Week will not preserve us from ourselves, this is the way it is going to be, it's not going to get any better in my lifetime? Was there one special moment? Or was it so gradual that you never noticed it? Like middle age?

> *Slán libh* – a simple Irish phrase
> Of parting but to meet again,
> 'Twixt comrades who through nights and days
> For Ireland's sake strove might and main.
> For her dear sake remember me,
> For her dear sake my faults forgive,
> God speed the fight for liberty – *Slán libh*.

This was your verse. In fact, as far as I remember, you used it as a chorus and sang it after the first verse as well. Watching you sing the final lines, nodding and muttering about your poor father as you reached for your drink, I always felt the song was soft-centred and sentimental, encouraging a dangerous surrender to sadness and loss and death. But weighing the words as Rory sang them, I was surprised to find that the song moved me – despite the conventional nods towards God and patriotism and heroic idealism. You never thought you'd hear me admit that, did you?

But your poor father, whatever else he was, was no daw. He wrote some good comic songs. He had done a day's work and had known what he was about when he took on the British Empire. He had drunk into the morning with some hard men and had learned how to pick out a detective in a crowd at fifty yards. He had acted and travelled with the Abbey and he had eaten stray cabbage leaves gathered in the street. The chances are he knew the score. Like the sisters and brothers, he had answered the nation's call but he was not deluded into thinking that they had succeeded in freeing Ireland: the fight for liberty must be continued. Your father contributes his one and only gift, deathless hope, eternal hope, the hope that will always be alive. Why deathless? Because the freedom they fight for will always be something to be hoped for. Why? Because by its nature it is never achieved: whatever this ideal freedom is, it is something more than a thirty-two-county republic. Fight on and fear not: God is just and all tyrants will eventually fall. Not that that's worth a lot to me: when the tyrant falls – when God is just? – I'll be no more than scattered dust. He wants to be prayed for. Why? To shorten his time in purgatory? No mention of this, not even what could be construed as a hint. He is about to pass into the night, not into an eternal day. There is no suggestion that when his bones are dust on earth some other part of him will have soared or swooped to a heavenly or infernal afterlife. No: the only life after death which he can think of is in the memory of his friends, those who shared his dream; in the sacred name of the goddess for whom they fought, he asks them to preserve a kind memory of him. The song owes much more to the Irish pagan tradition than it does to the heroic Christianity with which the fight for independence was often cloaked. And is all the better for that. For what did they strive might and main? Certainly not for what they got. And not, I would suspect, for any structure the historians or the politicians could identify. Men like your father, the small, hard, quietly indomitable men, were obsessed by an *aisling* that transcended the forms of conventional politics. The fight for independence from England was the closest approximation they had to hand: in their inner hearts they were enraged at the tyranny of things-as-they-are, maddened at having glimpsed things-as-they-might-be. For men like him, taking on the British Empire was the easy part – dying for Ireland would have been a cinch – it was the return to normal that was frightening.

When did this strike you? Could it have been a day in the early thirties that Con once told me about? Do you remember – you would have been about sixteen – going to the funeral of one of the Revolutionary Heroes? It was from High Street; you were there with your father and Con. Your father was chatting with Sean Farrelly when a big black limousine pushed imperiously through the crowd, taking some Big Shot up to the church gate. As the car moved past, it suddenly came to a halt and out got Big Mister Large, a old IRB friend of your father's, one of the few who had done very well out of the revolution: chauffeur, black topper, overcoat with velvet lapels. You know who I'm talking about; the name escapes me for the moment. Anyway, he made his way through the crowd, disregarding the shy salutes of the others, heading straight for your father. A big smile on his face as he took off his hat and stuck out his hand:

– How are you, Peadar?

– Ask me arse.

Your father spat the words out and then turned away to continue his conversation with Sean Farrelly.

There's a saying in our family that pride feels no pain but I wonder what you and Con felt as Big Mister Large retired to his car. I think I know what your father felt. Things were still as they had always been. All he could hope for was that when his bones were dust his friends would remember him as one who had kept his word. Remember me. Eventually it's all any reasonable human being can hope for. Even Joyce, who went further than most, asked no more in the end.

And there's no doubt about it: you remembered your father. I don't suppose you ever saw yourself as being a loyal and devoted son – I wouldn't be surprised if you sometimes felt that you had betrayed the political cause – but you were there where the real fight was taking place. I'm not thinking about your time in the army or your sporadic

gestures towards political plasterworks. I'm thinking about your lifelong
guerrilla campaign against the mean-minded and pompous brigades of
common sense. I'm thinking of your refusal to give an inch to things-as-
they-are.

And there's no doubt about it but I'll remember you. And, until I pass
into the night, I'll always keep you alive in my mind. You won't always
be singing 'Slán Libh'. You'll be going through your repertoire – grinning with aggressive crabbiness, rearing up to your full five foot nothing
to pour scorn on the pretentious, rising from your chair like an unlikely
lost leader to guide, with thumping fist and glistening eye, the rest of
us into the only heaven we have ever imagined:

> For it's a grand ould country every time,
> With its trees and rivers, rocks and soil and clime –
> We're God's own people
> And we shout from tower and steeple:
> It's a grand ould country every time.

Silence. Inertia. Enormous waves of guilt and regret. The
rugged rocks of inability.

For the first time since I began this grotesque epistle I feel
devoid of energy and have to convince myself to remain here
in my cell. It is now almost exactly half past five and I have
spent almost all day reading and re-reading the Pearse section
of the typescript, wondering if there is any point in all this.

I am an old monk in his scriptorium, smiling as he scrapes
away on his vellum, exposing with elegantly suppressed malice,
article by article, the misconceptions and mendacities of the
latest heresy to sweep some remote semi-barbarian land. The
image has returned continually today, each time showing the
old hermit at a greater angle from his desk, looking at his work
from a greater distance and with more perplexity, eventually
writing nothing at all. It is not that he is less convinced of the
errors of the heresy but the whole business of written
refutation now seems infinitely more difficult than it did when

he straightened out that first sheet of vellum, bent over it and scraped his greeting to those few remaining faithful in that godforsaken part.

Was there ever an Uncle in your life? Was there, lurking somewhere in that world of ballet and best schools, horse-riding, deportment, elocution and music lessons, somebody whose secret wink enabled you to endure those straight-backed hours of family Christmas conversation or the chatter of another relation who visited once a year on your mother's birthday, passing the same remarks and asking the same questions? Was there somebody, not necessarily the brother of your mother or father, who always slipped coins into your hand, knowing as well as you did that this had been strictly forbidden by your parents? Somebody who whispered to himself – aware that you and you alone could hear him – that some young relation had all the makings of a proper little bollix? Who, according to your father, could have made a success of himself if only he had bothered to impress the people who really mattered? Whose failure to live a quieter, safer, saner, more comfortable life was a mystery to most people? Except, of course, to you.

Maybe everybody has an Uncle. (It's a nice thought.) He may vary in shape and size from family to family – just as the heads on the coins he slips into little hands may differ from place to place – but the value is always the same: priceless.

It comes as a surprise to some people that Uncles are the eldest of their families. It's not that they look younger, more that they acquire the aura of being junior to the younger, steadier brother who represents the family socially, legally and ecclesiastically, speaking at christenings and weddings, holding official documents, accepting condolences at funerals.

And I suppose it comes as something of a surprise when Uncles die. It's not that they don't look old or that they hadn't begun to break down more often and take progressively longer to get back on their feet; it's just that, having looked so shaken for so long, they acquire an aura of battered invincibility. Everybody is convinced that he will pull through this time as he always has in the past, that he will soldier on for a while yet, that there's life in the old dog still.

And we are all surprised to find ourselves hanging about outside the church some cold January morning, talking about the last time we saw him in good form, his old self, before he took bad this time. And during the vacancy of the requiem mass, as we try not to be embarrassed by the incongruities of the ritual, we are wide open to the awful funeral feeling, not of loss – because all must be lost in time – but of regret at not having had one more meeting, one more jar, one more laugh.

ERW

Today's section of the typescript is entitled ERW, the initials with which Eugene Rutherford Watters often signed himself. I must have mentioned his name to you in the past but you have probably forgotten.

By the time I had begun to draft the piece on Pearse I knew that I would go on and write something about Eugene. I don't know why I was so sure. It crossed my mind once or twice that maybe everything I had written previously was merely a run-up to whatever I wanted to write or do about Eugene. There's probably no knowing for sure at this stage.

There were rumours of distant cousins muttering about the unfair and ungrateful treatment of the Pearse character – Uncle Nick – in the book but nothing sufficiently specific to bother me. On the other hand, I had myself heard and read comments on the Eugene character – George Rivers – which left me in no doubt that the novel projected a portrait of Eugene that

I considered imbalanced or partial or perhaps even false. This did bother me.

Frank McCann probably thought that my reaction to his comments in Grogan's was the result of wounded pride or professional vanity: that I resented his failure to praise and approve my work absolutely. If so, he was absolutely wrong. At the time I did not feel that degree or that kind of responsibility for the book. I hadn't read it and knew even less about it then than I do now. I had, of course, deduced a certain amount: the structure of three movements and epilogue based on primary, secondary and third-level education plus graduation, the general similarity with the facts of my own life, the foregrounding of characters whom any member of my family, any close friend or indeed anybody who put his or her mind to it, could identify as based – however obliquely – on people I had known when growing up. But at the launch I was still very hazy on the details and didn't know precisely which particular episodes had been used in the novel and which omitted. (The more I learned of this selection the more I was convinced that in many cases where there was a choice to be made, the choice was not the one I would have made.) One of the first things I learned about the book was that George Rivers was the name given to the man who taught Casement Kelly during his last year at primary school and steered him to a boarding school in Galway, remained in very close contact with him while he was away at school and later while he was at UCD. This George Rivers was a friend, an academic adviser, and he also encouraged young Kelly's literary endeavours. I don't think I ever came across any comment on the George Rivers character that did not include some amazement at the fact that he encouraged this youngster from a modern sprawling Dublin Corporation housing scheme to study – of all things – Greek! Merciful hour!

That much is true inasmuch as it is – at least in summary – a fair reflection of what happened between Eugene Watters and myself. What is not true is that I could ever describe Eugene, as readers of the book have described George Rivers, as 'an eccentric schoolmaster, something of a cold fish, something of a hermit, a Svengali, a quasi-academic snob or a mediocre writer happily convinced that lack of recognition was the surest sign of his greatness'. My memories of Eugene during the years covered in the book are of a good man, severe in some ways but almost always kind, an inspired teacher, a magician with words.

Though I knew – even before I had ever met him – that he had the name of being unusual, I wasn't a month in his class before I understood that he was exceptional rather than eccentric.

And Eugene was a most unusual man. He was intellectually first class and could, I believe, have been an outstanding scientist, an outstanding professor of classics, Irish or English. He won university scholarships but his family couldn't afford to keep him in digs in Dublin or Galway and so he had gone to the residential St Patrick's Training College in Dublin and qualified as a teacher. Later on he attended UCD by night and was awarded an MA. He was a distinguished writer of poetry, plays, fiction and critical prose in Irish and English. He was extremely well read in Irish literature and in English literature from the earliest texts up to Eliot. He never lost the fervent respect for Greek and Latin which he had acquired at school. Though he had never studied modern languages he could find his way in French and in Italian. He was, as anybody who ever discussed literature with him would testify, an incisive reader: his perceptions were consistently spot-on and flamboyantly free from cant and jargon. Married to a painter, he was a student of European art. He was a chess problemist whose compositions were praised in the respected chess column of the *Tablet*. But even if he had done nothing else but teach class in a primary school he would have been unusual. He was the most wonderful teacher I have ever had or even heard about. I remember verbatim things he taught me almost thirty years ago and I have never come across a student of his – guys who for the most part endured school less easily than prison and who would have been happy to forget all about those who taught them – who did not remember him with some kind of respect and affection.

Not that anybody would have confused Eugene with the menfolk of Finglas, the fathers of his pupils. I remember reading a short poem of his that described his arrival at the door of a pupil's house. (I don't know why but I always think of Mellowes Avenue, a block down from where Seamus Routledge lived.) In the poem, still unpublished, I think,

Eugene reveals his hatred of and inability to overcome the awe in which he is held by the young working-class mother who would have left school when she was fourteen, who would never have begun to imagine the possibility of secondary education, who would only have associated a visit from 'the master' with one thing – trouble at school. Eugene was a teacher when, in the eyes of most Finglas parents, all teachers were 'different' – middle class, stuck-up, country people who spoke a different dialect, who knew nothing of the lives lived by people in places like Finglas, who looked different, dressed different, talked different, who tried not to be contaminated by the life of Finglas, none of whom lived in Finglas and whose efforts were designed to enable the luckiest of the kids to escape from Finglas. (Where education failed, emigration often succeeded.) I myself can recall several teachers who made no effort at all to conceal their disgust for the culture – not that the term would have been permitted in the circumstances – of the pupils they were being paid to teach, teachers who habitually mocked the working-class Dublin accents of working-class Dublin boys in working-class Dublin. There were, to be fair, some decent teachers, who were kind and who made us feel that they were interested in us: I can think of one from Waterford, one from Donegal, one from Monaghan. There was another, a famous Kerry footballer who was probably doing his best, but it took us the whole year to get over his accent and by then he had managed to get back to Kerry. It goes without saying that there were no teachers from Dublin; you might as well have looked for a Dublin policeman.

Eugene cared for his pupils to an extraordinary degree, spending his own money to buy books and things which he knew most of the parents could not afford or would not buy. He also took the class to the Abbey Theatre to see the Christmas pantomime for which he had written the prize-winning script. The other teachers never dreamed of spending a penny on the boys in their classes, they stuck rigidly to the syllabus and considered Eugene mad for wanting to teach Shakespeare and Latin to the gurriers of Finglas; the other teachers dissociated themselves completely from the school at three o'clock in the afternoon – apart from the one or two who trained the hurling and football teams – and would not have cared to be seen in the company of the snotty-nosed jackeens it was their professional duty to teach. Looking back, I imagine that most of the teachers would have considered Eugene to be brilliant but eccentric, dangerously outspoken when the talk turned to matters which they thought of as more properly the concern of the church or the department of education. And, of course, he wrote poetry.

The term 'Svengali' I found offensive, not only to Eugene but also to me. It was first used by one of Kate's friends, a doctor whose confidence I had often found to be irritatingly in excess of her intelligence. We were having a drink in Henchy's one night, talking about schools or education or something. I was paying very little attention to her until she looked at me and made a reference to 'the old-fashioned national school teachers, the real tyrants, something like that marvellous character in your book, what's his name, the Svengali-figure'. Against all my instincts and inclinations I insisted that I could not possibly see how she could use the term 'Svengali' in relation to the book. Not having read the book, I was hardly in a position to argue the toss but she didn't know that. I must have insisted with some force because suddenly the subject was dropped.

Something similar happened a few weeks later. I was sitting at home, talking to the woman who is writing a literary biography of Eugene. She had phoned me and asked if I would help by answering some questions, mostly about Eugene as a teacher. It was a fine afternoon when she called and I found her pleasant and easy to talk to. I became a little anxious when she produced a copy of the book with several pages marked by slips of paper but I made it clear that I would rather talk about the man I knew than about a character in a novel. She accepted the point readily enough and put the book away, mentioning that she had enjoyed it. And then back to her questions. I was happy to recall the sunny days in St Fergal's Boys' National School on the Cappagh Road, sitting at the desk beside the window, utterly enchanted by the intimate manner and the universal knowledge of Mr Watters the master. I spoke of going to Spiddal and staying in his parents' house in Ballinasloe *en route*.

– You make him sound even more fascinating than in the book, more . . . fatherly.

– He was an extraordinary teacher.

– He must have been. And did the rest of the class feel as you did about him?

– Hard to say. Yes and no. He could be great fun but you wouldn't want to upset him: he could be quite severe if you broke his rules.

– What kind of rules?

– I don't know really. I suppose he got annoyed when anybody was disruptive, when somebody interfered with his teaching.

– What would he do? How would he punish them?

– Clattered them with his hand. Just lashed out. It was common enough in those days.

– Did it shock you when he became violent?

– 'When he became violent' is not accurate: it's too modern a phrase and gives the wrong impression. He wasn't particularly hard on his students; it's just that every now and then he lost his temper.

– But did it shock you when he lost his temper?

– Maybe the first time but I can't remember. I wouldn't have cared much anyway. After a few days in his class I just wanted to learn. I wanted to know everything. He seemed to know everything. I idolised him. I was very young.

– It was a real adoption, wasn't it?

And my first reaction was to protest strongly against the use of the word 'adoption'. Of course I did no such thing. I paused, smiled and demurred mumblingly before going on to clarify what actually happened. He took a special interest in me, certainly, and we became close over the next few years, very close, but you certainly could not use the term 'adoption': that suggested some sort of diminution of my relationship with my own family and nothing could be further from the truth because we were a very tightknit and happy family.

– But it was because of him that you went to school in Ballinasloe, that you concentrated on Greek and Latin, that you played rugby and all that sort of thing, wasn't it? I mean, it was almost as if he mapped out your life for you.

Again, I had to prevent myself from reacting too strongly. There were other boys in the class whom Eugene hoped to steer to secondary school; more cogently than anything else, what distinguished me from them was the support of my family, the fact that I had parents who were willing to make sacrifices themselves so that I would have the opportunities which they had been denied.

I had no idea what was going on when Mr Watters called to see my parents for the first time. I was in Mr Devlin's class at the time, the class ahead of Mr Watters's, and was due to leave the school at the end of the year. Mr Watters called back to the house a couple of times and had long discussions with my parents. I was not allowed to be present at these meetings but Daddy began, gradually, to let me know what was happening and to find out how I felt about it.·I was really too young to go to secondary school, everybody said that. (But·Terry Cooney was going and he was only a few weeks older than me.) Mr Watters was suggesting that I stay on for another year: he would be taking seventh class that year. The plan was that I would sit for the Dublin Corporation Scholarship and also for various other scholarship examinations, including Gormanstown, a school in County Meath, and another place somewhere in Galway of which I had never heard, Garbally or something like that, where Mr Watters had gone to school.

Boarding schools! Like in the *Eagle* and the *Tiger* and the *Adventure*. Pillow fights in the dormitories! Secret groups of boys who dressed up at night and used mysterious signs in their campaigns against the school bully and his evil companions outside the walls of the school! Striped blazers and cricket and all that kind of thing! (They hardly played cricket in Meath or in Galway?) And maybe I would understand those words in the comics: forms, dons, prep and so on. How would I get on with blue-eyed, blond-haired boys whose parents had cars and purchase-houses and whose sisters were in schools that looked like castles and were called names like Wychfield Towers? And where they lived there was no roaring at children in the morning to get up and eat their porridge, no daddies cycling to work, no neighbours who hit each other and called each other awful names, nobody like the bootmaker across the road who staggered home from the pub every night so that nobody – not even his own children – paid the slightest attention to him but just moved out of his way as if he was a blind man. Melchester. Wychfield. There were lovely level pitches for games and everybody had proper jerseys and knicks and the team always won in the end.

Listening to Mammy and Daddy, I knew that I would have to work hard if I was to get the scholarships: it would mean coming in from school and getting straight down to the books. Sometimes I overheard them or half heard them talking downstairs and they were worried about whether they could afford all the things I'd need. Mr Watters had said that he would help out with the money but Daddy said there was no question of that.

I suppose it had always been taken for granted I would go to secondary school, that my parents would not have wanted me to leave school at fourteen to go working for a couple of quid a week like the others. I knew of only one boy who went to secondary school, to St Vincent's CBS in nearby Glasnevin. Terrible stories were told of this school: how the Brothers were mad about Irish and mental arithmetic and how they battered the boys with the legs of chairs. If I had to choose between that and boarding school . . .

There was only one problem with all this: Mr Watters. It was difficult to make out exactly what his own class thought of him. One minute they were saying that he was great gas; next minute he was a savage. The whole school knew about his stories. All the teachers read stories at some stage or another but mostly they gave you kids' stuff to read while they buried themselves in the newspaper. Mr Watters got the whole class to read together and to act it out and everything. But when he was out in the yard he wasn't that funny at all: he walked in straight lines like a soldier, always smoking and it was as if he was spitting out the smoke, and when he'd roar at somebody they'd jump – *watch it, sonny* – and he'd hit you a clatter across the face as quick as he'd look at you. And he never helped the teams with hurling and football. He'd only turn up at the sports – but then nearly all the masters turned up at the sports – and he'd put on this big act at the high jump, showing off.

He lived up Cappagh, beyond the hospital, at the crossroads. Me and the other fellows were always going up there. Sometimes we'd take the Blanchardstown road, turning left past the Dunsink quarry, the Observatory, Lady Finny's estate and then across the fields and the new houses to come out on the Cappagh Road; sometimes we'd go straight up the Mulhuddert road, but then you had to come back the same way. You never saw many people up there, even around the farmhouses and the cottages, but when you did they were looking at you as if you were robbers or something. They'd be roaring and shouting if they saw you in the cornfields in the summer. Martin at the entrance to Cappagh hospital went wild if we went in and tried to knock chestnuts off the tree in the middle of his field. It was gas so long as he didn't catch you. There he'd be, hopping with temper and us all singing away and laughing Hey Martin! the cat's fartin'!

Mostly we just walked up the Cappagh Road to look for birds' nests or to get forks for slings or to get branches for bows and arrows. We'd have the dogs with us but no girls. Sometimes we dug up cowslips but that was a waste of time: they always died. We knew every inch of the fields, where the best blackberries were, where we could be seen from houses. Sometimes we made slings and tried to break the cups on the electricity poles. Sometimes we just threw stones at them. As we passed by the bungalow at Cappagh Cross I always imagined Mr Watters walking up and down, over and back, marching really, like a soldier, spitting out the smoke and muttering to himself.

But he wasn't there when we passed by during the holidays. He spent all his holidays down the country, somebody said, fishing. He must be rich. He had a car: ZH 6103. He drove past our house every morning. To look at him at times you'd think he was asleep.

And now he was going to take me down to the Irish college in Spiddal, with him and Mrs Watters in the car. We were going to spend a few days in Ballinasloe in his father's house. Mammy and Daddy told me to behave myself and to look after my things and to write home. It was hard to know how to behave with a master and his wife but he was very friendly, kind of funny in his own way all the time. Mr Watters's family were all very nice to me. His father had been in the British Army and had been wounded in the First World War; he showed me the canaries and finches in his aviary. His brother Tom was married to Bridie and she made beautiful cakes and bread every morning and I was always hungry there because we were out fishing and because the food was so good and I even liked the tea although I never drank tea at home. Granny Watters was a real old lady; she told fortunes by cutting the cards. The nine of hearts was your heart's desire. You couldn't keep saying Mr Watters and so I began to call him Eugene – but not to his face, only to other people. Everybody laughed when I said I was going down to the village to post a card to my family: Ballinasloe is a town, not a village, even though there are only six or seven streets or so. Lots of the people say wesht and lasht and Chrisht but the funny thing is they think the way I talk is very funny; when they want to jeer me they say Dooblin, which is, of course, nothing like the way we say it.

Eugene, or Mr Watters, doesn't do anything like anybody else. He doesn't talk like the others. He has no interest at all in football. He says he doesn't even know when Galway are playing Dublin. It'd be hard to believe that if anybody else said it but with him you wouldn't know. He knows that other people get excited about who they are and where they come from and how they stand up for their own, but he just laughs at anything like that. It's not that he's not friendly – he is really friendly with everybody – but it's just as if he didn't care about things like that. Once when Bridie and I were joking – we were only joking – about Dublin and Galway and Bridie was saying the usual Galway things about the Dublin team being dirty jackeens, Mr Watters – Eugene – just smiled to himself and said that it was strange how the need for these primitive tribal rituals persisted in the latter part of the twentieth century. He was always saying things like that, you know, the twentieth century, as if it wasn't so much today or tomorrow or Monday or Tuesday or even last year but as if he knew the future as well as the past and knew exactly what was going to happen. It was the same with things like music or clothes or anything. He could have dressed any way at all but he just wore a pair of trousers, a jacket and a pullover that you couldn't say anything about. He didn't seem to know anything at all about modern music, only about old music like Mozart; of course he never listened to the radio or read the papers so it wasn't surprising that he was out of touch. And yet he wasn't out of touch at all, it was just the way he talked about things. Once when I went over to the radio in the kitchen because they were playing Guy Mitchell, Eugene smiled and said something about the 'chants of the tribe'. It took you a while to work out what he meant by this tribe business; nearly everything that you got excited about, he'd just smile as if it was childish or as if it was something like Indians doing war dances or putting on feathers. He wasn't Fianna Fáil like Daddy.

Spiddal was great fun but I was dying to get back to school in Finglas and to have Eugene as a teacher. And it was great because we were moving into a new school, a huge new two-storey building that was all bright and shiny and not like the little three-room school over in Ballygall. And Eugene was even better than I ever imagined: all he had to do was explain something and you knew it for ever. Not that he ever explained things like other masters: no, he asked you questions and before you knew what was happening you had figured it out for yourself. Geometry was dead easy once you knew that it was a way of working out who owned what fields in the Nile delta when the floods had wiped out the boundaries. And when you knew that the county of Cavan was shaped like a goose – Mr Watters had made a map of Ireland that was a jigsaw puzzle with the bits in the shapes of the counties – you could easily draw it for yourself and remember where the brown smudge of the mountains was and where the blue lines of the rivers flowed and where the black dots of the towns were. All he had to do was say a list a few times and you could write it down no bother. Naas Athy Maynooth Kildare. Bacon boots and leather. Manchester Oldham Bolton Bury and Preston.

One sunny afternoon at the beginning of summer he told us the story of Séamus Dall Mac Cuarta, the blind poet who lived up in County Louth, and who heard the cuckoo on a day like this and he was gladdened to hear that spring was coming in but a little sad, too, that he could not see it for himself.

> Fáilte don éan is binne ar chraobh
> Labhras ar chaoin na dtor le gréin
> Domhsa is fada tuirse an tsaoil
> Nach bhfeicim í le teacht an fhéir.

Mr Watters went through each verse when he had it written on the board so that he could check it for mistakes and the slow boys could catch up.

> Cluinim cé nach bhfeicim a ghné
> Seinm an éin darbh ainm cuach
> Amharc uirthi i mbarraí géag
> Mo thuirse géar nach mise fuair.

He kept the story going so that you could see the old man turning his closed eyes to the sunny sky somewhere up beyond Mulhuddert and arranging the poem with the word at the end of one line rhyming with a word in the middle of the next.

> Gach neach dá bhfeiceann cruth an éin
> Amharc Éireann deas is tuaidh
> Blátha na dtulcha ar gach taobh
> Dóibh is aoibhinn bheith dá lua.

Before he wrote the last four lines on the board he told us how the old blind man ended his poem by changing his metre, going up a gear and expressing his loneliness in long lines of pain. This verse was called the *amhrán*.

> Mo thuirse nach bhfuaireas bua ar m'amharc d'fháil
> Go bhfeicinn ar uaigneas uaisle an duilliúir ag fás
> Cuid de mo ghruaim – ní ghluaisim chun cruinnithe le chách
> Ar amharc na gcuach ar bhruach na coille go sámh.

You could see old Séamus Dall, hearing the crowds of people as they listened to the cuckoo and then started talking among themselves. Mr Watters said there would be a shilling for the first boy who could say it by heart, that he would give the class five minutes and then go over it once more before looking for contestants. That's what I thought I heard him say although I couldn't believe him: did he think we were all slow or something?

– Sir!

– Fintan?

– Can I have a go now, sir?

– Already?

– Yessir.

– Back to the board?

– Yessir.

– Well, boys: it looks as if we have a contestant. All right, Fin: up here and let's hear it.

It didn't make any difference really, not being able to look at the blackboard, because I could still see it all as clear as if it was in front of me. Not only that: I could also remember every word that Mr Watters had said about the poem and about Séamus Dall and about the old district up in County Louth and about the way the verses rhymed and the change in the last verse or what was called the *amhrán*. There were words I had never seen before but they were no real problem. You could make some of them out from the way they were used – like *caoin na dtor* – or else Mr Watters had explained them: *blátha na dtulcha* was difficult until you knew that it was the genitive plural of *tulach*. But it wouldn't have mattered had the poem been in double Dutch: when Mr Watters told you about something, you remembered it. Some of the fellows in the class were laughing at me for a bit of gas and when I saw Dermo Harvey making faces I thought for a minute he was going to make me burst out laughing but I just closed my eyes and then I could see the words on the blackboard and at the same time I could see ould Séamus Dall sitting on a nice soft bank on a sunny day and working out his verses from line to line until he finally found a way out and could make a good poem out of his own misfortune.

Some of the fellows in the class thought they could cod him but that just showed how much they knew. Mr Watters missed nothing – even though he did give the impression that he was a bit out of touch with things. He knew that copies were being knocked off out of the press when he was outside the room but he said nothing about it; that was because he thought that maybe only the fellows who were very poor would knock them off. He was very good like that. He bought a big load of books – there was one for everybody in the class and some left over – and rented them out at three pence a year. There was *The Merchant of Venice* by William Shakespeare. I tried to read it all when I got my copy – that's what I always did with new books – but I just couldn't stick it. It was written in what they called 'blank verse' but it wasn't like poetry at all; it was all stuck-up and showing off. People didn't talk like that in olden London, did they? No: nobody spoke in poetry; so why go on with it like that? The story seemed very childish at first but after a while we were amazed at how good it got. We all hated Bassanio and hoped that Morocco would win. Mr Watters said he was like the world heavyweight champ, big and strong and brilliant looking, but you knew that Morocco would pick the gold and be wrong. In the beginning we booed Shylock but as things went on you began to feel sorry for him. Especially when the posh fellows turned his own daughter against him: she was a right one, Jessica, robbing her own father. Dermo Harvey would put on his Tony Curtis look and say *Wo-ho Jessica: get up on your boom*. Whatever that meant. It meant nothing but we all said it all the time. The nicest bit in the whole play was said to Jessica:

Sit, Jessica – look how the floor of heaven
Is thick inlaid with patens of bright gold,
There's not the smallest orb which thou behold'st

But in his motion like an angel sings,
Still quiring to the young-ey'd cherubins;
Such harmony is in immortal souls,
But whilst this muddy vesture of decay
Doth grossly close it in, we cannot hear it.

Yea, that was nice. You'd have to admit that that was good. It was exactly the way it was on a night that was dark and bright at the same time, a night when you felt warm even though you knew it was cold, and you looked up at the sky and it struck you that all the stars were together, each one in its place, but together. It was like the night on the lorry at the bottom of the Lower Cappagh Road singing 'Adeste Fideles' and feeling the words going up to the stars. Only warmer than that night. That was Christmas and the sides of the lorry were so cold that they burned your hand if you grabbed them to steady yourself; this was more like a summer night when grown-ups could sit out. Grown-ups like Portia who were rich and had palaces and that sort of thing. Their palaces were like the church with marble floors and huge high ceilings and smooth golden dishes like the patin I used to hold under the chins of the people receiving communion.

He said all great art was based on the facts. He was always going on about the facts. Most of what we saw around us, most of what we heard on the radio and read in the papers, most of what we were given as the gospel truth, was boloney if you sat down and thought about it. Like the statue of Saint Patrick in the corridor. I ask you, boys, can you imagine the lad who herded sheep on Slieve Mish sauntering around Ireland in that lovely cream and green chasuble? Can you see him rushing along the old bog road in a November sleet dressed like that? Agh no: we may not know a lot about Saint Pat but he wasn't like that, not that kind of a saint at all.

There was nothing he couldn't make interesting but when it was anything to do with language he was pure magic. Various kinds of plurals – heroes, echoes, men, women, children, geniuses or genii, mice and lice. Strong and weak verbs. An adjective qualifies a noun; an adverb modifies a verb or an adjective. I couldn't get enough of grammar. I didn't like to let on to the other fellows but more than anything else I loved parsing and analysis. I would have given up anything else to watch him taking apart phrases like 'would have given'. Auxiliary verb to form the conditional; infinitive of the auxiliary to form the perfect; past participle. Syntax: how words were joined together and hammered into sentences.

I loved to hand him my compositions and hope that he wouldn't find the kind of mistakes he had found last week. Just give me the facts, the facts, as simply and as precisely as possible, no padding. Ask yourself if it is absolutely necessary and if it is not, cut, cut, cut.

Terror. Ask yourself, is this the word I want? Is this the word which comes closest to describing precisely what I have in mind? Does it suggest exactly the physical sensation you experienced when the dentist asked you to open your mouth and your teeth were to be examined for the first time? (Matteradamn, Fin, that you've never been to a dentist, matteradamn: you've read enough and heard enough and seen enough in the films to enable you to imagine it.) Is it a bit soon for terror? Doesn't that come when your eye follows the hypodermic in his hand, from the plunger on his thumb to the long and pointed steel of the needle, and you see him turning around and coming in your direction? Were you hot or cold? Were you shaking or absolutely still? Try again.

Panic? Too much action, a little too melodramatic.

Fright? Too brief, too little movement in the word, it's all over within a second and it closes sharply on the final *t*.

Scared is not quite right either.

Petrified is too stiff and anyway, although the idea of being turned into stone with fear was originally wonderful, it has lost most of its charge and is a bit worn at this stage. No: you want a word or a phrase which will suggest the growing fear, starting in the pit of your stomach and spreading throughout the entire nervous system until the hairs on the back of your neck stand up.

Anxiety, mmn, something like it, although while the sense is perfect the sounds are a little too thin and sharp for what we are trying to communicate and, make no mistake about it, Fin, the sound is very important, maybe even all-important; but that's a subject for another day, what we want now is a word or a phrase which begins like the vaguest suspicion of a possible discomfort and gradually develops into some kind of conviction that things are not at all likely to look up in the immediate future. What's that?

Apprehension? Perfect! Bingo! Give him the cigar, Barney. Open your mouth. Aaaaaaaaaaaaa. What have we here? Somebody is poking about in my mouth and he has begun to concentrate on that lower left molar. The whole body tenses up, the muscles of the stomach contract, the skin tightens, fingers seize up into fists. And it's all there in the word, sound and sense, words and music. Imagine you are lying back in the chair, being told to open wider and you half say, half pray, *agh, please, stop this tension. Apprehension.* Bang on! Bull's-eye! Ninety-nine out of a hundred! (Nobody ever scores a hundred, Fin, not the greatest writer there ever was: the writer always thinks that he could come up with an even better word or phrase.)

Aaaaaaaaaaaaaprehension!

I was delighted when he told us to take out the Latin book and began to tell us all about the Romans. Europe was basically a Roman idea, he said. What he meant was that the Roman Empire gave the same laws and the same roads and the same customs and the same language to tribes all over Europe. Rome civilised Europe. But was it the same way as England civilised Ireland? Mr Watters said that it always was and always would be necessary to knock a few heads together if the state was to be run for the good of most people. He said things like that and it was hard to argue with him. But what England did to Ireland wasn't knocking heads together. He said that the English were doing the same to some of the English people, that everybody who didn't obey the law got the same treatment. He also said that given half a chance the Irish would have done the same and worse to the English – and still would if they could. But I wouldn't let anybody away with that and I told him that when the Irish went into other countries it was to educate them and to bring them religion and culture: we were known as the island of saints and scholars.

– The island of saints and scholars! And who was the first of those saints?

– Saint Patrick, sir.

– And from what part of dear old Ireland did this Patrick fellow hail from?

– He wasn't from Ireland, sir. He came from somewhere in France, sir.

– Somewhere in France? Precisely where in France?

– Nobody knows sir. Some people think he came from England or Wales, sir.

– This seems a very hole-in-the-corner state of affairs one thousand years after the flowering of Greek civilisation. But leaving aside all these minor details such as who he was or what he was or where he came from before he came to this island of saints and scholars –

– No sir. It wasn't the isle of saints and scholars before he came. He made it like that.

– So he came over here to give the inhabitants of this murky island the option of being either a saint or a scholar, is that what happened?

– Yes sir.

– And wasn't it a very fortunate event for us that this kind-hearted man from God-knows-where decided that it was the Irish he wanted to help. Where would we be if he had gone instead to the black babies or the fuzzy-wuzzies? Why do you think he came here? Did he take down the atlas and get a map of Europe and stick a pin in it?

– No sir.

– Aha! We are on to something. There is some item of knowledge, some fact associated with this Frenchman or Welshman or Englishman or whatever he was. He did not choose Ireland by the use of a pin. How, I ask you, did he pick us out?

– He had been here before sir, herding sheep on Slieve Mish.

– I beg your pardon?

– When he was a boy sir.

– A boy? How old?

– About twelve sir.

– Twelve! By the blessed wagtail! Agh, you're codding me? And what did his mother and father think of him skidaddling off across the water to become a trainee sheep farmer in Ireland at the age of twelve? Fin, it is your good fortune to have parents who take great care of you: what do you think the ma would say if you went home and told her that you were slipping over to some out-of-the-way mountain in the back of beyond to mind some Welshman's sheep?

Of course by that stage you knew that he had you. The Irish had done their bit of oppression when they had the chance. And even if he annoyed you by always standing up for everybody except the Irish, you had to laugh at the way he'd do it – bringing in mothers and fathers and things into history. He was always doing it, making the heroes and warriors talk like ordinary people. And he nearly split himself over Dermo and Patrick Sarsfield. Mr Watters was examining us one afternoon just after the break when we were all a bit sleepy and he was marching around the class, firing questions. I loved trying to be first with the answers.

– And the main casualty of the Siege of Limerick was Patrick Sarsfield. Right?

– Sir, sir, sir, sir!

Some of us would be out of our desks with one hand in the air and one hand still on the desk; you had to have something touching the desk.

– Eamonn!

– No sir. Sarsfield didn't die at the Siege of Limerick.

– That's a relief. May I take it then that he is alive and well and living in Lucan?

– Sir sir, sir sir, sir sir sir!

– Georgie!

– N–no s–sir. He d–d–died in 1693.

– That would explain why there was no mention of it in the paper. Where did the unfortunate event take place? In Cappagh hospital, fortified by the rites of the church?

– Sir sir sir sir sir sir sir!

– Eddie!

– No sir. He died at the Battle of Landen.

– At the what where?

– At the Battle of Landen sir, in Belgium sir, in the country we now call Belgium sir.

– A sudden heart attack, I presume. Couldn't take the noise of the heavy artillery?

– Sir sir sir sir sir sir sir sir sir!!!

– Felim!

– No sir. He was shot.

– The lord have mercy on him. Another great man who died for Ireland.

– Sir sir sir sir sir sir sir sir sir sir!!!!!

– Michael!

– No sir. He was fighting for France.

– Indeed? So he had conveniently forgotten about the island of saints and scholars, had he?

– Sssssssssirrrrrrrrrrrr!!!!!!

– Dermo, you haven't got your hand up but I know from the light in your eyes that you want me to ask you this time. Had Mr Sarsfield forgotten all about us?

– No sir.

– And what makes you say that, Dermo?

– Sir when he was dying he said would that this were for Ireland sir.

– Take it easy, Dermo. Hold your horses. He said what?

– Would that this were for Ireland sir.

– But you are answering for Ireland, Dermo.

And we all laughed and we knew that Mr Watters was in good humour and that he wasn't going to try and catch somebody out. Dermo was smiling back at him:

– No sir. Sarsfield says it sir. He said it sir. At the Battle of Landen sir. When he was shot sir. It says it in the book sir.

– It says so in the book? So it must be right?

– Suppose so sir.

– You suppose so, Dermo? Are you not sure?

– No sir. Yes sir.

– You are not sure, Dermo.

– No sir.

Mr Watters let on to be shocked and annoyed but we knew he was only gamming on.

– What we have here is nothing less than a crisis in the study of European history. Finglas youth questions conventional historical account. Mr Dermot Harvey, cross-examined by the masters of arts of the universities of Paris, Bologna, Oxford, Cambridge and Trinity College Dublin, said he could not lend full support to the traditional account of the death and dying words of the late Patrick Sarsfield. The maximum sentence is being asked for. Gentlemen of the jury, we must decide. But let us question the defendant. Mr Harvey.

– Sir.

– The scholars tell us that on the point of death Mr Sarsfield observed the blood of his heart staining his uniform – which was that of an officer in the French army – and uttered the words 'Would that this were for Ireland.' You accept, I presume, that Mr Sarsfield did die at the said battle in the said place in the said uniform as a result of wounds received?

– Yessir.

– But what you do not accept is that he said the words that are traditionally attributed to him?

– No sir. I mean yesssir. I don't believe he said that sir.

– Indeed. And why not, may one ask?

– It's stupid sir. You wouldn't say that if you were just after being shot sir.

– And tell us, Mr Harvey, what you would say if you were just after being shot sir.

– I dunno sir. But not that anyway.

– What do you think you would say?

Dermo looked around the class and then up at Mr Watters and then he just shrugged his shoulders and smiled and said it.

– Jaysus I'm shot!

Nobody knew what to do for a while. We were wondering how Mr Watters would take it, the Lord's name in vain just like that, but then Mr Watters began to laugh and you never heard anything like it, it was worse than when he tried to sing, and the class went mad altogether and into total uproar. And Mr Watters did a war dance up at the top of the class slapping his mouth with his hand and whooping like the Indians in the pictures. It was gas. Eventually, of course, things quietened down and he just stood there looking at Dermo like the rest of us and then he put his hand on his top pocket and pretended to feel something wet and he said, very quietly, Jaysus I'm shot, and he exploded laughing again until he was helpless and at this stage it was at Mr Watters that we were splitting ourselves and not at what Dermo had said.

– Give him the money, Barney, give him the money. Dermo, I have to hand it to you. I have read all the great historians from the ancient Greeks down to the present day and I will say this much, not since the Greeks have I come across a little piece of history as clear, as precise and as unquestionably convincing as your dramatic footnote on the death of P. Sarsfield. I know from this moment onwards that yours is the true account and the historians of the universities can pack up and go home because they're wasting their time as far as the Battle of Landen is concerned. I declare the defendant innocent of the charge and I declare anybody who says otherwise to be as nutty as a fruitcake. Case dismissed with costs and compensations to Mr Harvey. Give him the money, Barney; give him the blooming money.

You never knew whether he loved Ireland or not. Hibernia, he'd say, the wintery island. Lads, the Roman was no fool, even if he was afraid of elephants. Agh no, lads, your Roman mammy didn't rear many thicks. Your Roman fought his way through the bogs and swamps of Gaul, biffing the hairy fellows left, right and centre. Then across the channel to Britain and, mother of all snotty orphans, what did he find there? A lot of fuzzy-wuzzies yahooing all over the place and not only were they up to their bellies in slime but they painted the same bellies blue. Boys, you've heard of the yellowbellies; these were the bluebellies. Mother of Jupiter, muttered Marcus and his pals, here we go again: another bunch of savages that need to be taught that there's something better than tribalism and cannibalism and bluebellyism. It was like the Normandy landings only this time it wasn't John Wayne but a chap by the name of Caius Julius Caesar who was in charge. Now, as well as being one of the great writers, an astronomer (what is the difference between astronomy and astrology?), a soldier, a leader, as well as all that and more, he was a nautical (from the Greek work for a ship) engineer and he organised an armada to get all his soldiers and horses and pots and pans and statues and spears and carts and axle grease and the whole shooting gallery across the channel and up to the white cliffs of Dover and the white eyes of the bluebellies as they hopped and bopped and screeched and yodelled to their various gods, goddesses and assorted totem poles. Sweet Juno tonight, the Roman lads muttered, here we go again, sharpen up the tools of the trade. And they got stuck into each other good-o and there was wigs on the green and a right *rí-rá agus rúille-búille*. And Julius Caesar had a hard look at how things were going. Now, he was no stranger to fighting: he had fought the best of them throughout the known world and he had come across a few colourful characters in his time. But Julius Caesar looked at the boys in blue knocking lumps out of the superbly organised troops of the Roman legions and he thought for a while and then he muttered to himself, nodded his head, called over his secretary and told him to take a note: *Bellum semper Britannis gratum fuit*. War was always the delight of the British. If you asked a British boy what would you like for Christmas, what would he say? A fishing rod? No. A model chariot? Not at all. A box of chocolates? Not on your life. What did he want? A little bit of a war or, failing that and if things were hard, a battle or two. Men, women and chisslers, it was all the same: the light of their lives was war. Now who tells us this? A hermit? A schoolteacher? Not on your nanny: one of the greatest warriors of all time, a great commander of men in battle, a general who had seen to it a hundred times that whoever was going to come off worst in the rucks and the mauls, it wasn't going to be his chaps, a man who'd have your tripes in three seconds if you stood between him and what he wanted, a man whose career had been built on his ability to kill people of all ages, colours, shapes, creeds and classes. So we can take it from his remarks that the British were indeed fond of the odd scrap, that they were given to the biff and the barney. And so having shown the bluebellies what was what, Julius was thinking to himself, now I wonder if that's my lot in these parts and I wish to Janus it was because to tell you the God's honest, lads, I have a pain in the *gluteus maximus* with these madmen and it's time I rambled back to civilisation and a bit of decent weather. So he asks the intelligence boys if the job is done. But they shake their heads: Sorry Caesar but there's still the other island. You're codding me now? 'Fraid not, sir. To the west of Britannia. Shortest crossing is from the island of Mona. Wild-looking place. Utterly savage. Nothing more than a collection of small primitive tribes involved in constant warfare with each other. Celtic. You're joking me, lads? Tell me you're having me on. 'Fraid not, sir. Well, mutters Caesar, I suppose I'd better finish the job now that I've started it but I can tell you this much, lads, by the cackling geese of the Capitoline Hill, I've had me *dux-belli*-ful of this lot. Haven't we all, sir, haven't we all. And so Caesar drives up to Holyhead to make final plans for the invasion of this island. And all around him he has his general staff, the experts, the people who know about weather, boats, food, weapons, land transport and, of course, the secret service who have been spying on the enemy. And Caesar asks them all to give their reports and he listens to them. And then he goes out to look across the water to see what he can see. And what can he see? Rain. Nothing but rain? By no means. He can also see sleet and drizzle and the odd bit of hail – but mostly rain. And he shivers in his toga as he feels the wind whistle up his drawers and him wishing

to Urania that he was somewhere warm or at least headed in that direction. Tell me again, he says, what we know of the crowd over there.
And they tell him. And he whistles between his teeth and says: Be the
bolts and balls of the Balearic slingers, boys, but whoever named that
place knew what he was doing. (For your information, Mr Harvey, the
slingers from the Balearic Islands in the Mediterranean, where you may
spend your summer holidays when you have made your first million,
were among the crack assault troops of the Roman army in the armoury
of which the sling was an important weapon.) Where was I? Ah, yes.
Hibernia: the wintery place. And do you mean to tell me that the crowd
over there is as bad as the hairy fellows over here? If not worse, sir.
Worse! Ah come on, lads, between you and me and the forum, I doubt
if there is much we could do for them. I think, when all is said and done,
that it would be a holy and a wholesome thought to gather up the pots
and pans and get over the Alps before the winter sets in in earnest. And
there and then was heard the biggest cheer ever heard in these parts and
Caesar decided that he had enough material for his book and that the
section on Hibernia would have to wait. And so, lads, it's an ill wind
that doesn't blow somebody some bit of good because at the moment
of Ireland's greatest tragedy there were some of the happiest Roman
soldiers the world has ever known.

You couldn't let him away with something like that.

– Sir, Ireland's greatest tragedy was when the English invaded us.

– Do you think so? Do you really think so, Fin? Agh no: Ireland's
greatest tragedy was that the Romans didn't invade us and thus deprived
us of the benefits of European civilisation.

– The benefits of being killed 'd be more like it.

– Not really, Fin. Of course, it might have been necessary to knock
some sense into the thicks who'd prefer to hide up trees and howl at
the moon rather than enjoy the advantages of irrigation, viaducts,
aqueducts, heated swimming pools, fruits and vegetables from all over
the world, law and order, good roads, schools and universities and, most
of all, the great writers like Virgil and Horace and Catullus and Caesar
himself. Agh no: there'd always be the gobaloons who wouldn't want
to have these things because they were foreign and who would want to
travel by wading through muck because that was what their fathers did
– agh but sure eventually people would get sense and they'd tell the

gobaloons to shut up and stop making loodramawns of themselves.

Some of us made the mistake of laughing at the English and calling
them bluebellies but Mr Watters told us to think before we did things
like that. The bluebellies were the British, the Celts who had been
pushed out of England when the Anglo-Saxons arrived. The Anglo-
Saxons drove them out to the outskirts so that they survived mostly in
Wales and Scotland. And most of us were British.

No, no, no: maybe you're British but I'm Irish – my grandfather
fought to get the British out of Ireland.

But Mr Watters explained that originally British just meant Celtic and
I was Celtic, wasn't I?

I knew I was but I said nothing.

It's not that he was against Ireland. He was great at teaching Irish,
especially Irish poetry, and he wrote poetry and plays himself in Irish.
He loved the high crosses and the famous manuscripts, especially the
Book of Kells. He told us all about the way the books were made and
how famous they were and how they were known all over Europe.
He said they were the greatest expression of the Irish mind but I
couldn't understand that. Which was very unusual because normally he
could explain things that other teachers only made you learn by
heart.

The Greeks were his real favourites. You never heard him say a bad
word about the Greeks. If there was anything good it came from the
Greeks. Words like history, geography, geometry, astrology (who
remembers the difference between astrology and astronomy?), politics,
drama, tragedy, poetry – all these words went back to the Greek and that
was because the Greeks had invented all these things. He loved the
stories of Ulysses and Penelope and of the Trojan Horse and of Orpheus
and Eurydice. He'd say the names in English first and then he would say
them in Greek and it was like as if he could look out the windows and
see the temples of Athens in the distance where the rest of us saw Cabra
West.

One day when he was on about the Greeks I asked him to say some
Greek for me and he said the opening lines of the *Iliad*. I was expecting
it to sound like music, like an orchestra, but it was just ordinary, not

even beautiful like French or Italian. You had to know it well, I supposed, like Mr Watters. I was dying to learn Greek but first of all I would have to get the scholarships to go to Garbally. In the meantime I'd just have to study hard and hope and wait.

But I didn't have to wait as long as I thought. One evening in his house, a few weeks before I went to Garbally, he asked me if I would like to learn a bit of Greek, just to have something to do before I went away. He wrote out the letters of the alphabet – from the first two letters alpha and beta – for me to take home and study. And then he wrote out the definite article, singular and plural, masculine, feminine and neuter, and I was to study that too. I knew that he thought we had done enough for one night but I wanted more and so he got another piece of paper and on it he wrote ὁ βασιλευς.

ὁ βασιλευς normally meant 'the king' but βασιλευς without the definite article, had a special meaning: *the* king, the ruler of the vast Persian empire. The Persians loved everything that was on a grand scale – millions of people, millions of acres, millions of gold and silver coins, huge palaces that glistened in the sun, stuffed with all the trophies of their wars – vases, cloths, animal skins, jewels, the lot. The bigger the better. The more the merrier. They loved the flashy things and the biggest and the best and the flashiest of all was Darius, the man the Greeks called βασιλευς. His Resplendant Majesty, the Head Buck Cat of the Persians, the Big Chief Number One of the Medes and the Metro-Goldwyn-Mayer of his day. To the Greeks the Persians were all βαρβαροι, barbarians. Βασιλευς was not amused and decided to teach these little Greeks a lesson they wouldn't forget. But it was the little Greeks who taught the Persians a lesson κατα γην και κατα θαλασσαν, by land and by sea; the Persians found out that the mighty hordes of their empire were no match for Greeks fighting in defence of their own little patch of mountain grass and their own way of running their affairs. It was the big issue of the day: east versus west, a mainly naval force against a land army, crack commandos against vastly superior numbers. It inspired the first history known to man.

Then he asked me to get the book that was on the mantelpiece. It was old and the yellow cover was almost brown from use.

THE WARS OF
GREECE AND PERSIA

Selections from Herodotus in Attic Greek

Edited with Notes, Vocabularies and English Exercises

by

W.D. LOWE

Inside, the paper was shiny like in books in the olden days and it was all in Greek.

Herodotus sounded great. He loved to travel and hear tall tales and couldn't wait to come back and amaze the Athenians with his descriptions of life on the fringes of the known world but, for all that, he had a Greek mind and while he was having a good time for himself and having a few jars with the lads on the docks and formal dinners with the professors, while he was doing this, Herodotus was most of the time thinking of one thing. How did this bad blood between the Greeks and the Persians come about? What can the intelligent person learn from the study of events such as this? He put all his researches into a book which was known simply as *The History* and that, Fin, is what it was – *the* history – the only bloody history there was until somebody came along and read Herodotus and said, come here a minute, you could do the same kind of thing about what happened between X and Y. This thing was history, *histoire, stair, historia,* the study of the past, and Herodotus had invented it.

The next night I brought the alphabet and the definite article all written out. I had linked the letters as in written English and I was amazed to hear that the Greeks hadn't thought of that. I could write out the alphabet and the definite article by heart but what I wanted was to read Herodotus.

ὁ Κροισος ἦν Λυδος. Kroisos – or, as he's known in English, Croesus – was a Lydian. Even today we say 'as rich as Croesus'. ουτος ὁ Κροισος. This Croesus fellow. πρωτατιστατος. The superlative, a real mouthful: the absolutely very first bar none. τινας των Ἑλληνων: some of the Greeks. At last. ὁι Ἑλληνες. As opposed to ὁι βαρβαροι. The other crowd – me and you, Fin – the yahoos. And, of course, our friend Croesus. For all that he was the very first to conquer some of the Greeks he was still βαρβαρος.

Croesus had his palace in Lydia, on the coast of Asia Minor, across the Aegean from Greece. One day he heard he had a visitor. Solon – as wise as Solon – the lawgiver from Athens, paying a courtesy call, seeing how the other half lives, had arrived in Sardis. The red carpet treatment, ministers, bishops, smoked salmon, caviar from the Black Sea, chilled white wine, all the trimmings. Down to see this curiously quiet chap from Athens.

Croesus entertained him hospitably in the palace and three or four days after his arrival instructed some servants to take him on a tour of the royal treasuries. Three or four days? I wonder, Fin, was Solon sitting there with his host, discussing what he thought would be of common interest to both, such as how to live the good life or how to organise the state for the greatest good of the greatest number of people? Or maybe even mathematics? And your man there, sitting in all his silks and satins and gold and silver and jewels with African eunuchs bringing in exotic fruits and nuts and half-naked Lydian flute-girls tootling in the background. And all the time is Croesus asking himself, when in the name of the Seven Snotty Orphans of Sardis is this Athenian going to come to the point and ask me to show him all my wealth? I wonder, Fin, if that's why it was 'three or four days' after Solon's arrival that Croesus got fed up waiting and, how does our shrewd old friend Herodotus put it, 'instructed some servants', note that, 'instructed' the flunkies to show Mr Solon something that will bring the old coot to his senses and put an end to his guff and blather about moderation in all things. Give him the works. Fin, can you imagine it? Chests of gold, coffers of silver, jewels given by and taken from the kings of the known world. Bales of the most expensive cloth, cloth only kings could afford to wear and then only on state occasions, statues, icons, you name it and he's got it, not one but thousands, not any old kind but the best, the biggest, the longest, the brightest, the lot. And that's only the beginning. Then come the accountants, showing how many millions of tons of corn, how many million jugs of olive oil, how many million boxes of Black Magic come in by the week from the four corners of the Lydian empire. Pause for a glass of wine and then we're off again: how many thousands of soldiers, how many ships, how many bullocks and oxen, horses and camels, dogs and cats, pens and pencils, milk and sugar, Laurel and Hardy, and would you please follow me, Mr Solon.

And as Solon comes into the most sumptuous room of the palace, marble halls and walls and pillars hung with golden ornamental armour and the devil knows what, there's Croesus lying on silk cushions and smiling the biggest smile you've ever seen.

– Well, my Athenian friend, I have heard a great deal about your wisdom, and how widely you have travelled in the pursuit of knowledge. I cannot resist my desire to ask you a question: who is the happiest man you have ever seen?

Solon, being an Athenian and a philosopher, a lover of wisdom, thinks carefully before he says anything. It's his instinct: you might say he does it without thinking. Who is the happiest man I have ever seen? The happiest. Happy. Not an easy concept. Hmmn: what is happiness? And he's thinking to himself first of all what the right answer is and second of all what will happen if the answer he gives is not what King Croesus thinks is the right answer. Croesus believes that Croesus is the right answer, no doubt about that. And mind you, to look at the innocent poor devil you couldn't deny that here and now he is very happy with himself. The question is: will he be happy with me if I don't tell him what he wants to hear? These kings would take the head off an Athenian lawgiver as easily as most men would take the head off a pint. You can imagine how he was fixed, Fin. What to do? Time is running out. One last check on the question – the happiest man I have ever seen. OK, check: answer. 'An Athenian called Tellus.'

Begod Fin, you could have heard a pin drop. The servants couldn't understand why Solon was still standing. Croesus was fit to be tied but he just managed to control himself. Herodotus gets it across perfectly: just listen to this. 'And what, he asked sharply, is your reason for this choice?'

Meaning that unless, Mr Hotshot from Athens, unless you have a bloody good explanation you can tear up your return ticket. I've never even heard of Tellus the Athenian. Tellus the blooming Athenian. I'll give you Tellus the Athenian.

'And what, he asked sharply, is your reason for this choice?'

Tellus. Humble man. Saw his children and grandchildren grow up. Died in his old age fighting for Athens and the Athenians gave him their highest honour: a funeral where he fell, at the public expense.

Good God, look at the time. Fin, you should stop me when it gets past midnight. Twenty past one and here we are in Asia Minor and you having to get to the Cappagh Road before Mrs Kearney sends out a search party.

– Can I come up tomorrow night?

– Tomorrow night. Tomorrow night. Tomorrow and tomorrow and tomorrow night. Yes, Fin, by all means. Come up tomorrow night and we'll see if Solon can come up with an explanation that will enable him to save his soul without losing his head. Will you be all right getting home at this hour?

– 'Course I will.

Pushing the bike on the gravel to the gate. Great trees shifting in their sleep. Eugene at the door, a shadow with a moving glow of cigarette, voice gravel in the navy blue air:

> What may this mean
> That thou, dear Fin, upon those rusty wheels,
> Revisits thus the glimpses of the moon,
> Making night hideous, and we fools of nature
> So horridly to shake our disposition
> With thoughts beyond the reaches of our souls?

Moving past McDonnell's lilac tree and swinging left around the corner, past the gate, with the hospital wall coming up on the right, hoping there are no tinkers there with dogs, accelerating down to the hospital gate and down the straight to the sweeping corner, to the main hospital gate and Martin the Cat's Fartin', then down to Smith's Corner to see the street lights of the Cappagh Road, past the foundations, the last house of the first block, around the back, dog barks over in Mellowes Road garden, into the kitchenette, not a mouse stirring, all asleep. From kappa to Cappagh, from Finglas to Phrygia. As happy as Tellus. Can't wait for tomorrow night.

– Well, Fin, where were we in the far backward and abysm of last night or early this morning? Solon was in a bit of a tight spot. Who is the happiest man you have ever seen? And who did he say?

– Tellus.

– No. You tell us, Fin.

– An Athenian called Tellus.

– Agh yes, of course. Sorry about that, Fin. The gastric juices are still working away on the dinner. Oh that this too too well-fed flesh would melt. It was, as you say, Tellus.

Una clears away the dinner things on a tray and takes them out to the kitchen. He lights another cigarette and then narrowing his eyes, looks out the window and exhales: 'And what, he asked sharply, is your reason for this choice?'

Poor Croesus was flummoxed, didn't know what to think, what to make of all this. Had he heard him properly? A nobody, a common soldier, battle-fodder, hundreds like him get bumped off every day of the week. So he had sons: big deal. If that's what counts, says poor Croesus, I've hundreds of sons, father of a thousand sons. A funeral at the public expense. I can just see it: stingy low-key affair costing a few thousand. Nothing spectacular, nothing like the Hollywood extravaganza that you'll see when I go. Solon was going on with more of the same but poor Croesus had had enough and he no longer tried to hide how fed up he was.

– That's all fine and large, my Athenian friend, but what of my happiness? Is it so totally insignificant that you won't even mention me in the same breath as common scruff of the kind you have been talking about?

Solon tries to explain to the poor devil. το θειον εστι φθονερον. Very difficult to translate. After all these years, over all those miles, through the centuries of barbarism and renaissance and the muck and tangle of the revolving planet. το θειον, whatever that is, εστι φθονερον, whatever that is. το θειον: that which has to do with the gods, as opposed to mere mortals. Difficult to find an English word for it or any other kind of word if it came to that: the god-thing. Or maybe even in the last resort: the good. But let's look at the rest of it. φθονερος, the common word for envious. Whatever the hell it is that's out there and is in some way connected with human affairs, whether you call it god or the gods or the devil knows what, let's call it το θειον for the moment, but whatever it is, it seems to be envious of human beings. When everything in the garden is rosy, Bang! Somebody drops a bomb on it or a late frost comes and wipes out the flowers or the neighbour's goat gets in and goodbye to the garden. No matter how good you are, how careful you are, how wise you are, how brave you are, how tall you are, how rich you are, matteradamn what you are: just when you least expect it, the roof comes in on top of you. Why? Dunno. When? Dunno the hell.

What is happiness?

Solon's answer is in two parts and the first is a definition: health, freedom from trouble, good looks and healthy children. But that's only the beginning. The real test comes later:

– Now if a man with these gifts dies as he has lived, he will be just the man you are looking for, the only sort of man who deserves to be called happy. But note this: don't use the word 'happy' until he is dead. Until he is dead he is not happy, merely lucky.

It's a peculiar bloody way of looking at things, Fin: count no man fortunate until you know how he ended his days. It's everywhere in Greek literature, from Homer to Sophocles, this sense that no matter how well things are going, you had better know that το θειον has still to be reckoned with. Of course Croesus with all his millions in the bank couldn't make head nor tail of this: after all, what could happen to him? What did happen to him?

Croesus did not fare well. He lost everything when he was defeated by the Persians under Cyrus, and when he was about to lose his life he muttered the name of Solon to himself. Cyrus insisted on hearing the full story and was so moved by it that he spared Croesus. And so Croesus lived to know the truth of what Solon had said. You know not the day nor the hour when our friend, το θειον, will come down on you – out of the blue – like a ton of bricks.

Not an easy idea to accept but there it is. χαλεπα τα καλα: the beautiful is difficult. Whether it's facing the facts or making a chair or painting a door or solving a chess problem, to do a really good job is always difficult. It may not look difficult to somebody else: Alekhine or Capablanca might just seem to glance at the board and do the obvious but . . . was it obvious before the Master did it? Or is it only afterwards, when we know how it works, that we are in danger of thinking of the move as obvious? It may only have taken Capablanca a second to check the situation and make his move but a thousand hours of thoughtful study, of painful trial and error, lay behind that apparently casual glance. All the greatest masters, from Plato down to Kyle . . .

He loved doing that sort of thing, talking about art or philosophy or something to do with culture and then suddenly bringing in something from the old pictures or from sport. From Plato down to Kyle. He had written a poem about Jack Kyle playing for Ireland. When he gave me the poem to read I couldn't make much of it but when he read it out and explained bits here and there I could see it all clearly. Whenever he talked about Kyle it was special, worth listening to, no matter how you felt about rugby. When he spoke about Kyle it was as if the attention of the whole world was on that shy little man with his hands buried in the pockets of his long knicks. It wasn't like being at any match I had ever been at: there was a beautiful quietness about everything and you suddenly understood how the moves followed each other.

> Feet, feet, light, and the tramped grass,
> a foe that no weariness
> makes falter in this long fight:
> these things have been our birthright.

I had seen Kyle's picture in the *Sunday Press* in Jack Arigho's column, his quiet face and wavy hair, looking fairly small in those old-fashioned knicks, but I had never seen him play. And yet I felt as if I had, as if I had been out there beside him on some wet wintry Saturday afternoon, when the pitch was six inches of muck and the ball was soap. The big men, the packs, were wrestling like hippos in a swamp, the steam rising off them, pushing and pulling, making a few feet and then being shoved back, over and over again, getting nowhere, getting tired, really looking forward to a wash and a rest, beginning to think of giving in, taking it easy for a few minutes. What's the point? We've tried everything, done our best, and there's no way through. And, anyway, look at the time.

> Not much time, there never is
> much time, the lengthening
> of the shade marks the minute
> and there is no decision.

But for some reason, somebody makes a special effort and they get the ball and somehow, though the ball weighs a ton at this stage, somehow somebody gets the ball out to Kyle. There's a little shout from the crowd but not much. The people who are leaving pause for a second but then keep going: like everybody else they've given up, they've settled for a draw and now they want to get home and thaw out before a big crackling log fire.

Unredeemed shall we go hence
leaving this field to silence
content with what we have seen
of the day's round, the routine?

Kyle takes the ball on the run. Not a big fellow, not a particularly fast
fellow, no sprinter, he moves into the attack and his centres move up
alongside him. The defence are immediately on the alert. There might
be only a few minutes to go and they're as tired as everybody else but
as soon as they see Kyle with the ball, they're on their toes and wide
awake. This is the attacking probe for which they have developed all
necessary defensive manoeuvres. They know they are facing a football-
ing genius. They have been told at training sessions, told again and again
and again till they've a pain in the face from listening, how this man Kyle
has turned matches in a matter of seconds, producing something special
when all seemed lost, how this strangely gifted man, this artist, can lull
you into sudden, inexplicable carelessness, can make you lose your concentration for a split second, just for one split second, for less than it takes
you to blink, or cough, or wipe the sweat out of your eye, for as long
as it takes to think about the time, or glance outside you to see if the
other centre or the winger is there just in case, for as long as it takes the
idea of just-in-case to flash across your brain. So the defence is doubly
alert and ready to counter all known forms of attack. The two sets of
backs advance towards each other, each man and his marker, no side
with any numerical advantage. We've been through this so often all
afternoon and we know the inevitable result: stalemate. Early on in the
relative brightness before three o'clock, there would be a huge surge of
nervous energy in the crowd when Kyle got his hands on the ball but
that all seems ages ago now, a hundred good tackles ago, a hundred
breakdowns ago: it's long since the feeling of hopelessness has begun to
hover on the wings of the Irish attack, long since their opposite numbers
have begun to play with the relish of men who know that they have
done well to get away from Dublin with a draw. Kyle gets the ball.
What can he try that hasn't been tried before? What is there left for him
to do except play out the game, let out the ball, go through the motions,
knowing that the attack will end with his winger being tumbled into
touch for the umpteenth time?

But the moment comes again and in our time
far out as ever in a wilderness
of effort and spent breath the quick grace
breaks quietly and he has crossed the line.

What's happened? The place has gone stark staring raving roaring mad: grown men are throwing their arms around each other and dancing up and down like children.

But what's happened? The Irish players are clapping Kyle on the back; some of the other team are holding their heads in horror as if they have just seen the unthinkable happening before their eyes.

But what happened? Did you see it? I was just fixing my scarf and getting ready to head off when there was this almighty roar.

What happened? Did you see it? Nobody can say for certain what happened. Sure: thousands of people saw what happened. It was simple, too blooming simple. It was as if it happened in slow motion, as if, strange to say, at some stage you actually knew it was going to happen, as if the whole game was leading up to it. At the same time, when it did happen you couldn't believe your eyes.

What actually happened? Well, Kyle got the ball from a scrum to our right on their twenty-five and he just ran the usual four or five strides, straightening up the line, drawing their out-half and then letting the ball out. Except that he didn't actually let the ball out: he looked as if he was *going* to let it out and then he looked as if he actually *had* let it out, and it was only when your eyes travelled on to the centre that you saw that the ball hadn't arrived and then you twigged: Kyle hadn't let the ball out at all. Mind you, you weren't the only one in that position. The centre looked surprised that he did not have the heavy sensation of slithery leather on his fingers. But strangest of all, the other team too seemed to think that Kyle had actually passed the ball: the out-half suddenly lost all interest, as if his job had been done, the centres came up at speed, the back row and the fullback made beelines for the far wing. The whole business had a dream-like quality. Was there a sudden silence? you asked yourself afterwards.

But what happened? That's it. That's all. One minute – what am I saying? – one microsecond Kyle was loping along in a pretty hopeless position, the entire opposition ranged across in front of him. A microsecond later he had already begun to slow up and trot in over the line, not a soul within a mile of him: he could have taken out his hanky and blown his nose before scoring bang under the posts. I suppose he must have produced a sudden burst of speed but if he did I didn't notice it: all I saw him do was, eh, more or less, em, kind of shake his head. He made it all look so easy. He had that look on his face as he ran back, you know that look of his, a mixture of pleasure and amusement, happy to have done his job well but bewildered by the reaction, surprised that anybody should be surprised. After all, he seemed to be saying, it was only a matter of picking the right moment: once you got that right, the rest just happened.

Only a man in a million, in a billion, more likely, could have waited for the right moment. You or I, Fin, would have tried it earlier and given the game away: the pressure would have been too great and the wing-forward would have noticed the anxious look we flashed at the scrum-half, the suspiciously casual way we straightened a sock, tightened a lace. How did Kyle know when to break? Nobody knows. It's possible, indeed it's more than likely, that he didn't know himself at the time, not in the conscious sense, that it was much more like an intuition, a blindingly confident intuition, an absolute certainty that for no good reason known to man, woman or child, this was it. What the artist calls inspiration, something in the air around you, a feeling you breathe in, the sudden sense that you are being looked after.

Garbally had rugby but Garbally was not everything I expected. It wasn't posh like the schools in the comics. It wasn't nearly as proper as Eugene made out. Mammy and Daddy thought I would be lonely but most of the time I wasn't: there were new books to study and new boys to meet and it was a great place for games. I saw the seniors playing rugby and I couldn't understand how nobody got killed. Tim Plummer and I became best friends. Some of the bigger boys were bullies and you had to learn to stay out of their way. But some of them were OK. There was only one other boy from Dublin in my class but he was different: he had no interest in games and he smoked and got into trouble. The ordinary food was disgusting, everything except the bread puddings on Tuesdays and Thursdays. We all looked forward to the great hog on November's Day – roast goose and everything – but first of all we had to do the November examinations. I was really worried and prayed hard that I would do well for Mammy and Daddy and Eugene and when I came first in the class I was delighted and everybody said I was a shot. We were all counting off the days till the vac and saying that we were more than halfway but November seemed to drag on and on, getting darker and colder until you didn't even want to think how many days were left. And then one Sunday after a boring afternoon we all went into the oratory and tried to stay awake through the hymns and the incense with nothing to look forward to except the study hall and we all stood up for the final hymn as the priest left the altar. What's that? It is, yes it is. 'Adeste Fideles'. The first Sunday of Advent. Christmas is coming. Up the vac! And suddenly we were all wide awake and singing our heads off and smiling at each other and pretending to shout. And I could do nothing in study that night: I was trying to imagine what it would be like to be at home again and I couldn't believe that I would ever be home again . . .

That first Christmas vac. As the train roared through the cold dark winter air, my head stuck out the little carriage window, waiting to catch through watering eyes the first familiar landmarks on the outskirts of the city – the canal at Cabra, Broombridge, Auntie Maureen's house, the Brian Boru, Croke Park. Then the panic, the sudden realisation that the unimaginable had actually happened: you were back in Dublin. And more panic: would there be anybody to meet you? And a final moment of profound fear: was that Daddy walking towards you? Were you sure? A moment of such frightening possibility that it would never entirely lose its power to lance the heart. And then a moment of such release, the slightest recollection of which causes the eyes to stream: when the man smiled and it was Daddy and we both ran towards each other and I buried myself in his overcoat and for a while I couldn't say anything but then when I began to tell him all the things that had happened I couldn't stop, not even when I was eating my second plateful of food back in the house and the girls began to snigger and Mammy tried to threaten them behind my back but Daddy was laughing too and then everybody was laughing and I realised that they were laughing at the way I was talking and they were all asking me if everything was all right and it was a trap to make me say *sound* and when I said *sound as a bell*, which is what we said at school all the time, they were all in stitches and at first I was annoyed because it was all so stupid and I didn't say it anything like the way they said I did, but sure what harm, wasn't it great to be back with them again after being away for so long, two and a half months, longer than any of us had ever been separated before.

And Eugene and Una dropped in afterwards for a few minutes to say hello and ask how I was getting on and to give me a typewriter for Christmas. They were going to Ballinasloe the following day and I wouldn't see them until they came back in January. It was easy knowing that they had no children. I mean, it was good of them to give me a present but with this thing you had to twist a wheel for every single letter; it was just a child's toy and not really a typewriter at all.

Almost as soon as we got back to school we began counting off the weeks, the classes, the days, the meals until the next vacation. But sometimes the vacs dragged for me. I wasn't going home to a village or a small town where everybody knew me and where I had an allotted place in the social arrangement, where going away to school was taken for granted. During my year in Eugene's scholarship class I had withdrawn from normal life: coming in from school, having something to eat and then getting down to study for the rest of the evening. For a couple of years afterwards I kept in touch with three or four boys from the class but the only one I was real close to was Seamus Routledge. In my second or third year at Garbally we moved house; we remained in Finglas, moving a mere half-mile or so, but for me it meant that I lost all contact – however tenuous it had become – with the people of the Cappagh Road and came home from Garbally for an Easter vacation to find myself living on a road where I knew nobody and was not likely to get to know anybody. I don't think there were many boys of my age around; I know that there were none at secondary school. Neighbouring women nodded at me with a kind of helpless deference which was painfully embarrassing, maybe seeing me as a future priest. One thing was very clear, very quickly: though I still lived where I had lived since I was six, things had changed. I was no longer one of them.

When I came home from school I had the solid support of a close family but once outside the gate I was to a great extent on my own: my people had no experience of this.

But though, especially during the first two or three years, my vacations were not crowded with companions of my own age and interests, and though I can recall moments when I looked out of a boring afternoon through drizzled windows and wished myself in a factory or an office or anywhere else, I managed fairly easily to fill the gaps and I don't imagine anybody ever thought I was less than delighted with my lot.

I loved films, often going to two cinemas on the one day, and was mad about popular music. Adolescent, addicted to popular films and popular songs, I spent a good deal of my time indulging myself in luxuriously romantic fantasy. The physical absence of a girl next door – blond, blue-eyed, alluring – did not constitute a problem for me: it allowed me to invent her in as many guises and as often as I wished and made her powerless to resist my invitations. The church frowned on my affairs and I knew I should give them up but fear of hell, though very real, was not quite as real as the girls who shared my private life and seldom prevailed against them for very long.

And there was football: Croke Park, the Dublin team, meeting Pearse afterwards. Daddy took me to all the games. I roared and shouted my heart out and swore at every loss that I would never love that team again. But I did. I just managed to hold back the tears towards the end of the 1955 All-Ireland when they were beaten by Kerry. I just let them flow in 1958 when Dublin made it at last, beating Derry, but I was far from the delirious crowds on the Hill: I was listening to an illicit transistor at school, surrounded by lads who wished every misfortune on the Dublin team. Not that I gave a tinker's curse what they said. Towards the end of the game I didn't even know they were there: I was thinking of Daddy going mad with excitement and wondering how we could cope with such happiness. Afterwards in the oratory, during the benediction hymns, I had to smile because I could see Daddy over in the Manhattan, with his hair tossed, his tie loosened, a pint in his hand; he was singing 'Down by the Liffeyside' with gusto and I could hear it so clearly that I almost joined in on the last line of each verse.

Before leaving for Ballinasloe with Una, Eugene used to call to the house and leave a collection of books for me to read during the vacation. Nothing heavy, novels mostly. One day, having waved them goodbye, I was checking through the bundle, trying to decide which was the best to begin with. Who was this Emma Woodhouse, handsome, clever and rich?

She was the youngest of the two daughters of a most affectionate, indulgent father, and had, in consequence of her sister's marriage, been mistress of his house from a very early period. Her mother had died too long ago for her to have more than an indistinct remembrance of her caresses, and her place had been supplied by an excellent woman as governess, who had fallen little short of a mother in affection.

What in the name of God? I was at secondary school, reading Euripides and Shakespeare, Caesar and Xenophon, the great poets of the world – what were they up to leaving this for me? There must be some mistake: this *Woman's Own* stuff could not have been intended for me. Of course: it was one of Una's books, light reading for the holidays, accidentally put in the pile for me. We'd have a laugh together, the three of us, when they got back from Ballinalsoe.

The two of them had a laugh right enough. I honestly thought he was joking when he started going on about Jane Austen being one of the great writers, one of the great poets, with a command of the language unsurpassed by anybody – with the possible exception of Chaucer. What was he saying? Was he really saying that this stuff was better than Shakespeare? Who was he trying to cod?

I agreed to give it another try. He mentioned that somebody had divided the human race into two types, those who appreciated Jane Austen and those who didn't. I knew which side he was on and I wanted to be there among the enlightened too.

But it didn't really work, much as I wanted it to: I couldn't feel comfortable over there with those who knew the brilliant from the boring. Highbury was too cold and too clean for me. The book was always on its best behaviour. In some ways it would be nice to live in one of those houses they showed on boxes of chocolates – all neat and tidy, no babies crying or children whinging, the whole family sitting down together at the table and eating the meals that the servants brought in, everybody so polite, nobody interrupting anybody else – but not for long: you'd soon get fed up living in your good clothes all the time and having nothing else to do but read a book or visit the neighbours for tea. And you'd miss a good laugh, too, and you'd miss the feeling, whatever it is, that you get when the family is together in the house at night, the girls playing on the floor, Mammy doing the ironing in front of the fire, Daddy reading the paper in the corner by the radio. Did those people in Highbury ever snuggle each other? I doubt it very much: not in a world where a mother's caresses had been more or less forgotten and – what was it? – 'her place had been supplied by an excellent woman as governess, who had fallen little short of a mother in affection'. That sort of thing went through you like a knife, and it was all over the book.

During the Easter vacation of 1960 I was in Easons in O'Connell Street, browsing among the books, not looking for anything in particular, just passing the time before the cinemas opened for the afternoon. Among the orange and white Penguin paperbacks I picked up a slim volume because the name of the author rang a bell. I checked the biographical note and found that I was right: the book was by this Dublin writer who was famous outside Ireland. On the cover it said that he was unique among writers in that he wrote nothing but masterpieces; from what I had heard somewhere he was a strange writer who had got into all sorts of trouble with the Catholic church. He was an oddball, to judge from the little photograph. I bought the book, stuck it in my pocket and went off to the pictures. Later on – it was dark – I was going home to Finglas on the 40 bus, sitting upstairs, when I decided to pass the time by reading a bit of the book. But it wasn't like reading at all, more like hearing a voice talking to me. I felt the heat rush into my face, the sweat on my skin. I was alone in space, in danger of floating away into the dark blue silence. I had to force myself to experience the swinging motion of the bus, to hear the breathing of the man on the seat beside me. I was almost afraid to glance over my shoulder, half expecting to see a stern man staring at me through little round glasses. I had to wipe the condensation from my own glasses. I tried to put the book away but I couldn't. It was all about me.

I don't know how much of it I managed to read on the bus but when I got home I more or less went straight up to bed and read it from start to finish. I couldn't wait to tell Eugene about this book. *A Portrait of the Artist as a Young Man* was like nothing else I had ever read; the following morning after breakfast I went up to my room, lay on the bed and read it through a second time.

And nothing was ever the same again.

In almost every detail my circumstances were different from those of the young Stephen. His family was posh and he himself was a bit of a sissy. (I didn't know what age Stephen was supposed to be when he went to Clongowes: I assumed it was around thirteen.) Compared to Garbally, Clongowes was very grand. But the most amazing thing was that, despite all these differences, Joyce had expressed the feelings of a young Irish boy at boarding school so well that I felt as if somebody was writing about me. I had probably read hundreds of stories of English boys at English schools but they were just stories, words in a book or comic; this was real and the more I read of it the more real it was. I knew what this book was about, what the writer had felt like when he was a child and when he was my age. I knew how he dreamed of meeting the girl with the golden hair, the girl next door, and being in love with her the way people were in love in pictures, always smiling a little sadly as they looked into each other's eyes and the whole orchestra would swell up. He had been an altar boy and had carried the incense boat at benediction – what we called being 'first master'. He had eaten fried bread and dripping: one morning there was nothing for him except the crusts that his brothers and sisters had left on the table. He knew what it was like to step out of the confession box as if you were walking on air, as if you were walking into a different world, or not so much a different world as the same world which you had never really seen before, never realised how beautiful it was. He knew what it was like to watch your own mother ironing in front of the fire and want to give her a huge hug and take her out and get her all the things she would like to have for the house and for herself, things we couldn't afford. What it was like to walk around Dublin and look at all the grown-ups and wonder what you'd be when you grew up. I knew Dollymount and the Bull Wall and the view over to Howth. The Finglas bus passed near Belvedere and then stopped almost outside the Jesuit House where the older Stephen wondered which window would be his if he ever joined the order.

I was no longer alone. Somebody had been through all this before me and he had written a book about it that was famous all over the world.

Daddy had heard of him and all. He looked a bit anxious when I told him about the book and he muttered about Joyce becoming very bitter about Ireland and about the church. But he told me that Tom Pugh, a great friend of his father's, had known Joyce well. Had actually known James Joyce! That was the strange part of it: James Joyce had lived all his early life in Dublin – how else could he know the place in such detail? – but still it was strange to think that you knew about somebody who had actually known Joyce. It was like – I don't know...

What had I read at that stage? The usual young boys' stuff, I suppose: Stevenson's *Treasure Island* and *Kidnapped*. And even more than either of them I liked Ballantyne's *The Coral Island*.

Uncle Kevin gave me my first Penguin, *Carry On, Jeeves*. I loved Wodehouse from the very first paragraph. He was probably the first witty writer I ever took to; the next was Evelyn Waugh. Waugh was one of those writers – Chesterton, Belloc, Greene and Newman were others – who were advertised at school because they were Catholics. Belloc's *The Path to Rome* was highly recommended, and we were told that Chesterton was the funniest writer in English; Newman was, despite the unwillingness of the English to concede it, England's greatest philosopher – although he was too difficult for now. Ronald Knox and Archbishop Cushing were admired all over the world for their wit – even by non-Catholics. Waugh was the only one of these who really had it. I loved the sharpness of his tongue and, most of all, the way he could lacerate people without losing his temper altogether; that was how he managed to get his dig in so brilliantly.

But though I continued to read and enjoy Wodehouse and Waugh, they were somehow different: they weren't what I thought of as *literature*. They were good popular writers, like Stevenson and Ballantyne, but they weren't *artists*. Waugh had tried hard in *Brideshead Revisited*: I suspected, in fact I hoped, that that was *literature* and that the writing of it had qualified Waugh to be called an *artist*, but I felt that in my heart of hearts I was only hoping.

I was the ideal buyer of Penguin books. I wanted to read modern classics, Penguins defined what they were, I bought them. I read people like Hemingway and Steinbeck and enjoyed them as I had enjoyed *The Coral Island* but I had to try and convince myself that they were essentially different because even I knew that R.M. Ballantyne was not an *artist*. I was always reading and was always encouraged to read – I remember Daddy recommended O. Henry and Mark Twain as having been among his father's favourites – but there is no point in going into such details: compared to Joyce, no other writer was in the ha'penny place. *A Portrait of the Artist as a Young Man* became the standard by which all other books were judged. Unless it featured a sensitive young man who wished to become an artist, a novel was consigned to the second division; even if a novel satisfied that requirement, unless the atmosphere was anguished, *déclassé* and paranoid, it was confined – like Moore's *Confessions of a Young Man* – to the lower reaches of the first division.

Stephen Dedalus, despite all the differences between us, was the character in literature who meant most to me. I never wanted to be like him in every way. I was shocked at his absolute rejection of family and religion, of nationalism and the Irish language. I laid no plans to fly by those nets because I did not believe they were such a threat to me as they had been to him. My family was, if anything, on the way up; my parents were loving, understanding and not at all inclined to force me to fulfil what they would have thought of as my religious duties. They reminded me of them and left it at that. From about the age of seventeen onwards I absented myself from the house and walked in the general direction of the chapel; at school, where absences from mass or benediction would have been a very serious offence, I went through the motions and thought of other things. In my private world I could share Stephen's coolness, luxuriate in his paranoia, practise his icy disdain of intellectual and moral cowards, but I found it a hard road to follow in company. I still roared my tribal war cries at Croke Park, jived and jittered to music on the radio, became utterly enraptured by films that I would later describe as silly. My whole soul ached to be loved by Debbie Reynolds though I knew it was blasphemous even to think of her on the same day as Emma Cleary.

And then there was the Nevin, the record hops held twice a week in the Glasnevin Lawn Tennis Club. One summer vacation Seamus Routledge casually asked me if I was going to the Nevin on Wednesday. The what? Was I hearing him properly? Or was he joking? A dance? Normally with records rather than a band but always with real girls. And Daddy said yes. And on the first night I went, just before I left the house I had to ask Mammy for the money because Daddy was out at work, and she got a bit flustered and rooted in her purse and asked me what I needed and she gave me that and then opened the purse again and gave me some more and I could see that she wanted to say something to me but she couldn't and so I gave her a kiss and said thanks and then all of a sudden she blurted it:

– You treat those girls with respect, do you hear!

As if she was annoyed with me. As if I had done something wrong already. And I hadn't even seen the Nevin, wasn't even sure where it was.

I lived for those nights. Nothing could cool my devotion to the place and the girls and the beat of the music. Despite my first awkward efforts at jiving, despite the sullen silences of girls who had hoped to be asked up by somebody else, despite my failures to strike the right note in conversations, despite my lack of experience, despite my inability to get Margaret Fagan to walk home with me (despite my inability to ask her to walk home with me), despite my failure to get her beautiful brown eyes to look at me with some kind of interest, despite my glasses, despite my face, my size, my clothes, my ears, my scholarships, my nose, my knees, my hands – despite the full range of human imperfection, I loved the Nevin and retained an absolute hope. What, short of crucifixion, could have tempered my religious zeal for the hallowed hall in which I first put my hand between a girl's naked shoulder-blades and pushed her gently but firmly to the rhythm of what we called a semi-demi? And was crucifixion itself, orthodox, upside-down or sideways, a lot to pay for that moment of ecstasy, that phase of transfiguration, that soar into free flight, when you nodded at a girl you had asked out two or three times before and she smiled as she stepped towards you, and as you went to hold her in the usual way for a slow dance – one hand on her waist, the other holding hers out – you saw – or thought you saw – her raise her two hands and put them around your neck and, yes, you felt her skin on your neck and knew that she wanted you to put both your hands around her waist. Stephen Dedalus himself could have been calling me from the edge of the floor, asking me to join him for a ramble as far as the Bull Wall, and I wouldn't have heard him. They could have set a match to the entire works of James Joyce, they could have offered money or a place on the Irish rugby team, a life's supply of cigarettes, a guaranteed scholarship in the Leaving, but it would have been in vain: the world did not hold anything that could have turned my attention from that gradual advance into intimacy, the pressure of her breasts, her stomach, her thighs, the scent of her hair, the warmth of her breath on my cheek. And then, the end of the first record, the raising of the lights and you stood there: your right arm still around her waist, hopelessly happy. And knowing that when the lights went down again and the second of the three records began – Del Shannon and 'The Answer to

Everything', please, somebody have requested it, please – you started where you had finished the first record and the possibilities were infinite: her head on your chest, her head moving on your chest, her right thigh between yours, her body moving against yours in counterpoint to the basic leaning of the dance. Her name, something of her story, a regular or not, next night, probably. You'd be there. Having walked home with the others, dazzled by the beauty of the street lighting, noticing almost for the first time what great company your friends were, good skins all of them, especially when they started on at you about that one with the dark eyes and you told them all to go 'way. And you hated it when you said the last goodbye and walked to the house but when you were by yourself you could smile and even jump in the air without embarrassment. Night Mammy. Night Daddy. Night son. Night love. Trying to stay awake all night to go over time and time again the thousand things that you find so nice about her, her eyes, so interesting, her smile, great to talk to, and her voice too, kinda husky, she likes nearly all kinds of films, except war films, Jesus, maybe she wanted you to, maybe that was her way of hinting...

And when you woke in the morning life was ordinary for a few minutes until... And you had to check that it wasn't another dream. Irene. And she'd be there the next night. God, that was four whole days, four whole days that stretched out like a desert, that yawned like outer space, an empty infinity of waiting, four nights of warm thoughts in which the rough hairs of the blankets became the soft down of an angel's wrists...

To my recurrent amazement the days always passed. I suppose I read a good deal, rambled through town, checking the bookshops before going to the cinema, dropped into the amusement arcades before getting the bus home, listened to Radio Luxembourg, always waiting for some encounter that would repeat my dreams, always hoping that she would be there at the Nevin, walking towards me even as I walked towards her, smiling at me as if she too had been waiting for me to walk towards her.

In the vast gaps of time between nights at the Nevin, if Eugene and Una were at home I would cycle up to Cappagh after tea, knowing that the light would be on in the front room and that I would be welcome.

Eugene is stretched out on the chair beside the fire – he is always sleepy after a meal and they have their dinner in the evening – a book open on the table or maybe a chessboard and a pad of chess diagrams with the solution to a problem scribbled in on the top sheet. Behind him is the radiogram. Una is sitting up at the far side of the fire, mending. Over the fireplace is a painting by Una, an Annunciation of medieval simplicity. There are several of her works on the walls: they change from time to time but for the moment they include her *Silken Thomas* and a poem by Eugene, beginning 'Style is a knife', which Una has inscribed on parchment. In the far corner by the door is a bookcase, beside it – under the front window – a sideboard with more books, including Lecky's *History* in several volumes, and there is another series of brown volumes, the work of some philologist: we have never discussed either. The fire crackles and Una asks some polite questions as we wait for Eugene to stop his intermittent postprandial humming, draw in his legs and reach – with automatic hand – for the packet of Player's and the box of matches.

– Sorry to be so rude, Fin, but the old gastric juices, you know. Beg your pardon, in God's garden, won't do it again, till the next time.

And then we were off. How did it begin? He'd ask some question, I'd say something back, Una would clear away the dinner things and take the tray out to the kitchen, and in no time at all we were into books and writers and poems. He knew them all. There was nothing I had read, at school or on my own, that he couldn't talk about in a way that made them flash with new significance. And always he was talking to me, not teaching, asking me many more questions than I asked him.

I have two pencil sketches that Una did of me. They are dated Jan '59 and Jan '63, and show me as I sat in the front room in Cappagh during my first and final Christmas vacs from Garbally. It was Una's idea to do the first one: maybe she and Eugene had discussed it before I came up, maybe I angled for it, but I remember it as Una's idea. It was done with a rather fine pencil and shows a thirteen-year-old boy absolutely transfixed: schooltied, snubnosed, longheaded, looking away from the artist, solemn with attention for the somebody or something that is outside the frame, looking for all the world like a child at the altar rails, awaiting the priest. The second, I know, was done at my request: with some extraordinary cheek – for which I will always be grateful – I asked Una to do it in order to have two sketches marking the beginning and ending of my years at Garbally. The second one never pleased me as much as the first – at least not until recently when, for the first time, I placed the two side by side. The pencil is thicker, the outline less precise. It occurred to me, even then, that maybe she was less interested this time, that I had caught her cold. But no: she was on to something and got it. Only my adolescent vanity could have been less than pleased with this portrait. The subject is probably recognisable as the disciple of the earlier sketch – same nose, same hair – but he has changed. The lips are not merged in the same repose but seem about to open in speech. The angle of the pose is changed, the face slightly turned to the front although still undeniably focused on some presence outside. The seventeen-year-old is wearing a pair of heavy black spectacles but they do not conceal the activity about the eyes. The eyebrows which were, in the earlier sketch, slight symmetrical arcs are now in a more dramatic relationship, the right rising in incipient interrogation above its more contemplative neighbour. The eyes are more alert, probing as well as receiving, one attending while the other waits for an opening. He is listening carefully but is about to speak: the face wants to give as well as receive, to argue as well as absorb. There is, despite the energy, no suggestion of anger or disrespect or – as far as I can make out – rebellion: something exciting is happening outside the frame and he wants to be part of it. But here is somebody who cannot be completely contained in the scene, somebody who lives another life outside the room. The rough strokes, the blurred outlines, capture the thrilling confusion, the complexion of adolescence.

A less involved inspector, somebody with a taste for history in art, would immediately point to the glasses. I had got my first pair of glasses during the Christmas vacation of my first year. (I was standing with some friends at the back of the school auditorium, watching a dress rehearsal for *The Pirates of Penzance,* when it dawned on me that the others could distinguish faces where I could only see colourful smudges of costume and wig.) These were my second pair and marked a crucial advance. The first were general issue, round brown frames, but these were something else: they were Buddy Holly specials, heavy black frames containing strikingly narrow lenses that seemed mere horizontal slits. I longed for those glasses, begged my parents to share my contempt for the other pair, lusted after the exchange that would allow me to shed the emblem

of the studious stewpot and assume the mark of the one who trembled
with excitement for Peggy Sue and who had put into words and music
my irrepressible dream of the perfect night at the Nevin:

> All my love, all my kissin',
> You don't know what you've been a-missin',
> Oh boy! When you're with me,
> Oh boy! The world will see
> That you were meant for me...

Inside, sitting opposite Eugene at the fire, we studied older forms:

> Bright star! would I were steadfast as thou art –
>   Not in lone splendour hung aloft the night
> And watching, with eternal lids apart,
>   Like Nature's patient, sleepless Eremite,
> The moving waters at their priestlike task
>   Of pure ablution round earth's human shores,
> Or gazing on the new soft-fallen mask
>   Of snow upon the mountains and the moors –
> No – yet still steadfast, still unchangeable,
>   Pillowed upon my fair love's ripening breast,
> To feel for ever it soft fall and swell,
>   Awake for ever in a sweet unrest,
> Still, still to hear her tender-taken breath,
> An so live ever – or else swoon to death.

Oh boy!

I moved constantly between the rhythms of Virgil and Horace, of
Shakespeare and Keats, and the more insistent beat of rock-'n'-roll. I
don't think I was ever perplexed by this dualism.

Within the chiaroscuro of the Nevin I tried to make some use of my
status as boarding school boy: to be away at school, to be considered
bright, was quite all right provided it was kept under control. What was
not all right, what was very unhelpful, was any suggestion of dedicated
study, the least hint of an interest in a subject for its own sake; it wouldn't
have been altogether damaging to drop casual remarks about a career in
engineering or business, but even I – in all my innocence – knew that
to mention Greek or Latin would be to advertise oneself as a square and
to place oneself outside the one true church of rock-'n'-roll. In the

world of the American film and the new 45 r.p.m. single, there was a ready-made role for the scholarship boy with the glasses. It was not a role I wanted: I wanted the girl with the gleaming smile and the ponytail.

> Don't know much about history
> Don't know much biology
> Don't know much about science books
> Don't know much about the French I took
> But I do know that I love you
> And I know that if you loved me too
> What a wonderful world it would be.

But into the wonderful world of the Nevin came tiny moments of sudden silence, as if somebody cut the sound and I could see the dancers miles away from me. And not only in the Nevin, but also when I was alone. Most of the time these silent moments passed quickly but they left a disturbing echo and they seemed to be coming more frequently. There had always been such moments in my life. Way way back in my childhood, as far back as I can reach, I used to be overcome by strange qualms. They too came suddenly and quietly, normally when I was looking at somebody who seemed sad or left out of things – or who struck me as bound to be pushed around by those who were tougher and less considerate – and as the qualm spread from my scalp down my neck and out across my shoulders, my whole self melted in a feeling for that person. This feeling was not restricted to my own family but was more often extended to boys and girls whom I didn't particularly like and also – and I even felt this when I was very young – to many who would not have thanked me for my sadness. I often stood at the Nevin, surveying the ranks of girls across the floor, looking as ever through the mass of heads – some bobbing in conversation, some demurely dissatisfied – for the blond fringe and ponytail, the flashing smile and the eyes which said yes, do ask me, please, and finding instead that I was looking at some plain girl and suddenly feeling myself all the hurts and pains and tears that she must surely experience in the open market of the dance hall. I had to wake up and remind myself that some of these delicate plants had, while dancing with me, shown themselves to be in-finitely better able to look after themselves than I could ever hope to be; it also occurred to me more than once that as an object of melancholy sympathy I myself would probably serve better than many of those who caused me to stand and stare in sadness.

I spoke of these silences to nobody but I knew that if I ever mentioned them that Eugene would understand them. Eugene was an experienced citizen of the other world into which I sometimes skidded, the world behind the hung clouds, the struts and painted scenery, the world I entered fleetingly during those quiet phases. Though I was clearly aware of the difference between the everyday and the other world, I was never troubled – perhaps I should have been – at the thought of commuting between the two. My family knew that there were some things – to do with study and literature and so on – which I shared with Mr Watters; Eugene knew that there were other things, most of my life, which I shared with Mammy and Daddy, with Maura, Eileen and Eva, with Pearse and some other relations, with my few friends in Finglas, with my many more friends at Garbally. There was no sense of an absolute division: Eugene and Una became close friends of my family, we exchanged visits and, the ultimate seal, Mammy and Daddy and Eugene and Una went over to the Manhattan to have a drink with Pearse; most of my close Finglas friends had been in Eugene's class with me.

Even at Garbally I was aware of Eugene. In some ways he was the only one with whom I discussed literary texts. Those who taught me Greek and Latin and Irish and English were delighted with my interest but, when all was said and done, they had the whole class to steer through the state examinations. It was good to have a student who was excited by literature but first things first and that meant methodical preparation for the examinations: accurate translation, grammatical and historical notes, names and dates, the central theme and the principal ideas. And so sometimes in the study hall at night, jaded by syntax or classical allusions, I would hear Eugene's voice, sharp, chuckling unmusically as he surveyed the hordes in the school yard.

Looking at them, Fin, you realise how short a time it really is since homo sapiens was swinging from tree to tree with the help of a good strong tail. And yet look again, Fin: look at the hands, how gracefully and effectively they can be used to appease the itch at the edge of a crusty old wound on the patella or extricate irritating shards of mucus from the nostril – with no apparent effort whatsoever. These are the hands that will master all kinds of tools and brushes and machines, hods and handsaws, cold chisels and monkey wrenches, hands that will create new tools and new grips for new materials and new problems. Look at the eyes, some flickering with excitement, others so absorbed with what they see that they seem asleep, viewing and reviewing, perceiving and apperceiving, sending back invaluable information to the brain, but not merely sending it back, presenting it in a unique way, creating a unique world. So many of them, Fin, and every single one of them, from the snottiest little snidgin in Low Babies to the biggest bruiser serving out his sentence in Seventh Class, every mother's son of them the centre and sunshine of his own infinite universe, every mother's son of them as important in his own eyes as anybody who ever has or ever will live, and why not? Every single one of them a potential Plato, a Shakespeare, a Keats, a Ballygall Beethoven, an out-half for Ireland, a mid-fielder for Dublin. If they get the chance, the chance in a million. Make no mistake, Fin. Pick out and observe the grimiest, squintiest-eyed urchin with the most soul-searingly stupid kisser on him: he is a pearl. If you don't believe me, take a trip to the zoo; then come back here and listen to the miracle of speech. Never forget that. A miracle: that which amazes us, takes our bloody breath away. And in order to write, Fin, you have to unlearn all the learning and see the world as a child sees it. Unless you be as little children and so on: he was dead right there – as he very often was when it came to questions of inspiration and creation: which of you by thinking – by intellectual exercise – can raise yourself by one tenth of an inch? But the learning has to be learned before it can be unlearned and it leaves on the *ka* or the soul or what you will a character or spiritual mark which lasts for ever. Unless the writer can – like the child – see this life as it really is and not as adults paint it, then the writer cannot hope to enter the kingdom of heaven: he's only wasting his time and ours.

I had always enjoyed writing essays and at Garbally it began to dawn on me that I would follow Dedalus from school to university, from the study of the great writers to the writing of my own books. It was all pleasantly vague, off in the misty sunshine of a future; meantime, though in the privacy of thought and reading I approved of Dedalus's chilly and callous isolation, my public behaviour was more conventional.

Because I was having a marvellous time. I got an Inter scholarship, first class, in 1961 and proceeded, well pleased, to become a senior at school. The year between Inter and Leaving was traditionally something of a joke; it was called Senior Stick, stick being the college slang for failing an exam. It was a most enjoyable year for me and brought what I had longed for: some success at games. I had always been sports-mad but I had never really made the junior teams, probably because I was too small, too slow and too fearful of physical contact. Sometime around my sixteenth birthday I developed enough speed and enough confidence and eventually made the teams at football and rugby. And so there I was in Senior Stick, full of myself and thriving generally, a regular at the Nevin, an admirer of Joyce and playing the part of Dick Deadeye in the Christmas opera. I was asked to contribute an essay to the school magazine; I proposed an essay on Eugene, an Old Boy beginning to make a name for himself as a writer, and this was accepted. For me it was the opportunity to write about something I knew and, at the same time, to spread the gospel about Eugene. My super-ego has failed to delete all knowledge of the essay, probably because of a coincidence: when I sent a copy of the magazine to Eugene I enclosed two other pages.

It was the spring of my life in the spring of the year 1962. It was during second study which lasted from 8.15 until about 9.45 but in actual fact it happened between 8.30 and 9.00. I was sitting about five desks from the senior end of the row nearest the wall on the yard side of the study hall. To begin with, it was a physical thing, an overwhelmingly physical sensation. One minute I was doodling lethargically, fighting off sleep, and then suddenly my whole body was gripped by a cold constriction of the skin. My tongue and my eyes felt dry, my palms seemed to be pumping perspiration, my limbs to have lost all coordination. It was as if I was totally alienated from everybody and every familiar thing about me, as if I was a spaceman wearing a glass bubble helmet and a pressurised suit, hearing nothing but the thumping of my own heart and the wheezing of my own breath. I wanted to scream and scream and scream as loud and as long as I could, I wanted to explode the calm of the study hall; and yet I knew that I should control this urge, that I must resist the temptation, that I must hold out, because to give in now would be to give in for ever, to hold out now would be to be safe for a long time. I was in actual physical spasm: muscles in my legs and on my shoulders were cramping for a second or so at a time. Then I began to write. I wrote very quickly and had completed the ten lines in about fifteen minutes. Rigid with fearful excitement, I asked for and received permission to go out to the toilets: the only place where I could, legally, be alone. My sweat seemed to freeze in the night air – though it was a relatively mild night. My fingers shook as I lit a cigarette, illegally, in the toilets; my whole body vibrated as I inhaled the smoke and tried to relax by leaning against the wall. I looked out at the stars and hungered to have somebody read what I had written on the blue-lined page.

I remember that I got into bed that night and lay on my back, expecting to be kept awake for hours by this body-quake, but suddenly a great wave of exhaustion spread through me, the kind of tiredness that comes after long hours of physical labour, the kind of total disintegration you suffer after playing your heart out in a long losing match.

As soon as we went up for classes the following morning, I arranged with a day-boy to post a packet for me. I sent Eugene a copy of *Gearrbhaile* and enclosed a copy of my ten lines and a brief covering note. He replied by return:

Cappagh Crossroads
Sat. 30/3/62

Dear Fintan,
Muchas gracias. Your 'portrait of the author' is quite brilliantly written, and to have it done in the magazine of my old school by my own pupil of a different school – this is a most gratifying experience. It was very kind of you – and quite penetrating of you – to include Una in the portrait: you mention the 'muse' in your poem: believe me, it's no mere figure of speech with the poets.

The muse is the moving power of poetry, a wind of energy – brainstorming – which the poet finds blowing within himself and which he personifies (per-sona) as a goddess – the external, objective form of an internal, non-personal, unconscious power which he finds infusing itself up into consciousness – in emotions not understood, tremblings, ecstasies, melancholy, up

in the air & down in the dumps – a madness, in fact. A
madness which may overwhelm the person (this is the
meaning of a neurosis – it happened my old teacher, Paddy
Joyce) unless the poet can objectify it and discipline it in a
rhythm as a poem, a play, a painting, a sculpture, or a
symphony. (Notice the meaning of poet – ποιητης: the
maker).

Why this lecture? Because, chum, your heart is bursting
with a power unproved. You have been swept by the Muse –
it can be a pretty grim experience – it's plain in every line of
your poem. It happens everybody at some time, more often
with some & to a greater extent than with others. The only
cure is to make something of it – a poem, a fortune, or a
birdcage. That is what is meant by making (ποιησις): it is the
finding of a satisfactory external & personal form for what is
impersonal, inchoate, internal. Eliot calls it a search for the
objective correlative. It is never found in its purest form (the
artist is never satisfied with his work) but when (by hard work)
it is found in a nearly adequate form, the maker feels he has
brought something beautiful to birth, & there is no joy on
earth equal to it.

Now, as to your poem, FIRST LIGHT.

(1) The shape, the metric, is extremely interesting. The
brainstorm has been disciplined into a short and strongly
articulated form (look up *articulum*). The verse-shape of ten
lines is divided into 2 parts by the rime-scheme, but these two
fives are rebound together into a complete whole by the
assonantal pattern. This assonantal pattern is an (unconscious)
Gaelic influence from *meadaracht na n-amhrán* working across
the English pentameter. If one were to make a complete map
of both vowels and consonants and join all the like elements by
straight lines and loops, the result would be an extraordinary
complex spider's web with a dominant pattern. The important
thing is that this complex has been achieved by ear alone – I
doubt whether the writer was aware of anything more than his
end-rime sounds.

The rhythm is equally interesting: there is a very daring

resolution of the iambic pentameter in line 3:

$$- \mid - \mid - \cup \mid \cup - \mid \cup -$$

This is not properly catalectic (the loss of one or more metrical elements): it is a real resolution; – in the 1st 2 feet the iambs have been resolved into one long stress, throwing the whole weight of the voice on the 2 words, *rich, ripe*. A similar effect is achieved in the last line:

$$\cup - \mid \cup - \mid \cup \cup \cup \text{ (from the de) } \mid - \mid \cup -$$

Here again the whole stress of the meaning is thrown on the *light*, but the *muse* holds its own because it is buttressed by all the preceding Us and U sounds in the poem.

Line 9 has too many extra-metrical elements which have the effect of hurrying the body of the important word 'melancholy' out of existence: one might prefer –

That deep down melancholy: I still refuse –

with such a precise use of the colon the awkward 'but' becomes unnecessary: –

That deep | down mel | ancholy: | I still | refuse

$$\cup \quad - \quad\quad - \quad - \quad\quad \cup - \cup \quad \cup - \quad\quad \cup -$$

This is but a small flaw. Metrically, here is a poet who knows his business.

(2) Materially, or from the point of view of subject matter, the poem is not quite so successful. The 'names', the characters who take part in the drama, are too abstract: heart, soul, power, music, brands, melancholy, muse. In bodying forth the demonic muse, it is necessary to give these (very real) powers & energies an external form, otherwise the lyric remains on the purely subjective and private level, & fails to communicate.

Another way of saying the same thing: the poet must not attempt a direct statement of his internal storm, but some external image of it that shall show it 'obliquely', as a reflection, say, in water: find an exact time, an exact place, a nightingale, a Pyrrha, a study hall, an echo of a desk lid clapped

to, the rebound of a handball, the cold white sheets, a caning
for a misguided subjunctive, the breaking of new buds near an
old wall, the copula clanging between 2 railway carriages, the
white cap of a housemaid, the sum to infinity of a harmonic
series, the bell clanging until it clangs within the brain
maddening, infuriating, and the absolute want, vacancy of a
windbitten Saturday, or the finding of a lovely image in a song.

This is, of course, a general criticism from a very adult point
of view. The adult knows bloody well of the deep-down
melancholy: from your point of view, it is a relief to have
given it such satisfactory metrical shape; but the adult wants
more, he wants the poet to re-create the melancholy in
tangible form, which means objective embodiment in images
that are unique for that poet in the place & time concerned.
Place & Time are the two co-ordinates of poetry, as well as of
being.

This is meant as encouragement. I am struck by the very
palpable sincerity of this poem, as well as by its metrical power.
But, and it is a big but, – don't wear your heart upon your
sleeve, speak to them in parables, learn to talk about the dog-
eared grammar and the grass gouged into the rugby field when
all the time you mean the brands which maim the soul & the
storms which trample on the teeming brain.

Salve, Poeta. More in a few days when I shall send you
L'Attaque.

Valedictions
Eoghan & Una

I wasn't quite seventeen when that letter came; it is possible that I
received it on Eugene's forty-third birthday. *L'Attaque* had been
awarded a special prize by the Oireachtas the previous year and he had
been all over the papers. Orpheus was coming out of the undergrowth.
At last people were beginning to recognise what I had known for years.

Eugene was a successful dramatist in Irish when he wrote *L'Attaque*
but a historical novel drew more attention and admiration than a play.
Reviewers wondered if it marked a beginning for the modern novel in

Irish; I knew that it would be the first of a series of great novels which would eventually make the name Eugene Watters famous throughout the world. My only regret was that so few people – a few hundred – would be able to read it because it was in Irish. If only it could be read and reviewed in London and Paris, Berlin, Moscow and New York . . .

I agreed totally with the image of the lonely artist toiling in isolation but I wanted him to achieve the fame he had earned. I wanted him to be famous so that he could write more and better and not have to worry about the future. I never put it to him quite so bluntly and I suppose I was ashamed of myself for wanting that kind of success for Eugene. I knew how he would react. χαλεπα τα καλα. Popular applause is perhaps the greatest threat to the artist. Poor Shakespeare writhing in disgust having made himself a motley to the view of the groundlings and the noble pups. Remember Johnson and Lord Chesterfield.

But I knew it was simply a matter of time. Eugene smiled as if he could read my mind. I was nineteen, in my first year at college, enjoying kinds of success I had long longed for; Eugene was forty-five, struggling to make a living from his writings, having given up his permanent pensionable teaching post. I was floating, almost independent of space and time: closer to Catullus than to Thomas Kinsella. I knew that Chaucer had smiled to be seen as the poet of Sir Topas, that Shakespeare had been tickled at the thought of himself as an upstart crow, that Jane Austen had put her manuscript out of sight when neighbours called to take tea and talk balls, that Keats had been dismissed by the men about town, that Joyce had not liked what he saw on the bandwagon and slipped away to do his own thing in the back of beyond, that Eliot had put on a pin-stripe and the mask of a clerk, that the barrows outside Hanna's and Greene's were bending under the gilt volumes of forgotten successes. χαλεπα τα καλα. I felt sorry for those who had, without realising it, made themselves a motley to reviewers. το θειον εστι φθονερον. I had stood at some distance from the Martello Tower in 1964 and grinned in agreement with Eugene's caption: 'The Mecca of the Mod. Lit. Mulligans'. Why could they not see it too?

Easier said than done, Fin, but above all, shun praise and publicity. Remember how poor Brendan was thrown to the wolves. Then fly our greeting, fly our contact, fly . . .

And meanwhile Eugene and Una worked away in Cappagh and

seemed well on the way. Una was beginning to be known as a painter and illustrator and her design 'A Celtic Sword of Light' was selected as the official emblem for the fiftieth anniversary of 1916. Eugene was utterly immersed in a new project: a novel in Irish on the 1916 rising. He envisaged it as an Irish version of *War and Peace*, a new national epic, and he flung himself into the research that he felt was necessary if he was going to rediscover the physical facts under the morass of lies and political exploitation. Begin with the facts: gimme the facts, sonny. No pleasure like it, Fin. God, how I envy you in the luxuriance of your research libraries. But χαλεπα τα καλα. Gimme a pick and shovel: dig down beneath the top soil of myth. The weather, what they were wearing, what they had for breakfast, the material, the weapons, the precise numbers, the exact times. What big games were on, what people were talking about, what the headlines were, what accounts pass the test when you take them in your hands and walk the bloody streets and alleys. The bricks and mortar without which all the purple passages are only a waste of everybody's time. The facts.

He was ready to begin in February and he slaved away through the summer and autumn, set on having the book completed in time for Easter 1966.

One Sunday morning in November my father was called to the front door. A neighbour. Something he heard announced at mass. And knowing we were friends, like, and in case we hadn't heard. My father's voice high with anguish, calling me from the kitchen. Granny Watters was dead, had died last night in the bungalow up in Cappagh. But the neighbour thought it was his wife, not his mother; he couldn't be sure but he'd swear... Agh no, sure Una, his wife, was a young woman; it was his mother; she must have been staying with him. But thank you very much for telling us. Mary, poor Granny Watters is after dying up in Eugene's house; Fintan and I had better slip up there immediately.

When we got out of the car I was apprehensive, asked Daddy to go in first. Walking slowly on the gravel. Eugene coming around the side. Nodding at us to come in. His face a grim mask. The neighbour was right. Una was dead at forty-seven. I could not bring myself to go with Daddy. I could not face that fact. Some dread prevented me from accompanying Orpheus to the opening of the underworld. το θειον έστι φθονερον – if proof were ever needed.

At the time I was probably closer to Eugene than anybody else was and yet I was too young, too callow, too inexperienced to know what was happening to him. I remember thinking that he was bearing up very well, hoping that within a few months of Una's death the wound would have lost its primal sting. Amazingly, he continued to work on the 1916 book. Though he had envisaged it as a much longer work which would cover the seven days of Easter week, he eventually settled for one day, the Monday. *Dé Luain* is the Irish for Monday but in this book the reader is reminded of the phrase, *Lá an Luain*, the Day of Judgment. The book resonates with the dull alienation of death. Perhaps the writing of the book saved him from something worse: it enabled him to continue working, passing the long hours in the empty house, keeping him going while the shock wore off and he became used to the echo of utter desolation. Perhaps it would have been better had he ripped up his contract and burned the notebooks and typescript, had he – for a few months anyway – taken up drinking in crowded bars and going back to sob and snuffle in friends' houses.

And then he gave up writing: after *Dé Luain* not a word. Orpheus was in the underworld. It would be three or four years before he emerged again.

But that is no part of the present story which ends, depending on your point of view, in 1966 or 1967.

I spent a lot of time with Eugene in 1966: there are photographs of him on the steps of Earlsfort Terrace when I was dubbed a Bachelor of Arts. There were lots of things we didn't need to talk about: by then we knew each other well enough to communicate quite adequately in silence. We spoke about sport or the texts I was studying at UCD, from both of which he felt himself a million miles removed; he smiled a distant smile when he recalled that other world, that previous existence in which such things seemed to have been interesting. He was trying to right himself, trying to practise a stoical acceptance of the blow a cruel fate had dealt him. Must stick it out, face the facts, reject all easy solutions out of hand. My Lord, I hope we have rejected these solutions indifferently well; to hell with your indifferently well, reject them altogether. The facts of life, of life as it is and always has been lived on this strange and temporary planet. The facts: what has been done, what has been established beyond reasonable doubt. *Facta* are no flatterers.

Important to see that, to perceive it, to understand it with feeling and, even though it might stick in your gullet at times, with gratitude, with thanks. For what, you might ask? For wisdom. For good counsel, that bloodywell feelingly persuades us what we bloodywell are and, equally if not more invaluably, what we bloodywell are not.

In the summer of '67 I think I came close to or actually got one foot into what is commonly called a nervous breakdown. I don't know what the underlying causes were; the trigger was an English girl in London who ended our relationship. Buzz-buzz! Not that there was much of the antic disposition in my behaviour: I doubt if anybody other than Eugene noticed anything other than that I seemed to be a bit down in the dumps. Mammy and Daddy must have wondered what I was up to when I suddenly rang them up from London and told them that I was flying home that night. What did they make of my unusually muted mood when I arrived and stayed up all night in the front room listening to *Sergeant Pepper's Lonely Hearts Club Band*? Presumably they guessed that I had been disappointed in some way and then they put two and two together – but they never asked anything straight out, never looked for an explanation, for any details. That was not our way.

Nor, of course, did Eugene. That wasn't his way either. He simply waited until I was ready to speak, always making it clear that he was willing to listen but not willing to push me. One night he suggested a drink at the airport.

It sounds a strange choice now – it is tempting to see him taking me as close as possible to the London affair in order to bring my memories to the boil – but in those days the airport was quite a popular nightspot. Eugene loathed pubs and the airport lounge was about as different from your ordinary pub as you could get. We sat up at the bar, smoking during long intervals of silence. Each knew exactly what the other was thinking and feeling. Eventually I said that I was sorry if I had been a bit of bore recently but that I was not exactly feeling on top of the world. No cause, no cause. I didn't want to bore him further by digging up the past. It helps to speak, but one must decide whether to speak to the trees of the forest or to a friend. And so, as planes landed and took off, parting and reuniting friends, drowning parts of my narrative in their monstrous howls and leaving me to pick particles of tobacco from my mouth, I told him what had happened. I doubt if I told him the whole story – I can't imagine anybody ever doing that, least of all myself – but I set the scene, listed the characters and summarised the action from some arbitrary beginning to the unavoidable final curtain.

One Sunday afternoon on the cliffs at Howth I noticed Eugene looking at me in a very strange manner and I realised that he was afraid I would throw myself off; I smiled to think how mistaken even Eugene could be.

Ever since Una's death Eugene had thought aloud about the options facing him. Stick it out, face up to it, see it through and, if you are very lucky, you will begin to understand that it is good: that was the beginning of wisdom. That was Eugene's line but I lacked his faith. I thought that if I was in his situation I would skidaddle – somewhere, anywhere – but I said nothing. When he mentioned the idea of leaving the house I wanted to tell him that he should get to hell out of it as soon as possible or, as we used to say, ὡς ταχιστα, but I still said nothing because I couldn't bring myself to contest his sacred principles. It is absolutely necessary to stick it out. That which had been moulded by years of human fulfilment was beautiful, to be respected, not to be abandoned.

But if he was going to stick it out, to see the thing through, changes were necessary. By turning the little garage into a bedroom he was able to sleep in the only room in the bungalow that was not throbbing with memories. And then shortly after the night in the airport he decided on a more radical alteration.

One afternoon I arrived up in Cappagh and as I pushed my bike up the gravel path I saw clouds of dust issuing from the kitchen window and heard disconcerting sounds. I looked in the window and there was Eugene in a choking swirl of dust, pausing to lay a sledgehammer on the floor and break for a smoke. The kitchen had been emptied of movables and some attempt had been made to cover the appliances with sheets. Eugene was all smiles when he saw me. I was just what he wanted, an excuse to stop for a fag and a cup of tea and a chat. It was heavy work in this weather; your man had hammered the sledded Polacks but that, remember, was on the ice.

The old house was going, giving way to the new design, giving way to the sledge. I joined him in a cup of tea and a cigarette, tried to return his quips and quotes, but I couldn't take my eyes from the tiny aperture through which I could see into the front room where I had sat at the table and first glimpsed the possibility of seeing through the squiggles of the Greek alphabet. The fire, the fruit moved to the sideboard, the smoking cigarette in the ashtray beside the typewriter on the table. And it was always warm, in summer or winter, always shining with excitement like the brasses by the fire, always busy but always neat. I could now for the first time see exactly what the kitchen wall was made of: under the paint was a thick skin of white plaster and under that the basic blocks. There was dust everywhere. Even though he had only made a beginning on the wall, knocking off a square foot or so of plaster and making a token penetration with a long chisel, it was as if a bomb had gone off. Five minutes there and your mouth was coated with dust, so much so that you thought the cigarette was stale; tea seemed a great idea until you tasted it and it clung to the back of your mouth like a cobweb. A bomb could not have changed the room any more: the acoustics were different and it was suddenly a dump, a place that had been deserted for years. I barely managed to prevent myself from spitting on the floor – as I had often done while working on houses in London.

I did my share of swinging the sledge and wheeling rubble out in the barrow. I was helping Eugene. Did I ever believe in the new place? I don't know. Did Eugene? For how long? Deep down, did he ever intend or want to do anything other than destroy the old place? Was he – were we – aware that having done the simple destruction we lacked both the will and the ability to begin to build again?

In late August I was in Galway on holiday, working on a poem and listening to the Pastoral, when a letter arrived from Eugene. The naked energy of the opening paragraph amazed me.

K. Xrds. Mon. 21/8/67

Fin, it's happened. Biro's begun to flow. Herewith the first
fruits. It was the doorway of some ancient celtic church,
standing in the wilderness, white and red sandstone. She had
discovered it in her solitary walks in the countryside beyond
the Barrow. Incomparable, celtic, comic, classic, abstract as
Plato himself. The classic arch inscribed with celtic doodles,
noodles, & scripture. Narrow, a gash, opening on the rainbright
Irish sky. Quaint as the *Miller's Tale*. Pure art.

It was the surprise of finding it, following the girl with
amber sandals through the nettles and dock. To write the verse
took an immense effort to overcome the paralysis. Kept saying,
if Kearney can do it why can't I? Began then, sat up in bed, &
had the first draft finished in an hour. Am now for whole
volumes in folio. I prithee do not mock me fellow student –
don't laugh at this verse, it may be a poor thing, but my own.
And it's the first.

How are things in the wilderness? Don't be too eager. The
doorway is always gifted suddenly, quietly, surprisingly, *luce
ducente.*

No hurry with the Mini, for another fortnight at least, but
move whenever the spirit moves you.

Love to the family,

E.

I devoured the poem. Knowing the code, I could translate the secret
history, could see his guarded heart reflected in the white quartz, could
sense his fear of opening the heart again to the envy of το θειον. But it
had happened.

and heart rises ridiculously.

And then a vision of the new found land? Or a waking dream?

Look – but we have looked so many thousand times –
yet look, consider this enlargement,
release of the hills in mist of light and stone
and all man's patchwork of his days and fields
resolved in a design of delicate distances.
So what? Now bend,
kneel, smiling at one's simplicity,
and kiss the cold breast of her
upon its sharpest bit, saying:
Lifegiving bitterness, mother of the good,
temper us, thieves and adulterers,
now in this nick of time
and in the empty moment of our truth...

I knew then that he would leave Cappagh. The bungalow was a thing of the past. We were both on the move. With his flowing lines still echoing in my ears I went back to my own halting effort, 'The Will and Testament of Larry Lynch', and tried to finish it off.

> I feel the foliage of the Abscissatic Ocean,
> The calm of the already dead,
> Devoted to the sloping fields
> Which overlook the river of my school days.
> Say, when new lymphs are bathing in the pools,
> Which of the daughters of the daughters of Eve
> Will feed to what new family
> The strange cabbage of me?
>
> The old men shuffle off but I remain:
> Only son of an only son, end of a harmless line,
> The name will live in telephone directories,
> Conjuring up the black protruding tongue
> And the rude expression of disentangled eyes.

In a way, I was the one who stuck it out: come October I was back in UCD picking up lists of tutorial students and planning a sustained crash course that would last the best part of a year and would result in a travelling studentship.

Eugene had begun his three years' wandering in the desert. My three years were spent in an old and beautiful university city. We never lost touch: we were in constant correspondence and still used the discourse we had evolved over the years. On two or three occasions he included stinging remarks in his letters but they never seemed to matter very much. I knew now that he had been hurt deeply, no matter how he tried to disguise it. I was growing up a little myself. I realised now that much of what I had understood as eternal wisdom had been part of his defence against a world which had always sought to exclude him. He had every reason to believe that the gods were envious. Just when he had scraped and slaved his way to where he wanted to be – writing in Cappagh while Una painted in the next room – the bomb had gone off. Who could blame him if he was convinced that somebody who had had it all as easy as I had was due for an awful fall? Who could blame him for believing that the difficult was beautiful? Who could blame him for believing that the empty desert was preferable to the gothic politics of university life? . . .

Eschew criticism (except to make a few bob now & then when things are tight). Criticism is good gymnastic (same as the paradigms of the Greek irregular verbs), & helps to clear one's own ideas. But the best criticism is anonymous, hidden in the texture of some rumbustious parable for the groundlings. Write everything and anything that comes your way (you have never sent me crap). Learn to know about people & things. Discern the difference between mud & muck. Watch patterns emerging – but slowly, do not try to shape the pattern of things: the emergence of pattern in a life or a work is the unplanned, living element: the inspiration. Then, in your forties, you may, by some sheer accident, produce a *Robinson Crusoe*, a *Lear*, a *Diabolical Comedy*, a *Siege of Syracuse*, a *Nana*, or an Acts of the Apostles. Or even if you left one little Lucy verse before going down into the empty moment of our truth.

We want makers more than mod. lits. Immerse yourself in scholarship, then go right out into the world, & make all the attempts & mistakes in the Bloody Book, not worrying too much, taking things as they come, gradually getting rid of wants (μνησε τον Σολωνα), & remembering that you are watched over in your sleepwalking at every crisis in your life.

August 1982. Drove to Ballinasloe for Eugene's funeral. Drank whiskey in the house of death. Thinking of bullfinches and almond slices, I exchanged formulae with friends and neighbours. I imagined Granny dealing out the cards as I read one of the lessons at the requiem mass, hearing my voice assure the upper air of the church that I would fear not death. There was music and prayer, handshakes and nodding of heads. None of it seemed real to me. It was only when some graveyard eulogist addressed the remains as Eugene that tears dribbled down my cheeks and I had to swallow the knowledge that Eugene was dead: I would never note those little manners of voice and thought again, never again be startled by that darting intelligence, never again be unnerved by his adamant gentleness, his sovereign humanity, his absolute kindness.

Il maestro di color che sanno was gone from me: I could never again consult him, knowing that he would know. The walks and sacred spots at Cappagh were buried beneath the junk and jumble of another story: where he had looked across at the copper spires and slate roofs of the Brightcity ravaged, there was the scrap metal currency of another family trying to make its own way, *lares penatesque*, the pots and pans of another world. The Sibyl's things were swaying on a makeshift clothesline where the roses had edged the little tennis court. The blackbird in the pine-wood was singing to the bereft. That tone of voice, that way of his, drawing the lids together over those protruding eyes and issuing a jet of cigarette smoke. Heads lowered and teeth set as the lid of the coffin snarls like a snare drum under the pebbles. Sedimentary, my dear Fin. Perced to the roote. Observe carefully the little ways of the tribe, note especially the eyes and the gestures, those miraculous hands, miraculous the only bloody word for them, the keys to the kingdom, the great play that dwarfs all our little dramas. To what two gifts may the seven gifts of the Holy Ghost be reduced? Wisdom and understanding. Sure, Fin, but the trick is to distinguish between the two and to work out what is meant by *and*.

> and going by the doorway discovers
> a canebrake of raspberries, late ripening,
> kindling in a dusk of leafgreen and underlight
> breastbuds hang hid.

And what is it? Agh yes: and heart rises ridiculously. Upon me solemn oath, you'd have to laugh. The patch of ice in the school yard sharply and overwhelmingly discovered: the sudden enlightenment, the aftershock shooting up the vertebrae, the fall of our fathers which determines all our faiths and forward passes, our poets and our stand-up comics. Open the box. I wouldn't have missed this for a wilderness of monkeys. Gimme the facts, sonny, the precise facts and cut the technicolour. *Sunt lachrymae rerum*: Jaysus I'm shot! Would that this were for Disneyland. Make a shine of the curst. What wild ecstasy? Will no one tell me what she sings? Did he ever think of asking her? Listen to what the other man says: I cannot see what flowers are at my feet. Well, in the case of this most precisely observant of young men, we may certainly ask: why not? He too guesses, but note the precision. Tried to describe it scientifically. Science: *scio, scire, scivi, scitum*: I know, to know, I knew, known. Not quite as easy as *amo, amare, amavi, amatum*. And I don't mean the conjugation – or maybe I do. Odd phrase: negative capability. We're all attracted to the QED lark but you'd be at it till you were blue in the face and still you wouldn't be much the wiser. Those are pearls that were his eyes. Now you're talking, Barney, give him the money. The oddest thing on God's earth, Fin, but . . . oh jay, look at the time it is: you better be going back with the others.

Eugene!

> A sunk track suddenly shadowed,
> hovel here once, the door is unhinged,
> one thrusts through thorns as far as the threshold
> dank mouth, empty, floor dark with dung
> where earthchildren once lay along the earth
> flushed in the delight of the fire's flaming.
> A touch of tears for things, one turns away
>
> and going by the doorway discovers
> a canebreak of raspberries, late ripening,
> kindling in a dusk of leafgreen and underlight
> breastbuds hang hid.

What will you – or anyone else – make of that secret history? You see, I know where Eugene found that canebreak of raspberries. I have a fair idea of his feelings at the time. I can hear him drafting the poem in his mind, can feel the tears welling up behind his eyes, can see him turning away and putting a brave face on the finale: the use of the impersonal 'one turns away' is a dead giveaway.

Eugene stumbles into the overgrown hovel and imagines a history. It is hardly surprising that the history is based on his own experience, partly on his own happy childhood around the fire in Ballinasloe but to a much greater extent, I feel, on his more recent memories of the bungalow in Cappagh. He

and Una had had no earthchildren of their own: they had
never known what it was like to see the eyes of their children
flashing around the fire. All those nights and days that I spent
up there. Did it ever occur to Eugene or Una that I was...?
Did it ever occur to me in those days? *Sunt lachrymae rerum* and
no mistake.

Eugene and I drifted apart when he went into the wilderness
and I went away to experience, as you know, the joys of being
a doctoral student in Cambridge in the late sixties. I didn't
know at the time that we were drifting apart – we wrote to
each other quite frequently and I spent a weekend with him
during some Christmas vacation – but things would never be
quite the same again. Back in Ireland, I was always in written
contact with him and once every couple of years I arranged for
him to come to lecture at UCC – but now even I knew that
things had changed. In fact both of us had changed a lot.
Though I still looked up to him as to nobody else, I was no
longer a student: I was married with a wife and children of my
own. Eugene had changed too but in a more subtle way. In
some ways he hadn't changed at all – I could often, for
example, anticipate precisely what his reaction would be, even
what phrases he would use – but in fact he was a different
person from the man who lived with Una in Cappagh. Una's
death had changed him; for all his show of stoicism he never
came to terms with it. More and more he came to base his life
on loss.

If only Una had lived. If only Eugene had been sufficiently
successful to enable him to forget about success and failure. If.

But Una's death confirmed some part of him. Not only was
her death a horrible wound, it was also a vindication – maybe
even a definition – of his sense of το θειον. The Greeks had the
situation sized up four thousand years ago. καλα τα χαλεπα.

8.00 pm. After all those ifs and I-don't-knows I decided to
take a walk. For a while I continued to play with the puzzle
that is the final phase of Eugene's life. Suddenly I heard a
glorious run of birdsong and was lucky enough to locate the
source: a luxuriant goldfinch. I smiled at the irony because it

was Eugene's father in Ballinasloe who first introduced me to the song and the colours of the goldfinch. And I smiled again when I remembered that I had forgotten to add to the Eugene typescript a translation of the poem about the cuckoo by Blind James McCourt. The rest of my walk was in a daze as I tried to come up with some kind of a decent version of the Irish. As you will see below, I failed.

WELCOME THE SWEETEST BIRD

Welcome the sweetest bird on the boughs
Singing sunwards from the fringe of the bush!
It lengthens the anguish of my hours
Not to see her when the spring grass comes.

Though I cannot see her shape I can hear
The sound of the bird they call the cuckoo;
The sight of her on the tips of the branches
Is something, sadly, I have been refused.

People who enjoy the sight of the bird
And the Irish landscape north and south
And the flowering hillocks everywhere –
How lucky they are when they recount them.

If only I'd been granted the gift of seeing,
To see all alone the grandeur of growing leaves;
It's part of my sadness not like others to speed
For a sight of the cuckoo serene on the edge of the trees.

No shilling for that translation. Mind you: it's not as easily done as I expected. There are all kinds of little effects in the Irish which you don't notice until you try to translate the words or phrases which contain them. You'll have to take my word for it: the original is not a bad poem. Nor is it as simple as it sounds: at the end you are surprised to realise how well the little pastoral vignettes have revealed the inner darkness of the poet.

Out on my walk, trying to translate and count syllables and search for rhymes and then trying to fit it together verse by verse, I often closed my eyes and whenever I did I saw Eugene sitting on the grassy bank opposite the bungalow in Cappagh on a fine early summer's day in the late fifties. I remembered the sunny classroom and thinking that the road to Omeath – where Blind James lived – would have passed by Eugene's bungalow. Did the brain-charged schoolboy ever think of Eugene as Blind James? Or has that vision come from my present musings?

And suddenly, shooting across time and space, an apocalypse: it was in this very house I first heard that Eugene was dead. How could that have ever slipped my mind? Yet it did. Not once in the past four or five days had I recalled what happened in this hallway in August 1982. Almost to the day.

Kate and the girls and I were on holiday with our American friend, John, staying in a rented house about ten miles from Clifden. There was a phone in the house but it was a primitive affair and we were not even sure if it worked at all; we had tried it several times, cranking it up with one of those old starting handles, but we never got anywhere with it. The lack of a phone didn't bother me but John wanted to be available for calls from San Francisco and so we were in the habit of using the post office phone in a nearby village. One morning John came back from the phone with a confused message which seemed to suggest that somebody from America had been trying to contact me urgently. I drove over to the post office where – of course – the person who had been taking the calls was no longer on duty. All I could think of doing was asking the local operator to put any call for me through to Bernard in Clifden: he would have enough cop-on to find out what was happening. We were barely back in the house when Bernard arrived over from Clifden with the news that there would be a call for me at lunch time. And here we were drinking tea and beginning to doubt the status of these mysterious calls from America when the phone rang. Kate and John applauded, I identified myself to the operator and heard her tell somebody to go ahead. It was my father. He had almost given up trying to get me. Eugene was dead. Knowing I was in Connemara with an American friend, my father had had me paged on the local Irish language radio station. The funeral was in Ballinasloe the following day. I would head over there immediately and stay the night; I didn't know where, most likely with Tom and Bridie Watters. And him? He would drive down with my mother for the funeral and see me there.

And so I got into the car and headed for Ballinasloe. I turned off the road at Moycullen so that I could drive through Spiddal and along the coast road to Galway – reversing the journey that I had first taken with Eugene in his Ford Anglia ZH 6103 in the summer of 1957. A quarter of a century had passed. And more.

BRENDAN

THURSDAY: 11.00

Weather fine. Unlike me. Felt I had to get out of the house
when I had finished writing my comments on the previous
section. Wanted to get away from memories of Eugene and the
confused thoughts they generated. Walked into a restaurant in
Clifden and ordered a big dinner and a bottle of Burgundy.
Had two vodkas while waiting for the meal but neither the
vodkas nor the Burgundy banished the spectre of Eugene. Kept
thinking about him. Would Solon consider him happy? Or
merely unlucky? Wondered if he was doomed in some way,
maybe from birth or beyond, if his horoscope had been drawn
before the geometry of the Nile valley. 'A definitive biography.
Imagine that, Fin: a grown man using such a meaningless
phrase.' Bought another bottle of the same Burgundy from an
adjacent off-licence and rambled back to the house babbling of
the green fields of Finglas and Garbally. Didn't really intend to
open the second bottle. Lay on the sofa and tried to do a deal

with sleep. Sudden nightmare. Eugene-like figure fishing a
deep swirling pool. Me – in short trousers – standing beside
him. Eugene reeling in with difficulty as if he is bringing up a
log from the bottom. But it is no log at the end of the line:
it's a body, hooked at the back of the neck, being dragged
along the surface. Inches from the bank, the body rolls over
and there is the white face of Una's first sketch. I finished most
of the second bottle before I passed out.

I will spare you the details of this morning's alcoholic
poisoning. I wish I could do the same for me. If my head
wasn't so sore I would laugh at the ironic situation that sees
me here, racked with a hangover, about to raise the spectre of
Brendan Behan.

The character of Decco Deane attracted more attention than
any other in the book. Predictably, I suppose. It was the only
one based on a personality of international reputation. The
comments didn't bother me a lot one way or the other. I had
deduced early on that the general tone of the book was
somewhat cooler than that of my own recollections. ('Sharp', as
I have already told you, was the favoured adjective.) Apart
altogether from nuances of tone, I was reasonably certain that
not all the Behan episodes of the book were quite as I
remembered their actual correlatives. There was nothing in the
general commentary to generate the kind of unease I had felt
in the case of Eugene.

As far as I can make out, there are five episodes in *Gone The Time* in
which Declan Deane, notoriously rumbustious guerrilla-turned-
dramatist, plays a prominent part. He takes the central character,
Casement Kelly, *aet.* fifteen, to the races at Leopardstown on Stephen's
Day; shortly afterwards he visits Casement at boarding school and
charms his clerical instructors out of their anxiety; he writes to Casement
from America and includes a ten-dollar bill; he takes Casement – now
a student at UCD – into McDaid's where, having put on a spellbinding

performance, he gets obstreperously drunk and is put out and barred; while attending a drama festival in Galway, Casement hears of Deane's death in hospital in Dublin. Again, as far as I can make out, the papers tended to exaggerate the role of Deane within the novel. In the popular press in Ireland – especially the *Herald*, the *Evening Press*, the *Irish Times* and the *Sunday World* – the writers, both staff journalists and 'imported' academics and theatrical folk et cetera, all seized on the character of Decco Deane with such gusto that some of their constant readers – for example, the elderly unemployed in public libraries – could easily have come away with the idea that the book was primarily about the relations between Casement Kelly and Declan Deane.

It is hardly surprising that the media people made much of Deane; it would have been surprising if they hadn't. After all, the person on whom – by common consent – the character was based had served his time as a journalist and had always been good for a headline quote and five hundred words of marketable copy. Apart altogether from such professional courtesy and distinct from his literary achievement, Behan was the most memorable Dublin character of the century, not only warm in himself but a source of warmth in others, glowing like a naughty deed in a classroom world. Even today, when less than half the population would ever have heard the noise he made, any mention of his name will cause people to pause and look and listen in anticipation of some story of irreverent generosity.

Almost everybody seemed to notice the episode in which Declan Deane takes the young Casement to the races: the boy is tickled to be at the centre of so much attention and to be tasting the high life – rambling in the paddock, gorging himself in the restaurant, backing winners and going home by taxi. It was like a day in the garden of paradise. Even the weather was perfect. I remember a big blue sky and a warm sunlit day although I know it was cold because it was Stephen's Day and Brendan was wearing a thick black Crombie coat; I never felt the cold and so how could I remember it? The first horse I backed was called Annabelle and she romped home easily – so easily that I thought there was another lap – earning fortunes for Brendan and me. I had two bob each way with the tote; to judge from Brendan's victory dance and his lyrical testimony to my beginner's luck, he had plunged a little more deeply with the bookies. And then, our pockets bulging with money, we rambled into the restaurant where Brendan demanded and got the best of attention and service. Some of the other customers were piqued at the presence of a jumped-up gurrier who cared little for the nuances of the class system but before long Brendan had them in fits of laughter, crunching and masticating amounts of raw celery thunderously and informing all who cared to listen that amongst the upper classes of Bulgaria the quiet chewing of one's celery was a social solecism on a par with farting in the royal presence. And as they all haw-hawed, simulating varying degrees of shock, he turned to me and gave as his considered opinion that he and I were the only people in the restaurant who knew what a fucking solecism was. Some of my elders and betters exchanged knowing glances when Brendan called for a waiter and ordered Club Cola for his cousin here and a soda water for himself. Even I could see that many of them assumed that his carelessly gregarious performance was fuelled by something stronger than soda water and that he had made some sort of an arrangement with the bar. But they were wrong. It was soda water. Brendan was on the wagon, in good physical shape and enjoying his fame, breaking the silence of the stiff and the sullen with outbursts of irresistible misbehaviour.

Several of the more 'literary' reviewers made much of the episode in which young Casement, having been asked by a priest in confession if he has ever thought of the religious life, goes into the refectory where he finds waiting for him a letter from Decco Deane which contains – along with a ten-dollar bill – an account of dining with Marilyn Monroe. The episode is a strange series of variations on what actually happened. There was at least one occasion in which a priest asked if I had considered the possibility that I had what used to be referred to – with confident simplicity – as a vocation, but I don't remember a letter from Brendan arriving so closely on the heels of such a confessional confrontation. I do remember at least one ten-dollar bill, and a note from Hollywood that mentioned Jayne Mansfield. I know he met Marilyn and Arthur Miller – he also met the Marx Brothers and Norman Mailer – but I can't recall any letter referring to Marilyn.

Not that all the episodes are factual: far from it. For example, I was never with Brendan when he was thrown out of McDaid's; strange to relate, I can't ever remember being with Brendan in McDaid's. In the late forties and fifties he had been amongst the most prominent of the bohemian set that frequented McDaid's and it is the pub with which his name is most commonly linked, but I was never with him in McDaid's and I have the feeling that he did not go in there very often in the years in question. Why not? I could guess at a hundred reasons but the most likely is that, *mutatis mutandis*, just as I do not frequent McDaid's now because it is clearly no longer the kind of place it was when I was a student, so Brendan may have avoided it then because it was so different from the place in which he had set the table on a roar in years gone by. I have read accounts of his performances in McDaid's and in the Catacombs and I can easily believe how extraordinary they were because I have seen him turning a bar full of strangers – many of whom resented his intrusion into their privacy – into an audience of happy, smiling, laughing people who could not believe their good fortune in being present at the greatest little free show on earth, a non-stop routine of song and dance and stories dramatised with grotesque actions and outlandish mimicry. And I have seen him fail to do so: a lumbering hulk of a man, trying to rise from the mental mire of alcohol and despair, falling back on the old routines and realising that the timing was gone, the delivery was slurred, the memory was gapped, the audience turning away. And I have seen this prince of good humour collapse into arrogance, aggression and obscenity, abusing customers and bar staff as if he wanted to be beaten up and kicked out. It wasn't always quite that bad. Sometimes a friendly old barman would size up the situation and ensure that Brendan was away in a taxi before he got any worse. In many ways the most painful experience for him was to be refused service not because he was drunk or disorderly but because, given his reputation, nobody wanted to give him the chance. But it was nearly always a question of how drunk he was, how capable he was of taking the blows. It was appalling to have to drag him out of a pub with a barman offering pushes and insults from behind. It was almost enjoyable if Brendan was sober enough to castigate his opponents, dismissing the establishment as nothing more than a kip and the employees as so many arse-licking lackeys and informers, and then out into the street with his head thrown back and his left fist pumping:

Arise ye starvelings from your slumbers,
Arise ye criminals of want,

For reason in revolt now thunders
At last ends the age of cant;
Now away with all superstitions,
Servile masses, arise, arise!
We'll change forthwith the old conditions
And spurn the dust to win the prize.

Nor did Brendan ever make it to Garbally à la Decco Deane. He often promised to drop in the next time he was going to Connemara and I often imagined what it would be like to be told that I had a call and to rush up to the house and find Brendan laughing and joking in Irish with the president. When his blood was up about Irish history or politics or imprisonment or the Communist revolution he could foam at the mouth and fulminate against the black bastards of druids but when he got anyway close to a priest who would talk or listen to him he was the soul of courteous good humour. There were some priests at Garbally who would have been happier to stay out of his way but on the other hand there were some who would have liked to meet him, one or two who would have enjoyed a jar and a joke with him, and the president during my time, Father Page, was such a devotee of the Irish language that he would have welcomed and fed Mao Tse-tung if he'd had a smattering of Irish. It would have been a howl: Brendan and Father Page in the president's room, Father Page tidying up the place and wondering what to do next with this strange visitor, Brendan with a big cut glass of whiskey in his hand, chuckling away and explaining the subtle differences between a diocesan seminary boarding school and a borstal institution.

That's the way I imagined it would be and as far as I can make out that's the way it is in *Gone The Time*. But as a matter of historical fact, it never happened that way or any other way.

Which reminds me of the surprisingly energetic review in *The Economist*. This anonymous piece – entitled 'Roman sans Clef' – began with the statement that *Gone The Time* would be read, especially in Ireland, as 'a puzzle in the form of prose fiction'. Even a mere Englishman could see that the character of Decco Deane was a very thinly disguised version of Brendan Behan, and the same mere Englishman would wager a pint or two of Guinness that the rest of the characters were equally thinly disguised versions of real people. But could it be, wondered this *Anglicus ignotus*, that the author was laying a false trail? That, for reasons best known to himself, he was inviting the reader to conclude that everything in the book was based on historical actuality? And that, as a consequence, he could more or less do what he liked without ever losing credit with his reader?

> Take, for example, the scene towards the end, when Casement Kelly hears of the death of his relation, Decco Deane, the famously gifted but suicidally alcoholic dramatist who is so blatantly based on Brendan Behan. Where is Casement when the news breaks? About to go into a theatre. How come? He is at a varsity drama festival where he has just won a special award for – wait for it – his translation of the choral odes of *Oedipus Rex* into Gaelic! Grief-stricken, he sits in the almost empty theatre with his girlfriend, the theatre where he has just heard, in his own words, the thoughts of Sophocles on the rise and fall of brilliant men. The *mise en scène* is elegant and economic but the style is anything but naturalistic. The coincidence of the death of one dramatist with the first success of another would, in a realist text, be extreme; the location in the empty theatre, the choice of Sophocles, would be unacceptable. But, the technique claims, it must be true: Decco Deane is Brendan Behan and therefore everything else in the book coincides with an historical fact. I would resist such a presentation of the book and prefer to believe that the passage is true in the sense that it is utterly convincing but such truth is more likely to derive from a carefully creative arrangement of possibility rather than from simple exercise of memory.

One brief comment: my memory of first hearing of the death of Brendan Behan is precisely as in the account of *Gone The Time* given by the reviewer in *The Economist*.

But back to the beginning. There I was, fifteen at the most, scrubbed and rubbed, the scholarship boy intent on a serious literary experience, arriving at his house in Ballsbridge. Did I by any chance think I knew what I was doing when I picked up the large stone (or small rock) which clearly lay in the porch for that purpose and knocked on the knockerless door of this notorious relation whose successes and whose sins had been sensationalised in all the newspapers?

Twice he had barrelled into my childhood. Once – it would have been about 1950 – I was over in the Behans' house, 70 Kildare Road, with my mother – was it winter time or merely late in the evening? – when Brendan was announced and in he came all dark and loud and merry. He was off to France with nothing but a toothbrush in his top pocket and before he went he stood over in the corner holding a bottle and a glass of stout and everybody was asking him to sing 'My Lagan Love' and after a while there was a hush and he sang it, looking all serious and sorrowful. Not long afterwards, a year or two at the most, Mammy and I were walking up Grafton Street when we met this strange man. I remember him as being loose – long hair falling over his forehead, his shirt open on his chest, his clothes all baggy, his voice heard above all the noises of the street – and as he was going away he gave me sixpence and laughed and shouted out so that everybody turned to see what was wrong: 'Don't tell your ou' fella.'

The untidy figure who now answered the door knew who I was and the first thing he did was to tell his wife Beatrice what great people Con and Maisie were and how lucky I was. That was it: before I got my coat opened he was telling me to sit down and shut up for the sake of Jesu, ordering Beatrice to rustle up a bit of breakfast, assuring me that there was no need to go on with good manners or with any of that old bollox with him, that I could save all that for the druids down in Galway.

I wasn't sure how to take the bit about the druids. As luck would have it, I was in the only religious phase of my life and was disposed to defend the one, holy, Catholic and apostolic against all comers. At the age of nine I had touched the communion wafer with my teeth and had been afraid to confess such an appalling sin. Between that crime and a long confessional talk with the retreat priest during my first term at Garbally I had lived in constant nightly terror of sizzling for all eternity. While the memory of that moment of infinite reprieve lasted I was a grateful and loyal member of the Roman Catholic church. Consequently, I felt Brendan was being a little unfair – comparing Garbally with borstal and the priests with witch doctors – but you couldn't help laughing at him when he said things like that. Everybody laughed when Brendan ridiculed anybody. Even people who did not want to laugh, people who wanted to dislike him. He didn't care about what other people cared about: he didn't care about which knife and fork you were supposed to use, and he would shout across the road, across the room, and he just said exactly what he wanted how he wanted and if somebody got stuck up and spoke down to him, Brendan would tell the old bollox to go 'way for jaysesake and let the rest of the people get on with enjoying themselves which was hard enough anyway without some dull scruffy crawthumping creeping Jesus with a poisonous drip at the end of his miserable nose and his long informer's face like a horse's hole trying to put a damper on things: go home outa that to your unfortunate long-suffering wife and stop spending the money you got when you pawned her rings, go way for jaysesake, you're the same as your ou' fella that got six months for fraud, the grabbing huer, going round with a collection box and telling everybody the money was going to Little Willy. Little Willy me arse, the money was going to Dolly Fawcett, not that the decent girls there'd rather go hungry than to let the mean bastard get up on them, not bejayses if his little willy was studded with diamonds. Go on, off with you now, before I tell the decent citizens here how your grandfather threw the brick at poor James Connolly and him being dragged a cripple to Kilmainham to be shot.

> Tooralooralooraloo
> They're looking for monkeys up in the zoo
> And if I had a face like you
> I'd join the British Army.

And so after the bit of breakfast we spoke of school and studies and what I wanted to be when I grew up.

– Your father says you're interested in books. Would you like to be a writer?

What thoughts crossed my mind? Did I want to provoke him? Did I want to avoid giving the impression of flattering him? Of behaving like a child? Like a fan? Or did I still feel myself indebted to the Passionist preacher who had given me the greatest gift I had ever received, the freedom to look forward to bed at the end of a long day?

– Whatever I decide to do, I have to consider my end.

– Your what?

– My end.

– What do you mean?

– I mean that I have to consider how I will feel about it when I am dying, when I look back at my life and . . .

Brendan was moving his head up and down slowly, as if he had difficulty in believing what he was hearing:

– So it's your last hour you're worried about?

I nodded my general approval of his interpretation and was about to explain that it wasn't so much a matter of being worried as of –

– Beatrice!

The room exploded as he stood up, scattering newspapers and a milk jug, stammering with exuberance, consumed with comic delight, roaring at Beatrice to come in from the kitchen.

– Beatrice, drop whatever you're doing and come in quick; come in for the love of Jesus and listen to this. There's this young fella here going on about his end and I declare to Christ it isn't his arse he's talking about at all!

And even I had to laugh – and thank Jesus that there was somebody who could make me laugh in the aftermath of such a declaration, thank Jesus that there was somebody who was kind enough to want to make me laugh, someone who could hear me talk of death in my little treble voice and still want to learn more about me. We got on to books and writers – but not his books, not his writings, nor had he heard of Eugene Watters – and then it was time for the races. I had never been to a race meeting. Well that, me young *scoláire*, is a deficiency which will soon be remedied. Let us ring for a taxi. You go and ring the taxi; the number is beside the telephone out in the hall.

And so we had our day at the races.

I never again saw him in such unflawed good form as on that first day. There were other times when he wasn't actually drinking but he was never as happy and healthy as he was the day of the races. Were there days when he drank a lot and got drunk in a normal way? I only remember the days when he got drunk so quickly and so totally that it was frightening. One brandy and he was gone. Goodnight, Joe Doyle.

But I only thought how sad it was that when he could have been talking and singing and reciting and joking he was slouched there unshaven in the corner of a bar, muttering and stumbling about in the haunted labyrinth of the past. I didn't know or understand or even fear very much. I didn't know then what a young man he was – about thirty-seven when we went to the races, only forty-one when he died; I had no comprehension of what it felt like for a working-class Dubliner who had spent most of his adolescent and adult life in prison to hit the literary jackpot, no notion of the temptations offered by the international media, only the vaguest idea of the claims that his Irish past refused to waive.

Of course I felt sorry for him, sorry that he suffered so much, but I always thought he would survive, that he would walk out of hospital as he always had, posing and quipping for the press, giving them a headline with death in it, pulling his jacket over his head, joining his hands, his eyes to heaven and his mouth puckered with devotion as he intones 'To Jesus' Heart All Burning'. I never knew how much his heart was burning with the terrible certainty that he wasn't going to pull out of it because he didn't want to pull out of it, that he had lost hope in his ability to write again and that, as he said himself, he was nothing if not a writer and so, if he couldn't be a writer, he would be nothing.

But that was the very end. There were intervals during which the media reported his triumphs, his defeats, his firm purposes of amendment: his success somewhere or other in America, his witty encounter with some star, his plans for a new kind of show, his failure to turn up in some theatre, his night in some cell, his resolution to come home and drink soda water and write. And always the news, however painful, was accompanied by a good line. But the collapses were becoming more painfully squalid and the line more predictable.

And yet I always hoped we would have another day at the races. He wrote me several letters from America. The thrill of seeing his hand-writing. He always wrote to me in Irish and on hotel stationery – I think I still have one in blue from the Algonquin in New York – and always included five or ten dollars. And he always sounded in good form. Vassar he recommended as the ideal place in which to continue my studies.

Once he rang me at Garbally. The one phone, outside the president's room, was normally only used on the most serious and urgent business and so a summons was answered with trepidation and anxious fears for the welfare of one's family. I think I received two phone calls in my five years there. One was from a representative of Gateaux Cakes Limited in response to my written complaint about the poor quality of their tipsy cakes; the other was from Brendan. It was during second study, between 8.15 and 9.45, that I was told there was a telephone call for me up at the house and I ran out into the night, my heart pounding as my imagination produced an endless series of domestic disasters. I picked up the receiver and paused a few seconds to get my breath back.

– And by Jayses daughter, you sound to me as if you could give a good account of yourself. I'd say the boyfriend wouldn't be up to much by the time he'd got you home.

– G'way, Mr Behan, you're an awful man. I'd lose my job if anybody knew what you were saying to me.

– So long as you wouldn't lose your immortal soul or anything else that you couldn't replace. Ha? Have you me?

Relieved, I interrupted.

– Brendan, is that you?

– It is indeed, me oul' flower. *Ça va?* I was just talking to a lovely girl there be the name of Mary and I think you could do worse than get the full of your arms of the same *girseach*. Would ye be on, Mary, for a bit of *conas tá tú*, yourself and a lively young scrum-half with fluent Irish? Would you be on, Mary? Mary? She's gone. Ah, you would have liked her, Fintan. Tell us this much and tell us no more: how are ye getting on down there in the wilds of the County Galway?

He had just rung up for a chat. He had been meaning to do it for a while but never got round to it. He'd been to America: New York was a marvellous place. He would take me there some day soon. The show was doing very well but that's not what he wanted to talk about. Was I allowed have visitors there? Any time at all? What do visitors do? Sure I know Hayden's well. And would the druids mind? I mean, would they mind me? *Ara mo ghraidhin thú, a bhuachaill. Éist liom anois agus ná bac le cad tá ar siúl agam: an bhfuil tú ceart go leor ansin? Níl aon rud ag teastáil uait? Seachas an rud eile, ar ndoigh. Tá tú OK ó thaobh an airgid de? Sure? Look, scríobhfaidh mé chugat agus déanfaidh mé iarracht cuairt a thabhairt ort ansin amach anseo. OK?* (Me life on ye, boy. Listen to me now and don't mind what I'm up to: are you all right there? You don't need anything? Apart from the other thing, of course. You're OK for money? Sure? Look, I'll write to you and I'll try to come and see you there one of these days. OK?)

He never made it to Garbally, never charmed the president in the sweet and princely discourse of the Gael.

It was all over, though nobody knew it only himself. He must have known that he was finished as a writer. Under pressure from publishers whose advances he had already spent, he was forced to tape-record his books. The signs were there for those who could read them, even on that fine morning in August 1962 when – almost three crucial years older than the child who had gone to the races – I cycled from Finglas to Angelsea Road and was admitted by Beatrice who was on the phone in the hall. She smiled and indicated that Brendan was at home but that he was upstairs in bed; then she continued her phone conversation which was to the effect that yes the parcel had arrived and yes Brendan was going to do them and yes she had told him how urgent they were and yes she would keep at him and yes as soon as he came back she would ask him to call them but you know Brendan but yes she would do her best and yes he was well enough and would be going to London soon.

– Brendan! Fintan's here. And that was London again to say that you were supposed to have sent back that parcel weeks ago. You better do it this morning; remember we're going out this afternoon.

Brendan was coming down the stairs wearing only a pyjama jacket, muttering his *fáilte romhat*, looking healthy enough but not very happy. Beatrice reminded him again of what he was supposed to have done but he just waved her away and asked her to mind her own business and make some tea. I was happy to hear him ask for tea. It meant we could talk and there was a lot to talk about. *The Hostage* had been chosen in Paris that summer as the best foreign play and the papers had been going on about a new play and a new book. He was proud of his success in Paris, a city he had once been poor in, but that was as far as he would go on the subject of his literary career. The reports in the paper were all fucking rubbish: there was no new book. Beatrice interrupted to say that Brendan was only joking, that the book was a travel book called *Brendan Behan's Island* and it would be published within a few weeks. At this point Brendan became quite vicious, asserting that, as he was supposed to have written the fucking thing, he should at least be allowed to know some fucking thing about it and that, as far as he was concerned, there was no new fucking book; there was a sheaf of shit called *Brendan Behan's Island* due out soon but it was neither a fucking book nor was it fucking new. When I asked about the play that he was writing in Irish, he got up and walked out of the room.

– Am I to be fuckingwell persecuted with this shite, morning, noon and night? How is it that everybody on earth is supposed to know more about this than me? I get up for a bit of breakfast and it starts all over again. Now every fucking eejit in Ireland gives me advice, every fucking schoolboy knows what's good for me.

– Brendan, that's not fair on Fintan.

– When I want to be told by you what's fair and what's not you'll know because I'll ask you but until I ask you I would be eternally grateful if you could to the best of your limited ability MIND YOUR OWN FUCKING BUSINESS! Do you hear me?

– Of course, Brendan. Will I make you a cup of tea, Fintan?

Brendan stormed out and I asked Beatrice if I should go.

– Not unless you want to, Fintan. Leave him alone for a few minutes; he'll be fine when he comes down again. He's not in the best of form for the last few days because he's not drinking at all, thank God. He'd be much better if that crowd in London got off his back about the new book.

She explained that the parcel out in the hall consisted of two hundred copies of the title page of his new book which Brendan had contracted to autograph for the American market. Brendan kept putting it off but he knew he had to do it and the longer he put it off the more London called him and the more cantankerous he got.

– Beatrice!

Brendan was in the front room and there was not the least trace of his recent temper in his voice.

– Where's that book I got for Fintan? You know, the *Only In America*? Agh, here it is.

Back he came into the dining room, radiant, politely accepting tea. I didn't even have to ask him to sign the book for me. Beatrice brought the tea things out to the kitchen and Brendan and I began to talk about school and rugby and the like. I don't know what led up to it but I remember telling him a story which he found fascinating to a degree which amazed and pleased me in equal measure.

A friend of mine had incurred the wrath of a prefect who threatened to report him to the president.

– The dirty little bollix of an informer! Go on.

There seemed no way out until I came up with a plan which might or might not work but which was our only chance. I got a sheet of official college notepaper – we all used the same notepaper, priests and students – and wrote a letter to the prefect in the handwriting of the president.

– Saying what?

Saying that my friend had gone to the president and explained the situation to him, admitting his fault and so on, confessing everything and saying how sorry he was. And going on to instruct the prefect to forget all about the business. And it worked.

– He fell for it? He really believed the letter came from the archdruid?

Yes. You see the president had a very distinct style of old-fashioned writing and all the students had seen it somewhere before – on reports and on notices.

– But how were you able to imitate it well enough to fool the grassin' bastard?

It was no problem. It was easy: very clear, very square and very straight.

– But how did you know that you could do it?

Some of us often messed about like that, imitating each other's hand-writing. It's easy after a while.

– Bejaysus and if you find it that easy you might have to watch it or you'll find yourself in another sort of boarding school altogether.

The phone rang and Brendan said that if it was them fuckers in London, he wasn't here. In fact it was a woman who was ringing up to say that she had just had a call from her brother who was a priest in America who had met Brendan in America somewhere and got his phone number from him with the encouragement to call on him if he ever got back to Ireland and though he didn't think he would be in Ireland in the immediate future he wanted Brendan to know that he had enjoyed meeting him and looked forward to seeing him some day soon either in America or in Ireland and that was why he had asked his sister who lived and worked in Dublin as a buyer in McBirney's to call him, just to say that he was thinking of him and although maybe she shouldn't say this ha-ha he was also praying for him sure what harm can it do and if it does good well and good and who's complaining.

– The same fucking druids have me destroyed. If I by some stroke of fortune manage to escape to hell for all eternity it will be the biggest defeat for the druids since Karl Marx began to put the skids under them and the biggest waste of prayer since the eucharistic congress.

– Listen to him, Fintan. You'd swear he did anything to discourage the priests. You should see him in America – and not only in America, Brendan, you're the same in Connemara: any priest, doesn't have to be Irish, mind you, but it helps, any priest that comes along is sure of a sign-ed book for himself and a generous contribution for the building fund. There's no such thing as a priest in America who is not building a new church, am I right, Brendan?

– Sure at least they're giving employment to the working class.

– Oh of course, and you'd say the same if the priest in Donnybrook asked you for a donation.

– Divil the much danger there is of those bastards coming near me unless they were well armed with bell, book and candle, malice and aforethought. They'd lose their regular customers if they took anything from me other than abuse. But, you know what? I thought your woman on the phone was a sister of that mad huer in California. Remember the priest in San Francisco who took us out to see his new church?

– I do. You went with him by yourself and left me drinking coffee in the Irish consulate. Tell Fintan the story.

– Wait till I see. Agh yes, when would it have been?

– What does that matter? It was last –

– Will you shut up, woman, and let me think: when was that strike-breaking scab beatified or whatever you call it?

– When was who what?

– Matt Talbot, Matt Talbot, for jaysesake. Who did you think I was talking about?

Beatrice was confused for a while and then she got it.

– Oh yes, now I see what you're getting at.

So now I was the only one confused – until I gathered that the story concerned Matt Talbot and had nothing to do with San Francisco . . . at least not to begin with.

At some crucial stage in the recognition of Talbot's special status – Brendan recognised him as special too but not for the same reasons as Rome and without any of the hesitation that characterised the actions of the Curia – the Dublin Corporation, in anticipation of crowds of devout visitors, decided to clean up the room in which Matt Talbot had spent his latter years, mortifying his flesh in many ways, not the least of which was by sleeping on a bare board of some kind.

– Now on whose graceful shoulders should the responsibility – or maybe I should say 'the honour' – of this task fall but on those of the ou' fella. Which indeed only goes to support the received opinion that the ways of the Lord are exceeding strange. Anyway, some guy in the corpo, directed by God or by somebody with a sense of humour, take your pick, decides that Frank Behan is the man for the job. Just give the place a bit of a dusting and a lick of paint where necessary, Frank, just so as they won't be able to say that the place was a pigsty when the visitors came to say their prayers and do whatever else they do in such places on such occasions. So off with your Uncle Frank and of course he's thinking in his own little pleasant way that if it was up to him Matt Talbot's bedroom would not be cleaned up, it'd fuckingwell be blown up. But howandever, he rambles over to the room and knocks on the door and this poor woman comes out wondering what's happening. Of course she's heard of Matt Talbot, yeah, who used to live here, yeah, Jayses it'd give you the creeps the thoughts of what he was up to betimes, God forgive me and him almost a saint. To clean the place up? Will I have to pay for it 'cos if that's the idea you can tell the corporation to forget about it right now. For nothing? Lovely. I ask you, who'd believe it and me just saying to me sister last Monday that the oul' place was beginning to get me down. And are you going to do it? Now? Lovely, come in. The what? That he used to sleep on? Looka mister, there was no bed here when I moved in and that's the truth, honest to God, mister. What? Oh Jesus, Mary and Holy Saint Joseph, what am I after doing? Oh Jesus, mister, you mean the plank? Oh lamb of Christ tonight! We burned it last winter, remember how cold it was after Christmas? Will I get into trouble, mister? Oh I hope you're right. Oh, that's right, don't tell anybody. Oh, you're a star, mister, but what are you going to do?

– Wasn't the poor oul' wan after burning the plank or whatever it was that the other oul' shite had been sleeping on or staying awake on or whatever it was he was doing on it for the greater glory of God in the small hours of the morning when he wasn't scabbing on his fellow workers or trying to break strikes for the greater profit of the employers

in the broad light of day. Not that this knocked a bother out of the ou'
fella. He just shagged off up to Inchicore, to the CIE railway works,
more than likely pausing to clear his mind in the Black Lion, and he arranged the immediate delivery of item one railway sleeper. He must
have been amused: a sleeper. And with nobody but the oul' wan the
wiser, he places the sleeper where he thinks a saint would like it – how
he worked that out is more nor the limitations of the human brain could
cope with, but however – he lays out the saint's bed and goes over it
with glasspaper to give it that slept-in look and then he touches up the
place here and there and then, his good deed done, he goes home for
his dinner.

– *Bhí go maith agus ní raibh go holc.* Or so I am reliably informed by
those who are better informed of such things than I am. The people
came in their thousands from all airts and parts, from Bantry Bay up to
Derry Quay and points much further afield, holy fathers, reverend
mothers and children of Mary, and all panting for the divine grace that
was to be showered on anybody who ejaculated in the presence of the
relics while muttering, in public or in private, dear devout dilapidated
Jesus, please make poor Matt a saint. Sure you'll never get the Irish out
of Ireland. Come in Dungannon we know your knock. And who
should come into the odour of sanctity but one Larry Qualter, late of
Loughrea in the County Galway but at present trading under the name
of Father Laurence Qualter CC and fighting the good fight out of the
parish of Nuestro Señor de las Putas somewhere on the outskirts of San
Francisco in the state of grace and California and no more bother to the
bould Larry to be nipping back to Ireland maurya to get a rub of the
relic of the Blessed Matt but no doubt he used the opportunity of the
pilgrimage to say hello to the plain people of Loughrea, to kiss the mammy and to take tea and biscuits and maybe a touch of something stronger
with the sister – she who rules the roost in McBirney's and who better
to do it? And up to the upper room he made his way, the holy blissful
martyr for to seek, and it was as if he was overcome with the gift of grace
for having kissed the bed on which the saint was wont to lie, the bould
Larry fell upon it and almost foamed at the mouth, such was the intensity
of his transport, or so it seemed to them as was queuing up behind him
wishing to Jayses he'd get his skates on and get moving and let somebody
else get a gick at the relic.

– Time which waiteth for no man passed on apace. And in the fullness of that same sovereign time it pleased the Lord in his infinite wisdom to send his servant Brendan – not the navigator but your humble scribe whom you find here before you – across the water to Amerikay and across Amerikay to the city of the Golden Gates. And there I was like stout Cortez gazing at the Pacific and at a few other things besides and passing the time of day in the congenial company of hacks and whores of all descriptions, all out to make a buck as quickly and as quietly as possible, preferably without having to work up a sweat or having to get up too early in the morning. This is as true as Jayses, Fintan, not a word of a lie. There we were labouring away beside the swimming pool of some hotel and I'm telling you, if you had been there, no matter what the druids of Garbally Park might have told you, you would have had to be dragged off some of the lovely birds that were there, doing nothing more than brightening up the scenery and driving some of us to an early grave from excess of lecherous thoughts. And here I am trying to disguise the effect which all this is having on me which is not the easiest thing in the world to do when all you're wearing is swimming togs and sunglasses and at the same time I am endeavouring to simulate an interest in what somebody is telling me about some matter pertaining to the art of letters but he might as well have tried to interest me in a translation into Urdu of the weather forecast for Arseholes, Missouri. Anyway, all this is just by the way, a touch of the *mise en scène*, as we say in the trade. This guy comes up to me and says hello and I says hello and suppose that he is some good-looking Jewish kid in the entertainment business but then he introduces himself and though he is not Jewish he is more or less in the entertainment business but then again who isn't in California? But soon I am apprised of the fact that standing before me, wishing me well and coming out with no end of ould chat about the fair hills of holy Ireland, standing there before me large as life and at least twice as ugly is the aforementioned Reverend Laurence Qualter CC. Now what he is doing by the pool of the Hotel Excelsior I cannot tell nor do I know anything except that he was there with ne'er a trace of a Roman collar or e'er a bit of black: he looked more like a film star or some young buck with nothing better to do than knock off the crumpet that was so plentiful about the pool. But to cut a long story short, between the jigs and reels, it transpired that he knew all about me and

mine and was related to several friends of mine in Galway city and environs and he made it clear to me that I would never be forgiven – either
in heaven, for which I did not give the proverbial fuck, or in Galway,
which was a possibility to be reckoned with – I would not, he said, be
shriven or forgiven if I did not visit the little church he was after building
not more than five minutes from where we were sitting or lying or
lounging or whatever. So of course, ever polite to our pastors, I pulled
on a shirt and pair of trousers and off we went to look at his little church.
Little church! Bejaysus, you could lose the pro-cathedral in it. You've
no idea. Eye hath not seen nor for that matter has the ear heard of what
the one true church can offer by way of accommodation in the city of
San Francisco. A huge fucking thing, all brass and glass, more like
something from outer space than the received notion of what a chapel
should look like. And there's the hard man from Loughrea, dressed
more like a film producer than a priest, taking me on a conducted tour
of the place, pointing out the little treasures here and there and there
am I oo-ing and aah-ing and saying that I have seen stations of the cross
in my time but these take some fucking beating. We did the lot, from
the confession boxes to the air conditioning – far from fucking air conditioning you were reared, Larry, says I to meself, but sure no matter: I
can tell you this much, if the one, holy, Catholic and apostolic could
lay on a service like this over here well bejayses the problem wouldn't
be how to get the faithful into the church on Sunday morning but how
to get them out on Sunday night. Well, as I was saying, I thought I had
been through the lot and I was telling Larry that he was lucky to have
such a premises but then he winked at me. Now it's not often men wink
at me and I tend to be a bit leery when the owner of the eye is a druid
of any description but I need not have worried. Not that I was, by the
way; but to get to the point. What, I asked myself politely, is he up to
now? Come this way, he beckoned. This, he said, while opening a door
stage right of the main stage, is my pride and joy. I couldn't wait. In we
went and he stands beside a kind of display case, just like you'd find in
a jeweller's shop only this was the de luxe model, a golden frame, gleaming glass, and a purple velvet display cloth within it. Jayses, I thought to
meself, he must have a real rarity: I wonder if I am about to fulfil a life's
ambition and glimpse a bit of the divine prepuce, the authentic foreskin,
or what. Well, Brendan, he said, whatdya make of that? Of what? says

I, still looking down into the case and seeing nothing. I thought you would like this, Brendan. I'm still gaping bug-eyed into the fucking glass case and getting more afraid by the minute that I'm going blind or something. I don't let anybody touch it, he said, but here, you can touch it but try not to move it. And he took my hand, or rather my finger, and put it down on the velvet and started moving it along and suddenly I saw that there was something there: it was like a tiny bit that you might break off a match to clean your teeth only it wasn't white and clean like a match but dirty and black. Ever one to be solicitous for the feeling of mine host I curbed the desire to ask him how long it was since he had seen his psychiatrist. But there he is smiling away like a mother with a new baby: Brendan, says he, I know it was wrong of me to take it but I can truthfully say to God that in my opinion the good it does by being here cancels the wrong I did by bringing it here. Agh good night, Joe Doyle, says I to meself: this was beginning to sound like holy water on the fucking brain. Sure I no more knew what he was talking about than I knew the irregular verbs of double Dutch. And then what does he do? He stands back and points to something on the side of the glass case, inviting me to follow with my eyes, which I did, and there inscribed on a little golden plaque were the words: *True relic of the bare bed used by the future saint of God, Matthew ('Matt') Talbot of Dublin. Pray for the cause of his canonisation. We welcome all subscriptions for the maintenance of this room of prayer and meditation.* And there underneath the glass case was another case well designed to protect the spondulicks that a credulous public were in the habit of stuffing into it through a slit small enough to frustrate the most adept young lad with the most flexible knife.

– Well be the living Jayses, I thought I'd never get out of that church without laughing. I thought I was going to split meself. True relic of the bare bed? True relic of me bare bollix: true relic of a railway sleeper that the ou' fella picked up in Inchicore. And then, blushing like the cute culchie he was, he told me the whole story: of how he visited the room where Matt the Self-Thresher had lain anights waiting for the churches to open, of how he suddenly got the great idea and went away and bought a Swiss army knife – which he still has and showed and I told him that that too was a relic if only class two – and came back and joined the queue again and when it was his turn to touch the bed he let on to be carried away but the only thing that was carried away was the bit of the plank that he cut off with the Swiss army knife unbeknownst to all and sundry except the all-seeing God on high and he was happy to explain all to Him at a time to be arranged later. And thus was the relic transported to San Francisco. What would you make of that, me oul' scholar, what?

– Did you tell him?

– Did I tell him? O callow youth, what takest thou me for? An unfeeling bastard who would burst the bubble of a poor Galwayman trying to make his way in the jungle of California? Do you think I'm a fucking informer? Of course I didn't tell him. If the fucking eejits of wherever it was are happy to bend the knee and bow the head before a sliver of railway sleeper, sure are they any worse than them as believes that the son of a Palestinian chippy was able to transform common H_2O into the best of good wine? Zounds, my boy, and by the holy rood, whatever else they teach you in that druidic institution they go easy on the Christian charity: live and let live and fuck the begrudgers and their friends in America. Beatrice, is there e'er a chance of a drop of tea?

– Brendan, we'd better be going or we'll be late. Fintan, we have to go to lunch. It's Brendan's doctor who has invited us; other than that you could have come with us but... you understand, don't you?

Of course I understood, and anyway I had my own plans for later that afternoon. I was just back from holiday in the Galway Gaeltacht – a final brush-up for the Irish before starting off the year of study that would culminate in the Leaving Cert – and I had met a girl called Yvonne. She was due to spend the afternoon shopping with her mother and then to meet me at five o'clock outside the Metropole. I had enough money to pay in for myself but not for her: I wasn't sure that I could just come out and tell her the truth – it never struck me as the thing to do, not unless all else had failed – and I was thinking in terms of parking the bike and going for a stroll along the river with the general intention of stumbling accidentally into the Phoenix Park et cetera.

Brendan was looking for his pen, the one he had used to sign the book for me, as I was saying goodbye to Beatrice.

– Hold on there a minute, take it easy for a minute and come here. You were saying that you copy people's writing. What about that there? Let's see what you make of that. Here: you can use my pen.

Brendan's signature was very easy: I had already studied it at school and it was no bother to me. He was somewhat surprised at how well and how quickly I wrote out his signature.

– Beatrice, will you come in and look at this.

Beatrice was not all that interested: she gave my forgery a cursory glance but she was more concerned with getting Brendan to the lunch on time and the doctor was due to collect them at any minute. And then, of course, she could not see into Brendan's mind.

Nor, for that matter, could I.

– Hey, me ould china, how would like to earn a flim for yourself, *cúig phunt glan*, eh?

– How?

– Oh, you needn't fucking worry. You won't have to peddle your virtue or your immortal soul or your mortal hole or anything like that. It's a literary job and won't take you more than a few hours. And you'll be doing me a favour.

– In that case I would be happy to do it for nothing.

– Will you for the love of the crucified Christ give over that *Boy's Own* bolloxology. Don't ever work for nothing. If a fiver's not enough just out and fucking say so. If a fiver's fine, fine. OK?

– OK.

– Just sit down there and hold my pen and wait till I come back. Where did you say these fucking things are, Beatrice? Out by the phone? Jesus, there must be hundreds of the bleeding things. Clear off the table in there, Fintan, till I show you what's to be done.

He ripped open the parcel to reveal the title pages which Beatrice had mentioned. He handled them with visible disgust, as if trying not to see them.

– Now what this is, need not concern you. It doesn't matter a fiddler's fuck anyway and you're better off not knowing. You have one thing to do on each of these and that is to write my signature the way you did a few minutes ago. OK?

– OK.

– Good, now I don't know how many there are but do you think you can do them all today?

– I'll get them done in a couple of hours, by three anyway.

– Great. And we'll be back shortly afterwards. There's the fiver in case you want to shag off beforehand.

- Brendan, come on. Here's the car.
- Thanks a million, kiddo. See you.
- See you.

I picked up his pen, tested it on a piece on blank paper, took a title page from the top of the bundle and, with what I took to be a becoming display of haste, habit and insouciance, I scratched out the words 'Brendan Behan'.

My first allograph.

Two hours later I had done the lot, some two hundred and fifty as far as I remember. After a few minutes I had worked myself into the nervous pattern of the scrawl and ceased to feel any personal concern for the schizoid tendencies of the *d* or the *h*; then I was free to appreciate the dramatic possibilities. I imagined being crowded at some reception by hordes of happy book buyers who sought my autograph. I could see all their faces, gauge their true feelings, notice how pleasantly or imperiously they made their requests. Each was rewarded according to his or her – especially her – charm. (After all, I was seventeen.) For some I scribbled 'my best wishes', for the slightly more favoured 'my very best wishes'; I honoured those who were elderly and cheerful with 'mo ghraidhin thú' or 'mo cheol thú'; I got my own back on one frozen-faced oul' fucker by writing the extremely dubious 'B. Behan' and then, while underlining it, pretended to be bumped by another customer and put the line right through the name. When the ink supply to the nib got choked I just shook the pen over the page; the blobs would lend a certain touch to the signature that was bound to appeal to buyers of Behan. I was sorely tempted to enliven the proceedings still further by scribbling down the odd bit of obscene Irish now and then but that would have been to take a risk which might have rebounded on Brendan and so I played safe and behaved myself and stuck to forgery uncompounded with any other offence against decency or the trades descriptions act.

Beatrice had said that there were some nice Irish tomatoes there if I wanted to make a sandwich. Allographing being thirsty work, I sank my teeth into the tomatoes and sucked the juice. A little salt goes well with new Irish tomatoes, as hard as rocks and as full of flavour as anything made or grown. And there is only one thing better than a new Irish tomato and that's another one and so before I knew what was happening

I was groping in the bag that had once held two pounds of tomatoes and failing to find e'er a one. Sweet Jesus, I prayed, I hope I'm gone by the time Beatrice decides to have the tomatoes for her tea.

But I wasn't. When they came back all Brendan wanted to see was the work but Beatrice was looking ahead and looking in particular for what was left of the tomatoes. I turned red when she asked me if I had eaten them all. Brendan was inclined to fuck the tomatoes: there was tomatoes to be had in every tuppenny ha'penny shop in Ireland but a good forger was a rare treasure and was to be honoured as such with whatever he wanted be way of tomatoes or anything else that helped him concentrate on his work. And Beatrice was relieved to know that when those people in London rang next she would be able to say that the parcel was in the post.

With their best wishes ringing out behind me I cycled away from the house. I had done my good deed for the day and made somebody happy into the bargain and with the help of God my good deeds for the day were only beginning. And this was none of your bob-a-job stuff: stuffed safely in my trouser pocket was a five-pound note. I was rich, as Daddy used to say, beyond the dreams of Avarice, whoever he was. I rode up along Leeson Street in the afternoon sunshine as if I owned it all, houses, shops, bridge and everything, loving the whole world, luxuriating in the feeling of one who has not only done a good day's work but has been well paid for it into the bargain.

Lamplighting Christ, I was thinking, forget about walking up by the quays. We'll push out the boat: ice cream in the Rainbow, followed by whatever was on in the Metropole, followed by chips wherever she wanted afterwards. Even then I'd still have about four pounds left. I was rich for ever.

Normally the thought would cross my mind – what if she's not there? – but not this time: I knew she would be there and there she was.

Dear Yvonne, with whom I sat on the sand at Spiddal harbour, with whom I sauntered out the Moycullen road, if only I could hear you tell me now what you remember about that August afternoon in O'Connell Street. What did you make of me jumping off the bike and locking it to the railings that surrounded the trees? Running across the traffic, pulling my trouser-ends out of my socks, pushing my glasses back up along the bridge of my nose, sweating with happiness and anxiety? And then,

big mister large, the last of the big spenders, asking what you would like
to do? What did I mean? Just that: where would you like to go or what
would you like to do? Such as? Coffee, ice cream, chips. Of course we
were going to the pictures. I mean as well as the pictures. As well as the
pictures! Don't worry about the money? Did I rob a bank? Pause and
enigmatic smile before slow cryptic reply:

– No: not quite.

Boom! Buzz-buzz.

We rambled into the Rainbow and ordered two tall and colourful
extravaganzas that came with spoons a foot long. A fiver! The waitress
wanted to know if it was the smallest I had. It was all I had on me.
Where did you get that? Don't worry: let's see if we can get something
played on the jukebox. Each table had an individual facility for booking
tunes on the jukebox but you had no idea how far down the line you
were or even if your record was in fact your booking. But who cared:
we were talking about Spiddal and all the incidents of the summer there
when along come two guys who say hello to her in posh accents. Hellos
all round. Trying to keep their eyes off the knickerbocker glories. These
guys were living near her in Merrion. Why don't they just shag off back
to Merrion the pair of them and mind their own business. No she wasn't
going home for a while; we were going to the pictures. Hadn't decided:
probably the Metropole. And, I muttered as I looked through the
jukebox list, we'll probably have something to eat afterwards. Robbed
a bank? Humorously, maybe even triumphantly, rather than cryptically:

– No: not quite.

Boom-boom! Pick the bones out of that. And when you have
digested it –

– Actually . . .

Get a load of the adverb.

– Actually, I've just been paid for some stuff I wrote.

New balls please.

The cinema door closes and there is a moment of total darkness back
here. Crucial moment. No matter what happens, I must make sure that
she is sitting on my left. No matter what happens. I have always felt
myself to be unidexterous – or, more correctly, unisinister – when it
came to physical encounters of the amorous kind.

So far so . . . good.

Sit. Help off with cardigan. All right? Fine. Sit back. Elbows touch. Excuse me. What? Smile and say something. What's that? Whisper. Faces close. Feel the wisps of her hair on your forehead, catch the sense of powder on the skin.

When to kiss? And then, having decided when, how? How to make that terrifying journey of the head out into the uncharted space between her face and yours where so much can go wrong, where the smallest misunderstanding, the least mistiming, the slightest move, can reduce the ultimate ecstasy to a silent idiotic farce.

But first, the arm around her shoulders.

The arm around her shoulders.

The arm.

Was paralysed.

I could whisper in her ear. I could push my shoulder into hers. But when I went to raise my left arm and describe that adventurous arc in the infinite space of the cinema . . .

I was paralysed. I did everything. I threatened myself. I mocked myself. I encouraged myself. I cursed myself. I cast doubts upon myself. I bullied myself. But to no avail.

I told myself I was seventeen.

I told myself that I was sorry for speaking to myself like that, there was no need for panic, that there was no great hurry, that I didn't have to do anything just for the moment: I was going to count slowly to ten and then, and then there would be no delay, no messing, no excuses. I must have counted a million but never once did I get to ten: as soon as I hit nine, I ordered a recount on the grounds that I had been counting too fast, that I had left out four, that it would not be a good idea to make a move during a romantic part of the picture, that it certainly would not be a good idea to do so during a funny part of the picture, that there was no point putting my arm around her when my mouth was bone dry.

And then the intermission came and the lights came up and the girl with the ice cream came and Yvonne went to the toilets and I lit another cigarette and then got more ice cream so as not to have the taste of tobacco on my breath when the moment came. If the moment came. Dark again for the feature.

Still nothing. I began to feel the seeds of panic sprouting in my stomach.

The perspiration of barely confined anxiety rolled down my body and seemed to glow in the dark. I was wretched. I was useless. I was wasting a glorious opportunity. It even struck me that I, however hopelessly beyond redemption, should at least think of my unfortunate companion: why should she feel partly responsible for what was entirely my fault? A phantasmagoria of guilt and accusation passed before my eyes. The characters of the screen seemed to be looking at me, sometimes pityingly, more often contemptuously: some of the lines in the film seemed directed at me and my inadequacy.

Suddenly I thought of Brendan and his chuckle and the laughing way he'd talk about getting the full of your arms of girls, girls who were on for anything, girls who were just my weight.

Out and make way for the bould Fenian men!

With the courage of the desperate I sat up straight, turned around to my left, threw my left arm out into space and around till it caught her shoulder and pulled her towards me. She needed little encouragement and just before I closed my eyes, having taken aim, I saw her face, rigid with the passionate surrender which was the hallmark of a superior convent education, give itself to me and my intentions. But what was that? A finger stabbing me between the shoulder blades! I turned in fright to see an elderly woman behind me, her eyes glinting with some zeal that was not for me. Her voice high and authoritative as her husband looked on with admiration.

– There will be none of that carry-on here, boy. This is a cinema where people come to watch the picture and not to be distracted by goings-on like that.

A look of terror on Yvonne's face as she recoiled from the attack, glanced at me and then looked straight ahead at the screen. So this was it: just when things were going right some oul' one had to come along and spoil everything. In my bollox, I said to myself and then turned around in the seat.

– Will you go 'way outa that, woman, and stop making a public eejit out of yourself. Who do you think you are?

I could hardly believe that I was the one who had sent those words out into the whispering darkness. The woman rose in her seat and glared dramatically.

– How dare you! I'll soon let you know –

– And I'll soon let you know that you can fuck off with yourself, you hatchet-faced strap, and take with you whatever unfortunate you inveigled into taking you here in the first place. Fuck off with you now before I call the manager and tell him what you're up to in the cinema. Watching the picture, me bollox, if you were watching the picture you wouldn't know what anybody else was doing. Watching the picture me arse.

– I'm going to get the manager.

She and her husband stood up in high dudgeon.

– Good, be God, and that'll save me the trouble of getting him but, dear dilapidated Jayses, you better have a fucking good excuse when I tell him what you and that jewel beside you there were up to.

Though she was fuming dangerously, he advised her that they would be better off leaving the cinema and not getting involved with a pup like me who was more than likely drunk, that they would only be wasting their time. It was time to strike.

– That's right, blame the drink. How well you'd think of blaming the drink, you dull scruffy creeping Jayses, and look at you, look at the pair of yis, hardly able to stand never mind fucking walk, and yis full to the gills. Look at the walk of him; no wonder he wants to get out as quick as he can.

And, of course, in the circumstances, what with her hopping with rage and him trying to keep her quiet, him helping her on with her coat and her grabbing the coat from him in temper, and both of them trying to get out at the same time, it was no wonder that they nearly did knock each other over. I had carried the day, fair fight and no favour, lurry him up he's no relation.

It was one thing to carry the day, quite another to sit down in the sea of embarrassment and attempt to continue what I had come here to do and only so lately begun to do. My first thought was that a well-bred middle-class girl like Yvonne would run at the first opportunity consistent with anonymity. I paused, waiting for my heart to get back below the ten-beats-per-second mark, before looking at her. Quiet amazement in her eyes, in her voice:

– Oh, that was terrific. How did you do it? Where did you learn to do that, to talk like that? It was like... It was out of this world!

– We'll be out of this world and out of this cinema if they bring the manager.

– They won't dare.

– You think so?

– I know so.

When she snuggled into me, what could I do except put my arm around her again and pull her towards me with a last-ditch daring, noticing just before I closed my eyes and the lights went out that she had responded with Pavlovian speed, once again assuming that look of polite passion on her face. And so we met in the flesh, my mouth unaccountably landing on the bridge of her ,nose. But I was not to be gainsaid on this day of days: sure, didn't I know that her mouth was just below her nose and, to save time and be certain and to put an end to all delay, I just slid down along her embarrassed nose and landed on her lips to the relief of all. And, safely anchored there, I set out to get in the last quarter of an hour the three hours' entertainment I had paid for.

Dearest Yvonne, did you go on to be a nurse? Or am I confusing your afterlife with that of somebody else? No matter. Me life on you, Yvonne girl! Girt around by cruel foes and attacked by embittered begrudgers, you stood your ground in spite of all and showed a spirit that, blind as I was, I never thought you had.

(And blind as I was, I never learned the lesson of the Metropole but went on trying to win various Helens with my imitations of various young stars who mixed – or so it seemed to me – four parts tortured sensitivity to one part machismo when I would have been much better off getting rid of the fucking sensitivity and . . .)

Still, for all that I knew you so little and have such a slight recollection of being with you in Spiddal – why didn't we keep in touch? – I'll no more forget the evening I spent with you in Dublin than I'll forget the morning I spent with Brendan and Beatrice all those years ago in August 1962.

August 1962. Within a year and a half Brendan was dead. Those last months were like the final moments of a bull in the corrida. Battered and bleeding from umpteen mortal wounds, he stood up only to be beaten down again and it seemed as if he understood that the sooner he stood up again the sooner he'd be bludgeoned down for the last time. There is some footage somewhere which contains a clip of Behan as he approached the end: some American was filming general shots of the Grafton Street area when who should stray into shot but BB looking like a baby dinosaur. He sways about, a creature from a previous epoch, not knowing what to do or where to go, utterly alone in the milling crowds, utterly alien among the consumerist ants of the twentieth century, almost totally disregarded by the hundreds of people around him as if they had decided by some silent vote not to see him. He had very few friends towards the end and what friends he had were friends from other days. Everybody was surprised when he died – because he had come back from the brink so often before – but there were few who knew him who did not welcome it as a release from the grimmest period of imprisonment he had ever suffered through.

That was the general murmur among the thousands who lined the route of his funeral, that it was all for the best, that he was well out of it. I was down in Galway at the drama festival when I heard the news; I hitched up the morning of the funeral and barely made it in time. Apart from nodding to people here and there I kept myself to myself. I didn't want to sit in a big black car or be part of anything official. I had come to the funeral to suffer the required amount of sadness but when I saw the traffic stopping to allow the cortège through, when I saw bus drivers pull over and stare silently at the coffin, when I saw hundreds of women interrupt their shopping to line the route, shaking their heads and blessing themselves and muttering about poor oul' Brendan, when I saw the dealers and delivery men, artists and bookies, publicans and republicans, upper class and working class, rich and poor, media men and messenger boys, religious and irreligious, young and old, when I saw all Dublin turning out to say goodbye to their favourite quare fella, their one and only prodigal son, I couldn't be anything but glad and I wanted to enjoy the occasion. It was the ultimate award for Brendan and one he would have appreciated a million times more than any Nobel Prize or any Prix des Nations. His spirit was there as he himself had been there the day at the races, not only lively in himself but a source of liveliness in others.

As the coffin was lowered down I realised that I still found it hard to think of Brendan as dead.

Thinking that everybody would head straight for the Brian Boru, I had a look into Murphy's: it was crowded of course but not impossible. There was a large table in the centre of the lounge around which women, young and old, were sitting, each guarding a chair for a man who was up at the bar ordering quantities of pints and shorts. The only talk was of who was drinking what and who wasn't all right and whether there was a seat there for somebody. At the table sad-faced women nodded to each other with knowing resignation and handled their drinks, waiting for the company to assemble and commence drinking with proper order and ceremony. Those who did not live close to one another or who did not see each other regularly asked briefly of common friends and were assured, equally briefly, that they were grand. I stood behind the men at the bar, contented to wait for my pint as I listened to them intone the litany.

– And didn't he have a great turnout all the same?

– I was just saying that.

– And the lovely day and all.

– How many would you say was there? Thousands?

– Aw yis, easy.

– And more.

– Well, if you counted all the people who came to see the funeral pass.

– Sure you'd be talking about tens of thousands.

– Easy.

Drinks were brought back to the women at the table and things got under way.

– I didn't know half the people there.

– Where?

– Around the grave.

– Oh, to tell you the truth, neither did I. I suppose Shay would have known most of them.

– Did you, Shay?

– Did I what?

– We were just saying that you probably knew most of the people who were around the grave and that.

– I did in me arse.

– What do you mean?

– What do I mean? I know what I mean.

– What?

– I mean that there was some people there who had no right to be there.

– True for you, Shay. I'm with you there.

– I'm not. What does he mean?

– What he's saying is, unless I am greatly mistaken, is that there were people up there who could not be classed as close friends of Brendan's. Am I right, Shay?

– Too true, Liam.

– And that some of the people who were doing most of the pushing to get right up beside Brendan's coffin were the same people who, not so very long ago, not so very long ago, mind you, who would have gone up a side street if they seen Brendan coming in their direction.

– Aha! If you'd an air to that you could sing it.

– Lovely. Who's going to sing?

– In a minute, Mammy.

– I only asked.

– Somebody will sing in a minute, Mammy. Take it easy. No rush.

– Oh I don't mind waiting.

– Jimmy, will you get your mother a drink.

There was a further adjournment by several of the men to the bar and it was considered rude to introduce any serious matters into the conversation in their absence. One of the younger women finished off her first vodka and orange, shivered and asked her father to ask the barman not to put so much orange in the next, and then turned merrily to the other women.

– Jaysus, I wish somebody would sing a song.

Her granny looked up from her handbag.

– Be careful. I asked for a song and I had the snot cut off me.

Granny's son looked sideface on at his daughter.

– For the love of Jesus, Breda, will you take it easy. Here's your vodka. See if it's all right for you.

– Pardon me for living. It's grand. Thanks.

– The snot cut off me.

– Nobody cut the snot off you, Granny.

– 'Deed an' they did not, Mrs Mac, 'cause if they did, I'd be a'ter telling them, so I would. They'd have me to answer to. Are you drinking your sherry?

– Why wouldn't I? Is there something wrong with a body taking a drop of sherry at a funeral?

– 'Course not. Enjoy yourself while you can.

- I'll mind me own business, that's what I'll do.
- Is everybody fixed up now? Can I sit down?
- We're all grand. Sit down and relax.
- Carry on with the coffin.
- The corpse will walk.
- Agh, indeed, poor ould Brendan.
- He'll never be dead.
- Never. Never.

There was a long pause which I could not fathom until I rose up in my seat and noticed that gradually, two by two, the eyes around the table were all heading in the direction of the man they called Liam. Liam rubbed his chin a good deal, looked down at the table, raised his eyebrows and sniffed three times with diminishing violence. He extended his hand slowly till it gripped his pint. Then he remained motionless, transfixed.

- Are you all right there, Liam?
- I'll be grand in a minute.
- Are you sure you're all right?
- Leave him alone for a minute. He's all right.
- I'll be fine, don't worry. I was just thinking.
- About what?
- Leave him be. Let him take his own time.

Liam raised the pint to his mouth and took a slug. Then he sniffed twice, pulled on his cigarette, allowed the grim set of his face to re-form in sardonic interrogation and, having expelled a long thin jet of smoke through pursed lips, he cleared his throat, smiled wryly and looked up and around at the company.

- I was just thinking to meself there about something that happened. When would it have been? Let me think. It was just before his first play went on. When was that? In the early fifties sometime?

Just as I was settling down to enjoy Liam's tale, who should come in the door and salute me only Mick and Izzy, two distant relations whose present proximity was about the last thing I wanted. They were both snobbish and a little slow: they would have considered their presence at the funeral an act of generous tolerance. When Izzy took off her glove to shake my hand I knew that I would have to get them a drink before I could get rid of them. As I ordered a small Jameson and a pale sherry

I could hear snippets of Liam's story and this made my behaviour with Mick and Izzy even more muted than it would normally be. They assumed that I would know where the important mourners were; I assured them that anybody who was anybody would be in the Brian Boru. By the time I convinced them to go there – explaining that I would follow them as soon as some friend of mine arrived – Liam had come to the end of his story. Once again I was with the men at the bar as the next round was arranged.

– Are you all right for sherry there, Mammy?

– Are we goin'?

– No, Granny. Daddy wants to know if you want another sherry.

– Well, I suppose if we're stayin' I'll take one more anyway. I may as well.

– True for you, Mrs Mac. Why wouldn't you? Sure we'll all have one more anyway. Won't it be there after us?

There was another interval in which the men went up to the bar and came back with pints for themselves and various shorts for the women. Shay was the first of them back into his seat and he was demonstrating once again how confident he was of the date of the opening of *The Quare Fellow*.

Liam lit his wife's cigarette and his own and then sat down behind a pint and a small one.

– You're dead right, Shay.

– I've a fairly good head for dates.

– I'd say you have, mind you.

– Like I could almost pinpoint to a day the time something very funny happened to do with Brendan.

– When was that?

– Well, it's not today nor yesterday.

– Give him a chance.

– I'd be talking about October 1949 and the reason I'm sure it was October 1949 is that Peg's brother got married just before our Mary was born – I remember Peg there wasn't sure that she should go to the chapel – and our Mary was fourteen on the twentieth of October last. You can work it out.

– Go on. We believe you.

– It was a Saturday and it would have been about the twelfth or the thirteen of October – or maybe even a little earlier, the fifth or the sixth.

– Go on anyway.

– We'll say it was the sixth of October.

– We'll say anything for a quiet life.

– It was a Saturday morning and herself had sent me to town to get a few things for Tommy's wedding – a pair of shoes, I think, and socks and maybe a tie – I don't know, but I probably had about a pound on me. Which was very different from having a pound today. I'm talking about the time when the pint cost a shilling or so.

– That's right. And you'd get ten smokes for a tanner.

– Agh you would not get ten smokes for a tanner.

– I'm telling you, you would.

– Anyway, things weren't too hot and I'd been given the knock. The only reason that I had the quid was because Peg had saved it up, knowing that there was a wedding in the offing and having a fair idea that I wouldn't be earning. To tell you the truth, herself and meself were after having a barney about the same wedding and the need to get dolled up for it. Am I right, Peg? 'Member?

Peg smiled and lifted her eyes to the ceiling but kept her lips sealed. Shay acknowledged her corroboration and proceeded.

– I thought that we'd be better off spending the money the way we wanted to spend it and not to be spending it in order to please other people. But Lady Muck here couldn't give her crowd the pleasure of seeing me in leaky shoes. And so, as usual, she let me have my say and then ordered me into town to do as I was told. And off I went.

– Did what I was told! The devil pull it out of you.

– A model husband.

– Jesus, Peg, were you long looking for him?

– I didn't look half long enough.

– Anyway, I got off the bus in College Green and I was walking down Westmoreland Street towards McBirney's when who should I see coming round the corner by the ESB there but the bould Brendan. Shay, says he, his face lighting up, and how are the balls of your feet? Great, says I, and yourself, Brendan, how is the world treating you? Shay, says he, if I was any better I couldn't stick it.

– He used to say that, right enough.

– Agh yes, that was one of his.

– I can hear him say it as clearly as I can see him standing there. If I was any better, says he, I couldn't stick it. Up to any good? says I. Devil a bit, says he, I just looked into the Palace. Jaysus, says I, and are you sure that a look was all you had there? I regret to have to inform you, says he, that a look was the sum total of what I had there. I was hoping, says he, that I would bump into a citizen who might advance me a few bob on a thing I'm writing but things didn't work out; what are you up to yourself? Nothing much, says I; only getting a few things for Peg's brother's wedding, shoes and socks and things. I wasn't going to say any more on the subject because I didn't think Brendan'd want to hear about weddings or shoes or whatever – but that's where I was wrong. Shoes, says he, looking all business and rubbing his chin. Socks, says he, scratching his head as if he was thinking real hard about something. Pricey enough these days, says he. Don't I know, says I. That lot, says he, is going to set you back a few bob. And so I tell him that I have the quid or whatever it is that Peg has given me and that's the lot. And there he was – I can still see him, as plain as anything – looking at me and sucking his teeth and whatever few bob I told him I had, well, he wasn't sure that it was enough to get what I wanted with it. You could have a problem there, says he, but I think that as luck would have it I can help you out in this one. There's a fellow working in Clery's who was in the Curragh with me, a decent enough skin, and if anybody is able to kit you out for what you have in your pocket he's the one; but sure, says Brendan, we can but try. And so over we go to Clery's and I needn't tell you that Brendan is getting the odd funny look as we go through the shop. But, no fool Brendan, he turns to me and asks me to ask where Mr Whatever-his-name was. I'm the one who's getting the suspicious looks now 'cause of course they're talking to me but every second second they're looking over at the fellow with the long hair and the shirt open all down his chest. But, howandever, we eventually find the fellow we were looking for and himself and Brendan start lashing out the Irish at each other to beat the band. I've no idea what they're going on about – it's all mahogany gaspipe to me – but next thing Brendan tips me the nod and a wink and gives me to understand that the job is oxo. Your man asks me the kind of stuff I want and so on and then he heads off to the shoe counter and the stocking counter and so on. As soon as he's gone Brendan sidles up to me and tells me that his pal will do the lot for a quid and throw in a tie as well for luck, so that I was getting the lot for almost half-price 'cause the shoes he's getting me are no ordinary shoes but the best, nothing but the best, Lee shoes, made down in Cork, shoes that normally went for about thirty-five bob a pair. 'Course I'm delighted and tell Brendan that I won't forget him. Forget it, says he, what are friends for? But come here, says he, me friend thinks that I'm buying them for you and so don't let on otherwise; slip us the money when nobody is looking and I'll keep him happy. Anyhow, back your man comes, as good as his word, shows me the shoes, lets me fit one of them on, waves the socks and the tie in front of me for a split second and then, before you could blink, he had the whole lot wrapped up and under me oxter. Brendan asks me if everything is OK and I say yes and then he gives me the nod and so I stay out of things for a bit, rambling down the shop, while he takes your man up the shop a bit and does his business with him. It was half past three on the dot when we came out into the street. That was a handy bit of business, says Brendan. It sure was, says I, and it was lucky I bumped into you. Thanks a million, Brendan. Forget about it, says he; any time. Now that you've done your messages, says he, would you be interested in a pint? Wha'? says I. Would you like a pint? says he. I didn't know what to say; I was a bit embarrassed because I assumed that he had no money and I thought I had made it clear that all I had was the money for the shoes and stuff. And so I'm stood there like a Burton's dummy and he asks me again: are you fucking deaf, says he, or how often do I have to ask you if you want a drink? I've no money, says I. What harm? says he; I've a few bob and, Shay me ould flower, you're more than welcome. It's awful good of you, Brendan, says I. 'Deed and it is not, says he; what in the name of Jaysus are friends for if they can't do each other a good turn without making a song and dance about it – will you come in here quick out of the street before we're arrested and charged with causing an obstruction. What could I do? In we went into Ryan's of Marlborough Street and that was the start of it. Such a day of it as we had. Up marches Brendan to the bar, waving and saying hello to all and sundry as if he was Alfie Byrne and then, lo and be-bleedin'-hold, out on the counter he throws a ten-bob note. Two pints, says he, and may the giving hand never falter. Well, I needn't tell you that it didn't stop at two pints or at four pints either. We got well oiled in Ryan's and then we headed over to the Tower Bar in Henry Street. We were grand there until Brendan started to sing and when he did we were invited to take ourselves elsewhere. Which we did: we went up to Ma Murphy's.

– Poor oul' Ma Murphy. She was just around the corner.

– The very place. Agh lamb of Jesus tonight, what a session we had. I don't think I ever enjoyed meself so much in all me born days. Laugh? There was never anything like it. Do you know what I'm going to tell you? You know what? To my dying day I'll treasure the memory of that day. That day was Brendan for me. They can write what they like about him, they can say what they like about him, they can claim he was this, they can claim he was that but, as far as I am concerned, that day was the true Brendan. Anyway, were was I? Ah, yes, we moved on to some other place. Don't ask me where it was because I don't know. I could never put it away like Brendan in those days and somehow or another, jarred and all as I was, I told Brendan I was off. He asked me what in the name of Jaysus for, but I just said I was off. He walked out to the door with me and so on and I kept telling him how I'd make it up to him one of these days, that we wouldn't be down for ever and so on, that with the help of God...

Shay stubbed out his cigarette, lit another, took first a short sip then a long draught from his pint, wiped his lips, sniffled and exhaled at length.

– How I got home I do not know. When I got home I do not know. It was late and your woman there was in no humour for me. I mentioned Brendan's name and that, as the man said, was how the battle was lost. How could you do it? says she. And me the way I am, says she. Don't talk to me, says she. Don't even come bleeding near me; the smell off you is enough to turn me stomach. I was going down the stairs to sleep on the sofa – at that stage I could have slept on the floor and not been any the wiser – when she shouts down. Did you get the stuff? says she. I did, says I. That itself, says she; bring it up till I have a look at it. Jesus alone knows, says she, what you got if you had Brendan Behan with you. Hold on a minute, says I. Hold on, a minute. And then it suddenly struck me: I couldn't remember bringing home the parcel with me. I searched the room high up and low down but I knew I was wasting me time: I must have left the stuff either on the bus or in the last place we were in, in Moore Street. What's delaying you? she shouts down; have you fallen asleep? Fallen asleep, says I to meself, I wish to Jayses I'd fallen under a bus. And to make matters worse, wasn't I trying to walk up the stairs as careful as I could, so as not to let her know that I was as far gone as I was, when I lost me bleeding balance and down I went with such a clatter. Jesus, Mary and Joseph tonight, she screams, jumping out of bed and her almost due. Jesus, Mary and Joseph, he's dead. No such luck, says I to meself, but bad and all as I was, I knew that the best thing for me to do was to pretend that I was banjaxed altogether – in the hope that she might go easier on me.

 – Oh, Breda, I'll never forget it as long as I live. I genuinely thought he was a goner; I really did that night. And then, of course, just to put the tin hat on it, didn't I think that I had started, that all the excitement had brought it on.

 – And had you?

 – Not at all. I was another week waiting.

 – But I'd say the fall down the stairs saved my life. At least I got to sleep that night. Needless to remark, the following morning at the crack of dawn I was up and over to CIE to ask about the parcel, just in case it had been left on the bus. Not a sign of it; nobody knew anything about it. Then down to Moore Street and, as luck would have it, it was Sunday and so the place wasn't open even though it was a market pub. And so I've nothing to do except traipse around town with a splitting headache and an ankle that's black and blue and yellow and five times its normal size. I was never so glad to see doors open as I was when that place opened. They remembered me all right from the previous night. Yes, of course they did. I was with Brendan Behan. Right, says I. Did I leave a parcel behind me here? Your man asked around but nobody knew anything; they looked under the bar but no sign of any parcel. I was on me way out when this ou' fella staggers up to the bar, hardly able to walk with the shakes. Excuse me, says he, but I couldn't help hearing you talk about a parcel. Yes, says I; what about it? Did I hear right? says he; was I with Brendan Behan last night? I was, says I; what about the parcel? Well, says he, Brendan had the parcel with him and him leaving. And the reason, says he, that I know that is that he was going off without the parcel when I noticed it and called him back and told him that he was going off without his parcel. And what happened?

says I. Nothing, says your ou' fella: he just takes the parcel and goes off.
Thank God, says I, in me own mind: the parcel is safe. And so I thanked
the ou' fella for taking the load off me mind and I asked behind the bar
if they had any idea where Brendan had gone last night. They weren't
sure but somebody thought they heard him say something about
Grafton Street. Try McDaid's, says somebody, and off I went and up to
McDaid's. I was thinking that either Brendan would have left the parcel
in McDaid's or that somebody could tell me where he was staying – he
wasn't living in 70 at the time – or when he was expected. As soon as
I mentioned Brendan's name in McDaid's there was a silence and I knew
that he had been a bit out of order and so I played dumb. Was I looking
for Mr Behan? asks this fellow who looks and sounds as if he was the
owner.

– Ould McDaid. Mr Mac himself. Cheerful Charlie, maurya.

– Ould Sobersides: an awful damper. But, go on.

– Not really, says I, just wondering if he was expected. And all the
time I'm looking around for me parcel. He's not expected today, says
your man; in fact, he's not expected for some considerable time. In me
own mind I'm terrified that what he's telling me is that Brendan has
been picked up for drunk and disorderly or something but all I say is:
Oh? No, says your man, not for some considerable time. Why's that?
says I. He's gone away, says he, on his holidays. His holidays? says I, not
knowing whether your man is having me on or what. He's gone on his
holidays to France, says your man, just as if he was telling me that
Brendan was gone out to Inchicore. As God is me judge, I just stood
there, not knowing what to say, not knowing what to think, and I'd be
there to this day, I'd say, if this guy hadn't come up to me, one of the
customers who looked as if he was curing himself, and he says he's sorry
et cetera, but that he couldn't help hearing what I was saying and so on.
Am I a friend of Brendan's? he asks. I am, says I, and it's out before I
know what I'm doing but no harm: this fellow is also a friend of
Brendan's and he wants to know what I'm having and there's no point
in telling him that I don't want anything because there's a pint coming
for me. And then he starts to laugh and tell me what a night they had
there last night. Brendan was only flying, had the place rolling with
laughter. There was this story Brendan had and I 'clare to God it was
the funniest thing you ever heard and the funniest thing of all about it

was that Brendan swore a hole through an iron pot that it was the gospel truth without a word of a lie added to it. I must tell you, says your man and off he goes with the story, or at least as much as he can remember, and half the time you can't hear him because he bursts out laughing and then he starts coughing and spluttering. But the story is that Brendan sails in in the best of good order lateish last night having been heard singing from the bottom of Grafton Street. In he comes and no looking about but straight up to the bar and it's a pint and a small one. Begod, says somebody, have you been working, Brendan? I have, says he, I've been in the money market. So we all know from the way he says it that this is only by way of being an introduction to some tall tale or other. Now I'm the worst in the world to retell a story but the gist of it is this. Brendan meets some guy who's buying a suit of clothes or something or maybe it was shoes or something but anyway that doesn't matter, it doesn't affect the story one way or another. Brendan meets this guy, hears that he is about to spend money on whatever he's about to spend money on, and Brendan decides that whatever this guy was going to spend money on, it was a waste of good money. So he comes up with this stunt. He knows a fellow, some guy he was in the nick with, who works in Clery's –

– Sacred heart of Jesus tonight!

– I don't believe you, Shay!

– Let him go on. Ssh!

– A bit of shush.

– Go on, Shay.

– And Brendan lets on to this guy that he has to buy whatever it is for the other fellow and that he has no money and that he'll come up with the money in a week or so if your man will let him have the stuff on tick for the moment. Which your man does; being an old amigo of Brendan's from the nick he's not bothered because he's not going to pay for it anyway and if Brendan should come up with the money later on – most unlikely – well and good and so much the better. But what the guy behind the counter doesn't know is that the other fellow has given Brendan the money; and what the other fellow doesn't know is that Brendan hasn't given the guy behind the counter the money at all. But everybody's happy. Your man has his clothes or whatever, Brendan has the few bob and the fellow in the shop is not particularly bothered one

way or another. Brendan and his friend head off and start living it up
on the proceeds – all unknown to the friend of course, who has no idea
where the money came from. Brendan is in his element, drinking and
singing and no better man. After a few hours, when Brendan is just getting warmed up, the friend has had enough and more than enough and
just wants to get home before he passes out and falls by the wayside.
Brendan stays to the bitter end of his ill-gotten gains and is about to head
off himself when somebody gives him a parcel. A parcel? What fucking
parcel? You've guessed. Your man is gone to God and has more on his
mind than the parcel of stuff: he's forgotten all about it. Never one to
look a gift horse in the mouth, Brendan says thank you very much for
the parcel and then, quick as a flash, nips out of the pub they're in and
into some nearby boozer where, without further ado and in double-
quick time, he sells the stuff for ten bob – no problem at all down there
– and then it's up here with him to have another lash and keep us all
in stitches until it's time to go and then it's a fond farewell from him
to all of us because he's down to the docks and off to France for a change
of air. Well, Jesus, I nearly died laughing. Even you'd have to admit, Mr
Mac, that it was as good as a play. I was sore from laughing. If I'd laughed
any more I would have given meself a hernia: I was relieved when he
went out that door and that's a fact. Am I telling a word of a lie, Mr
McDaid?

– Well I for one, says oul' McDaid, was relieved to see Behan go out
that door. I'd always rather see him going out the door than coming in
through it. If he never came back from France it'd be too bloody soon
for me. Although I hardly expect the unfortunate fellow whose stuff he
stole and sold to feel the same as I do. That is, of course, if he was telling
the truth, which is most unlikely, because in my opinion that man has
never told the truth in his life except maybe by accident.

– Well, I needn't tell you that that pint nearly poisoned me: I nearly
choked on it and the more your man told me how Brendan had them
all in stitches with his story the more I wanted to throw up. I couldn't
wait to get out. I thought I'd never get out that door quick enough.
Jesus! when I thought of that other huer, probably passed out on some
bloody glorified barge between here and bloody France, and a big smile
on his face thinking of the great stroke he was after pulling off. Me
lovely Lee shoes.

– And poor you, you must have felt an awful eejit.

– You could say that. In actual fact, the loss of the bloody shoes and the rest of the stuff was the least of me troubles – I couldn't care less what me in-laws thought of me; I'd been knocked off and that was that, nothing to be ashamed of – but I had to live with your woman here and her not exactly in the best of form with Madge about to arrive.

– I'd say you gave him lackery, Peg.

– Wouldn't you, in my position?

– I certainly would.

– If I'da been able to get my hands on that Brendan Behan – God forgive me for saying it here today and him just buried – if I'da got me hands on him for two minutes, pregnant and all as I was, I would have made him remember the time he got drunk on my money that I had been putting by for months.

– How long was it before you saw him again?

– Sure it was no time at all.

– And did you go for him?

– 'Deed and I did not. Sure what could you do with him?

– I don't know about that.

– Tell them, Shay, tell them what happened.

Shay put down his pint, threw out his hands in a gesture of helplessness and allowed the smile on his lips to degenerate into slightly stifled laughter.

– Madge was born late in the afternoon and so I went down to the Rotunda to see Peg and little Mary Margaret as we called her then and then went across the road to have a drink with Peg's mother in Mooney's.

– A drink! Twenty drinks'd be more like it. The nurse didn't want to let you back into the hospital.

– Anyway, there I was in Mooney's having a few, mark me, a few jars to celebrate the birth of me first child when next thing I hear a very familiar sound and I turn round to see Mr Brendan Behan, large as life and back in Dublin, bursting in the door and him singing. I was still very touchy about what had happened a few weeks earlier and I'd had a few jars and so . . . well, we're only human, and I thought to myself, Brendan Behan, you're walking a very narrow line here, you're on tricky ground here; but what really made me blood boil was that he was singing in

French and that was more than I was prepared to stomach.

– What did you do?

– I put down me drink and walked over towards him and I shouted at him to shut up the singing if he knew what was good for him. Peg's mother tried to calm me down but I was going to settle up the score between myself and Mister Brendan Behan for once and for all.

– Your blood was up. I can just see you.

– He was jarred, that's all.

– Leave him tell the story, will yis, and shut up.

– Anyway, everything goes quiet and your man looks up at me with his big innocent face. I was looking for you, says he. I was looking for you too, says I. And there we are, me glaring at him, but is he glaring at me? Not on your nanny: there he is, standing there, with his two hands behind his back, looking as if butter wouldn't melt in his mouth, as innocent as the day is long. Fuck you anyway, says I to meself, but you're not going to get away with it this time, and I made a move towards him. But as soon as I did, out come his two hands from behind his back and he has something in each, a bottle in one and some kind of a packet in the other. That kind of stunned me, because I didn't know what he was up to. I just looked at him and next thing he starts smiling at me and walking over to me and him singing.

A soft smile spread across Shay's face as he spoke the words of the verse, lingering plangently between the phrases:

> My Mary of – the curling hair –
> the laughing cheek – and bashful air –
> A bridal morn – is dawning fair –
> with blushes in the sky –

And then, slowly and quietly at first, but gradually building up line by line to the release of a crescendo, they all sang together, raising their glass to each other and swaying the while:

> *Siúl, siúl, siúl a ghrá,*
> *Siúl go socair agus siúl go ciún,*
> My love, my pearl, my own dear girl,
> My mountain maid, arise.

– Lovely, lovely.

– Wasn't that lovely.

– Lord have mercy on him, I can hear him singing it as if he was standing there in front of me this very minute.

– But go on, Shay.

– Agh, yes. What happened then, Shay?

– What could I do? You know yourself what he was like: you couldn't hold a grudge against him. How is Peg? says he. Grand, says I. And how is little Mary? Grand, says I, although how he knew that we were going to call the child Mary Margaret is more than I could tell then or now. Are we going over to see them? says he. Why? says I, still trying to be annoyed with him. I brought them a little something from France, says he.

– Agh, tut-tut-tut. Wasn't that nice?

– Underneath it all he was as good as gold.

– And a real softie too, you know.

– What did he have?

– Here, says he, give little Mary a taste of that for luck, and he gives me a bottle of the very best champagne – none of your cheap stuff, the real Ally Daly. That's the best that money can buy, says he; not bejaysus, says he, that I paid full price for it but however... And then he gave me the packet: nylons for Peg.

– Oh gorgeous! Nylons!

– Again, the very best.

– Very hard to come by in those days.

– Don't I know! I think he got them from the American forces or something like that.

– Wasn't it very thoughtful of him?

– But sure that was Brendan for you. Next thing we had our arms around each other, the best of pals, singing our hearts out together as if nothing had ever happened. Not only that: just before we went over to see Peg, he mutters something about being sorry for the other business. Forget about it, says I. We're still friends? says he. Brendan, says I, it'd take more than a poxy pair of shoes to come between us; 'course we're friends, the best of friends, and always will be. Shay, says he, you're a star.

– All palsy-walsy again.

– Not only that. To give you some idea of what he was like. Walking across the road to go in and see Peg, I was telling him how I went into town that Sunday morning to look for the parcel, how I went from pub to pub and how I heard the whole story in McDaid's. Do you know what I'm going to tell you? We fell around the place laughing. That's why the nurse didn't want to let us in at first: she thought we were disorderly but we were only laughing. And the more I'd tell him what the fellow in McDaid's told me, the more he'd burst out laughing, and the more he'd laugh the more I'd laugh. And why was I laughing? I don't know: to this day I do not know. That was Brendan. Does anybody feel like a drink?

There was another break in which people resorted to the bar or the toilet or both. Everybody took some form of exercise except Mrs Mac who said she would have another sherry, emptied the glass she had and then began humming to herself a tune that nobody could identify with any certainty. What was certain was that she would very soon, if not prevented, bloom into song. Nobody else felt that the time had come for the singsong but neither was anybody willing to tell Mrs Mac that in so many words. People looked at Mrs Mac and then at Breda and smiled uncomfortably. Breda looked over at her father and showed all her teeth. Jimmy took a minute or so to realise what was happening but as soon as he twigged he put aside his tobacco and knife and spoke across the table at his mother.

– Mammy?
– What's wrong with you now?
– There's nothing wrong with me. I'm grand.
– Then why are you roaring at me?
– I'm not roaring at you.
– I'm not deaf, you know.
– Oh my God!
– Will you go easy, Daddy, or she'll hear you.
– Mammy?
– What?
– Why don't you tell the story of your Persian rug?
– I will not.
– Agh, go on.
– Tell it yourself if you want to; I won't.
– Go on, Mrs Mac.

- I will not make an eejit out of meself.
- You tell it, Jimmy.
- It's me mammy's story. Go on, Ma.
- You can ask me till the cows come home for all I care.
- Agh, Mammy.
- You start it for her, Daddy.
- He can finish it too while he's at it.

Breda nodded to her father and beckoned him to begin. Having glanced once more across at the stony face of his mother, Jimmy smiled resignedly.

- It was Christmas Eve 1946. Meself and Gertie – the Lord have mercy on her – were living with Mammy in Anglesea Street. Remember the place we had on the top floor? Sure you were all there at one stage or another. What age would you have been, Breda?
- Four.
- That's right. About four. And Ellen was nearly two. That's right: her birthday was on the seventh of January. Anyway, that was the really bad winter, remember?
- Says you, will we ever forget it? I won't anyway.
- I was working for meself at the time and doing reasonably well too. Gertie – may God be good to her – had been at me since Ellen was born to make her a rocking cot and I had been putting it off from week to week, nearly from year to year. But coming up to Christmas, Gertie put it to me that if I didn't make the cot . . . I was in trouble. It was no problem to make the cot but I just kept putting it on the long finger, saying I'd knock up a cot as soon as I had finished whatever paying job I was doing. Now that I think of it, I was doing a job for a certain party – a bookcase, I think – and the certain party wanted it the day before Christmas Eve. Anyway, to cut a long story short, I finished the bookcase the night before Christmas Eve, had it delivered on Christmas Eve morning, got paid for it, came back, gave Gertie the few bob to go out and do whatever shopping she had to do and then, in plenty of time, I threw the cot together – no problem to me in them days. I had it finished and painted and drying nicely when Gertie and Mammy came home late in the afternoon. Or I thought I had it finished. Of course, Gertie took one look at it and asked when I was going to put on the transfers. It was the first I had ever heard of transfers but I knew better

than to argue and so I had a quick look at the clock and decided that if I ran all the way I'd make it in time to this place up beyond Adam and Eve's where I could get some transfers. Off I went in the freezing cold – I think it was actually snowing at the time – and just as I was going past the Clarence who should I see walking along in an open shirt and without cap or cloak but?

– Brendan Behan.

– Correct.

– Come here: wasn't Brendan in the Glass House in 1946.

– Take your time. Listen and learn. *Éist agus foghlaim. An dtuigeann tú mé?*

– Whatever you're having yourself; mine's a pint.

– Go on, Jimmy.

– Brendan Behan, says I. The dead arose and appeared to many: I thought you were on the Curragh of Kildare. I was, says he, until a couple of weeks ago. But I thought, says I, that you were going to be there for a while longer. So did I, says he, but we all got out under a kind of a general amnesty. Fresh and well you're looking, says I, even if you are frozen itself; how are you feeling? Fine, says he, and he left it at that. And you know something? I thought for a minute that maybe the years inside had kind of knocked the stuffing out of him. And you have to remember that – what age was he then?

– Twenty-three or twenty-four.

– That's all. Twenty-five at the very most. And ever since he was sixteen he'd spent most of his life in prison.

– For Ireland.

– For Ireland, sure, but most of his grown-up life had been spent in prison. I knew Brendan when he was a kid – we all knew him when he was a kid – and there was never anybody as lively and as full of divilment as Brendan. He was a couple of years younger than me but I knocked around with him a bit when he came back from England – not as much as I used to but that was because I was getting married and trying to get a few bob together. I visited him once or twice when he was in the Joy and once when he was in Arbour Hill but I never made it down to the Curragh and I always felt a bit bad about that. And then when I saw him there on the quays on Christmas Eve, I felt kind of sorry for him. Here was this guy, a young fella like the rest of us, fond of a good time like the rest of us, a patriot like the rest of us but with this difference: some of us had done a little bit *ar son na saoirse* but Brendan had done more than his fair share and, you know something, this day he looked it. Brendan, says I, would you like to come back to our place and Gertie will rustle up a bite to eat. I'm not hungry, says he; I got something to eat over in the Star. Jesus, me heart went out to him and so I asked him if he'd like to come back and have a chat with us around the fire. (He looked frozen with the cold.) Agh no, says he, not on Christmas Eve; you'll all have things to do. I didn't know what to do for him. I knew I could spare him a couple of bob but I didn't want to do it out in the street in front of everybody. Can I buy you a pint? I asked him, or are you in a hurry? Not in any hurry, says he; I've time for a pint. Where will we go? says I. Suit yourself, says he; what about Cawley's? Why not? says I, and off we went to Cawley's.

– As soon as we got inside I called for a couple of pints. Welcome home, Brendan, says I; *sláinte. Sláinte 'gus saol*, says he. I had a good look at him when he took his first slug of the pint. I thought he was going to knock it back in one but no, he took the glass down from his mouth, very slowly, and then licked the froth off his lips. I needed that, says he. You did an' all, says I; I think you better have another one while you're at it. He didn't say anything but just put the pint up on his face again and finished it, drinking it slowly to the very last drop. You know what I'm going to tell you? It was like a sick man getting a blood transfusion just in the nick of time before he died. One minute he looked all beat and not like the old Brendan at all. Next minute he drained the pint, put it down on the counter with a bang, let a ferocious belch out of him and then his whole face lit up. Be Jayses, says he, I'd nearly consider go-ing back in for another five years if only to experience another pint like that. Go on outa that, says I, and get stuck into another pint. Are you not drinking with me? says he. Of course I am, says I. And of course I had to gollop off me pint there and then to catch up with him and then get on with the second. When the second couple of pints came along there was a baby Power beside each one of them. I was lost for a minute, wondering if Brendan had called for them. Brendan, says I, did you . . .? Not me, says he. I was taking the money out of me pocket to pay for the pints when the barman stood in front of us. On the house, says he. I didn't know what to say: I wasn't a regular there at all and so it could hardly be a Christmas drink. On the house, says your man again: never let it be said that one Irishman didn't do what he could to show his thanks for what another Irishman did for his country. Never indeed, says I to meself as I looked at Brendan and then at the barman. You're name is Brendan Behan? says he. That's what me mother told me, says Brendan. Well, Brendan Behan, says the barman, you've done your share and more than your share and I would be honoured if you would accept a drink from me and I would be more than honoured if you would allow me to shake your hand. And I, says Brendan, along with my friend Seamus here, am honoured to accept your drink and to take your hand, and the blessings of God on you and on all belonging to you. *Tiocfaidh ár lá*, says he, and him shaking Brendan's hand like billy-o. *Tiocfaidh go deimhin*, says Brendan and with that the barman broke the seals on the baby Powers, poured them into glasses for us, got a glass of the quare stuff for himself, lifted his glass up and then let fly with 'Out and make way for the bould Fenian men'.

– You're joking.

– I am not joking. There he was, standing to attention behind the bar, the rest of the bar looking at him in amazement, him singing away for all he was worth, grabbing Brendan's hand with his and swinging out of it.

– And what did the rest of the people do? Did they all keep quiet and listen?

– I'm telling you: it would have been the brave man who opened his mouth while your man was singing, a very brave and a very stupid man. Not only did they keep quiet and listen: there was a round of applause when he finished. Up the Republic, says he with a roar. Up the Republic, says the crowd in the bar. Then the barman raises his hand and there's silence again. Men, says he, I am going to call on Mr Brendan Behan, who has been falsely imprisoned both by the English and the Free State governments – God's curse on the bastards both – for fighting for a thirty-two-county Irish Republic, I am, on your behalf, going to ask him to give us a song. No better man, of course, than the bould Brendan. He finishes off the baby Power and makes a little speech, saying how moved he is by their welcome and especially by the kindness of the barman – I've forgotten what his name was – and he tells them all what a fine song the one they've just heard is but that there is another song about the bould Fenian men, a song written by his own uncle, the author of the 'Soldier's Song' and many other fine republican songs, and that's the song he's about to sing. And so he lets fly with –

– 'Down by the Glenside'.

– With 'Down by the Glenside'. Now in them days Brendan had a voice, a fine voice.

– Lovely. Lovely.

– And, be the Lord Harry, when he finished they pulled the place down and nothing would do them but another song. Give me time to draw me breath, says Brendan, and lubricate me vocal cords. Just then up comes the barman with two more pints and two more baby Powers.

– On the house?

– No. He leans across and points to a small fat man at the far end of the counter. The man up there, says he, wishes you a happy Christmas and a welcome home and he hopes you won't be offended if he sends up this to you. Not at all, says Brendan, and a happy and a holy Christmas to you and yours. And that was that. We were there for the duration. In no time at all there was drink flying at us from all directions and fellows asking Brendan to sing and him more than happy to oblige them. And then there were fellows coming up to shake his hand and tell him how happy they were to shake the hand of a true Irishman and all that sort of thing. Now Brendan couldn't take this sort of thing for long. He couldn't be a martyr for very long and soon he got going on the stories about the Curragh. Man dear, I never experienced anything like it in me entire life, not in all me born days. Stories! He had us falling all over the place with stories about prison. He made it sound like some kind of a holiday camp. And I wouldn't mind only the best stories always seemed to have to do with murderers who were about to be hanged, men who committed the most atrocious crimes and who were, if Brendan was to be believed, out-and-out headcases. If only somebody had written them down. I'll tell you this much: not even half of his stuff is in his books – as a matter of fact I would go so far as to say that not one quarter of his best stuff did he ever put down on paper, and that's the truth.

– You're right there, Jimmy.

– I suppose he is.

– Go back to your story though.

– Anyway and howandever, all good things come to an end and eventually it was closing time and out into the cold we went with the blessings and good wishes of everybody there. I was flutered and so I have only the vaguest notions of what happened between then and Christmas morning. I suppose that when the cold hit me I must have sobered up enough to remember that I had forgotten something. Holy God, the bloody transfers! Bad enough that I was palatic and could neither walk nor see nor think straight, bad enough that I had been out for five or six hours when I said I'd only be five or six minutes but, worst of all, I had forgotten to get the transfers and that meant that the cot would not be properly finished till after the Christmas and that meant that Gertie would not be wishing me a happy Christmas that night. What in the name of God was I to do? Come on, says Brendan, and I'll drop down with you just to say hello to Gertie and your mother. Serve me better, says I to meself, to drop down on me two bended knees and pray to the almighty for mercy. How we got around to Anglesea Street I do not know; how we got in and up the stairs I cannot remember.

– I can.

Mrs Mac's voice was economically belligerent.

– I can remember exactly what you were like. I remember poor Gertie walking up and down the room for hours, biting her nails and talking to herself all the time, one minute asking the Blessed Virgin to promise her that nothing had happened to you, the next minute saying what she'd do to you when she got her hands on you. Mrs Mac, says she, what do you think has happened to him? Do you think, says she, that he's had an accident or something? No, says I, I don't think he's had an accident unless you call meeting some crony and going off to some pub an accident. The poor woman was demented with worry and I couldn't get her to go to bed. There we were, me sitting by the fire knitting and her hopping up and down like a yo-yo. Next thing there's a noise in the street below and I knew it was Jimmy and whoever he had fallen in with. Your prayers are answered, says I; that poor husband of yours is down in the street. So she goes over to the window and opens it and looks out. Mrs Mac, says she, that's not Jimmy; there's only two drunks down there that can hardly stand up. True love indeed, says I to meself. Just as she is going to close the window, a voice comes up from the street. *Gertie! Mrs Mac!* Mary jewel and darling, says I, I know we live at the top of the house but your man down there must think we're up in the clouds. That's not Jimmy, says she. No, says I, that's the Christmas present that Jimmy is bringing home for us all. *Gertie! will you throw down the shaggin' key!* Poor Gertie nearly died when she realised who it was. Mrs Mac, says she on the verge of tears, I think that's Brendan Behan. God between us and all harm, says I; look out and make sure that Jimmy is there. So she bends out the window and looks down and asks Jimmy is he there. And the big voice comes up that'd wake the dead never mind the other people in the street. *Of course he's here. Where do you think he'd be at this hour of night? But if somebody doesn't let him in soon it's in a hospital ward he'll be with a bad case of frostbite!* Gertie shouts down for Jimmy to answer her if he's there and this tiny little moaning voice floats up – *throw down the key, Gertie, please* – and Gertie turns around to me, spitting fire, because it's obvious to a blind man that Jimmy is down there, stotious drunk and out of his mind. She throws the key down to them but sure she might as well have thrown down a grain of salt because after searching for ten minutes the two jewels still couldn't find it and Gertie had to go down herself and find it for them and help them up the stairs.

– Now by the time they arrived back up Gertie had told Jimmy exactly what she thought of him but sure I suppose it was a waste of breath because your man there didn't know whether he was coming or going. All he could do was wish everybody a happy Christmas and go on about the great time they had up in whatever pub they were in and what a good man Brendan Behan was and how he had done his bit for Ireland and all that sort of thing – none of which made Gertie any happier. Poor Gertie, the Lord have mercy on her, could be sharp at times but sure beneath it all she was as good as gold and she hadn't the heart to put Brendan out on the street on Christmas Eve even though there was nowhere for him to sleep except on the floor in front of the fire.

– That was poor Gertie all right. She wouldn't put a dog out on a night like that, Christmas Eve or no Christmas Eve. But tell them about the Persian rug.

Mother glared at son, who seemed to be reduced to the state of hapless guilt in which he had climbed the stairs in Anglesea Street almost twenty years before.

– Are you telling the story or am I?

- You are, Mammy. I'm sorry.

- Leave her alone, you. Go on, Mrs Mac, and pay no notice to him. Much he'd know about it.

Mrs Mac snorted to indicate her acceptance of these expressions of apology and her willingness to overlook the interruption and recommence her narrative.

- At the time I used to sleep on a sofa bed near the fire and Jimmy and Gertie and the children used to sleep in the back room. What we did that night was put Jimmy on the sofa bed in the front room and I got into the bed with Gertie. Brendan insisted that he would sleep on the floor in front of the fire, saying he was well used to sleeping on floors without any fire to keep him warm. And so Gertie and I got out the few presents and put them under the tree and then we were just going to get into bed when Gertie pulls me aside and, says she, I feel terrible about your man sleeping on the floor. Woman dear, says I, don't bother your head about poor Brendan sleeping on the floor; in about ten seconds he'll be unconscious and it won't matter a damn whether he's on the floor or on a feather bed. But, no, she couldn't rest thinking about it and I know from the look on her that she's up to something. Mrs Mac, says she, maybe we could let him sleep on the rug; would you mind if I let him? You see, I had bought her a rug for Christmas. She was always saying that the ould mat in front of the fire was very shook and so I had saved up a few bob and got her this lovely Persian rug around in McBirney's. Seven and eleven it cost me but I thought it was well worth it: it was lovely and thick and it was a gorgeous rich shade of crimson. Now the idea of your man stretched out on me lovely Persian rug and him looking as if he could do with a good wash . . . well you can imagine how I felt about it. But what could I say? I had given the rug to Gertie and I suppose she was entitled to do what she wanted with it and if she wanted to let this big drunken galoot stretch out on it for the night, well and good. So out she goes and puts down the rug and wishes Brendan good night and he mumbles something or other to her but even before she's gone out of the room he's sound asleep to the world, snoring like a train. Gertie and meself get into the bed and after all the waiting and the worry we're exhausted and so before long we're out for the count too.

Mrs Mac paused, sipped from her sherry, cleared her throat quietly, and closed her eyes for a brief moment to indicate the passing of time.

– I don't know how long I was asleep before all of a sudden I feel this grip on me arm and there's somebody whispering at me to wake up and listen. It was Gertie. Mrs Mac, says she, listen: can you hear anything? Gertie, says I to her, you must be having a nightmare. No, says she, I can hear voices. Where? I asked her. Out on the stairs, says she. I listened carefully and, though me hearing was never the best, not even then, I thought I could hear some noises. Gertie, says I, it's probably Jimmy and Brendan going out to the toilet. Will I look? says she. Go on, says I. She pulls an ould cardigan over her shoulders and creeps out into the front room. As soon as she opened the door I knew it wasn't your man there or Brendan. I could hear screams and shouts and everything. I got the fright of me life because the first thought that came into me mind was that there was a fire and so I jumped up and woke Breda and the baby. Gertie, God be good to her, ran back into the room and she was frantic. Come out quick, Mrs Mac, says she, there's people out on the stairs shouting in at us and I can't make head nor tail of what they're saying. I still wouldn't let the children go: I brought them out into the front room and there right enough I saw Jimmy on the bed and Brendan in front of the fire, both of them sleeping the sleep of the just and both of them snoring to beat the band. All the time Gertie was talking I was trying to see if I could smell any smoke; only when I was sure there was no sign of fire or burning did I pay any real attention to Gertie and what she was saying. Listen to them, Mrs Mac, says she. I could hear voices out on the stairs but I couldn't make out who it was or what they were saying. Who's out there? I asked Gertie. It's the Flanagans, says she. (The Flanagans were the people on the floor beneath us. Remember oul' Timmy Flanagan – used to lose his rag when people called him Banjo – married Dotty Sonnix from Thomas Street – Dotty be name and Dotty be nature – they'd only the one girl, Delia, but she was as much trouble as a family of ten, remember?) What time is it? I asked her. Three o'clock in the morning, says she. And what in the name of all that's high and holy are the Flanagans doing shouting and roaring at this time on this morning of mornings? They want me to go out to them, says she. Are they mad? says I. Will I go out? says she. You will in your foot, says I; stay where you are. Here, says I, get a hold of your children and let me over to the door and might I ask you, woman dear, why in the name of God the two of us are up here on our feet while those two brave men are stretched out over there? While I'm at the door, says I, will you see if you can wake up that snoring sot of a son of mine. Let me over to the door, says I, till I see if I can make out what all the shouting is about. I put me mouth up to the door and I shouted out as loud as I could and asked them what in God's name they were up to. They were all quiet for a minute and I could hear them whispering among themselves and then young Delia shouted up. *Are you all right up there? Are yis all all right up there?* Of course we're all right, says I, and why wouldn't we be? *Oh, Mrs Mac, thanks be to the living Christ that you're all right. Are Gertie and the children all right?* Of course they're all right; what are you all shouting and roaring about? *Open the door and show them to us, Mrs Mac.* I told Gertie not to open the door but to shout out to them and when they heard her voice some of them were thanking God and some of them were whispering that they couldn't believe what we were saying. I shouted out again that we were all all right and why wouldn't we be. *But, Mrs Mac, we know there's murder done, we know it. Who's dead and who's alive?* Sacred heart of Jesus, I couldn't believe me ears. There's nobody dead, says I. *Show us the children; open the door and show us the children.* What'll we do? asks poor Gertie; maybe we should open the door and set them at their ease. No, says I, you take the children over to the window and I'll talk to them. What I did was: I told the Flanagans that they could go down to the street and look up and we'd be at the window. Some of them went out and we could see them looking up at us and I got the children to wave, though the poor unfortunate children didn't know what in the name of God was going on. At this stage Jimmy and Brendan had woken up at last and the two of them were falling around the place hardly able to stand up straight and all they wanted was a drink of something. Serve you better, says I to your man, to go down and keep your neighbours quiet rather than to be staggering like a sight round the place in front of your own children on Christmas Night. So Jimmy went to the door and we all had a gick out at the Flanagans on the stairs. *Jesus, Mary and Holy Saint Joseph, Jimmy, who's been killed?* Nobody's been killed, says Jimmy; can't you see that we're all here and that we're all well. *Who's that fella there behind Gertie?* That's only a friend of ours who's staying the night, says Jimmy; there must be some mistake. Then young Delia Flanagan steps out in front of them and I can see her kissing her rosary beads like a mad woman: *Oh don't keep saying that; sure we've seen the blood.* What blood? says I; show us this blood you're talking about. I'd had enough of this and I was going to get to the bottom of it one way or another for once and for all. I went in and got me coat and threw it over me and then out I went to face them. Show us the blood, says I. That mad rip, Delia Flanagan, it's like she's having an epileptic fit, what with kissing her beads and blessing herself and kissing my hands and then blessing everybody and all the time she's down on her bended knees and scampering down the stairs like, God save the mark, the child up in number 28 that was born with no legs. But anyhow, Banjo and Dotty bring me down into their front room and point up at the ceiling.

– The ceiling?

– Sh!

– As I said, they take me into the front room and point up at where there was this patch on the ceiling as if there was something red seeping down through it. What do you make of that then? says Banjo. If that's not blood splashing down onto the floor, what is it? Jesus, Mary and Joseph, says I, when I saw what he was pointing at. There was a big pool in front of the fire and the drip from the ceiling was plopping into it, just like a tap. I didn't know what to say. It certainly looked like blood to me and there could be no doubt that it was coming down from above and the only thing that was up there was our place. And when mad Delia came in again and saw the stuff splashing away she lost the run of herself completely. *Sacred heart of Jesus, what are yis all standing round here for like eejits? Go up, go up quickly, and see where the blood is coming from. God alone knows who's lying up there with the life blood pouring out of them this very second.* So with that we all rush up the stairs and Gertie tells Jimmy to take the girls into the bedroom and the rest of us go to find out where the blood could be coming from. It must be somewhere in front of the fire, says Banjo as we reach the door. Next thing there's a noise from Dotty that nearly put the heart crossways in us. *There he is,* she screams as she points at Brendan; *there's the murdered man.* Murdered me arse, says I and God forgive me for using bad language like that; that's Brendan Behan and you saw him walking around here only five minutes ago. Him and Jimmy had a few drinks tonight, says I, and Brendan decided to spend the night here on the rug in front of the fire. He's so jarred and tired, says I, that he's after going back to sleep; if you don't believe me, go over and wake him up and ask him yourself whether he's dead or alive. You go over, Timmy, says Dotty, but be careful. (Timmy came from Cork. He had a very funny way of talking at the best of times but when the kids called him Banjo you'd swear he was talking another language altogether.) So Timmy goes over, all dramatic like, and he kneels down beside Brendan and nudges him to wake him up but to no avail and so he starts to roll him over and back but sure he might as well have been singing 'Adeste Fideles' for all the effect he had on Brendan. Then Banjo, the dirty eejit, he must have seen too many pictures, what does he do but listen to Brendan's chest to see if he's alive when a deaf man in the next room could have heard the snoring and moaning. Banjo turns around to us and holds out his hands as much as to say that there's no more he can do. With that there was another screech from Dotty and Delia fell down on her knees again and the both of them pointing to Banjo. *Look at his hands! Look at the blood on his hands!!* And as God is my judge and as true as I'm sitting here before you today after Brendan Behan's funeral, his hands were glistening red.

– Sacred heart of Jesus tonight!
– I never heard any of this before.
– And was Brendan bleeding?
– Ssh! Listen to her tell the story.
– But had Brendan cut himself or something?
– Cut himself? God forgive me for saying it but that night I wished to Jesus he had cut himself and cut his throat while he was at it.
– What had happened?
– Let Jimmy tell the rest of the story.
– Go on, Jimmy. Don't keep us in suspense.
– We're all on tenterhooks.
– Tell us what happened.
– Can you not guess? No? Brendan didn't cut himself. When it was time for us all to go to sleep Brendan lay down on the rug and passed out into a deep sleep. He was the next thing to unconscious and nothing on earth was going to disturb him, nothing was going to make him get up from his comfort; and so when, as a result of all the pints he'd had, it was necessary for him to empty his bladder he did... there and then in front of the fire, without moving a muscle. Saving your presence,

ladies and gentlemen, he just wet himself like a little baby. And the piss seeped through the rug and then through a hole in the lino – there was a burn hole there for ages – and then down through a crack in the floorboards and down through Flanagans' ceiling. But the thing was: when the rug became thoroughly soaked the dye ran and so what dropped down onto Flanagans' floor was not your usual yellow but blood-red. And that's what had the Flanagans out on the stairs and screaming that murder had been done.

There were various forms of laughter and other loud expressions of surprise, exhilaration and general wellbeing at having been kept interested and amused for some time. Just before there was another diaspora from the table towards bars and doors and toilets, Jimmy called them to order for his finale.

– By Jesus, I'll tell you this much. There very nearly was murder done that night, there very nearly was blood spilt that night – mine. When the Flanagans went downstairs, Gertie and me mother there got stuck into me and, I'm telling you, if I had one great night with Brendan I paid for it afterwards and I was never let forget the lovely Persian rug that me mother had bought for Gertie.

– Persian lamb's wool, if you please, and I didn't buy it for Gertie; I bought it for you and Gertie.

– One way or another, I wasn't let forget it. But do you know what the funniest thing of all was? While I was standing there getting the face ate off me and being told what kind of a husband I was, what kind of a father and what kind of son, there was the bould Brendan stretched out in front the fire – the rug had been hung over a chair to dry – a big stupid smile on his face and him lying there as if nothing had happened, lying there like an angel on a Christmas card.

Jimmy wanted to add some more but the length of the story and the nature of its climax made a visit to the toilet an absolute necessity, not only for the men around the table but for me as well. When I returned to my seat near the table, Breda was, despite the wishes of the others, trying to find a suitable key in which to sing 'Heart of My Heart', Liam's wife was insisting that it would be better if Liam sang something Irish at least, Shay was about to try and head Breda off by giving them a blast of 'Red Roses for Me' while, with a regal disregard for the rising chaos about her, Mrs Mac was saying that she would have a cigarette if anybody had the decency to offer her a tipped one. I was headed up to the bar to stock up for the singing when I noticed – and was noticed by – a group of relations on the other side of the bar and so I went out one door and in the other and was soon immersed in another school of song and story in memory of Brendan.

And that was the great thing about Brendan's funeral. It showed him to be, like a younger northside Falstaff, not only good company himself but the inspiration of good company in others. And through the years he would continue to walk in his lopsided way through the minds of people who had never known him, his head hanging back over a dropped left shoulder, his mouth twisted into an invincible smile, his eyes ready to dance – his whole self ready to sing grief rather than cry it.

Me life on ye, Brendan.

Many years after the funeral, when I had been several other people and only an impersonal memory of the seventeen-year-old who ate the tomatoes that August day in 1962, I found myself in the city of San Francisco, in an eminent university, delivering a lecture on – of all things – 'Brendan Behan and the Gaelic Tradition'. To tell the truth, I was amazed at the number of people who turned up to hear a lecture on such a distant topic, but there they were, the specialists in Celtic Studies, Anglo-Irish Lit and Mod Drama, the culturally curious, the supporters of things Irish, and all looking interested when I sketched the history of writing in Ireland, looking delighted when I quoted colourful passages from *Borstal Boy*. And afterwards, in the frank manner of the Americans, they came up to say how much they had enjoyed the talk, to tell me where they had seen *The Hostage* or on what TV show they had seen Behan, to ask me if I had ever met him, to hope that I was enjoying my stay in San Francisco. I was, in the uneasy manner of the Irish, trying to respond as gracefully and as convincingly as possible while at the same time making definite progress towards my host who was to take me to a room where there were ice cubes and alcoholic drinks. I was doing quite well until I noticed a very large man making his way through the press. Far from being satisfied to shake my hand and mutter some pleasantry, he put his huge arm around me and simply took me away from the others, telling me that he was Ronan FitzGibbon and telling the others that he would let them have me back in a minute.

Having seated me behind a desk he identified himself further as Father

Ronan FitzGibbon CC, originally from Cork where, he gathered, I came from myself.

No. Dublin. But I was teaching at UCC.

He supposed that maybe I was a bit surprised to find a priest dressed in jeans and tracksuit top. I told him that things were loosening up in Ireland too in the matter of clerical dress. He guessed that maybe I didn't expect to find an Irish Catholic priest from Cork at a lecture on Brendan Behan. I didn't expect to find an Irish Catholic priest from Cork at a lecture – or, if it came to that, in San Francisco. Did I know that Brendan Behan had been in San Francisco? I did and then . . . slowly and vaguely . . . a spume of memory began to weave itself into a pattern and I wondered: wasn't it in San Francisco that Brendan met the priest with the glass case containing . . .

– Oh yes, in fact he told me about being in San Francisco and, it's coming back to me now, about meeting an Irish priest out here and spending some time with him in his church, a new church.

– Is that a fact? What was the priest's name?

Holy Jesus, I thought to myself in sudden panic: it wasn't this fellow here, was it? If it was, I had better be careful about what I say if I don't want to have to keep a straight face while looking at a splinter from the Inchicore CIE works.

– Oh, I wouldn't have an idea. It was hundreds of years ago. How long are you here?

– I'll be here twelve years this fall. I had a spell in Baltimore before I came out here.

Thank God for that, I thought; it's safe to pass my time with this fellow by mentioning the splinter – but watch your language.

– Brendan was very impressed with this priest and the two of them got on like a house on fire.

– You don't say? I wonder who it was and if he's still around.

– What I do remember about him is that he had built a new church and that inside this church there was a special kind of side-chapel or alcove or something like that in which there was a relic of Matt Talbot.

Father Ronan shook his head agnostically and smashed his large fists on the desk.

– Well, isn't that something? Would you believe it? That sure is something.

My host had joined us to take me away to gins and tonics but I had to know what this something was and anyway I knew that Father Ronan was not about to let me go without telling me.

– Larry Qualter. That's who it was, sure as hell.

Yes. He was right. I could confirm the name because though Qualter was an uncommon name it was also the name of a friend of mine at Garbally. He was right.

– You're right.

– You're right I'm right. Larry Qualter. It was Larry, sure enough. Well ain't that something?

He was utterly bemused by what he had learned. I was utterly bemused by his utter bemusement. My host tried once more to prise me away from this seance, but in vain and he said that he would see how things were going at the reception and be back for me in a couple of minutes.

– Well, ain't that something? Ain't that really something?

I had to prod him to explain, just in case we ran out of time.

– What's so strange?

– What's so strange? Sure, go ahead and ask me what's so strange. I can hardly believe my ears, that's what's so strange. The story of Larry Qualter, that's what's so strange. Weird, that's what it is, weird.

He shook his head from side to side and then seemed on the verge of narrative only to wave a hand in token of failure or frustration and return to the shaking of the head. I was curious but I had the rest of my life to think about and so I put it to him.

– Maybe I could call you sometime.

A big freckled hairy arm on mine. Two enormous blue pupils rivetting mine to attention. The slow delivery of one who is normally allowed his own speed.

– You won't believe this, but Larry Qualter was parish priest in the parish where I am now. Larry Qualter was a great man. Larry Qualter was like a father to me when I came out here first. Larry Qualter was... *(various gestures, reminiscent of Brando, indicating the inadequacy of verbal language)*... an Irishman in the best sense. You know what I mean? The very best sense. None of the stage Irishman stuff. There's a lot of that over here but as far as Larry Qualter was concerned... forget it. A true Irishman and proud of it, he was proud of everything that was good and Irish. And, you know what I'm about to tell you? As straight as an arrow: straight.

– I'm sure he was.

– So Behan saw the Blessed Matt Talbot Chapel of Meditation and Self-Knowledge. He remembered it and spoke about it. What did he say about it?

– Well, just how ... how impressive it was, you know, and what an impression it made on him.

– Right. It is impressive. And can you imagine how much more impressive it will be when Blessed Matt is canonised?

– Indeed.

– If only poor Larry had known that somebody like Brendan Behan had been so impressed that he spoke about it back home. Shoot! Poor Larry, I don't suppose he believed that there was a bad Irishman. What a heart!

– What happened?

– What happened? Who knows? Who really knows?

Again he seemed lost for words.

– Larry never left the church. The last words he ever spoke to me were: Fitz, I'll never leave the church – no matter what they do to me or say about me. No: I guess if everybody was as full of faith as Larry, well ... Larry fell in love, I guess there's no other way of saying it. He fell in love with a lovely lady and he wanted to share himself fully with her. He would have stayed on here but he knew it wouldn't work out. So, you can guess what happened. He went south and got a job teaching in San Diego and set up home there but things ... things didn't work out too well. Two years ago I received a letter telling me that Larry was no longer with us. You know something: that guy had not seen me for years and years but left more or less everything to me. (The lady, his wife, had left him and I don't think the people in Ireland were anxious to keep in contact, if you know what I mean.) There was a couple of hundred dollars and some things, books mostly, and things like Waterford crystal and stuff. The money didn't cover the cost of transportation from San Diego.

That seemed to be the end of the sad story and I began to rise. He did not prevent me by fixing me under one of his huge hands and so I began to move away, muttering as suitably as I could. He waited till

I was on my way.

– When I met Larry first, the first time I was inside his church, he showed me the Blessed Matt Talbot Chapel of Meditation and Self-Knowledge, he took me in and showed it to me and told me the story of how he had brought it to pass. He said that he was convinced that the power of the future saint had been and would be manifested there. I asked him to explain but he said that there was nothing definite yet, nothing like the cure of a diseased organ; he was convinced that just being in that chapel had brought people closer to God and he was convinced that attestable miracles would be worked there. That's why, he said, it was so important that somebody would always take great care of the chapel. That's why, he said, I am asking you to be responsible for the chapel and to take care of the relic . . . if and when I am no longer here to look after things. They were his very words.

I nodded my head up and down in an effort to signal my understanding of the great duty that had been laid upon him. Then, as I turned around towards the door:

– I went through the books. I won't say that I read them, I didn't, I'm not really a great man for books although I like Irish history. Most of the books were connected with Ireland in one way or another. He sure thought highly of those books. I would be happy to show them to you, they're in my apartment and I'd say you'd be very interested in them.

Tactful but firm refusal of offer on the grounds that my time in San Francisco is short and is not really my own: all my time has already been scheduled.

– I thought as much and that's why I brought this along for you to see. I guess it was his proudest possession.

He reached into an Adidas sports bag and took out a large object which, having been told it was a book, I assumed to be a facsimile Book of Kells. But as I approached it, it seemed to be much smaller than a folio and very much thicker, almost three inches.

– You'll never guess what this is.

It was a large book, sumptuously bound in green leather with all sorts of pseudo-Celtic toolwork. Was it the *Ulysses* with the Matisse drawings?

– Nope. Guess again.

As I stood beside him, he carefully opened the book at a particular page and turned it to me for my inspection. And there I saw –

BRENDAN BEHAN'S ISLAND
An Irish Sketch-book
by
BRENDAN BEHAN
with drawings by
Paul Hogarth

and between this title and the name of the publisher was scrawled in ink that had already begun to fade:

Éire Abú!
Brendan Behan

I was moved. There was no need to pretend. The inheritor of the Blessed Matt Talbot Chapel of Meditation and Self-Knowledge was delighted to see the little jerk of emotion which I registered.

– You like it?

– Oh yes.

– You got this book?

– I have a copy but it's not autographed. Behan gave me a copy but never got round to signing it for me.

– Would you say there are many copies signed by Behan himself?

– Oh no, very few. Very, very few. I've never seen one.

– Even you don't have one, right?

– 'Fraid not. I'd love to have one but he's not signing them any more.

He smiled and put the book back in its holder and back into the Adidas bag.

– You know something? You've just made me very, very happy. Very happy indeed. I am grateful to you for that and I sure am glad I came to hear you. I'm sorry to keep you from the other people in there but I was sure you'd understand.

– Of course.

– Very happy indeed.

– *Slán leat.*

– *Slán agat.*

And so he left, turning not to the room where there was gin and tonic and much talk of things Gaelic but turning towards the front door of the building to make his way, I supposed, to the Blessed Matt Talbot Chapel for Meditation and Self-Knowledge, where, again I could only suppose, he would contact the spiritual remains of Father Larry Qualter and tell him how happy he was.

And why.

And why not?

POSTSCRIPT

FRIDAY MORNING: 9.30

Weather beautiful, even when it rains. It feels so great not to
feel as bad as I remember feeling yesterday morning. Virtue is
its own reward and that's fine by this new reformed Me. I was
in bed by nine o'clock last night and unconscious by five past
without the assistance of any narcotics. I will never know how
I managed to get through yesterday morning but I did; I
applied the remnants of my senses to the Behan section and
was eventually requited by the gods of industry and assiduity.

It was about half past one when I put away the typescript
and staggered out into the kitchen to consume a couple of
pints of water. Trusting the muted promptings of my
diminished brain rather than the pandemonium of my stomach,
I heated a small tin of tomato soup and swallowed it in fear
and trembling spoonfuls. Then I laid my head down on the
kitchen table and awaited sentence. And the sentence came:
with such a crazy clarity that my head throbbed with arrested

laughter. Ah, there's the agony. No pub open, but the bells battering your bared nerves and all you could do with the cold and the sickness was to lean over on your side and wish that God would call you. The text was from *The Quare Fellow*; the voice was that of Brendan Behan himself chuckling away as he delivered the lines with grotesque relish. I tried to exorcise his comic spirit but to no avail. I heard myself beginning to speak his words, assuring him that he would never be dead, that you'd never get the Irish out of Ireland, that he was the flower of the flock. And he replied with tumultuous peremptoriness, telling me that it was time to get up and get out of the house, to take the air and see the world at large and hear what the people were saying about us.

And so, having thrown a towel and togs and a few apples into my back pack, out I staggered and, as often happens when the chuckling ghost leads, I was rewarded with a little adventure.

I headed out of town but instead of turning down to the sea I found myself taking the road north. At first I thought my Director of Subconscious Operations was simply taking me for A Long Walk. But not at all.

I had known for many years that the main concentration of Joyces was in this part of Connemara, which is still known as the Joyce Country. More recently, while researching the activities of his immediate ancestors in Cork, I had begun to suspect that James's people may once have been involved with the marble quarries of Galway. At some stage last year I had queried Bernard on the subject and he mentioned a marble quarry a couple of miles outside Clifden. And so here I was stepping out the road absolutely convinced that the spirit was leading me to this Joycean quarry.

Great though my faith was, my vesture of decay was distinctly muddied and so I took the liberty of stopping a man on a tractor and asking for directions. No doubt about it: he had been placed in my way by the tutelary goddess and he pointed the gnarled limb of his index finger in the direction of a hill and then at a gate by the side of the road. There was nothing to be seen from the road but a rough path leading in and so I clambered over the gate and, piously placing one foot in front of the other, proceeded along the path. Soon the stones began to enlighten me, reflecting the sun's rays into my eyes with the green scintillation which is the mark of Connemara marble, and then, turning a corner, I saw the works: a large shed surrounded by broken slabs, lumps and bits of marble everywhere. There were sounds: engines whirring, the complaints of sheared stone, men talking, three of them in the large shed. Who were these three, I wondered, whom the goddess had chosen to strew in my way?

At first I did not approach. I nodded a salute to them in the manner of the area and they nodded slightly in response, looking up at me from under the peaks of their caps as if I was the one from another world. And I did feel uncomfortably a stranger – blue back pack, beige cotton trousers, hangover thoughts of James Joyce and the goddess. I looked over at the quarry and then turned back to the men and nodded over at the quarry in such a way as to seek their permission to inspect it. This they granted with a slight though gracious dipping movement of their cap peaks.

Have you ever seen a marble quarry? Have you ever wondered how marble is quarried? I had never seen one before and I realised as I looked at this one that inasmuch as I had ever thought about the extraction of marble I had assumed that it was blasted out explosively. Bottom of the class, Fintan.

Imagine a small Connemara hill covered with grass and stones and furze and so on. Now – if you are up to it – imagine that Somebody sliced it vertically in two and removed one half of it Elsewhere. You are left with a section such as you see in geological textbooks: on top a rough overcoat of the common vegetation I have described, underneath that a skim of brown soil and underneath that again a wall of marble – not rough and jagged but perfectly smooth because, as I am now in a position to tell you, marble is not quarried by chaotic explosions but by cutting and it is not extracted in a crazy variety of fragments but in neat cubes. Both the facing wall and the floor of the quarry were smooth planes. Even as I stood there I could look down at the floor where saws – lubricated with water – were cutting out the next cube. Presumably the cube is then hoisted out and swung into the large shed where it is cut into slabs and then into pieces of whatever dimensions the orders require. And how are these huge cubes – between two and three metres each way – lifted out? By means of the strong hoist on which I stood the better to look down into the quarry. And how did I react when I deduced this? With a wry grin. And why? Because the hoist was large and black and vaguely reminiscent of another piece of industrial mechanics that I had recently seen in a museum of modern art.

Having controlled my urges to laughter and photography, I turned and walked towards the men in the shed. I muttered a few remarks and they nodded vaguely. I hoped they hadn't minded me having a look. Very interesting and so on: I had never seen a marble quarry before. Then I broached my subject slowly and unsurely.

– Is there some connection between the Joyces and the marble?

Their only response was to look straight at me for a second and then back down at the slab of marble on the bench. Try again: some gentle pressure on the portal of discovery.

– Weren't there Joyces from Maam Cross involved with marble?

I knew there were but the taciturn trio were not about to confirm or deny it. Did my manner or my speech betray my condition? Had I – even with my few words – touched on forbidden ground? Maybe they were employees of the same Joyces. Maybe there was some trouble in the air. Time to go.

– I suppose I could always go over and ask there.

It was a reasonable request for permission to withdraw but even this was not forthcoming. How could I make it clear that I wasn't any kind of spy?

– It isn't so much the marble or the quarry I'm interested in but the people who used to work it years and years ago, well over a hundred years ago.

He spoke, the man in the middle with the blue overalls and the pencil behind his ear, as if we had been talking for an hour.

– If that's what you want there's no point in going over there.

– Why's that?

– They only bought in.

We all nodded, them at me in sympathy for my ignorance, me at them in total uncertainty. I decided to risk it:

– But there were Joyces working in the quarries at some stage?

The two on the sides smiled at the one in the middle. He took the pencil from behind his ear and used it to scratch the part of the back of his head just under the rim of the cap. The others continued to smile while he prepared to speak.

– There were Joyces here all right.

I jumped in with what I immediately regretted as uncivil haste.

– Here? In this quarry?

– Here. In this quarry.

– How far back, do you know?

His acolytes looked over at me and then down at the bench as if the man in the blue overalls was about to raise the chalice at the consecration. The celebrant brushed some dust from the slab before him:

– How far back? My father and his father and his father before him. Is that far enough for you?

In one sense, the academic sense, it wasn't but I was still interested.

– You're a Joyce yourself?

– I am.

– And you're talking about Joyces being here for almost a hundred years?

– And maybe more.

I tried to look at his face without seeming to do so. Was there any trace of the long jaw, the big hands, the sardonic blue eyes? I was interrupted by one of the acolytes.

– A hundred years and more. 'Tis something to think about.

– It is.

– It is that.

I was now at the crucial stage of my enquiries and had to be careful. Though the name of James Joyce has become sufficiently sanitised to be used by Bord Fáilte and though his books are widely discussed if not actually read and though his image is sold in Irish cities in poster and statuette form, nevertheless there are still parts of Ireland where people would not appreciate the suggestion that they were related to such a lewd genius. And it was possible I was in one of those parts. But it was worth a try.

– I should explain that the reason I'm here is that I'm interested in a man called James Joyce, a writer.

It was impossible to gauge from their responses if they had ever heard of him; but it was enough for me that they did not drive me from the quarry. I went on.

– As far as anybody can make out, his people came from around here but that was a long time ago. We know that they were stonemasons in Cork way back at the beginning of the last century. They had limestone quarries and that sort of thing. Anyway, James Joyce, the writer, believed his people came from Galway and not only that: he married a girl from Galway, from Galway city. In fact on one of his visits back home to Ireland he came out to Clifden by train...

I wasn't willing just to go on and on, though the men seemed quite content to let me. I wondered if any of them knew who I was talking about. But it was now or never. I looked straight at the man in the blue overalls, trying to produce a disarming smile as I spoke:

– Did you ever hear anything about being related to this James Joyce? Was there ever any talk of it in your family?

A little anxiously, I heard my question hover in the air among the sounds of machinery and awaited the reaction. He looked at me very firmly and began.

– Do you think...

Jesus, I thought, I've done it. There was such a direct and

confident ring to his obviously rhetorical question and such an authoritative angle to his gaze. And that confidence, I feared, was most likely to come from the kind of religious conviction that would not encourage an admiration or even an acceptance of James Joyce. Home, James.

– Do you think that if I had what that man had I'd be standing here today in overalls and cap?

My heart bulged. I wanted to throw my arms around him, look him in those eyes and tell him that he had – as they say around these parts – never lost it. But I restricted myself to a smile: he was a Joyce right enough, a chip off the same block. I took away with me as a remembrancer a large chip about the size of a man's head. Of course I asked permission and of course I was more than welcome.

And so I put it in my back pack, waved a last farewell and sauntered back to the house at my leisure. Inside, I placed the marble on the table here in the scriptorium and sent up before it a votive offering of a Willem II Optimum 100% tobacco which I bought by way of celebration on my return into Clifden. The stench of which offering – stale from its overnight stay – hangs in the air now as a relic of that strange pilgrimage.

But not for much longer because it's time to go, time to clear up whatever mess I've made in the past few days and return the house to Bernard's immaculate conception. There's not that much to do and every modern convenience with which to do it. A quick phone call to Kate to herald my return and then all I have to do is prepare this package for the post and wait to see what you make of it.

1 pm. Still here, still scribbling, still no clearing up done.

When I had finished writing earlier on I was full of zip but it didn't last. I stripped the bed but the sight of the phone reminded me to ring Kate. I only let it ring four or five times and put it down. I don't know why. Was there something else to be done first? Couldn't think of anything but I didn't ring again. Just in case my confused state was due to simple hunger I made a sandwich and waited for my sense of purpose to return. Obviously it wasn't simple hunger. I came into the scriptorium and began to tidy things up a bit. And then I remembered that I had intended taking some photographs before I left and I had decided that the ridge to the left of the lake was the best vantage point. My walk took me down through the half-hearted vegetable garden, across the stubble of the school football pitch and up to the narrow road, across the road and another stone wall and then up the ridge. I was wondering whether my pantings would be adequately rewarded when I turned around and saw the scene beneath me: the house, the town snuggled in the hills on my right, the lake down to my left, the sea further out in front. And guess what? The lake is not a lake at all, at least not in the way I assumed it was. It is not a sufficiently distinct entity to be a normal lake. (Am I dreaming or is there such a term as 'a marine lake'?) It's not separated from the sea by more than twenty or thirty metres. All lakes are, I suppose, ultimately connected to the sea by rivers but you wouldn't call this connection a river, merely a short neck of water. As I worked this out I realised why the rocks on the edge of the lake were marked as they are: the lake is tidal. This will strike you as a fuss about very little but I was amused to think that I had been staring out at this lake for the past week without realising that it was really a part of the invisible sea. That's all.

Except that I am going to treat myself to a sauna.

I had taken my photographs and was putting the camera back in the case when a slight drizzle began to fall. It was, as we joke in Ireland, the kind of rain that would wet you; by the time I had clambered back down and made my way across the fields to the house I was in that particularly uncomfortable state of being soaked with both rain and perspiration. And then it struck me: the sauna. ('What a jolly good idea!' as you used to enunciate in your perfect language laboratory English before you felt the baleful influence of a Dublin accent.) And that is why you must avert your eyes as you read this for I am quite naked as I write it. Bye for now: my sauna should be ready.

1.54. I feel odd. Maybe I shouldn't have had that sauna. One part of me wants to get out of this haunted house and yet I can't put this biro down. Whatever the hell is happening to me began in the sauna. For some reason or other the image of Pearse in Jervis Street hospital stuck in my mind and I couldn't get rid of it.

Pearse is lying on his side on the bed in Jervis Street hospital. The rest of us are standing around, whispering to ourselves and wondering if we should wake him. When I remember how I used to look forward to seeing him, how I enjoyed his free spirit, I have to go out to the toilet and cry. When I come back the others have gone and I stand at the bottom of the bed and though I know that he cannot hear me I tell him I am sorry that I never showed him the bits of the typescript that might have interested him. He turns in the bed and his face is suddenly vital: his brow furrows, his eyes sparkle, he coughs slightly and then he speaks.

> I can't describe what it is that I wanted – I never could – but part of it was wanting to be with Brendan, with Kavanagh and Cronin and Kernoff and that crowd in McDaid's. And Brendan never mentioned me in his books, not so much as a fucking mention, and all we'd been through together. I would have loved to have been a writer, loved it. But I could never have written books. I know I couldn't because I didn't. It's as simple as that: the only one who can do it is the fellow who gets up off his arse and fuckingwell does it. You can do it if you want to. But nothing. The time is long gone when you could have decided what and how to write. That's all settled now. The only question is will you or won't you do it. Do it. Do it for yourself – the best reason of all – but if that doesn't suit you, do it for me.

(No such conversation ever took place in Jervis Street or anywhere else. Pearse was beyond talking when I went to see him in Jervis Street. And I think I can truthfully say that not only did Pearse never mention any desire to write but I never even imagined that he had ever imagined himself in those terms.)

As I turn away from Pearse to see if anybody else is listening I see Brendan Behan passing by the door of the ward. He is wearing only the jacket of his pyjamas and his hands are joined in a parody of prayer. I expect to hear his raucous voice raised to Jesus' heart all burning with fervent love for men but I can't hear it. I run out of the ward and chase down the corridor after him. He is there as I turn the corner but he has changed. He is now fully dressed in scruffy overcoat, shabby trousers, untied shoes. I call his name several times but he doesn't seem to notice. When he bumps into a trolley he turns around and his face is all swollen and crusted with stubble and grime. I call his name again. I can't tell if he recognises me through those weary, bleary, bloodshot eyes. Again I call his name but he just waves me away and staggers on around the next corridor.

(Brendan was long dead when I visited Pearse in Jervis Street. It must have been about twenty years earlier that I saw Brendan walking half naked around Baggot Street hospital to the intense embarrassment of the staff. And the final image – that of the dazed death-marked man – could have come from many meetings with Brendan during his last years but the wave of the hand identifies it with that piece of film I saw some time after his death.)

And then I came on Eugene, dressed in striped hospital pyjamas and sitting up in bed, writing. I am shocked at his appearance: he was never other than thin, but now he is emaciated and looks as if he is very ill indeed. We smile at each other and he goes back to his writing. It is, apparently, a letter to me.

If you should meet some scholar from an antique land,
ask him to define for you the difference between Grace
and Beauty – in English. Why one sounds like the name
of a girl and the other like the name of a greyhound. And

why any metaphysical definition is a waste of breath unless it can include these physical facts.

Best of luck with the thesis. Nothing can stop it now except a nuclear fission. It will be that much done. Hope it has helped you to shed the last of your ridiculous youth, for the days are far too full of aging Ariels.

He reads over what he has written and then slashes his signature and puts the top back on the pen. It is as if the effort has exhausted him. He exhales vocally, relapses back on the propped pillows and closes his eyes. The unfolded letter remains on the bed.

(This again is mostly imagination. Parts of the letter I recognise – especially the bits about the greyhound and aging Ariels – but I can't remember ever visiting Eugene in any hospital.)

For a long time Eugene was a god for me, the only god I believed in, the graven image of writing. Everything I ever wrote (and a good deal of what I thought) when I was younger could be traced back to him. And yet – and I am not talking about anything as simple as age here – we were very different people. Strangely enough I always knew that. When I was a young teenager – not a word Eugene could ever have uttered without a circumflex of contempt – I assumed that I would develop into his reflection, that I would discard those elements which we did not have in common, elements that had to do with our very different sense of family and so on. But the older I got the more I suspected that I would not. It's not that I thought that my instincts were any better than his ideals – probably the opposite – but I discovered to my embarrassment that blood was as potent as the waters of Pieria. And so, cousin Fintan, you will never be a poet.

I have always considered myself strangely fortunate – one in a million – to have known two such writers as Brendan and Eugene who were, for all their differences, two men of what used to be called 'genius'. Now I am not quite so sure; it may have been a mixed blessing. I had great times with both of them, learned a good deal too, and even loved them in a childish hero-worshipping way. But there was a price to pay and maybe it will take me a lifetime to pay it off. A small part of it was seeing them die. The major part was seeing them writhe in torment in the years before they died. Even as I listened to them, even as I was under their spells, did I perhaps sense the whirlpool and turn away in childish fear as I did from sudden violence in the cinema? How long have I been recoiling from the sight of them both disappearing into the empty moment of their truth? I wonder. I wonder just how much fear of the hangman's rope I got from Brendan, how much fear of the protrusive eyes from Eugene. The last lines of Larry Lynch are heard above the tumult:

> Only son of an only son, end of a harmless line,
> The name will live in telephone directories,
> Conjuring up the black protruding tongue
> And the rude expression of disentangled eyes.

Jesus! How old was I when I concocted that charming little epitaph? Twenty-two at the very most. Talk about a farewell to the muse!

Am I making any sense at all? Can you see what I am getting at? Or rather what is getting at me? It's difficult to put into words and my shaking hand does not help. What is coming through to me with some force is a suspicion that my contact with Brendan and Eugene (Then fly our greeting, fly our contact, fly!) may have given me more than an admiration for their writings, more than an ambition to write, that seeing them both broken at the end may have vaccinated me with a rooted fear of the *belle dame sans merci* who led them out onto the cold hillside.

> Some died by the glenside, some died mid the stranger,
> And wise men have told us their cause was a failure ...

Not Keats. Two lines from one of my grandfather's ballads. His face appears, as in a drawing I have at home: the cynical stare of a man who has known fame and hunger in equal measure.

Though he is immobile I can hear the repressed coughs. Noises
off. Who else is coming to the wake? This is ridiculous! But
welcome, secret master James, to the hitherandthithering waters of.

Enough! Air!

But no: I don't want to turn away. Meet it is I set it down.

Were these the faces, friends' faces twisted in pain, that I
portrayed in *Gone The Time*? Did I for a moment see behind
the furrows of Pearse's brow anguish of a kind he had always
managed to conceal? Did I reveal the skulls beneath the skin,
discarding the muddy vestures of decay that had often warmed
my heart and set the benches on a roar in St Fergal's School, in
the restaurant at Leopardstown, in public bars *passim*? Had I
stirred the waters of the whirlpool so that the dissolving shapes
emerged from beneath the waterline of my mind as images of
expiration? Did I perhaps see my own face among them? Just
as I did the other night?

Was it a case of Larry Lynch all over again?

When I tried to kill off Larry Lynch I thought I was merely
burying the pain of a romantic infatuation but now I'm
inclined to believe that I was attempting to smother the aspect
of myself that had left me open to such pain. Eugene twigged
something of this when we were walking along the cliffs of
Howth Head: as I looked down on the jagged rocks in the surf
below I knew that his mind was on the dreadful summit of
Elsinore. Maybe he was right to worry.

(Useless footnote: I imagined Larry Lynch as a victim of
Hodgkin's disease, which can cause a swelling of the lympathic
glands and lead to death by strangulation. A more useful
footnote would explain why my imagination took such a
tender turn.)

And twenty years later did the ghost assume some other
horrible form to deprive me of my sovereignty of reason and
draw me towards madness? When I was trying to distance
myself far from the village, was I once again on the run? Was I
trying to kill something in myself? Maybe. It seems likely but I
cannot remember. When I try harder to remember I can see
things but whether they are the facts of memory or the fiction

of imagination I cannot say.

The answer is disappearing in the past. Eugene and Brendan and Pearse are dead and buried; I am alive. And yet for me they will never be dead: always they will feelingly persuade me what I am.

And what about you? I really feel bad about dumping out my entrails before you. It was no part of the original plan, believe me; you are supposed to be the nurse and me the patient. (Remember our courtyard table in the Museum of Modern Art? I came close for a while but never knew it.) Now things are changed and I am concerned about you and what you will make of these last few pages.

Flashback. Peas Hill. Sunny Sunday morning in October. Shortly after I met you. The two of us sitting opposite each other at my worktable. (Can you hear the bells? There must have been bells.) You are reading a magazine called *St Stephen's* and trying to be cheerfully polite about my favourite breakfast: fried eggs on malted crispbread. Remember what you were reading? It was a short story of mine. (Later I would think of it as my last.) And, trying to intercept shards of yolk-drenched crispbread as they exploded in your delicate mouth, you commented.

– Will you write a story about me?

I never wrote you a story. I had given up writing short stories at that stage; tortured verse was so much easier. I assumed then – as before and later – that I would write a story in which you and I would recognise ourselves but . . . well, you know the rest.

Thanks for being there, then and now. I'm sorry that I never wrote the kind of story you wanted then but maybe this will be an acceptable substitute for the moment. I'll call you soon to see what you made of it. And I'll send you a copy of the book – promise.